Praise for Minette Walters

The Ice House

'Terrific first novel with a high Rendellesque
frisson count'
The Times

The Sculptress

'A devastatingly effective novel'
Observer

The Scold's Bridle

'A gothic puzzle of great intricacy and
psychological power'
Sunday Times

The Dark Room

'A marvellous, dramatically intelligent novel.
It shimmers with suspense, ambiguity and
a deep unholy joy'
Daily Mail

The Echo

'It grips like steel . . . Passion, compassion,
intelligence and romance are what Walters offers
with no quarter for squeamish cowards'
Mail on Sunday

The Breaker

'Stands head and shoulders above the vast majority of crime novels . . . Existing fans will love *The Breaker*, new readers will be instant converts'
Daily Express

The Shape of Snakes

'Breaking all the rules of popular fiction, Minette Walters asks as much of her readers as many literary novelists, and yet she offers them a book as gripping as any thriller'
Times Literary Supplement

Acid Row

'Humane intelligence enables Walters to twist and turn her plot . . . *Acid Row* is a breathtaking achievement'
Daily Telegraph

Fox Evil

'*Fox Evil* is the work of a writer at the peak of her confidence and supreme ability'
The Times

Disordered Minds

'A powerful, acute and vivid work from a staggeringly talented writer'
Observer

The Tinder Box

'If there wasn't a recognised school of crime writing
called Home Counties noir before, there is now.
Minette Walters invented it and remains
the undisputed Head Girl'
Mike Ripley, *Birmingham Post*

The Devil's Feather

'One of the most powerful yet nuanced practitioners of
the psychological thriller . . . always keeps the narrative
momentum cracked up to a fierce degree'
Daily Express

Chickenfeed

'A marvellous little story, thoroughly intimate
with human nastiness'
Evening Standard

The Chameleon's Shadow

'No wonder Minette Walters is the country's
bestselling female crime writer. But even this label
does not exactly do justice to the scope and breadth of
her gripping, terrifying novels . . . *The Chameleon's
Shadow* is another classic'
Daily Mirror

Also by Minette Walters

The Ice House

The Sculptress

The Scold's Bridle

The Dark Room

The Echo

The Breaker

The Shape of Snakes

Acid Row

Fox Evil

Disordered Minds

The Tinder Box

Chickenfeed
(Quick Reads)

The Chameleon's Shadow

MINETTE WALTERS

The Devil's Feather

PAN BOOKS

First published 2005 by Macmillan

This edition published 2012 by Pan Books
an imprint of Pan Macmillan, a division of Macmillan Publishers Limited
Pan Macmillan, 20 New Wharf Road, London N1 9RR
Basingstoke and Oxford
Associated companies throughout the world
www.panmacmillan.com

ISBN 978-1-4472-0807-5

Copyright © Minette Walters 2005

The right of Minette Walters to be identified as the
author of this work has been asserted by her in accordance
with the Copyright, Designs and Patents Act 1988.

All rights reserved. No part of this publication may be
reproduced, stored in or introduced into a retrieval system, or
transmitted, in any form, or by any means (electronic, mechanical,
photocopying, recording or otherwise) without the prior written
permission of the publisher. Any person who does any unauthorized
act in relation to this publication may be liable to criminal
prosecution and civil claims for damages.

1 3 5 7 9 8 6 4 2

A CIP catalogue record for this book is available from
the British Library.

Typeset by SetSystems Ltd, Saffron Walden, Essex
Printed and bound by CPI Group (UK) Ltd, Croydon, CR0 4YY

This book is sold subject to the condition that it shall not,
by way of trade or otherwise, be lent, re-sold, hired out,
or otherwise circulated without the publisher's prior consent
in any form of binding or cover other than that in which
it is published and without a similar condition including this
condition being imposed on the subsequent purchaser.

Visit **www.panmacmillan.com** to read more about all our books
and to buy them. You will also find features, author interviews and
news of any author events, and you can sign up for e-newsletters
so that you're always first to hear about our new releases.

To Mick, Peggy and Liz

for all the good times we've had together

My particular thanks to Liz

for giving me *The Devil's Feather* as a title

CITY AND COUNTY OF SWANSEA LIBRARIES	
6000145040	
Askews & Holts	17-Jan-2013
	£7.99
LL	

Madeleine Wright and Marianne Curran
made donations to Leukaemia Research and the
Free Tibet Campaign to have their names included
in this book. I thank them for their generosity
and hope their characters amuse them.

'The secret of happiness is freedom; the secret of freedom, courage'

Thucydides (Greek historian, 5th century BC)

Devil's Feather (derivation Turkish) – a woman who stirs a man's interest without realizing it; the unwitting cause of sexual arousal

Barton House

The Devil's Feather

>>>**Reuters**
>>>Wednesday, 15 May 2002, 16:17 GMT 17:17 UK
>>>Filed by Connie Burns, Freetown, Sierra Leone,
   West Africa

Spate of brutal killings

Four months after President Kabbah announced an end to Sierra Leone's bloody civil war a spate of brutal killings in Freetown threatens to undermine the fragile peace. Police blame former rebel soldiers for the savage murders. Attacked at intervals since peace was declared in January, the five victims were found raped and hacked to death in their own homes.

A government source said yesterday, 'The killing of these women bears the trademark ferocity of the rebels. Sierra Leone has just emerged from a decade of savage conflict, and police believe a group of dissidents is responsible. We call on everyone to put an end to bloodshed.'

Detective Inspector Alan Collins of Manchester CID, who is in Freetown as part of a British training force, points to the serial nature of the murders. 'It's difficult to say how many people are involved at this stage, but the evidence suggests the crimes are linked. We are looking for a disturbed individual, or group, who acquired a taste for killing during the war. Rape and murder were commonplace then, and violence against women doesn't stop just because peace is declared.'

>>>**Reuters**
>>>Tuesday, 4 June 2002, 13:06 GMT 14:06 UK
>>>Filed by Connie Burns, Freetown, Sierra Leone,
    West Africa

Three suspects charged

Three teenagers, formerly members of Foday
Sankoh's RUF child army, were charged yesterday
with the murders of five women. They were arrested
after the attempted abduction of Amie Jonah, 14.
Ahmad Gberebana, 19, Johnny Bunumbu, 19, and
Katema Momana, 18, were caught and detained by
Miss Jonah's family when the girl's screams alerted a
neighbour.

A police spokesman said the teenagers were badly
beaten before being handed over to the authorities.
'They caused great distress to Miss Jonah,' he said,
'and her father and brothers were understandably
angry.' Fear has been rampant in Freetown since the
gruesome discoveries of five murdered women. All
were raped and disfigured by machete wounds.

In two cases identification was impossible. 'They may
never be named,' said Detective Inspector Alan Collins
of Manchester Police, who is advising the enquiry

team. 'The civil war saw nearly half of this country's 4.5 million population displaced and we've no idea which region these women came from.'

He confirmed that a request for a British pathologist to provide expert assistance has been withdrawn. 'I understand that Gberebana, Bunumbu and Momana have provided the police with full confessions. Investigators are satisfied they have the right men in custody.'

The three teenagers were given medical treatment before being transferred to Pademba Road prison to await trial.

Paddy's Bar

One

I DON'T KNOW if that story was picked up in the West. I believe some interest was shown in South Africa, but only because rape and murder had been high on that country's agenda for some time. I was transferred to Asia shortly afterwards, so I never learnt the outcome of the trial. I assumed the teenagers were convicted because justice, like everything else in Sierra Leone, was subject to economic restrictions. Even if the court went to the expense of appointing a public defence lawyer, confessions of guilt, with graphic details of how each victim was murdered, would attract a summary sentence.

I know Alan Collins was troubled by the indictments, but there was little he could do about it when his request for an experienced pathologist was refused. He was in a difficult position – more an observer than an adviser – with less than two weeks of his secondment left at the time of Amie Jonah's abduction, and the youths' descriptions of their crimes effectively sealed their fate. Nevertheless, Alan remained sceptical.

'They were in no fit state to be questioned,' he told

me. 'Amie's family had reduced them to pulp. They'd have said anything the police wanted them to say rather than face another beating.'

He was also troubled by the crime scenes. 'I saw two of the bodies in situ,' he said, 'and neither of them looked like a gang attack. Both women were huddled in the corners of the rooms with their heads and shoulders sliced to ribbons and defence wounds to their arms. It looked to me as if they were trying to protect themselves from a single individual who attacked from the front. A gang would have been slashing at them from all sides.'

'What can you do?'

'Very little. No one's been interested since the youths confessed. I've written a report, pointing up the anomalies, but there are precious few doctors in Freetown, let alone forensic pathologists.' He smiled ruefully. 'The thinking seems to be that they deserve what they get because there's no doubt they were trying to abduct young Amie.'

'If you're right, won't the killer strike again? Won't that exonerate the boys?'

'It depends who he is. If he's a local, then probably . . . but if he's one of the foreign contingent – ' he shrugged – 'I'm guessing he'll export his activities elsewhere.'

It was that conversation which increased my suspicions of John Harwood. When he was first pointed out to me in Paddy's Bar – Freetown's equivalent of

Stringfellows – I knew I'd seen him before. I wondered if it was in Kinshasa in 1998 when I was covering the civil war in the Congo. I recalled him being in uniform then – almost certainly as a mercenary because the British army wasn't involved in that conflict – but I didn't think he'd been calling himself John Harwood.

By the spring of 2002 in Sierra Leone he was dressed in civvies and had a bad reputation. I saw him in three fights while I was there, and heard about others, but he was never on the receiving end of the damage. He had the build of a terrier – middling height, lean muscular frame, strong neck and limbs – and a terrier's ferocity once he had his teeth into someone. Most of the ex-pats gave him a wide berth, particularly when he was drinking.

At that time Freetown was full of foreigners. The UN was coordinating efforts to put the country back on its feet, and most of the ex-pats worked for the international press, NGOs, religious missions or world charities. A few, like Harwood, had private contracts. He was employed as chauffeur/bodyguard to a Lebanese businessman, who was rumoured to have interests in a diamond mine. Once in a while the pair of them vanished abroad with heavily armoured cases, so the rumours were probably true.

Along with everyone else, I tended to avoid him. Life was too short to get involved with loners with chips on their shoulders. However, I did make one overture during the six months I was there when I asked him to pass on a request for an interview with his boss. Diamonds were a hot topic in the aftermath of conflict. The question of who owned them and where the money was going had been a bone of contention in Sierra Leone for decades. None of the wealth was fed back into the country and the people's resentment at their grinding, subsistence-level poverty had been the spark which ignited the civil war.

Predictably, I got nowhere near Harwood's boss, but I had a brief exchange with Harwood himself. None of the local women would cook or clean for him, so most evenings he could be found eating alone at Paddy's Bar, which was where I approached him. I said I thought our paths had crossed before, and he acknowledged it with a nod.

'You're bonnier than I recall, Ms Burns,' he said in a broad Glaswegian accent. 'Last time I saw you you were a little mouse of a thing.'

I was surprised he remembered my name, even more surprised by the backhanded compliment. The one fact everyone knew about Harwood was that he didn't like women. It poured out of him under the influence of Star beer, and gossip had it that he was in the tertiary stage of syphilis after contracting it from a whore. It was a convenient explanation for his aggress-ive misogyny, but I didn't believe it myself. Penicillin was too freely available for any westerner to progress beyond the primary stage.

I told him what I wanted and placed a list of questions on the table, together with a covering letter explaining the nature of the piece I was planning. 'Will you pass these on to your boss and give me his answer?' Access to anyone was difficult except through a third party. The rebel fighters had destroyed most of the communications network and, with everyone living in secure compounds, it was impossible to blag your way past the guards without an appointment.

Harwood prodded the papers back at me. 'No to both requests.'

'Why not?'

'He doesn't talk to journalists.'

'Is that him speaking or you?'

'No comment.'

I smiled slightly. 'So how do I get past you, Mr Harwood?'

'You don't.' He crossed his arms and stared up at me through narrowed eyes. 'Don't push your luck, Ms Burns. You've had your answer.'

My dismissal, too, I thought wryly. Even with a score of ex-pats within hailing distance, I didn't have the nerve to press him further. I'd seen the kind of damage he could do, and I didn't fancy being on the receiving end.

Paddy's was the favoured watering-hole of the international community because it remained open throughout the eleven-year conflict. It was a large open-sided bar-cum-restaurant, with tables on a concrete veranda, and it was a magnet for local hookers in search of dollars. They learnt very quickly to avoid Harwood after he hurt one so badly that she was hospitalized. He spoke pidgin English, which is the lingua franca of Sierra Leone, and cursed the girls vilely in their own tongue if they tried to approach him. He called them 'devils' feathers' and lashed out with his fists if they came too close.

He was rather more careful around Europeans. The charities and missions had a high percentage of female staff, but if a white woman jogged his arm he always let it go. Perhaps he was intimidated by them – they were a great deal brighter than he was, with strings of letters after their names – or perhaps he knew he wouldn't be able to get away with it. The less articulate black girls were easier targets for his anger. It persuaded most of us that he was a racist as well as a woman-hater.

There was no telling how old he was. He had a shaven head, tattooed with a winged scimitar at the base of his skull, and the sun had dried his skin to leather. When drunk, he boasted that he'd been in the SAS unit that stormed the Iranian embassy in London in 1980 and the scimitar was his badge of honour. But, if true, that would have put him in his late forties or early fifties, and his devastating punches suggested someone younger. Despite the strong Scottish accent, he claimed to come from London, although no one in the UK ex-pat community believed him, any more than they believed that John Harwood was the name he had been born with.

Nevertheless, if Alan Collins hadn't made his remark about the foreign contingent, it wouldn't have occurred to me that there might be more to Harwood's violence than anyone realized. Even when it did, there was nothing I could do about it. Alan had returned to Manchester by then and the murders of the women had quickly faded from memory.

I ran my suspicions past a few of my colleagues, but they were sceptical. As they pointed out, the killings had stopped with the arrest of the boys, and Harwood's modus operandi was to use his fists, not a machete. The tenor of their argument seemed to be that, however despicable Harwood was, he wouldn't have raped the women before murdering them. 'He can't even bring himself to *touch* a black,' said an Australian cameraman, 'so he's hardly likely to soil himself by dipping his wick into one.'

I gave it up because the only evidence I could cite against Harwood was a particularly brutal attack on a young prostitute in Paddy's Bar. A good hundred people had witnessed it, but the girl had taken money in lieu of prosecution so there wasn't even a report of the incident. In any case, my stint in Sierra Leone was almost at an end and I didn't want to start something that might delay my departure. I persuaded myself it wasn't my responsibility and confined justice to the dustbin of apathy.

By then I'd spent most of my life in Africa, first as a child, then working for newspapers in Kenya and South Africa, and latterly for Reuters as a newswire correspondent. It was a continent I knew and loved, having grown up in Zimbabwe as the daughter of a white farmer, but by the summer of 2002 I'd had enough. I'd covered too many forgotten conflicts and too many stories of financial corruption. I planned to stay a couple of months in London, where my parents had been living since 2001, before moving on to the Reuters bureau in Singapore to write about Asian affairs.

The night before I left Freetown for good, I was in the middle of packing when Harwood came to my house. He was escorted to my door by Manu, one of the Leonean gate-guards, who knew enough about the man's reputation to ask if I wanted a chaperone. I shook my head, but protected myself by talking to Harwood on my veranda in full view of the rest of the compound.

He studied my unresponsive expression. 'You don't like me much, do you, Ms Burns?'

'I don't like you at all, Mr Harwood.'

He looked amused. 'Because I wouldn't pass on your request for an interview?'

'No.'

The one-word response seemed to throw him. 'You shouldn't believe everything people say about me.'

'I don't have to. I've seen you in action.'

A closed expression settled on his face. 'Then you'll know not to cross me,' he murmured.

'I wouldn't bet on it. What do you want?'

He showed me an envelope and asked me to mail it in London. It was a common request to anyone going home because the Leonean postal service was notoriously unreliable. The usual routine was to leave the package open so that the bearer could show Customs at both ends that there was nothing illegal in it, but Harwood had sealed his. When I refused to accept it unless he was prepared to reveal the contents, he returned it to his pocket.

'You'll be needing a good turn from me one day,' he said.

'I doubt it.'

'If you do, you won't get it, Ms Burns. I have a long memory.'

'I don't expect to meet you again, so the situation won't arise.'

He turned away. 'I wouldn't bet on it,' he said in ironic echo. 'For people like us the world's smaller than you think.'

As I watched him walk to the gate, I was curious about the name I'd glimpsed on the envelope, 'Mary MacKenzie', and the last line of the address, 'Glasgow'. It flipped a switch in my memory. It *was* Kinshasa where I'd seen him before – he'd been part of a mercenary group fighting for Laurent Kabila's regime – and the name he'd been using then was Keith MacKenzie.

I must have wondered why he'd assumed an alias, and how he'd acquired a passport as John Harwood, but it wouldn't have been for long. I spoke the truth when I'd said I didn't expect to meet him again.

Two

TWO YEARS LATER, in the spring of 2004, I recognized him immediately. I was on a three-month secondment to Baghdad to cover the rapidly deteriorating situation in Iraq, which was about as long as any newswire journalist could take the stress of the unfolding shambles. Editors around the world were demanding instant copy since the publication of photographs showing US soldiers abusing prisoners in Abu Ghraib jail.

It was a dangerous time for westerners. Civilian contractors were being targeted for hostage-taking and execution, and private security firms were recruiting ex-soldiers by the thousand to bodyguard them. Iraq had become a bonanza for mercenaries. They were paid double what they could earn anywhere else, but the risks were enormous. Shoot-outs between private security agents and Iraqi insurgents were common, but they rarely hit the headlines. Discreet veils were drawn over the incidents to protect client confidentiality, for as often as not the client was the US government.

In the wake of Abu Ghraib, with the coalition lurching from one public relations disaster to another, a charm offensive was launched to mitigate the damage done by the 'torture' photographs. This involved bussing the press corps to different types of detention and training facilities with promises of full and free access. Being cynical hacks, few of us expected to hear anything that wasn't 'on message', but we went along for the ride just to escape the claustrophobia of our fortress hotels.

There was no venturing out on the streets of Iraq alone at that time, not if we valued our lives and freedom. With an al-Qaeda bounty on every western head – and women being targeted as potential 'sex slaves' after Lyndie England's part in the prisoner abuse – press accreditation was no protection. Baghdad had been dubbed the most dangerous city in the world and, rightly or wrongly, women journalists saw rapists round every corner.

One of these PR tours ended at the police academy, where they were pushing out five hundred newly trained Iraqi policemen every two months. The coalition authorities had briefed their people well, and we received the same human rights spiel at the academy as we'd heard everywhere else. The buzz phrases of the moment were: 'in accordance with the law', 'clarified chains of command', 'absolute commitment to humanitarian principles', 'proper checks and balances'.

They were fine-sounding sentiments, and honestly meant by the smart young Iraqi who pronounced them, but they were no more likely to prevent future abuse than the Nazi Nuremberg trials or the inquiry into the My Lai massacre in Vietnam. If I'd learnt anything from my forays into the world's conflicts, it was that sadists exist everywhere and war is their theatre.

Thoroughly bored, I glanced through an open office window as the press crocodile wound around the main building. In the centre of the room, several uniformed dog-handlers, with Alsatians on leashes, faced a man in civvies with his back to me. I'd have known MacKenzie's bullet head anywhere from the winged scimitar tattoo, but he turned as his listeners' attention was drawn by the voice of our escort and there was no mistaking his face. More out of surprise than any desire to speak to him, I came to a halt, but if he recognized me he gave no sign of it. With an impatient scowl, he reached for the handle and jerked the window shut.

I caught up with the guide and asked him about the civilian with the shaven head. Who was he and where did he fit into the chain of command? Was he training Iraqis to handle dogs? What were his qualifications? The guide didn't know, but said he'd find out before I left.

Half an hour later, I learnt that MacKenzie was now calling himself Kenneth O'Connell and was a consultant with the Baycombe Group – a private security firm that was providing specialist training at the academy. When I requested an interview, I was informed O'Connell was no longer on the premises. I was given a phone number to call the next day. As I made a note of it, I asked the Iraqi what O'Connell's speciality was. Control and restraint techniques, he told me.

The phone number turned out to be the Baycombe Group's main office which was inside a fortified compound near the bombed-out United Nations headquarters. I was given the immediate runaround when I asked for an interview with O'Connell, and it took a further week to set up a general interview with BG's spokesman, Alastair Surtees. I assumed Mackenzie was making his point about 'good turns' and, if so, I was supremely indifferent to it. In terms of what I planned to write – a hard-hitting piece on the calibre of personnel these firms were recruiting – I expected Surtees to be a lot more forthcoming than a Glaswegian bully who changed names whenever it suited him.

I was wrong. Surtees was urbane and courteous, and as tight as a drum when it came to giving out information. He told me he was ex-British army, forty-one years old, and had reached the rank of major in the Parachute Regiment before deciding to join the private sector. He reminded me that the agreed interview was thirty minutes, then filled the first twenty with a slick presentation of his firm's history and professionalism.

I learnt very little about BG's sphere of operations in Iraq – other than that they were wide-ranging and almost exclusively concentrated on the protection of civilians – and a great deal about the type of men that BG recruited. Ex-soldiers and policemen of the highest integrity. Tired of this spin, I asked if I could speak to an individual operative in order to hear his story at first hand.

Surtees shook his head. 'We couldn't allow that. It would make him a target.'

'I wouldn't use his real name.'

Another shake of the head. 'I'm sorry.'

'How about Kenneth O'Connell at the police academy? He and I know each other, so I'm sure he'll agree to talk to me. The last time we met was in Sierra Leone . . . the time before in Kinshasa. Will you ask him?'

The request clearly came as no surprise to Surtees. 'I believe your information's out of date, Ms Burns, but I'm happy to check.' He eased a laptop across the desk and punched up information on the screen. 'We did have an O'Connell at the academy, but he was transferred a month ago. I'm afraid you were wrongly advised.'

I shook my head. 'I don't think so. He was there a week ago because I saw him.'

'Are you sure it was Kenneth O'Connell?'

It was such an obvious question that it made me laugh. 'No . . . but it's the name I was given for the man I saw. In Freetown he was calling himself John Harwood, in Kinshasa, Keith MacKenzie.' I lifted an amused eyebrow. 'Which makes me wonder how you can vouch for his integrity. What name did you vet him by? He's had at least three to my knowledge.'

'Then it wasn't O'Connell you saw, Ms Burns. He was wrongly identified to you.' He tapped at his keyboard. 'We have no Harwoods or MacKenzies on our books, so I suspect the man you saw is with another firm.'

I shrugged. 'I asked the academy twice if I could do an interview with him – once that afternoon and again a couple of days later when I got through to their press office. On neither occasion was I told that Kenneth O'Connell wasn't employed there any more . . . which I should have been if he was transferred a month ago.'

Surtees shook his head. 'Then they haven't kept their records up to date. As I'm sure you're aware, everything's fairly chaotic in Baghdad at the moment.' He closed the lid of his laptop. 'We're meticulous about *our* records, so you can rely on the information I've just given you.'

I drew a Pinocchio doodle on my notepad so that he could see it. 'Where's O'Connell now? What's he doing?'

'I can't answer that. Company policy re our employees is no different from Reuters. Complete confidentiality. Would you expect anything less?'

'Then talk generally,' I encouraged him. 'What qualifies a man to teach restraint techniques to raw recruits in the most dangerous capital in the world? Knowledge of the law? A long and honourable career with Scotland Yard? A period in the military police, even? He appeared to be instructing dog-handlers, so I assume he has experience in that field? What sort of qualities does it need? Patience? A good control of his temper?'

He folded his hands on the table. 'No comment.'

'Why not?'

'Because your questions relate to a specific individual and I've already described the sort of people we recruit.'

I extended Pinocchio's nose. 'You must think very highly of O'Connell, Mr Surtees. He's one of your few employees who's *not* working in the private sector . . . or *wasn't* until a week ago. I'm assuming the coalition only takes consultants with scrupulously clean records?'

'Of course.'

'So you checked O'Connell thoroughly?' Surtees nodded. 'What's his background? Where was he born? Where did he grow up? With a name like that he ought to be Irish.'

'No comment.'

I watched him for a moment. 'When I knew him in Sierra Leone, he said he'd been with the SAS unit that stormed the Iranian embassy in London. Is that what he told you?'

Surtees shook his head.

'I knew it was a load of baloney,' I said amiably. 'That embassy siege was twenty-four years ago and the unit was chosen for its experience. O'Connell would be a good fifty now if he'd been one of them . . . unless the SAS was recruiting teenagers in the late seventies.'

'I'm not denying or confirming anything, Ms Burns – ' he tapped his watch – 'and you're running out of time.'

I turned over a page of my notebook and did a quick sketch of MacKenzie's feathered scimitar, showing it to Surtees. 'He told one of my colleagues that the tattoo on the back of his head is a symbolic interpretation of the SAS winged dagger . . . it's his personal tribute to a crushing victory over Islamic fundamentalists. Do you think it's appropriate for a man who holds views like that to train Iraqi policemen?'

Surtees shook his head again.

'Meaning what? That he never trained them . . . or it's not appropriate?'

'Meaning, no comment.' He unbuckled his watch and laid it on the desk. 'Time's up,' he said.

I tucked my pencil behind my ear and reached for my kitbag. 'He's working in a sensitive area. Control and restraint techniques are used to immobilize dangerous or violent suspects, and we've seen some graphic images of what happens when uneducated sadists end up in charge of detainees. I'm sure you recall that dogs were used to terrorize the prisoners at Abu Ghraib. It may not bother you if we have a repeat of it – you'll wash your hands of it with some creative record-keeping – but it'll bother me.'

The man smiled slightly. 'I'll leave the creative side to you, Ms Burns. I'm afraid I'm too slow-witted to follow your imaginative leaps from the misidentification of one of our employees to my being personally responsible for what went on in Abu Ghraib.'

'Shame on you,' I said lightly. 'I hoped you had more integrity.' I stuffed my notebook and pencil into my kitbag. 'MacKenzie's a violent man. When he was in Sierra Leone he couldn't restrain himself . . . let alone teach others how to do it. He had a Rhodesian ridgeback patrolling his compound which was even more aggressive than he was. He trained the dog to kill by throwing stray mongrels at it.'

Surtees stood up and held out his hand. 'Good day,' he said pleasantly. 'If there's anything else I can help you with, feel free to phone.'

I pushed myself to my feet and shook the proffered hand. 'I can't afford the time,' I said equally pleasantly, tossing my card on to the table in front of him. 'That's my mobile number in case you feel like talking to *me*.'

'Why would I want to?'

I rested my kitbag on my hip to fasten the straps. 'MacKenzie broke a drunk's forearm in Freetown. I saw him do it. He took it between his hands and snapped it against his knee like a piece of rotten wood.'

There was a short silence before the man gave a sceptical smile. 'I don't think that's possible, not unless the bone was so brittle that anyone could have done it.'

'He wasn't prosecuted,' I went on, 'because the victim was too frightened to report him to the police . . . but a couple of paratroopers – *your* regiment – forced him to pay some hefty compensation. You don't get broken bones set for free in Sierra Leone . . . and you sure as hell don't get benefit if you can't work.' I shook my head. 'The man's a sadist, and all the ex-pats knew it. He's not a type I'd choose to instruct raw recruits in Baghdad on how to do their jobs properly . . . certainly not in the present climate.'

He stared at me with dislike. 'Is this a personal thing? You seem very intent on destroying a man's reputation.'

I walked to the door and flipped the handle with my elbow. 'Just for the record, MacKenzie's victim was a half-starved prostitute who weighed under six stone . . . and I bet she did have brittle bones, because every cow in the country had been slaughtered for food by the rebels and calcium-rich milk was a luxury. The poor kid – she was only sixteen years old – was trying to earn money to buy clothes for her baby. She was tipsy on two beers which another customer had bought her, and she jogged MacKenzie's elbow by accident. As retribution, he dislocated hers and fractured her ulna by wrenching her arm open and snapping it backwards across his leg.' I lifted an eyebrow. 'Do you have a comment on that?'

He didn't.

'Have a nice day,' I told him.

*

In the end I never wrote the piece. I managed to get an interview with a bodyguard from a different security firm, but he'd only recently left the army and Iraq was his first freelance operation. As my original idea had been to show how demand for mercenaries far outweighed supply, with compromises being made in the vetting of recruits if numbers were to be met, a single novice didn't make a story. Also, the public appetite for 'war' stories was wearing thin. All anyone wanted was a solution to the mess, not more reminders that the coalition's grip was slipping.

With the help of a translator, I toured Iraqi newspaper offices and went through three months of back copies, looking for stories about raped and murdered women. Salima, the translator, was sceptical from the outset. 'This is Baghdad,' she told me. 'The only thing anyone's interested in is death by suicide bombing or, better still, acts of sadism on the part of the coalition. Women are raped all the time by husbands they never wanted to marry. Does that count?'

I pointed out that it would take twice as long if she conducted a running commentary all the way through.

'But you're being naïve, Connie. Even assuming a European could get close to an Iraqi woman without being spotted – which I don't believe – who's going to report it? Some parts of Baghdad are so dangerous that the Iraqi journalists won't go into them – it's not as if the bombing and shooting have stopped – so how's the death of a single woman going to grab anyone's attention?'

I knew she was right, so I don't know which of us was more surprised when we came across the first story. It was headlined 'Rape on the Increase' and was a statistical account of how the rape and/or abduction of women had risen from one a month before the war to some twenty-five a month afterwards. Based on a Human Rights Watch report, it pointed to the dangers women face when the moral and ethical bases of society are shattered by war.

'It says that rape was rare under Saddam because it was a capital offence,' Salima told me, 'then suggests it was the disbanding of the police force at the start of the occupation that put women's safety in jeopardy.

This will interest you.' She followed the text with her finger. ' "With thugs and bandits running lawless districts, women are forced to cower in their homes for fear of their lives and honour. Disgracefully, this is no protection. Fateha Kassim, a devout young widow, was found raped and murdered in her home last week. Her father, who discovered her body, said it was the work of animals. They destroyed her beauty, he said." ' She looked up. 'Is that the kind of thing we're looking for?'

I nodded. 'It sounds like a carbon copy of the Sierra Leone killings.'

'But how could he have got at her?'

'I don't know, but I'm sure it's part of the excitement. If he was in the SAS, he'd have been trained to move around without attracting notice. Perhaps he goes in at night. Alan Collins said the crime scenes in Sierra Leone suggested the women had spent some time with their killer before he took the machete to them.'

The second story, the only other one we found, was from a different newspaper, dated a month later. It was buried in the middle pages under the headline 'Mother Dies in Sword Attack', and was very short. Salima translated: ' "The body of Mrs Gufran Zaki was discovered by her son on his return from school yesterday. She was brutally slain by blows and cuts to her head. The attack was described as frenzied. Police are looking for her husband, Mr Bashar Zaki, who is said to suffer from depression. Neighbours say he had a sword, which is missing from the house." '

We looked for a follow-up to see if Bashar Zaki had been arrested, but the story had been overtaken by the events at Abu Ghraib jail and there were no further references to it. Nor did the murder of Fateha Kassim feature again. It was difficult to know what to do after that. There was no mileage in the women from an international point of view, so I didn't mention them or my suspicions of MacKenzie to Dan Fry, the Reuters bureau chief in Baghdad. We were snowed under with more immediate disasters, and shortly afterwards Salima, the only other person interested, was sent south to Basra with another correspondent.

More out of frustration than with any real expectation of a response, I unearthed my two pieces from Sierra Leone and had them delivered, along with Salima's translations of the articles on the Baghdad murders and a covering letter, to Alastair Surtees at the Baycombe Group. I also emailed them to Alan Collins via the Greater Manchester Police website. Surtees's only reply was a printed compliments slip, acknowledging receipt of the documents. Alan's, a week later, was rather more encouraging.

'My best suggestion,' he wrote in his email, 'is to contact DI Bill Fraser or DS Dan Williams in Basra. They're doing a similar training job to the one I was doing in Freetown. I've forwarded your email and attachments to Bill Fraser to bring him up to speed,

and will add his e-address at the bottom. No guarantees, I'm afraid. If the coalition sectors are acting
independently, it will be difficult for Bill to intervene
in Baghdad, but he should be able to give you some
useful names higher up the chain of command. Meanwhile, be a little wary who you talk to. MacKenzie's
inside the loop if he is/has been working with the
police, so he'll have no trouble finding out who's
accusing him. And even if your suspicions are wrong,
you already know he reacts violently when he's
crossed.'

His advice came too late. By the time I received it,
I'd changed my hotel twice and my bedroom three
times in as many days. It's hard to explain how the
constant invasion of your space can destroy your equi-
librium . . . but it does and it did. The door was always
locked when I returned, and nothing was stolen, but
the deliberate rearrangement of my possessions frightened me. On one occasion I found my laptop open
with my letter to Alastair Surtees on-screen.

I had no proof it was MacKenzie – although I never
doubted it – but I couldn't persuade the hotels to take
me seriously. It was impossible for a non-resident to
enter guests' bedrooms, they said. And what was I
complaining about, anyway, when no thefts had
occurred? It was simply the chambermaid doing her
job. My colleagues merely shrugged their shoulders
and quoted the 'thief of Baghdad' at me. What else
could I expect in this god-awful city?

The only person who might have taken my fears seriously was my boss, Dan Fry, but he'd chosen that week to go on R & R in Kuwait. I thought about phoning him and asking if I could transfer to his flat, but I was afraid I'd be even more isolated there than in a hotel full of journalists. There was no point in going to the police. Obsessed with suicide bombers and hostage-takers, they wouldn't have given me the time of day. And in any case, I thought Alan Collins was right. The police were the last people to talk to.

I didn't sleep. Instead I lay awake, clutching a pair of scissors, and watching the door with burgeoning paranoia. After four nights of it I was so exhausted that, when I returned to my room after a press conference to find my knickers with the crotches cut out, my nerve snapped completely and I applied for immediate sick leave on the grounds of war-induced stress and mental breakdown.

I hadn't spent more than two months in the UK since I'd left Oxford in 1988, but in Baghdad in early May 2004 all I could dream about was soft summer rain, green grass, narrow hedge-lined lanes, and fields and fields of ripening corn. It was an England I barely knew – drawn as much from fiction and poetry as real life – but it was the safest place I could think of.

I can't imagine why I was so stupid.

>>>**Associated Press**
>>>Monday, 16 May 2004, 07.42 GMT 08.42 UK
>>>Filed by James Wilson, Baghdad, Iraq

Reuters Correspondent Snatched

Just three days after Adelina Bianca, a 42-year-old
Italian television reporter, was taken hostage by
Muntada al-Ansar, an armed terrorist group, it's feared
that Connie Burns, a 36-year-old Reuters
correspondent, has suffered the same fate. Snatched
while on her way to Baghdad International Airport
yesterday, Connie Burns's whereabouts are unknown.
Her Reuters car was discovered, burnt out and
abandoned, on the outskirts of the city. As yet, no group
has claimed responsibility for her kidnapping.

Muntada al-Ansar, believed to be led by Abu Masab al-
Zarqawi, a senior al-Qaeda operative, was responsible
for the savage execution on video of American civilian
Nick Berg. They have now posted video footage of a
distressed and blindfolded Adelina Bianca on the same
website, with threats to behead her if Silvio Berlusconi,
Italy's Prime Minister, continues to support the coalition.

In the wake of these atrocities, Amnesty International has
issued the following statement. 'The killing of prisoners is

one of the most serious crimes under international law. Armed groups must release immediately and without any precondition all hostages, and should refrain from attacking, abducting and killing civilians.'

Colleagues of Connie Burns are devastated by her abduction. She is a well-known and popular correspondent who has reported on wars in Africa, Asia and the Middle East. Born and brought up in Zimbabwe, and a graduate of Oxford University, she worked on newspapers in South Africa and Kenya before joining Reuters as an Africa specialist.

'With the help of religious leaders in Baghdad, we're doing all we can to find out who's holding Connie,' said Dan Fry, the agency's bureau chief in Iraq. 'We ask her captors to remember that newswire correspondents are neutral observers of conflicts. Their job is to report the news, not devise the policies that make it.'

The last piece Connie Burns filed before she left for the airport was a moving tribute to Adelina Bianca. 'Adelina's a courageous journalist who never flinches from asking the difficult questions. As a powerful voice on the side of suffering, her writing has stirred consciences around the world . . . any attempt to silence her will be a victory for ignorance and oppression.'

>>>**Associated Press**
>>>Wednesday, 18 May 2004, 13.17 GMT 14.17 UK
>>>Filed by James Wilson, Baghdad, Iraq

Reuters Correspondent Released

The surprise release of Connie Burns, the 36-year-old
correspondent abducted on Monday, was announced by
Reuters this morning. 'We received an anonymous
phone call yesterday telling us where to find her,'
explained Dan Fry, her bureau chief. 'She had a difficult
time, and I took the decision to fly her out of the country
before making the details public.'

He went on to say that Connie had been in fear of
her life before she was abandoned in a bombed-out
building to the west of the city. 'When we found her she
was bound and gagged with a black hood over her
head. We believe her treatment was in revenge for Abu
Ghraib and we ask both coalition and dissident forces
in Iraq to remember that all abuse of power is a
crime.'

'Connie's first thoughts were for Adelina Bianca,' the
agency chief told a press conference. 'She was
informed by her captors that Adelina was beheaded on
Tuesday and was warned to expect the same fate. She

reacted emotionally when we said that to the best of our knowledge Adelina is still alive.'

It was a measure of Connie Burns's courage, he went on, that she spent three hours helping police before flying out of Baghdad airport. 'Her greatest regret is that she was unable to give them any useful information. She was blindfolded after being snatched from her car by masked men when her driver left the airport road and took her into the al-Jahid district.'

Police have issued a description of the driver. 'The car was hijacked minutes before it collected Connie from her hotel,' said Dan Fry. He confirmed that Reuters have issued tougher guidelines to their correspondents. 'In future, no one should assume a vehicle is safe,' he warned. 'It's easy to become complacent when you've been a passenger in the same car several times.'

He refused to give further details of Connie Burns's captivity. 'At the moment her primary concern is for Adelina Bianca. Connie is determined to say and do nothing that might jeopardize Adelina's release.'

The armed group holding Ms Bianca issued the following statement. 'The fate of Adelina Bianca will be decided by the Prime Minister of Italy. While he gives sustenance to American soldiers to occupy the sacred land of Iraq, the mothers of his country will receive only coffins from us. The dignity of Muslim men and women is not redeemed except by blood and souls.'

It is now over a week since Adelina was taken hostage, but the passing of Tuesday's deadline for her execution offers a glimmer of hope. There is considerable concern among moderate Iraqi religious leaders that the escalating brutality of hostage-takers is further damaging Islam in the eyes of the world. 'Islam does not wage war on innocent women and children,' said one. 'In the face of these atrocities, the shocking abuse at Abu Ghraib prison is being forgotten. These groups are handing the moral victory to America.'

Three

I watched Adelina's release on the television in my parents' flat after the crowd of reporters and photographers who'd thronged their road finally departed. By that time, a week after I'd left Baghdad, my own story was dead. I'd eluded the Reuters welcoming committee at Heathrow, failed to show up for a press conference, and buried myself in an anonymous hotel in London as Marianne Curran – an agoraphobic woman with no appetite and frequent nosebleeds, who never left her room, and whose stay was paid for in cash by the sugar daddy who visited her every evening.

God knows what the hotel made of me. The only request I made of them was the address and telephone number of the nearest STD clinic. Otherwise, I wouldn't let the chambermaids into the room, smoked like a chimney, spent hours in the bath and ate only when my father ordered sandwiches on room service. I put on a good show for him whenever he appeared, but I could see it concerned him that I only ate crumbs.

The story I gave him for my refusal to meet the

press was the same as Dan had offered in Baghdad: I didn't want to speak publicly about my captivity for fear of jeopardizing Adelina's chances. For his private peace of mind, I told him I'd been blindfolded throughout and had never seen my captors, but had been treated reasonably despite being terrified.

I don't know if he believed me. My mother certainly didn't when he smuggled me into the flat at three o'clock one morning. She was shocked at how much weight I'd lost, worried by my preference for darkened rooms and deeply suspicious of my refusal to talk to anyone, particularly Dan Fry in Baghdad and Reuters in London. However, as I locked myself in the spare bedroom every time she tried to question me, my father put pressure on her to let me deal with things in my own way.

Adelina Bianca was my single excuse. As long as she remained in captivity I had a reason for keeping quiet, so it was with mixed emotions that I watched her uncertain steps on television as she emerged from a mosque in Baghdad, dressed in a heavy black chador. Beside her was the imam who had negotiated her freedom. She was so hidden beneath the veil that I couldn't read anything from her face, but her voice was strong as she thanked everyone who'd helped her. She denied that the Italian government had paid a ransom.

Twenty-four hours later I sat glued to the set again as she gave a press conference in Milan. It was a bravura performance which left me ashamed of my own inability to talk about what had happened to me. I didn't have Adelina's courage.

*

As soon as Adelina was released, I scoured websites for rented property in the West Country. Of course my mother was unhappy about it, particularly when I told her I planned to take a six-month lease and asked if I could use her maiden name again. Why did I want to do that? What about Reuters? How was I going to live? Why did I keep telling her I was fine when I so obviously wasn't? What was wrong? And why was I going into hiding the minute Adelina was free?

Once again, my father stepped in. 'Let her be,' he said firmly. 'If she doesn't know her own mind at thirty-six, then she never will. Some wounds only heal in fresh air.'

I could – probably *should* – have told them the truth, and I wonder now why I didn't. I was their only child and we had a close and supportive relationship despite the often huge distances between us. But my father had so many regrets about abandoning the farm in Zimbabwe that I hesitated to burden him with mine. If he hadn't been married, he'd have stayed put and barricaded the house out of bloody-mindedness, but my mother forced his hand after one of their neighbours was murdered by Mugabe's Zanu-PF thugs.

My father never forgave himself for what he saw as capitulation. He felt he should have fought harder for what his family had bought and built, and what was rightfully his. He landed a reasonably paid job in London with a South African wine importer, but he hated the insularity of England, the claustrophobia of city life and the modest rented flat in Kentish Town that was a quarter the size of their farmhouse outside Bulawayo.

I take after my mother in looks, tall and blonde, and my father in character, determinedly independent. On the face of it, my mother appears the least secure of the three of us, yet I wonder if her willingness to admit fear shows that she's the most self-assured. For my father, running away was an admission of defeat. He thought of himself as strong and resolute, and I realized in the summer of 2004 how humiliating it had been for him to cut and run. He hadn't found the courage to confront Mugabe's bullies any more than I could find the courage to confront mine . . . and we both felt diminished as a result.

The excuse I gave them of wanting time and space to write a book was partially true. I'd produced an outline while still in Baghdad (in the aftermath of the Abu Ghraib revelations) and had been offered a publishing contract on the back of it. I saw how twitched I and my colleagues became when the West lost its sheen of moral respectability, and my idea had been to chart the world's trouble-spots through the eyes of war correspondents. I particularly wanted to explore how constant exposure to danger affects the psyche.

The original advance offered was a pittance but I renegotiated it on the basis that the book would include a full and free account of my kidnapping. It was straightforward fraud, because I signed the contract knowing I would never reveal the truth. Indeed, I couldn't see myself writing a book at all – I seized up every time I sat in front of a keyboard – but I had no conscience about persuading the publishers I was committed. It was the pretext I needed to take myself out of circulation while I stitched my tattered nerves together again.

I found Barton House on a Dorset agent's website and chose it because it was the only property available on a six-month lease. It was far too big for one person but the weekly rent was the same as for a three-bedroomed holiday cottage. When I queried this, the agent told me that holiday lets were unreliable and the owner wanted a guaranteed regular income. Since I could afford it, I accepted his explanation and forwarded a money draft under the name I'd used in the hotel, which was my mother's maiden name – Marianne Curran – but even if he'd told me the truth, that the house was in a poor state of decorative repair, I would still have gone ahead. I was obsessed at that stage with removing myself from the world.

I don't know what I expected – to be part of a small community where I could close the door when

I felt like it, perhaps – but that wasn't the reality. All the arrangements had been made by email and telephone until my collection of the key from the agent's office in Dorchester half an hour earlier. The photograph of Barton House on the website had shown climbing plants across a stone façade, with the roof of another building to the side (a garage as I discovered later). I had assumed, since the address was Winterbourne Barton, that this meant it was within the village boundaries.

Instead, it stood behind high hedges, well away from the nearest house, and with most of it invisible from the road. An absence of crowds was exactly what it promised – even isolation – and I halted my newly acquired Mini at the entrance and stared through the windscreen with anxiety fluttering at my heart. The human maelstrom of London had been a nightmare during the three weeks I'd spent with my parents because I'd never known who was behind me. But surely this was worse? To be alone, and hidden from view, with no protection and no one within calling distance?

The hedges cast long shadows and the garden was so wild and unkempt that an army could have been lurking there without my seeing them. Since the moment I'd landed at Heathrow, I'd been trying to conquer my fears by reaffirming what I knew to be true – *I was no longer in danger because I'd done what I was told* – but there's no reasoning with anxiety. It's an intense internal emotion that isn't susceptible to logic. All you can do is experience the terror that your brain has told your body to feel.

I drove in eventually because I had nowhere else to go. The house was pretty enough – a low rectangular eighteenth-century construction – but, close to, its tattiness showed. The sun and salt winds had taken their toll of the doors and window-frames, and so many of the tiles had slipped that I wondered if the roof was even waterproof, despite the agent's assurances on his website that the property was sound. It didn't worry me – I'd seen far worse, most recently in Baghdad, where bomb damage left whole buildings in ruins – but I began to understand why Barton House compared favourably with three-bedroomed cottages.

Does any of us know our breaking point? Mine was when the large iron key to the front door jammed in the lock and five mastiffs appeared out of nowhere as I tried to find a signal on my mobile. I was pointing it towards the horizon and only realized the dogs were there when one of them started growling. They took up guard around me with their muzzles inches from my skirt, and I felt the familiar adrenaline rush as my autonomic fear response kicked into action.

Half a second's thought would have told me there was an owner around, but I was so petrified I couldn't think at all. It didn't even register when I dropped my phone. You can reinforce your confidence as many times as you like, but it's a futile exercise when your

fear is so real that a single growl can reawaken nightmares. I'd never seen the dogs in the Baghdad cellar
but I could still hear and feel them, and they inhabited
my dreams.

I didn't notice the owner until she was standing in
front of me, and I mistook her gender until she spoke.
I certainly didn't take her for an adult. She was
wearing denims and a man's shirt that was too big for
her slight body, and her curiously flat features and
slicked-back dark hair made me think she was an
adolescent boy who was still growing. If she weighed
a hundred pounds I'd have been surprised. Any one of
the mastiffs could have crushed the life out of her just
by lying on her.

'Keep your hands still,' she said curtly. 'Birdlike
movements excite them.'

She gave a flick of her fingers and the dogs ranged
themselves in front of her, heads lowered.

'You look like Madeleine,' she said. 'Are you
related?'

I had no idea what she was talking about, and
didn't care anyway because I couldn't breathe. I
dropped into a squat, head back, sucking for oxygen,
but all I achieved was to set her dogs growling again.
At that point I gave up and scrabbled on all fours
towards the open door of the Mini. I dived in and
pulled it to, clicking the lock behind me, before
leaning back in a desperate attempt to get some air
into my lungs. I think one of the dogs must have

charged the car because I felt it lurch, followed by a sharp command from the girl, but I'd closed my eyes and wasn't watching.

I knew what was happening. I knew it wouldn't last and that all I had to do was stop the rapid, shallow breathing, but this time the pains in my chest were so bad that I wondered if I was having a heart attack. I groped for my stash of paper bags in the door pocket and clamped one over my nose and mouth, trying to ease the symptoms. I've no idea how long it took. Time didn't exist. But when I opened my eyes, the girl and her dogs had gone.

Extracts from notes, filed as 'CB15–18/05/04'

. . . I used to be afraid of the dark, but now I sit for
hours with the lights off. It felt as if red-hot pokers
were burning through my lids when Dan ripped the
duct tape away. He was upset when I refused to open
my eyes and look at him but I didn't know who it was.
He could have been anyone. The voice didn't sound
like Dan's. He didn't smell like Dan either.

. . . I do find it frightening that I can't bear anyone to
come too close. My invadable space has grown to
house-size proportions. Is that how the mind works?
I shut myself in little spaces but need a palace around
them to give me room to breathe. I can manage to sit
in a room with my parents, but no one else. I freak if
I'm in the street and a passer-by brushes against me.
I don't go out now unless I'm in my car.

. . . I told my parents I was going for counselling, and
it's odd how much better it's made them feel. I must be
OK if I'm in the hands of 'experts'. Despite my
mother's endless questions, I think she's secretly
relieved that I've rejected Reuters' help. The quid pro
quo for official support would have been an obligation
to deliver my 'story'. But she and Dad are private

people. It was hard for them when I was all over the newspapers and the phone never stopped ringing . . .

. . . Instead of counselling, I go to a church in Hampstead for a couple of hours every other day. It's cool and quiet and has its own car park. No one troubles me much. They seem to feel it's bad form to question why anyone would want to sit there. Perhaps they think I'm talking to God . . .

Barton House

Four

IN ORDINARY CIRCUMSTANCES I wouldn't have met Jess Derbyshire. She was so reclusive that only a handful of people in Winterbourne Barton had seen inside her house; and the rest were happy to spread the rumour that the local policeman went in once a month to check she was still alive. He didn't, of course. He was as scared of her dogs as everyone else, and he took the view that the postman would notice if she wasn't collecting her mail from the American-style box at her gate. She owned and managed Barton Farm, which lay to the south-west of the village, and her house was even more detached from the community than mine.

I discovered very quickly that Jess was both the most invisible resident of Winterbourne Valley, and the most talked about. The first thing any newcomer learnt was that her immediate family had been killed in a car crash in 1992. She'd had a younger brother and sister, and two thoroughly nice parents, until a drunk in a Range-Rover ploughed into her father's ancient Peugeot at seventy miles an hour on the

Dorchester bypass. The second, that she was twenty when it happened, making her older than she looked; and the third, that she'd turned her family home into a shrine to the dead.

There's no question she had an uncongenial personality, something she was happy to foster with her pack of thirty-inch high, hundred-and-eighty-pound mastiffs. It showed itself most obviously in her unfriendly stares and curt way of speaking, but it was the close relationship between her immature looks – 'arrested development' – and her morbid interest in her dead family – 'refusal to move forward' – that most people felt explained her peculiarity. Her 'loner' status made them wary, even though few seemed to know her.

My own first impression was no different – I thought her very strange – and when I opened my eyes I was relieved to find she'd gone. I do remember wondering if she'd set her dogs on me deliberately, and what kind of person would abandon another who was so obviously distressed, but it reawakened too many memories of Iraq and I pushed her from my mind. It meant I wasn't prepared for her return. When she drove her Land-Rover through Barton House gates fifteen minutes later and deliberately blocked my exit, alarm immediately coursed through my system again.

In my rear-view mirror I watched her climb out

with a metal toolbox in her hand. She walked to the front of the Mini and examined me through the windscreen, apparently to satisfy herself that I was still alive. Her flat, narrow face was so impassive, and the intrusive stare so unwelcome, that I closed my eyes to blot her out. I could cope with anything as long as I couldn't see it. Like an ostrich with its head in the sand.

'I'm Jess Derbyshire,' she said, loud enough for me to hear. 'I've called Dr Coleman. He's with a patient but he's promised to come straight on when he's finished.' There was a hint of a Dorset burr in her voice, but it was the deepness of her register that struck me the most. She seemed to want to sound like a man as well as dress like one.

I thought if I didn't reply she might go away.

'Shutting your eyes won't help,' she said. 'You need to open your window. It's too hot in there.' I heard something tap against the glass. 'I've brought a bottle of water for you.'

Desperate for something to drink, I opened my eyes a crack and met her unwelcome stare again. The sun was beating relentlessly down on the roof and my hair was plastered to my scalp with sweat. She waited while I lowered the window four inches, then passed the bottle through before nodding towards the door of the house. She twisted her hand as if to indicate that she was going to unlock it, then moved away to kneel on the doorstep. I watched her take a can of WD40 from her toolbox and spray a fine mist into the lock before sitting back on her heels.

In a funny sort of way she reminded me of Adelina, small and neat and competent, but without the Italian's expressiveness. Jess's movements were economical and spare, as if the method of releasing a key was something she'd practised for years. And perhaps she had.

'It always sticks,' she said, stooping to talk through the window. 'Lily never used it . . . she bolted the door inside and came in and out through the scullery. The oil takes about ten minutes to work. Were you given any other keys? There should be a mortise and a Yale for the back door.'

I glanced at an envelope on the passenger seat.

She followed my gaze. 'May I have them?' she asked, holding out her hand.

I shook my head.

'Try counting birds,' she said abruptly. 'It always worked for me. By the time I got to twenty, I'd usually forgotten why I'd started.' Her dark eyes searched my face for a moment before, with a shrug, she went back to the doorstep and squatted on her haunches in front of it. After a while she took a pair of pliers from her toolbox and used them to tease the key back and forth. When she finally managed to turn it, she twisted the handle and disappeared inside. A few seconds later, a light came on in the hall. After that, she moved along the ground floor, opening windows to let in the fresh air.

I wanted to get out and shout at her. Stop interfering. Who's going to close the place up again after I've left? But I'd become so comfortable with doing nothing that that's what I continued to do. I did watch the birds, however. I couldn't avoid it. The garden was alive with them. Flocks of house-sparrows, endangered in the cities, chattered and darted about the trees, while swallows and house-martins flashed in and out of nests beneath the eaves.

When Jess reappeared, she hunkered down beside my door to put herself on the same level as me. 'The Aga needs lighting. Do you want me to show you how to do it?'

I might have gone on ignoring her if I'd cared less about seeming rude or looking foolish, so perhaps counting birds did work. I ran my tongue around my mouth to produce some saliva. 'No, thank you.'

She tipped her chin towards the envelope. 'Are there any instructions in there?'

'I don't know.'

'If Madeleine wrote them, you won't be able to light the Aga yourself. She doesn't even know how to spark the ignition, let alone prime the burner.'

It was on the tip of my tongue to ask who Madeleine was, or even Lily, the name she'd mentioned earlier, but there was no point. 'I'm not staying,' I told her.

She didn't seem surprised. 'You'll need your car keys then.'

I nodded.

She fished them out of her pocket and held them up. 'I took them from your bag when I was looking for an inhaler. It was close to where you dropped your mobile.'

'I'm not asthmatic.'

'I guessed.' She curled her fingers round the keys. 'I'm going to hang on to them to stop you driving. You can't leave yet . . . not behind a wheel, anyway. If you want them back, you'll have to come into the house and get them.'

Her assumption that I would tamely do as she said annoyed me. I still thought of her as younger than she was, but there was a rigidity about her slight frame that suggested a strength of purpose I didn't have. 'Are you a policeman?'

'No. Just playing safe. You'll damage yourself as well as other people if I let you go now.' She searched my face again. 'Was it the dogs?'

I recalled how long it had taken me to drive through the entrance. 'No.'

She gave a satisfied nod before tucking the keys back into her pocket. 'The doctor who's coming – Peter Coleman – knows nothing about panic attacks,' she said bluntly. 'He'll probably tell you to take tranquillizers and write out a shopping list of anti-depressants to lift your mood. I only phoned him to cover my arse in case you tried to sue. You'd do better to put your faith in paper bags and break the cycle.'

A small laugh floated round my head. 'Are you a psychiatrist?'

'No, but I had a few panic attacks when I was twenty.'

'What were you afraid of?'

She thought for a moment. 'Not being able to cope, I suppose. I was left with a farm to run, and I didn't know how to do it. What are *you* afraid of?'

Suffocation . . . drowning . . . dying . . .

'Not being able to cope,' I echoed flatly.

It was a truth of sorts but she didn't believe it. Either my tone was wrong or my face was telling her something else. I wondered if she was offended that I hadn't confided in her, because she pushed herself to her feet and disappeared back into the house again. Some while afterwards, the doctor arrived.

He drew up alongside Jess's Land-Rover and I watched him ease himself out of the driver's door. He was a tall, dark-haired man, dressed in a linen jacket and cavalry twills, and I could see a golf bag propped on the front seat of his BMW. He stooped to check his tie in the driver's window before walking past me and into Barton House. I heard him call: 'Where the hell are you, Jess? What's this all about?' before his voice was swallowed by the walls.

If anything was guaranteed to set me panicking again it was the thought of all the fuss that was going to follow. Ambulances ... psychiatrists ... hospitals ... the press. I could predict the tabloid headlines: '*Distressed Connie Has Breakdown.*' It was the stimulus I needed to get out of the car because I knew I couldn't face the shame of disclosure again. I should have been as brave as Adelina.

Did you try to resist? No.

Did you ask the men who they were? No.

Did you ask them why they were doing it? No.

Did you talk to them at all? No.

Can you tell us anything, Ms Burns? No.

I eased my fingers out of a fist to reach for the door-handle, and found I'd been gripping the paper bag so hard that it had begun to disintegrate in the sweat of my palm. It's the little things that frighten. I had a sudden, terrible fear that this was my last bag.

It wasn't. My stash was still in the pocket to my right, a heap of folded brown paper that represented a lifeline. It's a trick I discovered on the internet. If you inhale your own carbon dioxide, the symptoms of panic begin to lessen. The brain understands that the body isn't going to die of asphyxiation, and the vicious cycle of terror is temporarily broken. As I learnt later, the means of managing her attacks had been Jess's key to stopping them, but, for me, paper bags were merely a last resort before I died of suffocation.

I wiped my hands fiercely against each other to rid myself of the shreds. It was Lady Macbeth stuff. 'Out, damned spot! Out, I say! Hell is murky!' But how did

Shakespeare know that troubled women need to clean themselves obsessively? Is it something we've done for centuries to purge ourselves of filth?

I remembered reading on the web description of Barton House that there was a fishpond in the garden. It wasn't visible from my car, so logic said it was round the back. It doesn't matter what drove me there to wash my hands, but I've often wondered since if the reason I became interested in Lily Wright's story was because I knelt to wash my hands where Jess Derbyshire had found her dying.

Five

FROM WHAT I learnt later, I don't believe Lily and I would have been friends. She had old-fashioned views about a woman's place, and would certainly have frowned on an unmarried war correspondent who put job before family. Her position in life was to play 'grande dame' to Winterbourne Barton because Barton House was the oldest and largest in the valley and her family had lived in it for three generations. While her husband was alive, and before the demography of the village changed with an influx of outsiders, she took an active part in community life, but after his death she became increasingly detached from it.

It was a slow process that went largely unnoticed, and most people assumed that her regular mentioning of close connections with Dorset's aristocracy meant she preferred her old associates to Winterbourne Barton's newcomers. Her daughter, Madeleine, who visited irregularly from London, reinforced this view by talking about her mother's social standing; and, since Lily glossed over her deceased husband's squandering of her fortune on the stock market and made a pretence of being wealthier than she was, it was generally accepted that her friends were outside the community.

She survived on a state pension and some small dividends that she'd managed to keep from her husband, Robert, but poverty was always lurking round the corner. It meant that Barton House was in a terrible state of repair – something I discovered as soon as I moved in – with bowed ceilings and damp walls, but as few visitors were allowed beyond the hall and drawing-room this wasn't generally known. Stains on carpets and walls were hidden beneath rugs and pictures, and wisteria was coaxed across the peeling paintwork on the windowsills outside. She dressed elegantly in tweed skirts and jackets, with her white hair twisted into a loose chignon at the back of her neck; and she remained a handsome woman until Alzheimer's stopped her caring.

Her garden was her passion and, though it was running wild by the time I arrived, the care she'd lavished on it was still obvious. The house remained much as it had been in her grandfather's time. There was no central heating and any warmth came from the Aga in the kitchen or had to be provided by log fires. Upstairs, the damp made the bedrooms cold, even in summer, and there was never enough hot water to fill the big, old-fashioned bath. Showers were nonexistent. There was an antiquated twin-tub washing-machine, a small fridge-freezer, a cheap microwave and a television in the back room where Lily spent most of her time. During the winters she wrapped herself in a great coat and blankets, which she discarded if anyone came to the front door in order to pretend she'd been sitting in front of an unlit fire in the draughty drawing-room.

Like much of Dorset, Winterbourne Barton had changed radically over the previous twenty years with house prices soaring and local people selling up in order to realize their most valuable asset. Two or three of the properties became second homes and remained empty for large parts of the year, but most of the newcomers were city retirees on good pension schemes who bought into Winterbourne Barton for its picture-postcard quality and proximity to the sea.

The village began life in the eighteenth century when a previous owner of Barton House used some unproductive land to erect three cottages for his workers. Built in Purbeck stone with thatched roofs and casement windows, these picturesque houses set the pattern for the hundred or so that followed until West Dorset council designated Winterbourne Barton a conservation area and further development was banned. It was this restriction on new building, as much as the roses and honeysuckle climbing up the pretty stone façades, that attracted pensioners. It seemed there was a cachet to exclusivity, particularly when a village was among the most photographed (and envied) in the county.

The explanation for Lily's continued isolation was

her own refusal to socialize. She invited anyone in who called, but the reception was as cool as her drawing-room, and the conversation was invariably about her 'chums' – the great and good of the West Country – and never about the newcomers in front of her. According to Jess, she was too proud to admit she'd fallen on hard times, which would have become obvious if she'd developed close friendships with her neighbours, but I think it more likely she shared Jess's indifference to people.

Her only regular visitor was Jess, whose grand-mother had been a maid at Barton House during and after the war years. This servant/mistress relationship appeared to have been handed down through the Derbyshire family, first to Jess's father, and on his death to Jess herself. Although neither was paid for what they did, it seemed they were at Lily's beck and call whenever anything went wrong, and even supplied her with free food from the farm to eke out her pension.

It was a state of affairs that Lily's daughter, Madeleine, apparently took for granted. Busy in London with a husband and an eleven-year-old son, she relied on Jess to perform a service that she couldn't do herself. Yet she made no secret of her dislike of Jess; nor did Jess hide hers in return. The reasons for the rift were unknown, but Winterbourne Barton's sympathies were definitely with Lily's daughter. Madeleine was an attractive forty-year-old who, unlike her mother and Jess, had an open, friendly personality and was popular in the village. There was also a general suspicion that Jess's motives in making herself indispensable to a wealthy woman were questionable.

Lily was first diagnosed with Alzheimer's in June of 2003. She was seventy years old, which made her comparatively young for the disease, but it was still in its early stages and, barring brief bouts of forgetfulness, there was no reason why she shouldn't remain independent for some time to come. Confusion led her to stray during the autumn, and several of her neighbours found her wandering in Winterbourne Barton. As no one had been told she had Alzheimer's, and she spoke quite sensibly when they pointed her in the direction of where she lived, they assumed it was mild eccentricity – only bad when the wind was north-north-west.

Her condition deteriorated markedly over Christmas and the New Year. On four occasions in January she let herself in through unlocked back doors while householders were watching television in the evening, and tiptoed upstairs. She used their flannels and toothbrushes to wash her face and hands and clean her teeth at their basins, then climbed, fully clothed, between their sheets and fell asleep. She reacted aggressively when she was discovered, but was quickly calmed by a cup of tea and a biscuit.

Still claiming to be unaware that Lily was seriously ill – despite her dishevelled appearance and bizarre behaviour – the four householders drove her home each time and took it no further. They described her as rude and unpleasant, and said she insisted on being returned immediately to Barton House, claiming the only help she wanted was Jess Derbyshire's or Dr Peter Coleman's. She dismissed her rescuers as soon she reached her back door.

The incidents were discussed in the village, but the consensus appeared to be that it was better not to interfere. If they didn't get the rough edge of Lily's tongue, they'd certainly get the rough edge of Jess Derbyshire's. Had Peter Coleman been around, they'd have raised the matter with him, but he was on holiday and wasn't expected back till the end of January. A message was left on Madeleine's answerphone, but she, too, was away, and no one felt confident about suggesting to Peter Coleman's locum that Mrs Wright was behaving oddly.

Afterwards, the finger of blame was pointed firmly at Jess. How could Winterbourne Barton know that she hadn't been near Lily since November? She'd fawned over the woman for years, knew better than anyone that Lily's mental condition was fragile, then abandoned her without a word when the consequences of Alzheimer's became too demanding. Why hadn't she told anyone?

Yet it was Jess who saved Lily's life. At eleven o'clock at night on the third Friday in January, she found her barely alive and dressed only in a nightdress beside the Barton House fishpond. Not strong enough to carry Lily to the back door, and with no mobile signal to call for help, she reversed her Land-Rover across the lawn, hoisted Lily into the back and drove her back to Barton Farm, where she phoned for a doctor.

There were no plaudits, only more suspicion. What was Jess doing in Lily's garden at that time of night? Why didn't she use the landline in the house? Why had she driven Lily to Barton Farm instead of the hospital? Why call in social services so quickly? Why accuse everyone else of neglect when it was she who'd neglected Lily the most shamefully? Conspiracy theories abounded, particularly when it became clear that Lily had secretly reassigned enduring power of attorney from her daughter to her solicitor. Jess was assumed to have been behind the decision.

In Madeleine's absence, Lily was sectioned for her own safety and placed in care over the weekend while efforts were made to contact her solicitor. Madeleine rushed down the following week on her return from holiday, only to discover that her mother's fate was out of her hands. Lily's solicitor had wasted no time in moving her to an expensive nursing-home, nor of announcing his intention to sell Barton House and the family heirlooms to cover the fees.

Depending on whom you believed, Madeleine was either a cold-hearted bitch who wanted her mother dead in order to inherit the house before it was sacrificed to Lily's care; or she was so uninformed about her mother's condition and precarious financial position that Lily's catastrophic decline and subsequent revelations of poverty came as a terrible shock. Being cynical, I found such ignorance hard to accept, although Winterbourne Barton pointed to the weekly allowance that Lily had been paying her daughter since she turned eighteen. Why go on with it if she hadn't wanted Madeleine to believe she was better off than she was?

In Lily's case, poverty was relative to the sale of Barton House. While it remained in her estate, her income was insufficient to meet her needs. Sold, it would realize upwards of £1.5 million. Not unreasonably, Madeleine resisted the sale. Her mother could die tomorrow or live for another twenty years, but to sell the family home on a gamble of twenty years was precipitate. A battle for control ensued between Madeleine and Lily's solicitor. The solicitor offered a compromise. If the house was let, and all the income from the remaining stocks and shares was diverted to Lily's care, then he would postpone the sale.

Which was where I came in as Barton House's first tenant. I knew nothing of its recent history as I stooped to wash my hands, and if I had I wouldn't have stayed. It was a place of anguish . . .

Extracts from notes, filed as 'CB15–18/05/04'

... I remember a woman in Freetown who roamed the
street outside my compound and shouted at herself.
I thought she was deaf as well as deranged until I was
told that she'd hidden under her house when a band of
rebels came to her village. The dozen fighters massacred
everyone, including the woman's husband and children,
and only left when the smell of the rotting bodies
became unbearable. The mother's response was to
berate herself publicly for being alive.

... I often think of her. The length of time she lay
under her house – motionless, terrified, silent – was
about as long as I spent in the Baghdad cellar. Did she
talk to herself to stay sane? And, if so, what about?
Did she argue the merits of saving her own skin against
leaving her children to perish? Is that when her loop of
madness began?

... There's a scream inside my head that won't go
away. Perhaps it's in everyone's head. Perhaps it's what
made the woman in Freetown shout. *Why does no one
care about me?*

Six

THE HALL WAS dark and cool after the brilliant sunshine outside. Doors on either side opened into rooms that didn't appear to lead anywhere, and a branching staircase rose in front of me. It was only when I heard a murmur of voices coming from somewhere to my right that I noticed a green baize door at the back. It was operated by a self-closing hinge and when I eased it open six inches, I could make out words.

'I still don't understand why I had to park beside your filthy old jalopy,' said the man's voice. 'Don't you think it's a little OTT to steal her keys *and* block her exit?' He spoke in a light, bantering tone as if teasing this woman-child came naturally to him.

Jess, by contrast, sounded irritated, as if his patronizing approach got on her nerves. 'She might have had a spare set in the car.'

'In which case she'd have left while you were phoning me from the farm,' he pointed out reasonably.

'Then it's a pity I can't see into the future,' she snapped. 'If I could, I wouldn't have bothered you at all. I was afraid she'd invoke the dangerous dogs' act if I didn't make a pretence of caring.'

'Who is she?'

'I don't know . . . she has keys to the house so I assume she's a tenant. I thought it was the dogs that frightened her, which is why I drove them home.' She gave a brief account of what had happened.

'Did you consider that she might be allergic to fur?'

'Of course, but I asked her if it was anything to do with the dogs, and she said no.'

'OK.' He must have been sitting down because I heard the sound of chair legs scraping across the floor as he prepared to stand up. 'I'll go and talk to her.'

'No!' said Jess sharply. 'She needs to come in of her own accord.'

Peter Coleman sounded amused. 'What's the point of my being here if you've already decided on the treatment?'

'I've already told you. I didn't want to be sued.'

'Well, I can't sit around all afternoon,' he said with a yawn. 'I'm on the golf course in half an hour.'

'There are other sorts of treatment besides pills, you know. You wouldn't think twice about cancelling your golf if one of your old ladies wanted a chat. It might tarnish your halo.'

Surprisingly, Peter laughed. 'My God! Do you *ever* give up? It's a shame no one's invented a cure for grudge-bearing . . . I'd have put you on a drip and pumped you full of it twelve years ago. Just for the record – *again* – you hadn't slept in five days and your heart was going like a hammer.' He paused as if waiting for a response. 'You know the sedatives worked, Jess. They gave you some respite, which was what your body needed.'

'They turned me into a zombie.'

'For all of a week, while your grandmother shouldered the burden. Don't you think I'd have given you a paper bag myself if that was all you needed?'

Jess didn't answer.

'So what's your prescription for the woman out there?'

'Slowlee, slowlee, catchee monkee.'

'What about my golf? I do have a life outside medicine, you know.'

But Jess wasn't interested, and a silence fell between them. I suppose I should have announced myself but it was a situation that was doomed to embarrassment whatever I did. Half of me hoped they'd up stumps and leave if I delayed long enough; the other half recognized that the longer the delay the more difficult the explanations. What was I going to say, anyway? That I was leaving? That I *wasn't* leaving? And what name was I going to use in front of the doctor? If he applied for Marianne Curran's medical records, they would show me as sixty-three.

I think it was standing in Lily's hall during that long hiatus that persuaded me to stay. It was impossible to ignore the tattiness – in one place three feet of wallpaper near the ceiling had come away from the Blu-Tack blobs that had been holding it in place – but in an odd sort of way it appealed to me. Apart from my stint in Iraq I'd spent the last two years in a minimalist flat in a high-rise block in Singapore, where space was limited, cream was the predominant colour and none of the furniture reached above my knees. It was hideously impractical – red wine was a nightmare – and hideously uncomfortable – I couldn't move without barking my shins – but everyone who saw it had commented on the designer's flair.

This was the opposite. Spacious, lofty and red-wine-friendly. The faded wallpaper in blues and greens, of Japanese pagodas, feathery willow fronds and exotic pheasant-style birds, was a good fifty years old, while the furniture, big and lumbering, was utilitarian Victorian. There was a battered chest of drawers under one branch of the stairs, a leather grandfather chair, sprouting horsehair from its seat, under the other, and an ugly oak table in the middle carrying a plastic pot plant. Perhaps the threadbare Axminster rug underneath it added a sense of recognition, because it reminded me of the one we'd had in Zimbabwe. My grandfather had imported it with great ceremony and then refused to allow anyone to walk on it.

The doctor's voice broke the silence. 'Does it never occur to you that you might be wrong?'

'About what?'

'At the moment, that woman out there. You're assuming she can pull herself together enough to come inside . . . but supposing she can't?' He paused to let her answer, but went on when she didn't. 'Perhaps her fears are real, perhaps she's frightened of something tangible? How much do you know about her?'

'Nothing, except that she talks with a South African accent and knows the paper bag trick.'

'Ah!'

'What's that supposed to mean?'

'It explains why you think she's going to come in. Paper bags are to you what leeches were to sixteenth-century quacks . . . the cure to everything.'

'They're a damn sight less harmful than Valium.'

Peter gave a snort of derision. 'It wasn't paper bags that cured you, Jess, it was getting to grips with running the farm. You conquered a steep learning curve through sheer bloody guts and an above average intelligence. Show me the paper bag that taught you how to shove your hand up a cow's backside to help deliver a calf.' He paused.

'What would you know about it?' I heard a door crash open angrily. 'I'm going out to see if she's still in her car.'

'Good idea.' There was another long silence.

I looked towards the front door, expecting Jess to come in that way, but I heard her voice in the kitchen again. 'She's not there. She must be in the house.'

'So what happens now?'

For the first time she sounded unsure of herself. 'Perhaps we should make a noise so she knows where we are. If we go to meet her she might take fright.'

'All right,' he teased. 'What do you want me to do? Sing? Tap dance? Bang some saucepans together?'

'Don't be an idiot.'

His tone softened as if he were smiling at her. 'If she's made it to the front door, I think you can safely welcome her in. I'll put the kettle on while you're doing it. Let's pray she's brought some tea bags with her. If Madeleine left any of Lily's behind they'll have grown mould by now. Go on, do your stuff. You never know, she might surprise you.'

It was only afterwards, when I found a mirror in the bathroom, that I realized how dreadful I looked. My T-shirt and long flimsy skirt did me no favours at all, clinging as they did to every angular bone and showing how skinny I was. My eyes had dark rings round them, my hair looked as if it had been doused in Brylcreem and my face was covered in blotches. I'd have taken myself for a depressed mental case, so it wasn't surprising that Jess and Peter both showed concern when they saw me.

I must have looked angry, too, because Jess's first instinct was to apologize when she came through the baize door and found me beside the table in the hall. 'I'm sorry,' she said after a small hesitation. 'I just wanted to let you know that we're in the kitchen.'

'Right.'

She nodded to the mobile, which I'd retrieved from the Mini's bonnet and still held in my hand. 'If you're looking for a signal there isn't one, I'm afraid. It's the same in my house. I can get one in the attic but that's about it. We're too low down the valley.' She jerked her thumb over her shoulder. 'The landline works if that's any help. I've checked it. There's a cordless phone beside the fridge.'

'Right.'

My one-word answers seemed to disconcert her and she stared at the floor. Not knowing her, I assumed she expected gratitude for her intervention, and it was only later that I discovered how much she relied on other people to make conversation. Peter blamed her introverted nature, but I always felt there was a level of arrogance in it as well. She was above the common courtesy of small talk, and it was left to others to struggle with her silences.

We were rescued by Peter, who appeared out of the corridor behind her and advanced on me with a smile on his face. 'Hi, there,' he said, reaching for my hand. 'I'm Peter Coleman. Welcome to Winterbourne Barton. I gather Jess's dogs gave you a bit of a fright.'

I tried to step back but his fingers had already swallowed mine. 'Marianne Curran,' I said, eyes widening as my skin crawled under his.

He released me immediately and stood aside to gesture me towards the corridor. 'I can't get it into Jess's head that the average person doesn't appreciate being slobbered over by those ugly great brutes. Their bark's a lot worse than their bite, of course – rather like their mistress.' His eyes lit with ironic humour as he ignored Jess's glare and shepherded me towards the kitchen. 'How far have you driven? If you've come from London, you must be exhausted . . .'

He sat me at the table and kept up an innocuous monologue until I relaxed enough to answer, although I was guarded in what I said, giving half-truths rather than outright lies. I told him I'd been born and brought up on a farm in Zimbabwe, that I'd fled with my parents to London when our neighbour was murdered in a racist attack, and that I'd rented Barton House for six months to write a book. I expected to be quizzed on details but Peter appeared entirely indifferent to what type of book I was planning or whether I'd written one before. Nor did he visit the reasons for my panic attack.

Jess took no part in the conversation but stood by the door to the scullery, chewing at her bottom lip. She wouldn't look at either of us and I did wonder if she had a soft spot for Peter and was angry that he was giving his attention to me. It made for an uncomfortable atmosphere and I wished the pair of them would go. I'd like to have told Jess she had nothing to worry about – a tactile doctor with perceptive eyes was of no interest to me at all – but I didn't, of course.

Instead, I searched for a form of dismissal that wouldn't sound too rude when Peter said in a warning tone: 'Don't even think about leaving, Jess. You're the only person here who knows how to light the Aga.'

Her hand was on the door knob. 'I thought it'd be better if I came back later.'

He was watching me as he spoke. 'I'm the one who has to go,' he said, rising to his feet. 'I have a surgery at four-thirty and I haven't had anything to eat yet.' He took out his wallet and removed a card. 'I'm part of a rural practice that covers a wide area,' he told me, placing the card on the table. 'There are three practitioners and our main clinic's about eight miles away. Jess can give you directions. But you'll have to take out a temporary registration to use it – ' he held my gaze for a moment – 'and that means you'll need an NHS number or some proof of identity.'

I ran my tongue nervously across my lips.

'The alternative is to call me on my private line – ' he tapped the card – '*this* one. I live five minutes away at the western end of the village. If I'm at home, I'll come out . . . if not the call will be diverted to the clinic. Just give your name and ask for me personally, and the receptionist will put you straight through.'

Why was he making up excuses to go? It was only twenty minutes since he'd talked about playing golf. What had he guessed about me? What was he planning to do?

He knew I wasn't Marianne Curran, I thought, but did he know I was Connie Burns? My bureau chief, Dan Fry, had told me he'd released a photograph to the international press, but he'd promised it was an old one, taken when I first joined Reuters. Shorter hair, rounder face, and ten years younger. I folded the card into my palm. 'Thank you.'

Peter nodded. 'I'm leaving you in good hands. Jess's only weakness is that she assumes everyone is as capable as she is.' He turned towards her so that I couldn't see his expression or his hands, and I wondered what he was signalling. 'Take it gently, eh? You know where to find me if you need me.'

*

I learnt later that it was my mention of Zimbabwe that had jogged Peter's memory. *The Times* had run a piece the day after my abduction which gave details of my childhood in Africa and my parents' enforced decision to quit the farm. He felt it was too much of a coincidence that an author with the same background, and roughly corresponding to Connie Burns's description, should turn up in Winterbourne Barton showing signs of acute anxiety. He confirmed it by searching archive coverage on the internet when he got home, where he learnt that my mother's name was Marianne.

Jess had no such recognition. All she could see was a similarity in looks between me and Madeleine. Tall, blue-eyed, blonde and pushing forty. Even my name – *Marianne* – was similar. When she felt more comfortable with me, she said my only saving grace was that I didn't appear to have Madeleine's vanity about my appearance. Even in extremis, Madeleine would have been at the face powder long before she reached the boiled lobster stage. She would certainly never have allowed Peter to see her looking less than perfect.

'She was all over him like a rash when he first came to Winterbourne Barton. My mother said it was embarrassing. Madeleine was twenty-five and desperate to get married, and she wouldn't leave Peter alone.'

'How old was he?'

'Twenty-eight. It was fifteen years ago.'

'What happened?'

'He conjured a fiancée out of a hat.' She smiled slightly. 'Madeleine threw a few tantrums, but it was Lily who was the most upset. She adored Peter, said he reminded her of the family doctor when she was a child.'

'In what way?'

'Breeding. She said doctors were a better class in those days. I told her it was a pretty stupid criterion – all I'm interested in is whether Peter knows what he's doing – but Lily trusted him because he's a "gent".'

It was part of Peter's charm, I thought, secretly sympathizing with Lily. 'He gives a good impression of knowing what he's doing,' I said cautiously, waiting to have my head bitten off. Jess's ambivalence about Peter meant I had no idea what she really thought of him. Any more than I knew what he thought of her. She'd hinted several times that she didn't trust him

over Lily's Alzheimer's, suspecting Madeleine's hand
behind his willingness to leave Lily to cope alone.

'He bloody well ought to know what he's doing,'
she said sarcastically. 'He's a qualified doctor.'

'Why are you so hard on him?'

She shrugged.

'What's wrong with him?'

'Nothing . . . apart from fancying himself something chronic.'

I smiled. 'He *is* quite attractive, Jess.'

'If you say so.'

'Don't you like him?'

'Sometimes,' she admitted, 'but Winterbourne Barton's stuffed with women who find him irresistible.
They're all in their seventies and their favourite pastime is massaging his ego. You'll be at the back of a
very long queue if you want to join in.'

'Is he married?'

'Was.'

'Kids?'

'Two . . . a boy and girl . . . they live with their
mother in Dorchester.'

'What's she like?'

Jess had a way of looking at me that was unnerving,
a little like having a scalpel slicing into my brain.
'Weepy, clingy and wet,' she said, as if that were also
her description of me. 'He wouldn't have strayed if
she'd beaten him up a bit more, or found herself a
job. She's the fiancée he produced to get rid of

Madeleine . . . and she took him to the cleaners when she discovered he was rogering a couple of nurses behind her back.'

'You mean two in a bed?' I asked in surprise.

It was the first time I saw Jess laugh. 'God! That *would* have been funny! He's a gent, for Christ's sake. He took them one at a time and sent them flowers if he couldn't make it . . . and now all three of them feel abused. I feel marginally sorry for the wife – except she brought it on herself – but the nurses haven't got a leg to stand on. They knew they were sharing him with one woman so why make waves about another?'

I thought rather guiltily of the married men I'd bedded. Particularly Dan. *What kind of relationship was that?* 'It's easier to compete with a wife. You know what you're dealing with. Another lover suggests you're as boring as the woman you're trying to depose.'

*

It was a good few minutes after we heard Peter's car drive away before either Jess or I spoke. I couldn't think of anything to say, other than 'Go', but she was staring at the floor as if looking for inspiration in the quarry tiles. When she finally opened her mouth, it was to express disapproval of Peter. 'I don't know why he did that. If you phone his private line you'll have to pay for treatment. I'll give you directions to the clinic so that you can get it for free.'

'Perhaps I'm not entitled.'

She frowned. 'I thought you said you and your parents had been given asylum.'

I reached for my keys from the other side of the table so that I didn't have to look at her. 'Ja, well, I still hold a Zimbabwean passport so I don't know what my status is. I think Dr Coleman was just trying to be helpful.' Over the years I've developed a mid-Atlantic accent that doesn't specify where I come from, but under stress my South African intonation takes over. I heard the 'Zim' of 'Zimbabwean' come out as 'Zeem', the 'think' as 'thunk', and the 'C' of Coleman as a hard 'G'.

Jess picked up on it immediately. 'Is it me that's worrying you? Do you want me to go?'

'I'm sure I can manage on my own.'

She shrugged. 'Are you planning on staying?'

I nodded.

'Then you'd better let me light the Aga first because you won't be able to cook without it.' She jerked her chin towards the door to the corridor. 'You might as well have a wander while I'm doing it . . . see if there's anything else you need help with. It'll be your last chance. I'm even less keen to be here than you are to have me.'

Looking back, it's odd that neither of us took these remarks personally. They were simple statements of fact: we preferred our own company. It hadn't always been so for me but for Jess it was natural. 'I get it from my father. He could go days sometimes without speaking a word. He used to say we were born into the wrong century. If we'd been around before the industrial revolution our skills would have counted for something and our reticence would have been taken for wisdom.'

Her mother had tried to teach her to be more forthcoming. 'While she was alive, she could always get me to smile – my brother and sister, too – but I reverted to type after they died . . . or forgot how to do it. I don't know which. It's a learnt skill. The more you do it, the easier it comes.'

'I thought smiling was an automatic response.'

'It can't be,' said Jess bluntly, 'otherwise Madeleine wouldn't be able to do it. Her smile's about as genuine as a crocodile's . . . and she shows more teeth.'

*

All this took time to make sense. That day, I was just an explorer. I remember standing in front of a poster-size photograph on the wall at the end of the upstairs landing with 'Madeleine' printed underneath it. The name registered because Jess had asked me if she and I were related, but still I didn't know who she was. It was a black and white shot of a young woman leaning into the wind with a turbulent sea behind her, and, but for the name, I'd have assumed it was an Athena print. It was striking, both for the girl's looks and the way the photograph was lit.

Madeleine was stunning. She was dressed in a long

coat and trousers with a black cloche hat pulled over her head. Her face was turned towards the camera and the definition of every feature was extraordinary. Her perfect teeth showed in the sort of triangular smile that American pageant queens practise for hours, but to me it looked genuine, reaching to eyes that danced with mischief. I came to understand why Jess didn't like her – there was no contest between Madeleine's Venus and Jess's Mars – but it was a mystery why Peter Coleman had turned her down.

I had no idea at that stage that Madeleine had been responsible for preparing Barton House for letting, but I do remember thinking that whoever owned the place had a very low opinion of tenants. It could have been so imposing – commanding ten times what I was paying – but instead it was hideously tacky. Every room showed evidence of cheaper, smaller furniture taking the place of something grander. Mean, narrow wardrobes had the imprint of a larger brother on the wall behind them, and indentations in the carpets showed where great beds and heavy dressing-tables had stood before their flimsier replacements had been imported.

To anyone with an ounce of creativity, the house screamed for a makeover. Given freedom, I'd have taken it back to its eighteenth-century origins, stripping the walls of their twentieth-century coverings and removing the fussy curtains to show, and use, the panelled shutters. Simplicity would have suited it, where frills, furbelows and vulgar furniture made it look like an ageing tart with thick make-up covering the blemishes. I discovered later that it was as it was because Madeleine refused to allow Lily's solicitor to squander her inheritance on improvements, but it did set me wondering about the owner. It seemed so obvious to me that any money spent now would pay for itself again and again through higher rent.

I was most puzzled by the sketches and oil paintings that hung in every room. They were a mish-mash of styles – abstracts, life drawings, eccentric representations of buildings with roots anchoring them to the ground and foliage growing from their windows – but they were all signed by the same artist, Nathaniel Harrison. Some were originals and some – the sketches – were prints, but I couldn't understand why anyone would collect so much of a single artist's work simply to hang them in a rented house.

When I asked Jess about it, her mouth twisted into a cynical smile. 'I expect they're only there to hide the damp.'

'But who's Nathaniel Harrison? How come Lily bought so much of his work?'

'She didn't. Madeleine must have imported them after she stripped the house of her mother's paintings. It would have been cheaper than having the house redecorated.'

'How did Madeleine get them?'

'The way she gets everything,' she said caustically. 'Sex.'

Extracts from notes, filed as 'CB15–18/05/04'

... I can't separate specific events any more. I'm not
sure if I've shut my memory down or if I was too
disorientated for it to function properly. Everything's
fused into time inside the cage and time out of it. I
described the cage to Dan and the police, and I said it
was in a cellar, but the rest ...

... The police thought I was being deliberately evasive
when I said I couldn't tell them anything else. But it
was the truth. When Dan asked me what happened,
I couldn't tell him either. It wouldn't have helped,
anyway. The police weren't going to arrest a man on
the evidence of smell. What sort of identification is
that?

... The artist Paul Gauguin once said, 'Life being what
it is, one dreams of revenge.' *I* dream of revenge. All
the time.

Seven

THE ONLY INFORMATION Jess gave me about the Aga was that the oil tank was outside and needed to be kept at least a quarter full. She took me to the back door and pointed to a wooden lean-to at the side of the garage. 'The tank's in there and there's a glass gauge that shows the level. There's also a valve that controls the flow, but I've turned it on and you shouldn't need to touch it. If you allow the oil to drop too low, you could run into trouble. The supplier's phone number is stuck to the side of the tank but if they're busy they may not come for a few days. It's better to order a refill early rather than later.'

'How full is it at the moment?'

'Up to the top. It should last a good three to four months.'

'Do I have to close the valve if I want to turn off the Aga?'

'You'll have cold baths if you do,' she warned. 'There's no immersion heater in this place. It means the kitchen's fairly unbearable in the summer but the Aga's the only way to heat the water. The house is pretty antiquated. There's no central heating and no boiler, and if you're cold at night you have to light a fire.' She indicated a wood store to the left of the outhouse. 'You'll find the number for the log supplier on the tank under the oil company.'

I think Jess was disappointed that I took all this in my stride, but it wasn't so different from the way I'd grown up in Zimbabwe. Wood was our primary fuel rather than oil, but we didn't have central heating, and hot water had been at a premium until a day's sunshine had heated the tank on the roof. Our cook, Gamada, had coaxed wonderful meals out of the wood-burning stove, and, having learnt from her, I'd never been comfortable with electric ovens that offered more touch controls than the flight deck of Concorde.

I was a great deal less complacent about the single telephone point in the kitchen. 'That can't be right,' I said when Jess showed me the wall-mounted contraption beside the fridge. 'There must be phones somewhere else. What happens if I'm at the other end of the house and need to call someone?'

'It's cordless. You carry it with you.'

'Won't the battery run down?'

'Not if you hook it up at the end of the day and recharge it overnight.'

'I can't sleep without a phone beside my bed.'

She shrugged. 'Then you'll have to buy an extension cable,' she told me. 'There are places in Dorchester that sell them, but you'll need several if you want to operate a phone upstairs. I think thirty metres is the longest DIY cable they make but, at a rough guess, it's a good hundred metres to the main bedroom. You'll have to link them in series . . . which means adaptors . . . plus another handset, of course.'

'Is it a broadband connection?' I asked, dry-mouthed with anxiety as I wondered how I was going to be able to work. 'Can I access the internet and make phone calls at the same time?'

'No.'

'Then what am I going to do? Normally I'd be able to use my mobile as well as a landline.'

'You should have gone for a modern house. Didn't the agent tell you what this one was going to be like? Send you any details?'

'A few. I didn't read them.'

I must have looked and sounded deeply inept because she said scathingly: 'Christ! Why the hell do people like you come to Dorset? You're frightened of dogs, you can't live without a phone – ' she paused. 'It's not the end of the world. I presume you have a laptop because I didn't see a computer in the car?' I nodded. 'What sort of mobile do you have? Do you have an internet contract with your server?'

'Yes,' I said. 'But it's not going to work without a signal, is it?'

'How do you connect? By cable or Bluetooth?'

'Bluetooth.'

'OK. That gives you a range of ten metres between the two devices. All you have to do is raise
the mobile high enough – ' she broke off abruptly in
the face of my scepticism. 'Forget it. I'll do it myself.
Just give me your bloody phone and bring your laptop
upstairs.'

She refused to speak for the next half hour because
I hadn't shown enough enthusiasm for groping
around the attic every time I wanted to send an email.
I squatted on the landing beside a loft ladder, with my
laptop beside me, listening to her stomping about the
attic before she came down the steps and repeated the
exercise in the bedrooms. After a while she started
shifting furniture around, angrily banging and scraping
it across the floors. She sounded like an adolescent in
a sulk and I'd have asked her to go if I hadn't been so
desperate for internet contact.

She finally emerged from a bedroom at the end of
the landing. 'OK, I've got a signal. Do you want to
try for the connection?'

It was a Heath Robinson set-up – a stepped pyramid
built out of a dressing-table, a chest of drawers and
some chairs – but it worked. It meant crouching under
the ceiling to make the link but, once established, I
was able to operate the computer at floor level.

'The signal's stronger in the attic,' said Jess, 'but
it'll mean climbing up there every time the battery
runs down or you want to log off. I didn't think
you'd want to do that . . . and you'd probably get

lost, anyway. It's not very obvious which room you're above.'

'How can I thank you?' I asked her warmly. 'Perhaps you'd like a glass of wine or a beer? I have both in the car.'

She showed immediate disapproval. 'I don't drink.' And neither should you, was the firm rebuke that I took from her expression. She was even more disapproving when I lit a cigarette as we went back downstairs. 'That's about the worst thing you can do. If you get bronchitis on top of a panic attack, you'll really be struggling.'

Delayed maturity and pointy-hat puritanism made a lethal combination, I thought, wondering if she'd cast me as dissolute Edwina from *Absolutely Fabulous* with herself as Saffy, the high-minded daughter. I was tempted to make a joke about it, but suspected that television was a focus of disapproval as well. I had no sense that there was room for fun in Jess's life or, if there was, that it was the sort of fun anyone else would recognize.

Before she left, I asked her how I could contact her. 'Why would you want to?' she asked.

For help . . . 'To thank you.'

'There's no need. I'll take it as read.'

I decided to be honest. 'I don't know who to call if something goes wrong,' I said with a tentative smile. 'I doubt the agent could have lit the Aga.'

She smiled rather grudgingly in return. 'My number's

in the book under J. Derbyshire, Barton Farm. I suppose you want help with the extension cables for the landline?'

I nodded.

'I'll be here at eight-thirty.'

*

This was the pattern of the days that followed. Jess would make a reluctant offer of help, come the next morning to fulfil it, say very little before going away again, then return in the evening to point out something else she could do for me. On a few occasions I said I could manage myself, but she didn't take the hint. Peter described me as her new pet – not a bad description, because she regularly brought me food from the farm – but her constant intrusions and bossy attitude began to annoy me.

It's not as if I got to know her well. We had none of the conversations that two women in their thirties would normally have. She used silence as a weapon – either because she had total insight into the reaction it inspired, or none at all. It allowed her to dictate every social gathering – and by that I mean her and me, as I never saw her in a larger group except on the rare occasions when Peter dropped in – because the choice was to join in her silences or trot out a vacuous monologue. Neither of which made for a comfortable atmosphere.

It was difficult to decide how conscious this behav-

iour was. Sometimes I thought she was highly manipulative; other times I saw her as a victim, isolated and
alienated by circumstance. Peter, who knew her as well
as anyone, compared her to a feral cat – self-sufficient
and unpredictable, with sharp claws. It was a fanciful
analogy, but fairly accurate, since the goal of Winterbourne Barton appeared to be to 'tame' her. Noncon-
formists may be the bread-and-butter of the media,
and loved by the chattering classes, but they're singled
out for criticism in small communities.

Over time I heard Jess described as everything from
an 'animal rights activist' to a 'predatory lesbian' –
even 'having an extra a chromosome' because of her
flat features and wide-spaced eyes. The Down's Syndrome charge was clearly nonsense, but I was less sure
about the animal rights and lesbian tags. She was at
her most animated when I asked her about the birds
and wildlife in the valley, always able to identify animals from my descriptions and occasionally waxing
lyrical on their habitats and behaviour. I also wondered if her twice-daily visits were a form of courtship.
To avoid wasting her time, I made it abundantly clear
that I was heterosexual, but she was as indifferent to
that as she was to hints about leaving me alone.

After a couple of weeks, I was close to locking the
doors, hiding the Mini in the garage and pretending
to be out. I'd learnt by this time that I'd been singled
out for special favours, since she never visited anyone
else, not even Peter, and I began to wonder if Lily had

found her as oppressive as I did. One or two people suggested that Jess's attachment was to Barton House, but I couldn't see it myself. I thought Peter's suggestion that she saw me as a wounded bird was a more likely explanation. In her strangely detached way, she appeared to be monitoring me for signs of renewed anxiety.

Surprisingly, I didn't show any. Not at the beginning, at least. For some reason, I slept better alone in that echoing old house than I had in my parents' flat. I shouldn't have done. I should have jumped at every shadow. At night the wisteria tapped on the window-panes and the moon silhouetted finger-like tendrils against the curtains. Downstairs, the numerous french windows invited anyone to break in while I slept.

My way of dealing with that threat was to leave the internal doors open and keep a powerful torch beside my bed. The beauty of Barton House was that every bedroom had a dressing-room with its own door to the landing, which meant I had a second exit if a prowler came along the corridor. It also had two staircases, one at the front and one at the back leading down to the scullery. This gave me confidence that I could outwit any intruder. I sprayed Jess's WD40 into every external lock on the ground floor, and embraced the doors and windows as escape routes rather than entry points.

Nevertheless, it was Winterbourne Valley that was the real healer. The contrast between the noise and chaos of Baghdad and these peaceful fields of ripening corn and yellow rapeseed couldn't have been greater. Passing cars were few and far between and people even scarcer. From the upstairs windows I could see all the way to the village in one direction and to the Ridgeway – a fold of land behind Dorset's coastline – in the other. This gave me a sense of security for, even though the hedgerows and darkness would screen a trespasser, those same concealments would hide me.

*

Jess was a dedicated conservationist. Apart from her hostility to social change, she farmed her land in much the same way as her ancestors had done by scrupulously rotating her crops, rationing pesticides, stocking rare breeds and protecting the wild species on her property by conserving their natural habitats. When I asked her once what her favourite novel was, she said it was *The Secret Garden* by Frances Hodgson Burnett. It was a rare piece of irony – she knew I'd identify her immediately with the difficult, unloved orphan of the story – but the landscape of the hidden wilderness was certainly one she liked to inhabit.

By contrast, Madeleine liked her landscapes populated. She was at her best in company, where her easy charm and practised manner made her a popular guest. Peter described her as the typical product of an expensive girls' boarding-school, well-spoken, well-mannered, and not overburdened with brains.

I thought her extraordinarily attractive the first time I met her. She had the sweet face and cut-glass English accent of the elegant British movie stars of the forties and fifties, like Greer Garson in *Mrs Miniver* or Virginia McKenna in *Carve Her Name with Pride*. It was the second Sunday of my tenancy. Peter had asked me along to meet some of my new neighbours over drinks in his garden. It was very casual, about twenty people, and Madeleine arrived late. I believe she came uninvited, as Peter hadn't mentioned her beforehand.

Despite the photograph on the landing at Barton House, I had no idea who she was until we were introduced. Indeed, I'm sure I assumed she was Peter's girlfriend, because she tucked her hand through his elbow as soon as she arrived and allowed him to lead her about the garden. His guests were genuinely pleased to see her. There was a lot of hugging and kissing, and cries of 'How *are* you?' and I was slightly taken aback to discover this was Lily's daughter.

'Your landlady,' Peter said with a wink. 'If you have any complaints, now's the time to make them.'

I'd been doing rather well up until then – with only the odd flicker of anxiety when I heard a male voice behind me – but I felt a definite lurch of the heart as I shook Madeleine's hand. If Jess was to be believed, she was a callous bitch who had driven her mother into penury and then neglected her. My personal view was that Jess's unaccountable hatred clouded her thinking, but the doubt was there, and Madeleine read it in my face.

Her immediate response was contrition. 'Oh dear! Is the house awful? Aren't you happy?'

What could I do, other than reassure her? 'No,' I protested. 'It's beautiful . . . just what I wanted.'

There was nothing artificial about the smile that lit her face. She removed her hand from Peter's elbow and tucked it into mine. 'It *is* beautiful, isn't it? I *adored* growing up there. Peter tells me you're writing a book. What's it about? Is it a novel?'

'No,' I said cautiously. 'It's non-fiction . . . a book on psychology . . . not very exciting, I'm afraid.'

'Oh, I'm sure it is. My mother would have been *so* interested. She loved reading.'

I opened my mouth to dampen her enthusiasm but she was already talking about something else. I don't remember what it was now, a reference to Daphne du Maurier, I expect – *'an old friend of Mummy's'* – whom she trotted out to new acquaintances as a close family connection. This seemed a little unlikely to me, as there was a considerable age difference between the novelist and Lily, and du Maurier had been dead for fifteen years, but Madeleine brushed such details aside. In the world she inhabited, meeting a person fleetingly at a party amounted to friendship.

She dropped names for effect in the same way that her mother was said to have done. I began to under-stand this when I commented on the paintings at

Barton House and learnt that Nathaniel Harrison was her husband. It made sense of Jess's remark that Madeleine had acquired the collection by sleeping with the man who owned them – even if 'married to the artist' would have been more illuminating – but it led to a definite withdrawal on Madeleine's part.

She spoke of Nathaniel as if he were up with greats, and to cement the impression she quoted David Hockney, suggesting he was a close acquaintance and a great admirer of her husband's work. To listen to her, Hockney was a regular visitor to Nathaniel's studio and always singing his praises to critics and dealers. I was genuinely interested, not just in how they knew Hockney, but in why he would champion an artist whose style and approach to painting were so different from his own.

'I didn't realize he spent so much time in England,' I said. 'I thought he was permanently based in America now.'

Madeleine smiled. 'He comes when he can.'

'So how did you meet him?'

'The painting world's a small one,' she said rather coolly, looking for someone else to speak to. 'Nathaniel's invited to all the openings.'

I should have left it there. Instead I asked her which other contemporary artists she and her husband knew. Lucian Freud? Damien Hirst? Tracey Emin? And where did her husband fit into the Britart scene? Had Saatchi bought any of his work? She continued to smile but it fell far short of her eyes, and I knew I'd overstepped some invisible line in etiquette. I was supposed to revere the absent Nathaniel, not demonstrate knowledge of other artists or question Nathaniel's close friendship with them.

It was all very childish, and I was amused at how she avoided me until Peter brought us together again. 'Did Marianne tell you Jess Derbyshire's been helping her settle in?' he asked, steering her towards me with a hand in the small of her back. 'Jess has built a hoist so that Marianne can access the internet via her mobile.'

I watched Madeleine's expression close at the mention of Jess. 'It's fairly ramshackle,' I said. 'We've discovered a signal near the ceiling in the back bedroom that allows me to operate my laptop underneath it. But it's not ideal, and I wondered if you'd have any objections to my installing broadband. It's available through the Barton Regis exchange and it would make life a lot easier. I've asked the agent and he says he can't see a problem as long as I pay for it. I'll happily leave the ADSL modem behind when I go.'

Peter placed a teasing hand on my shoulder. 'It's no good talking gobbledy-gook to Madeleine. She still uses a quill and parchment. It's a little box,' he explained to her, 'that separates voices from online connection . . . means you can use the phone at the same time as the computer. If Marianne's prepared to pay for it then my advice is to give her the go-ahead immediately.' He laughed. 'It'll make that old ruin of yours more attractive to the next tenant, and it won't cost you a thing.'

Madeleine's smile would have frozen the balls off a brass monkey, but it wasn't directed at Peter. It was directed at me. I had a strong sense that it was his hand on my shoulder that offended her, and not what he said.

*

I was surprised, therefore, when she came to Barton House, full of smiles, the next morning. 'I realized last night that I never gave you an answer to the broadband question,' she said gaily, as I opened the front door. 'Goodness! Is the key working properly now? Mummy only ever used the bolts because the lock was so stiff.' She walked past me into the hall. 'I paid a man to grease it but he didn't think it would last.'

I shut the door behind her. 'Jess lent me some WD40. I give it a spray every day which seems to be doing the trick.' I gestured towards the sitting-room. 'Would you like to go in here? Perhaps you'd rather be in the kitchen?'

'I don't mind,' she said, looking around to see if I'd made any changes. I saw her eyes flicker towards the piece of wallpaper that had peeled away from its Blu-Tack and was now, courtesy of Jess, firmly reattached with paste. 'Mummy was always very pukka about entertaining guests in the drawing-room. She thought it was non-U to expect her friends to put up with dirty crockery and vegetable peelings. Did you manage to light the Aga all right?'

'Jess did.'

Madeleine's mouth thinned immediately. 'I expect she made a song and dance of it.'

'No.' I opened the door to the sitting-room. 'Shall we go in here?'

Despite its size and sunny aspect, the room was too dreary to qualify as a drawing-room, and I hadn't been into it since my first day. Jess had told me it used to be full of antiques until Madeleine replaced them with junk from a second-hand furniture shop.

The carpet, a threadbare plush pile in muted pink, showed multiple evidence of dog accidents from when Lily had mastiffs of her own. According to Jess, she'd never exercised them enough, and had covered the marks with Persian rugs. Now packed away in storage, they were probably going mouldy if the musty smell of damp in the room was any indication of their state when they were removed. The walls were worse. They hadn't been decorated in years and the plaster was flaking above the skirting boards and beneath the coving round the ceiling. Irregular patches showed where Lily's paintings had been.

In an effort to distract the eye, Madeleine had hung two of her husband's originals and three Jack Vettriano prints on the inside walls – *The Singing Butler,*

Billy Boys and *Dance Me to the End of Love* – but all you could see of the prints was the sunlight reflecting on their glass. I couldn't understand why she'd put them there as Vettriano's film-noir style sat very uncomfortably with Nathaniel's fantasy pictures of rooted and foliage-laden buildings, and I assumed she'd bought them cheap as a job lot. It wasn't a subject I had any intention of discussing with her, however, as our tastes were clearly different.

'What do you think of Vettriano's work?' she asked, lowering herself to the vinyl sofa and spreading her skirt. 'He's very popular. Jack Nicholson owns three of his originals.'

'I prefer Hockney and Freud.'

'Oh, well, of *course*. Doesn't everyone?'

I produced my friendliest smile. 'Can I make you a coffee?'

'I couldn't. I've just had one with Peter. He has an espresso machine. Have you tried it yet?'

I shook my head as I took the chair beside her. 'Yesterday was the first time I'd been to his house. He wanted to introduce me to some of the neighbours.'

She leaned forward. 'What did you think of them?'

'Very nice,' I answered. It happened to be a true reflection of my views but Madeleine wasn't to know that. In the circumstances, I could hardly say anything else without appearing rude.

She looked pleased. 'That's a relief. I'd hate to

think Jess had turned you against them.' She paused before going on in a rush. 'Look, I hope you won't take this wrongly – I know it's none of my business – but you'll have a happier time here if you look to the village for friends. Jess can be very peculiar if she takes a liking to someone. It's not her fault . . . I'm sure it's the result of losing her family . . . but she latches on to people and can't seem to see how irritating it is.'

It was on the tip of my tongue to say it had already happened but it would have felt like a betrayal. I needed to resolve my issues with Jess face to face, not add to the gossip about her by fuelling Madeleine's curiosity. 'She helped me with a few things when I first arrived,' I said. 'I was grateful. I hadn't realized there was only one phone socket here, or that the mobile signal was so bad. That's why I need broadband.'

But she was only interested in Jess. '*Peter* should have told you,' she said earnestly. 'The trouble is he's paranoid about breaking patient confidences. It's not just the latching-on that's a problem . . . it's what she does when she thinks she's being rejected. It's obviously a legacy from the car accident – a need to be loved, I suppose – but it can be quite frightening if you're not ready for it.'

I found myself staring at her in the same detached way that Jess stared at me. For no better reason than that I didn't know how to respond.

'I expect you think I'm awful,' Madeleine went on apologetically, 'but I'd hate you to find out two months down the line that I'm right. Ask anyone.'

I shifted my attention to my hands. 'What am I supposed to ask them?'

'Oh dear! I'm not doing this very well. Perhaps I should have said listen. *Listen* to what they say.'

'About what?'

'The stalking. It starts with her turning up on the doorstep when you first arrive, then she's in and out all the time. She usually comes with presents or offers of help, but it's difficult to get rid of her afterwards. She plagued my poor mother for years. In the end, the only way Mummy could avoid her was by hiding upstairs every time she heard the Land-Rover on the drive.'

'Peter doesn't seem to have any problems with her.'

'Only because she doesn't like him. She's convinced he tried to turn her into a Valium addict after her parents died. It's when she fixates on someone that the problems start . . . and that's usually a woman.' She examined my face. 'I'm not being unkind, Marianne. I'm just trying to warn you.'

'About what? That Jess is inept at making friendships . . . or that she's a lesbian?'

Madeleine shrugged. 'I don't know, but she's never shown any interest in men. Mummy said she was close to her father, which may have something to do with it. Most people take her for a teenage boy the first time they see her . . . she certainly sounds like one. Mummy said her hormones went awry when she took on the mantle of farmer.'

Her use of 'Mummy' was getting on my nerves. I've never really trusted middle-aged women who choose that diminutive. It suggests their relationship with their mother has never developed beyond dependence, or they're pretending a closer and sweeter affection than actually exists. 'The only reason she showed up on my doorstep was because her dogs saw my car in the drive. She called them off when they surrounded me, otherwise we'd never have met.'

'How did they see your car?'

'Presumably she was exercising them along that stretch of road when I first arrived. Perhaps they saw me turn into the drive?'

'Is that what she told you?' She took my silence for assent. 'Then she was lying. She breeds from those mastiffs, so she's hardly likely to jeopardize them in traffic.' She propped her elbows on her knees. 'All I'm saying, Marianne, is be a little wary. Even Peter thinks it's strange that she happened to be passing that day.'

I gave a small nod which Madeleine could interpret how she chose. 'You said it was worse when she feels rejected. What does she do then?'

'Prowls about your house in the middle of the night . . . stares through your windows . . . makes nuisance phone calls. You should talk to Mary Galbraith about it. She and her husband live in Hollyhock Cottage, and they had a terrible time after Mary made it clear she'd lost patience.' She held out her hands in supplication. 'You must have asked yourself why people are so wary of Jess. Well, that's why. Everyone starts with good intentions because they feel sorry for her, but they always end up wishing they hadn't. Ask Mary if you don't believe me.'

I did believe her. I'd already experienced a lot of what she'd described. 'I'll bear it in mind,' I promised, 'and thank you for the information.' I reintroduced the subject of broadband. 'I'm very conscious of how isolated I am here . . . particularly at night. I'd feel a lot happier with a more efficient telephone line.'

Madeleine agreed to it immediately, adding: 'Jess's solutions never last very long. She was always rigging things up for Mummy that failed a couple of days later. I remember her trying to make a television work in the bedroom, but the picture was never good enough.'

At least she tried, I thought, wondering what practical help Madeleine had ever given Lily. I took a pack of cigarettes from my pocket. 'Do you?'

She looked as offended as if I'd offered her heroin. 'Didn't the agent make it clear this was a no-smoking tenancy?'

'I'm afraid not,' I said, popping a cigarette between my lips and flicking my lighter to the tip. 'I think he was so desperate by the time I showed an interest that he'd have handed the keys to an axe murderer as long as the deposit was paid.' I rested my head against the back of the chair and blew smoke into the air. 'If it's a problem for you, I'm happy to vacate immediately in return for a full rebate. Your agent's advertising a terraced house in Dorchester in his window that already has broadband.'

Her mouth turned down in irritation, as if my 'broadbands' were having the same effect on her as her 'mummies' were having on me. 'As long as you're careful about putting your cigarettes out. This is a Grade Two listed building,' she said rather pompously.

I assured her I was always careful. 'You must have been worried every time your mother lit a fire,' I murmured, glancing towards the hearth, 'particularly when her concentration started to go.'

Madeleine pulled a wry expression. 'Not really . . . but only because I didn't know how bad she was. She always seemed in such command when I came down . . . a little forgetful about small things, perhaps, but totally *compos mentis* about running the house. I'd have been worried sick if I'd realized she wasn't coping. This house has been in my family for generations.'

I expect I should have let that go as well, but generations suggested aeons instead of the seventy-odd years of actual ownership. 'Wasn't it your great-grandfather who bought the property? I was told he was big in armaments during the First World War . . . and bought the whole valley in nineteen-thirty-five when he retired.'

'Did Jess tell you that?'

'I can't remember now,' I lied. 'Someone yesterday, I think. How did your family lose the valley?'

'Death duties,' she said. 'Grandfather had to sell it off when his father died. He got virtually nothing for it, of course, but the developer who bought it made a fortune.'

'The one who built the houses at Peter's end of the village?'

'Yes.' It was obviously a sore point with her. 'That used to be our land until Haversham was given permission to build on it. Now his family owns one of the biggest building firms in Dorset while we're left with an acre of garden.'

'Did Haversham buy the whole valley?'

She nodded. 'Grandfather was lazy. He couldn't be bothered to farm himself, or even find tenants, so he let Haversham take the lot and sell the agricultural land in piecemeal plots for twice what he'd paid for it.'

'Who did he sell to?'

'I don't know. It happened in the late forties. I think my mother said it was split between four of the local farmers, but it's changed hands several times since. The north acreage was bought by a cooperative from Dorchester about three years ago.'

'What about the Derbyshires? Did they buy any?'

'Of course not. They couldn't have afforded it.'

'Except Barton Farm's quite big, isn't it? Peter told me it's one and a half thousand acres.'

Madeleine shook her head. 'She's a tenant . . . owns about fifty acres and the rest is rented. Jess's family were humble people. Her grandmother worked as a maid in our house after the war.' She looked at the fireplace. 'Old Mrs Derbyshire used to clean out that grate every day. Mummy said she had a squashed nose and flat face and looked like a mongol or someone with congenital syphilis.' She caught my eye. 'She wasn't either, of course, but it's obviously genetic or Jess wouldn't have the same problem.'

I blew smoke in her direction. 'And it was this lady's husband who owned Barton Farm in the fifties?'

I could almost hear the words 'She was no lady' forming in Madeleine's head. 'No, it skipped that generation. The husband contracted polio during the war and died of it shortly after he returned home – and there was a younger brother who died in Normandy, I think. Jess's father inherited it from his grandfather. Then *he* died, and Jess took it over . . . although what's going to happen when she goes is anyone's guess.'

'Perhaps she'll have children.'

She threw me a scornful glance. 'They'll be virgin births, then. She'd sooner lie with her mastiffs than a man.'

Ss-ss-ss! 'So what happened to Jess's grandmother?'

'When her son took over, she went to Australia to live with her brother. Before that she kept house for her father-in-law. He was a drinker . . . drove his wife to an early death and then made his daughter-in-law's life a misery. According to Mummy, it soured her relationship with her son – which is why she emigrated – although I expect the hope of a better life had something to do with it as well.'

'Did you ever meet her?'

'Only when she came back to help Jess through the funerals. She stayed about three months, but the whole thing was too much for her and she died of a stroke soon after she returned home.'

'That's sad.'

Madeleine nodded. 'Mummy was upset by it. She saw quite a lot of Mrs Derbyshire while she was over. They were different generations . . . and from very different backgrounds, of course . . . but she said it was fun reminiscing about the old days.'

'It must have been terrible for Jess.'

'It was,' she agreed, holding my gaze for a moment before looking away. 'She came up here with a carving knife and slit her wrists in front of Mummy. There was blood everywhere . . . although the doctors said it was a cry for attention rather than any serious attempt to harm herself. The cuts weren't deep enough to do any real damage.'

I didn't say anything.

'Poor Mummy was petrified,' Madeleine went on with a hint of apology in her tone as if she regretted having to tell me. 'She thought the knife was meant for her. It was such an odd thing to do . . . come all the way to Barton House to kill herself in front of an audience.' She paused. 'It's why I was so appalled yesterday when Peter said Jess was helping you settle in. He should have warned you about her mental state instead of encouraging her to fasten on you the way she fastened on to my mother.'

Extracts from notes, filed as 'CB15–18/05/04'

. . . I can't eat any more. I force myself to try but
everything tastes the same . . .

From:	Dan@Fry.ishma.iq
Sent:	Sun 11/07/04 14.05
To:	connie.burns@uknet.com
Subject:	Thank God!

Where the hell have you been, Connie? You promised
you'd keep in touch as long as I put you on the plane,
but all I've had is silence for nearly two months – zilch
. . . 00000000 – until a miserly 15-word email 2 hrs ago.
I'm so damned angry with you. I've been sick to my
stomach with worry since you left.

FYI: I've been bombarding London for info, only to be
told they know less than I do. Harry Smith had to ask a
colleague on a tabloid for your parents' address because
your next-of-kin details are out of date. All your father will
say is that you're 'out of London' and he's passing on
messages. So why haven't you answered any of them?
Where are you? What's going on? Have you seen a
doctor? I wouldn't have kept my mouth shut, if I thought
you were planning to deal with this on your own. Have
you any idea of the stick I'm getting?

I assume you used my private address to avoid the office
finding out. Well, OK, except you've told me nothing
apart from your new e-address and the fact that you're

'fine'. I can't/don't believe that. You *must* talk to someone. London had a counsellor lined up for you – they were willing to give you all the protection you wanted – but you blew them away. Why? Don't you realize what the consequences are likely to be? I still have nightmares about Bob Lerwick being shot in front of me, and that was ten years ago.

At the moment I'm beating myself up for not forcing you to accept help here. I thought I was doing the right thing by keeping it quiet, but now . . .

It's turning into a hell of a mess, frankly. I've been interviewed three times by a cynical US cop working with the Baghdad police [Jerry Greenhough] who's concluded the whole 'abduction' was a scam. He seems to think you're planning to demand huge sums in compensation or write a best-selling 'fiction' about something that never happened.

Write to me, Connie. Better still, phone. My number's the same.

Love, Dan

Extracts from notes, filed as 'CB15–18/05/04'

. . . Obedience comes quite easily after a while. Do this. Do that. Inside my head, I rebelled. If you let me live, then you will die. It was a way of staying sane . . .

. . . The truth was different. You belong to me. You die when I say so. You speak what I tell you to speak. You smile when I tell you to smile . . .

. . . At what point did I decide to be controlled for ever? When I realized that every shameful thing I did was being videoed? Why didn't I refuse? Was death by suffocation so bad that I'm prepared to live like this?

. . . There were no marks that would say what had happened. I bled inside but not outside . . .

. . . I'm lucky. I'm alive. I did what I was told . . .

From:	alan.collins@manchester-police.co.uk
Sent:	Mon 19/07/04 17.22
To:	connie.burns@uknet.com
Subject:	Keith MacKenzie
Attachments:	AC/WF.doc (53KB)

Good to hear from you, Connie. After your release, I tried to contact you via your mobile and old address but without success, so presumably some thief in Baghdad has them? I was shocked to read about your abduction, particularly as it happened so shortly after your email in May re MacKenzie. You say there was no connection between the two events, but, yes, you're quite right, I did wonder. To the extent that I contacted Bill Fraser in Basra and suggested he look into it. In the event, you reappeared, unharmed, before he was able to take it further.

You say your boss in Baghdad is interested in picking up the O'Connell/MacKenzie story where you had to leave it. I'm attaching my correspondence with Bill in full, as you requested, although some of it may not make pleasant reading for you. Bill tells me the situation in Baghdad is out of control. Foreigners have become a commodity, with most abductions being carried out by professional gangs who sell their hostages on to the highest bidder. As you say, you were 'fortunate' to be released when you were.

As you will see, Bill has spoken to his US opposite number in Baghdad re the two cases you found in the Iraqi newspapers. He has also had some email correspondence with Alastair Surtees re O'Connell/MacKenzie. Nothing conclusive, but interesting evasion from Surtees.

You asked if I kept a copy of my report on the Sierra Leonean murders. I did and I'm attaching it. I've also forwarded it to Jerry Greenhough (Bill's oppo in Baghdad) if only to point out similarities in the killer's/ killers' MO. Finally, I've been given a contact in the Kinshasa police who's agreed to check for similar murders there in 1998. It's a long shot – Kinshasa has 15,000 street children who die/go missing all the time – and teenage girls are particularly vulnerable. I'll let you know if I hear from him, but don't hold your breath. He paid lip service to international cooperation by answering my email, but I suspect my request was shelved. Old cases are hard/tedious work, particularly when there's no financial incentive.

My wife and family are well. Thank you for asking.

Finally, don't hesitate to write/call if there's anything I can help you with. Is there a reason why the only contact detail you've given me is your new email address? Or why you're choosing to act as a middle-man between me, Bill Fraser and your boss?

Kind regards,

Alan

DI Alan Collins, Greater Manchester Police

(Extracts from attachments)

Email from Bill Fraser to Alan Collins

. . . My oppo in Baghdad is an NYPD Captain called Jerry Greenhough. He did a stint in Afghanistan two years ago and was seconded to Baghdad in May. He's a decent enough bloke but I'm afraid he has reservations about Connie Burns. He wasn't in on her debriefing, but after listening to the tape he found her 'evasive and unconvincing'. On several counts: a) she told police virtually nothing, claiming her blindfold as the reason for her ignorance; b) she insisted that her boss, Dan Fry, sit in on the questioning with instructions to halt proceedings if she showed signs of distress – which she never invoked; c) she was examined by a doctor who found no evidence of rough handling or forceful restraint. This has led to some scepticism about the whole episode, particularly as her imprisonment was only 3 days' duration.

It's a difficult one, Alan. I don't necessarily share the scepticism – I can think of a number of reasons why a woman wouldn't want to talk about an experience like that – but, according to Jerry, there were too many inconsistencies in her answers. Nor did the abduction follow a recognized pattern. I passed on your suggestion re MacKenzie, but that has no takers either. Connie was 'self-possessed' and 'in control' throughout the interview, and adamant that nothing untoward had happened during her captivity. This seems to be backed by the doctor giving her a clean bill of health. I hear what you say about MacKenzie's MO, but releasing a woman unharmed isn't his recognized pattern of behaviour either.

Interestingly, I've had more success re Connie's suggestion that the two murders in Baghdad were a) linked; b) linked to similar murders in Sierra Leone; and c) might be the work of Keith MacKenzie aka John Harwood aka Kenneth O'Connell. Jerry has worked with the FBI on two serial rape cases and is at least willing to embrace the possibility. Any chance of sending him your report on the Sierra Leone victims? The downside is that investigations like this are complex and sophisticated, and I can't see raw recruits coping unless they have continuity and commitment at the top. FYI: I have less than six weeks left of my tour and Jerry goes home at the end of September, and even the most able Iraqis won't have the finances to conduct a cross-border inquiry.

I'm attaching a couple of emails from Alastair Surtees (Baycombe Group). I haven't met the guy but BG have about 500 security personnel on the ground and their reputation's better than some. My gut feeling inclines to Connie's view that Surtees is 'slippery'. His second email is more conciliatory than his first, following my request for copies of O'Connell's documentation/photo. To date, these haven't materialized, but I'll keep pressing for them because I want to know if I have a ringer on my patch. It's hard enough keeping track of the indigenous population without fake UK passports being thrown into the pot.

It's a big 'if' – but if the murders are linked, if the killer's a Brit and if he returns to the UK – that puts him on home turf where we do have the resources to nail him. I keep waking up of a night thinking what a perfect bloody crime this is, Alan. Life's so cheap in these war zones no one gives a damn if a psychopath gets his rocks off by chopping women into little pieces. It's been another bad day. 3 toddlers died and a 12-year-old kid got his legs blown off by an 'unexploded' cluster bomb. I hate this wretched slaughter-house . . .

Email (1) from Alastair Surtees to Bill Fraser

. . . I assume your interest has been sparked by Ms Connie Burns of Reuters, who engineered an interview with me in order to make unfounded and slanderous accusations against Mr Kenneth O'Connell. She claims to have known him under a different name in Sierra Leone, however it's now clear that the man she saw was wrongly identified to her. You have my personal assurance that none of our operatives was at the Baghdad police academy on the day Ms Burns visited it. I trust this settles the matter . . .

Email (2) from Alastair Surtees to Bill Fraser

. . . I'm sorry you thought I deliberately evaded some of your requests. I do not and would not condone the use of a false passport by any BG employee, however I thought my personal assurance would be enough to convince you that Ms Burns was in error. I have questioned O'Connell on two occasions since Ms Burns made her allegations against him, and I have *absolutely no reason* to believe that Kenneth O'Connell is an alias for John Harwood or Keith MacKenzie. The Baycombe Group is scrupulous in its vetting procedures and thoroughly examines the records of all its employees.

Kenneth O'Connell came to us with unimpeachable references. His history in brief: Sergeant, Royal Irish Regiment; service duty (multi-deployed) but including: Falklands and Bosnia; left the Army in 2000 (aged 36) to join the London Metropolitan Police (served 3 years); signed up with the Baycombe Group in September 2003. He has held two positions here in Iraq: 1) Lead trainer of restraint techniques at the Baghdad Police Academy from 1.11.03 to 1.02.04; 2) Personal Security Officer to Spennyfield Construction 14.02.04–ongoing. Spennyfield Construction are a UK firm, currently working out of Karbala.

O'Connell's documentation is held at our Cape Town office. I have requested a copy to be faxed to the number you gave me, with the proviso that his name, next of kin, and present location are blacked out. Faxes go astray or fall into the wrong hands and the safety of our personnel is important to us. I trust this meets your requirements and that any suspicions you have of Mr O'Connell can be speedily laid to rest . . .

Email from Bill Fraser to Alastair Surtees

. . . It is now two weeks since I requested information on Kenneth O'Connell. In the absence of documentary evidence supporting his claim to a legitimate passport, his name will be posted with the British Embassy and all attempts by him to exit this country will be blocked. Furthermore, if I have any suspicion that Mr O'Connell has left the country under a different name . . .

From:	connie.burns@uknet.com
Sent:	Tues 20/07/04 23.15
To:	Dan Fry (Dan@Fry.ishma.iq)
Subject:	Sorry!

Dear Dan,

I received your first email so you don't need to keep bombarding me with new ones. I'm sorry you've been feeling sick and I'm sorry that my long silences are making it worse. It has nothing to do with not trusting you, it's just that I'm finding it hard to write anything at the moment. The only reason I haven't given you a telephone number is because the lines here are hopeless and I'm having to use my mobile to email. As soon as I've worked out a better arrangement, I'll let you know how to contact me.

Please don't worry. I *am* fine. I've tucked myself away in a valley in the south-west of England where soft winds blow and people are scarce. It's very pretty and peaceful – rolling fields of golden corn, a chocolate-box village half a mile away and a tumultuous sea just out of sight beyond an upland. I spend most of my days alone, and I really do like it that way. The house is quite big, but very basic. There's even an old well in the garden – heavily disguised as a woodstore – though thankfully I'm not expected to use it. I do have running water and electricity, although the rest of the mod cons leave a *lot* to be desired. Hence the telephone problem. I've made friends with some sparrows. I've found that if I scatter birdseed around my feet, they appear out of nowhere to feed. It's only now that I realize I never saw a single bird in Baghdad. There's also a fishpond with no fish. I'm thinking of buying some so that I can sit and watch them in the evening.

As for Jerry Greenhough and the stick you're getting, can you please keep stonewalling for me? I honestly don't care what the Baghdad police and an unknown Yank think about me. It's all so far away and unimportant at the moment. They won't sack you, Dan, because you're too important. Also, you have broad shoulders, and I can't think of anyone better qualified to say 'get stuffed' to the men in suits!

I realized on the plane going home that it was going to be worse talking about it than *not* talking about it. I know you believe counselling worked for you but you're much stronger than I am and you don't mind admitting your weaknesses. It's a form of bravery that you and Adelina have . . . and I *don't*. Perhaps I'll feel differently in time, although I doubt it. My nightmares are never about what happened, only about the way I've gatecrashed other people's lives in seach of a story. Nothing is ever straightforward, Dan. I'm far more troubled by my conscience than a few forgettable events in a cellar.

I'll always be pleased to hear from you as long as you stick to other subjects and shelve your concerns about my mental state. If you don't, I won't answer! Let me thank you one last time for your care and kindness and end with love, Connie.

Eight

OF COURSE I looked for scars on Jess's wrists and of course I found them. They were only obvious if you knew they were there, and I did it as surreptitiously as I could, but she must have noticed my interest because she took to buttoning her cuffs. I compensated with over-friendliness, which made her even more suspicious, and she stopped coming after that. The odd thing is, her absences didn't register at first. Like a toothache that suddenly stops, it only occurred to me at the end of the week that the niggling irritation had gone.

It should have been a relief, but it wasn't. I started jumping nervously every time my parents phoned, and peered cautiously out of the windows as soon as darkness fell. For the first time since my arrival I felt anxious about being alone, and my mother picked up on it one evening when I refused to speak until she did. 'What's wrong?' she asked.

I told her the truth because I didn't want her imagining something worse. She was quite capable of populating Dorset with Iraqi insurgents and al-Qaeda terrorists. She listened without interrupting and, at the end, said simply: 'You sound lonely, darling. Do you want me and Dad to come down next weekend?'

'I thought you were going to Brighton.'

'We can cancel.'

'No,' I said. 'Don't do that. You're coming at the end of the the month, anyway. I'll be fine till then.'

She hesitated before she spoke. 'I expect I've got it back to front, Connie – I usually do – but from the way you describe them Jess has been a better friend to you than Madeleine. Do you remember Geraldine Summers . . . married to Reggie . . . they had two boys about your age who went to university in America?'

'Vaguely. Is she the fat one who used to turn up out of the blue with cakes that no one ate?'

'That's her. They lived about thirty miles from us. Reggie was a tobacco planter and Geraldine was a teacher before he married her. They met in England during one of his leaves, and she came home as his wife after only knowing him for a couple of months. It was a terrible mistake. Reggie had never read a book in his life, and Geraldine had no idea how isolated the farm was. She thought she'd be in the middle of a community and able to get a job as a teacher, and instead she discovered that Reggie and the radio were going to be her only source of stimulation.'

'I remember him now,' I said with feeling. 'Thick as two short planks, got sozzled on gin and told smutty jokes all evening.'

My mother laughed. 'Yes. He was worse after the boys were born. They inherited Geraldine's brains, and he had trouble keeping up with them. It turned him to drink even more, because he thought alcohol made him witty.' She paused in reflection. 'I always felt rather sorry for him. He'd have been much happier with a country bumpkin and two strapping sons who liked driving tractors.'

I wondered why she was telling me this story. 'What happened to them? Are they still together? Still in Zimbabwe?'

'Reggie and Geraldine? They went to South Africa. The last I heard, Reggie wasn't very well. I had a Christmas letter from Geraldine which said he'd been in and out of hospital most of last year. I wrote back but I haven't had a reply yet.' She returned to the point. 'The thing is, Geraldine drove me mad when she first arrived. She saw me and your father as the antidote to Reggie, and she plagued us with visits because she was so discontented. In the end, I had to be quite firm with her and tell her she wasn't welcome. It was all rather difficult, and she took it very badly.'

'What did she do?'

'Nothing too shocking. I received an unsigned letter about a week later, telling me how cruel I was, and one or two strange phone calls. I didn't see her again for two years . . . by which time her first baby had arrived and she'd managed to come to terms with her frustrations. Poor woman. We found ourselves at the same party in Bulawayo and she was terribly embarrassed . . . apologized profusely for being a nuisance and even owned up to the poison-pen letter and the phone calls.'

'What did you say to her?'

'That it was I who should apologize for being unkind. I felt far worse about rebuffing her attempts at friendship – even if they *were* annoying – than she could ever have felt about her letter. Geraldine was so thrilled to be back on speaking terms that she took to plaguing us again . . . and this time we had to put up with it. But you know, darling, she turned out to be the best friend we had. The Barretts and Fortescues – people we'd grown up with – wouldn't come near us when your father was accused of profiteering, but Geraldine and Reggie drove over immediately and stayed throughout the siege. It was very brave of them.'

I was out of Zimbabwe when this happened, but I'd kept in close touch via telephone. It was in the early days of Mugabe's push to evict white farmers, and a local Zanu-PF apparatchik laid trumped-up charges of tax evasion and profiteering against my father in a bid to stir up trouble. He had no chance of succeeding in the courts because my father kept scrupulous accounts, but the accusation was enough to incite anger among Mugabe's war veterans. For a week, a gang of over fifty camped on our lawn and threatened to overrun the house, and it was only the courage of Dad's own workers, who mounted a permanent picket in front of the veterans and refused to let them pass, that brought the siege to an end.

It was why my mother had been so keen to leave. She knew the intimidation would be worse a second time, and she didn't want to ask the workforce to intervene again. For Zanu-PF it was tantamount to treason for blacks to support their white employers, and Mum wasn't prepared to see anyone die for the sake of a few square miles of land. She and my father chose to overlook the Barretts' and Fortescues' refusal to help – 'they were afraid' – and turned out to support them when their own farms were invaded. But, privately, she never forgave them, and their life-long friendships ended with my parents' departure for England.

'So what's the moral of the story?' I asked with a smile. 'Don't judge a book by its cover?'

'Something like that,' she agreed.

'And if Jess produces a carving knife?'

'Your doctor friend should be struck off for negligence,' said my mother rather dryly. 'He shouldn't have left you alone with a dangerous patient.'

*

I suppose I could have checked with Peter, but there didn't seem much point. I decided my mother's logic was sound. We make our decisions in life on *who* we believe as often as *what* we believe, and I had no reason to think the local doctor would wish a disturbed lunatic on to me. I was a lot less sure about Madeleine's motives. There was no question she and Jess hated each other, and the old saying, 'Half the truth is a whole lie', applied to both. If I believed Jess, Madeleine had deliberately abandoned her mother to die of neglect; if I believed Madeleine, Jess was a dangerous stalker.

There was probably a grain of truth in both stories – Madeleine didn't visit Lily as often as she might and Jess visited too often, which suggested jealousy was at the heart of their hatred – but I was discovering at first hand just how quickly whispers become accepted as fact. According to Dan Fry's latest email, even Adelina Bianca was hinting that I'd faked my abduction. In an interview with an Italian magazine, she was quoted as saying: 'Of course there's money to be made out of pretending to be a hostage – the public loves horror stories – but anyone who does it belittles what the real victims go through.'

I've no idea if she was referring to me – there was a US deserter who faked his kidnapping before fleeing to the Lebanon – but that's how her words were interpreted. Dan told me that four of the main terrorist groups had denied holding me, and the Arab press was full of articles, claiming a foreign correspondent had sought to make money out of passing herself off as a victim. Thankfully, the western press ignored it – either from fear of a libel suit or because they knew my story hadn't appeared – but it made me even more reluctant to advertise where I was. It turned me against Adelina. I knew her words had probably been 'rearranged' to suit the editor's take, but I did wonder if the reason she was able to give interviews was because nothing much had happened to her.

When I finally went looking for Jess, she said she could always tell when Madeleine had been spreading her poison. It didn't matter who the recipient was, or how sensible they were, they never smiled as freely afterwards as they'd done before. She said I'd tried harder than most but I'd made my interest in her wrists too obvious. She took the hint after a couple of days and left me to get on with it. There were some things in life that weren't worth bothering with, and convincing strangers that she wasn't planning to knife them was top of the list.

It was an interesting rebuttal, since I hadn't told her I'd spoken to Madeleine. Was Madeleine so believable that everyone reacted in the same way? If so, it was frightening. I did ask Jess why she allowed half-truths to stand instead of coming out fighting, but she shrugged and said there was no point. 'People believe what they want to believe,' she said, 'and I refuse to be something I'm not just to prove them wrong.'

I couldn't follow her logic. 'In what way?'

'I despise them,' she said rather dryly, 'and I'd have to pretend I didn't if I wanted to change their minds.'

'You might feel differently if you got to know them.'

'Why? It won't change the fact that they believed Madeleine.'

This was part of a conversation we had in her kitchen after I plucked up the courage to drive to her house. There was no alternative, since she hadn't responded to either of my telephone messages, but I was terrified her mastiffs might be roaming free. I drove up the half-mile track to the farm and slowed to a halt in the middle of the yard while I tried to work out where her front door was. I had my window down because it was a rare day of sunshine in an otherwise wet month, and I heard the dogs barking furiously as soon as I put the gears into neutral. The sound was too loud for them to be inside and I looked around nervously to see where they were.

The house was separated from the yard by a beech hedge that was tall enough to mask the ground floor, but there was no obvious gap to suggest an entrance. To my left was a barn, and to my right the track appeared to follow the line of the hedge round a sharp corner at the far end of the house, although flashes of prowling mastiffs behind the beech trunks persuaded me that getting out for the purpose of exploration was a bad idea. As I was pondering my options, I heard the sound of a powerful motor and a tractor came roaring around the bend, towing a hay baler behind it.

I had a brief glimpse of Jess's scowling face before she swerved past me and into the barn. Half a second later, she reversed out again, missing the back of my car by six inches as the baler swung in the opposite direction from the tractor. She performed a neat three-point turn, with the tractor a whisker away from my wing mirror, before she reversed the whole contraption back under cover. She wasn't taking any prisoners that day, and I'm sure I did look scared as a couple of tons of metal looked like flattening my Mini.

She killed the engine and jumped down from the cab, whistling to the dogs to quit their noise. 'You're in the way,' she told me. 'Another time, park up by the hedge.'

I opened my door. 'Sorry.'

'There's nothing to be afraid of,' she said curtly. 'I wasn't trying to hit you.'

'I realize that. I'd have moved except I couldn't tell which way you were going to turn . . . and I didn't want to make matters worse.'

'The opposite of what you'd expect. I thought you grew up on a farm.'

'I meant the tractor.'

She crossed her arms. 'Did you want something?'

'No. I just thought I'd . . . see how you are. You haven't been around and you didn't anwer my messages.'

To my surprise, a slight flush rose in her cheeks. 'I've been busy.'

I pushed the car door wider. 'Is this a bad time? I can come back later.'

'It depends what you want.'

'Nothing. I just came for a chat.'

She frowned at me as if I'd said something peculiar. 'I have to unhitch the baler and grease it. You can talk to me while I do that if you like. You're not dressed for it, though. The barn's pretty messy.'

'That's OK. Everything's washable.' I climbed out of the car and picked my way across the rutted yard in my long wrap-over skirt and leather flip-flop sandals. She eyed me disapprovingly and I wondered what was offending her. 'Is something wrong?'

'You look as if you're going to a garden party.'

'I always dress like this.'

'Well, you shouldn't. Not on a working farm.' She nodded to some sacks of potatoes inside the barn entrance. 'You can sit on one of those. What do you want to talk about?'

'Nothing in particular.'

She eased the baler forward and worked it loose from the tractor tow before pushing it back against the wall. For a small woman, she had extraordinary strength. According to her, anyone could do anything when they needed to. It was mind over matter. Until it came to talking. Her expression said very clearly that if I expected her to start the conversation, I was going to be disappointed. I watched her take a handful of grease and work it into the twine-tying pivots.

'Do you have to do this every time you use it?'

'It helps. The machine's twenty years old.'

'Is it the only one you've got?'

'It's the only baler.' She jerked her chin at a combine harvester at the other end of the barn. 'That's what handles the crops.'

I turned to look at it. 'Dad had one in Zimbabwe.'

'It's pretty much standard these days. Some people rent them but I bought that secondhand at a farm auction.'

I watched her working. 'Why were you using the baler today?' I asked after a while. 'I haven't seen any crops being harvested, so there won't be any straw yet.'

'I'm taking the hay from the field margins while the weather holds.' She seemed to think it was an intelligent question because she decided to expand on it. 'The long-range forecasts are predicting more rain for August so it seemed sensible to bale what we could while we had the chance. We'll have trouble bringing in the wheat if the forecasters are right . . . let alone straw.'

We . . .? 'Do you have help?'

She put the lid back on the can of grease and picked up a rag to wipe her hands. 'Some. There's Harry who's worked here for years and a couple of lady part-timers – one comes mornings, the other afternoons.'

'From Winterbourne Barton?'

'Weymouth.'

'What do they do?'

'Whatever's on the rota.'

'Ploughing?'

She nodded. 'Anything to do with the crops. Harry and I look after the herds, the fencing and the woodland . . . but we all lend a hand where necessary.' She eyed me curiously as she folded the rag and put it on the grease can. 'Don't they have women farm-workers in Zimbabwe?'

'Thousands.'

'Then why do you look so surprised?'

I smiled. 'Because everyone in Winterbourne Barton describes you as a loner, and now I discover you have three people working for you.'

'So?'

'It's a wrong description of you. I got the impression you lived and worked on your own.'

Her mouth twisted cynically. 'That's Winterbourne Barton for you. They're completely ignorant about how much work is involved in running a farm, but then most of them have never lived in the country before.' She glanced towards the house. 'I'm making some sandwiches for lunch. Do you want to come in while I do it?'

'Will the dogs be there?'

Her dark eyes narrowed slightly, but more in speculation than contempt. 'Not if you don't want them to be.'

I stood up. 'Then I'd love to come in. Thank you.'

'You'll have to move your car in case Harry or Julie come back. If you park up there – ' she pointed towards the left-hand end of the hedge – 'you'll see the path to the back door. I'll meet you there after I've seen to the dogs.'

*

The farmhouse was a thin, straggling building, constructed in the same Purbeck stone as Barton House and Winterbourne Barton. The core, the rooms around the front door, was seventeenth century, but the extensions on both sides dated from the nineteenth and twentieth. In floor space it was almost as big as Barton House, but its piecemeal fabrication meant it lacked the clean lines and elegance of Lily's property.

We entered through the kitchen, which was larger, brighter and better appointed than Lily's. A plate-glass window gave a view of the garden, which was entirely laid to lawn, without a shrub or flower in sight. Six-foot-high wire fencing ran inside the beech hedge, preventing the mastiffs from escaping, and a large wooden kennel stood in one corner. At the moment, there was no sign of any of them.

'They're round the front,' said Jess, as if reading my mind. 'I'll let them back into this side when you go. My mother used to have flower borders all the way round but the first puppy I had rooted the plants out. It's easier like this.'

'Are they always out?'

'If I'm working. When I'm here I have them in the house. If you think of them as overgrown hearthrugs, you might not find them so frightening. Mastiffs are a sociable breed . . . they love being around people. The only thing they ever do is put themselves between their owners and a stranger, but they won't attack unless the stranger attacks first.'

I changed the subject rather too abruptly. 'This is a nice room, Jess. Much nicer than Lily's kitchen.'

She watched me for a moment before turning away to open the fridge door. 'Do you want to look at the rest of the house while I make the sandwiches? I'm sure you're curious . . . everyone else is.'

'Do you mind?'

An indifferent shrug was her only answer.

It was hardly the most fulsome invitation I'd ever had but I wasn't going to argue about it. The rooms we inhabit say as much about us as how we behave, and Jess was right, I was deeply curious about her surroundings. I'd been told variously that the house was frozen in time, that it was a shrine to her family, full of morbid souvenirs and with an emphasis on death in the shape of stuffed animals. I came across these immediately, to the extent that there were four glass cases in the hall, containing a pheasant, a fox cub, two weasels and a badger.

This was the seventeenth-century heart of the building and I could well believe it had remained untouched for years. The only natural light came from a window half-way up the stairs, but it wasn't enough to brighten the gloom of the dark oak panelling around the walls. The ceiling was furrowed with ancient beams and the flagstones worn into a visible curvature between the front door and the stairs.

The two rooms leading off the hall dispelled any sense of a house frozen in time. One, which was clearly Jess's office, had filing cabinets, a desk and a computer, and the other an old sofa and piles of beanbags that smelt powerfully of dogs. Against the longest wall was a steel grey designer hi-fi system with shelf upon shelf of CDs, DVDs, videos and vinyl records framing a plasma screen. I hadn't thought of Jess as a music, film or television buff, but she clearly was. She was even connected to Sky digital, if the unmistakable black remote on the sofa was any guide. So much for a shrine to the past, I thought enviously, wishing Barton House had more to offer than four terrestrial channels on one miserable little screen in the back room.

I almost stopped there. It's one thing to be offered free rein of someone else's house, another to exercise it. I was trespassing out of curiosity or, even worse, a childish desire to put one over on Winterbourne Barton by being able say I'd been invited in. It was the mismatch between what I saw and how it was described that drew me on, for I couldn't see where the ideas of morbidness had come from until I found a corridor full of photographs of Jess's family.

There was tier upon tier of the same four laughing people – a man, a woman, a boy and a girl – with variations on the same pictures occurring every two or three feet. Poster-size portraits. Postcard-size snaps. Enlarged headshots extracted from group photographs. Single prints of the children pasted alongside their mother and father to create a laughing group. It was a collage of black, white, sepia and vibrant colour on the continuous canvas of the corridor walls, and it was a glorious expression of life.

I thought of the pictures I had of my parents, the formal ones of their wedding, and holiday snapshots showing awkward smiles or squints of reluctance to be caught on camera. There was only a handful, taken unawares, when they were being entirely natural, and I thought how much better to duplicate the laughing ones than fill the spaces with self-consciousness and solemnity.

'What do you think?' asked Jess's voice behind me.

I hadn't heard her approach and turned a startled face in her direction. 'Brilliant,' I said honestly. 'It's the way I'd like to be remembered.'

'You don't look very impressed.'

'Only because you crept up on me. Who took them? You?'

'Yes.' Her dark eyes roamed across the pictures. 'Lily hated my gallery. She said it was unhealthy . . . kept telling me to let my memories go.'

Standard advice, I thought, but I couldn't see that

it applied to pictures. My mother had photographs of her dead parents on her bedside table, and I'd never felt they shouldn't be there. 'Why didn't you put yourself into any of them?'

'I did. That one.' She pointed to a postcard-size shot at the beginning, showing her parents arm-in-arm with a girl who I'd taken to be her sister.

I moved back to look at it. 'I didn't recognize you. When was it taken?'

'On my twelfth birthday. Mum and Dad gave me a camera and I let Rory use it to take that photograph.'

'How old was he?'

'Eight then . . . fifteen when he died. Sally was two years younger.'

'What about your parents?'

'Both in their late forties.' She pointed to a poster-size photograph half-way down the corridor. 'That's the last picture I took of them. It was about three weeks before the accident.'

I walked past her to stand in front of it. It was in colour, there was no sea in the background, but the composition and the way the sunlight lit the sides of the couple's faces reminded me of the black and white image of Madeleine at Barton House. 'Was it you who took the picture of Madeleine on my upstairs landing?'

'Maybe.'

'It's the only thing worth looking at in the whole house. The rest is tacky as hell . . . including Nathaniel's paintings.'

It was a compliment but Jess didn't take it as one. 'It looks nothing like Madeleine,' she said crossly. 'I only did it to make Lily happy. She needed to believe that something good had come from the Wrights. If it was an honest photograph her bitch of a daughter would look like the portrait of Dorian Gray – ugly as sin.'

'Your mother's pretty,' I said, in an effort to distract her.

Jess ignored me. 'You know, I sometimes wonder if that's what Madeleine's at. As long as Nathaniel puts her viciousness into his paintings, she can pass herself off as sweet.'

It was a strange analogy. 'Except his paintings aren't vicious, they're just not very good. If he had any talent, he'd have sold them and they wouldn't be gathering dust in Barton House.'

'Then it's a vicious destruction of talent,' she said flatly. 'He used to be good before he married Madeleine. Peter has one of his early paintings. You should look at it.' She opened a door at the end of the corridor. 'Did you get this far?'

'No.'

'This is the best room.'

I thought she meant it was best in terms of decor and size, or 'best' as in reserved for visitors, so I wasn't prepared for what I found. There wasn't a stick of furniture inside. It was a huge shuttered room with a woodblock floor, white walls and a series of slim floor-to-ceiling panels set asymetrically down the centre with mini speakers attached to them. I had no idea what I was supposed to be looking at until Jess touched a series of buttons on a panel by the door and the room came alive with moving images and sound.

For a few sickening moments, as the farm appeared on the wall at the end, I thought I was about to see her family go through a series of repetitive loops on video. In that case I'd be agreeing with Lily. What could be more morbid and unhealthy than sitting in the dark, watching dead people perform bursts of activity at long-forgotten parties or school plays?

'It's the life-cycle of the weasel,' said Jess as different footage played across the screens. 'That female was nesting under the house for a season . . . she moved into Clambar Wood when the dogs sniffed out her entrance. Those are her kittens . . . she's teaching them to hunt. It's probably where the myth of weasel gangs comes from. In fact they're incredibly territorial and only come together for mating. Look at that. Do you see how beautiful they are? Farmers should encourage them instead of killing them. They'll go for eggs and chicks if they can get them but their favourite prey is mice and voles.'

'It's amazing,' I said. 'Who took it?'

'I did.'

'Did you set up the room as well?'

She nodded. 'I made the panels light enough to move to produce different effects. Some films are more effective if the screens form a continuous arc . . . like birds in flight. I've some great footage of crows leaving their roost in the morning, and it's stunning to watch them wheel around the arc. The weasels work better in a staggered formation because it shows how territorial they are.'

'Can I see the crows?'

She glanced at her watch. 'It'll take too long to set up. I'd have to realign the projectors as well.' She touched the buttons and plunged the room into darkness before easing me out and closing the door. 'I'm working on the soundtrack for the weasels at the moment, but maybe I'll set up the crows when that's finished.'

I allowed myself to be shepherded back towards the kitchen. 'But what are the films for? Are they for schools? What do you do with them?'

'Nothing.'

'What do you mean, nothing?'

She took some sandwiches, wrapped in clingfilm, from the worktop and tucked them in her pocket. 'It's just a hobby,' she said.

I looked at her in disbelief. 'You're crazy! What's the point of making films that no one sees? You should be showing them . . . finding yourself an audience.' I paused. 'It would be like me writing columns that no one reads.'

'I'm not like you. I don't have to be admired all the time.'

'That's not fair.'

She gave an indifferent shrug.

'What's wrong with showing you've got talent? You're *good*, Jess.'

'I know,' she said bluntly, 'but what makes you think I need you to tell me? How much do you know about filming? How much do you know about weasels? Anything?' She gave a dismissive laugh when I shook my head.

'I was only saying what I honestly felt.'

'No, you weren't.' She opened the back door and ushered me out. 'You were being patronizing – probably because you feel guilty about listening to Madeleine. In future you'd do better to keep your mouth shut.'

It was like walking on eggshells. I couldn't see what I'd done wrong except compliment her. 'Would it have been better if I'd said it was crap?'

'Of course not.' She flicked me a scathing glance. 'I hate liars even more than I hate arselickers.'

From:	connie.burns@uknet.com
Sent:	Wed 21/07/04 13.54
To:	alan.collins@manchester-police.co.uk
Subject:	contact details

Dear Alan,

Journalists are notoriously jealous of their stories. I don't trust my boss not to cut me out of the O'Connell/ MacKenzie loop and pass off all my research as his! I'll let you know my address and phone number as soon as I've found somewhere permanent to stay. At the moment I'm living out of a suitcase.

It was ever thus!

Best wishes

Connie

PS. I can't believe how bad the mobile signals are in this country! I think I've signed up to the wrong server!

Nine

JESS AND I parted on superficially good terms but there was no invitation to return, and she gave a noncommittal nod when I said I hoped to see her at Barton House. It was all very confusing. Rather than go straight home, I drove to the village to see if Peter was home. When I spotted his car in the road, I pulled in behind it and rang his doorbell. I had second thoughts while I waited, mostly to do with rumour-mongering and disloyalty, but I was too curious to give in to them.

'Are you busy?' I asked when he opened the door. 'Can you give me ten minutes?'

'Is it a medical visit or a social one?'

'Social.'

He stepped back. 'Come in, but you'll have to watch while I eat my lunch. There's only enough for one, I'm afraid, but I can rustle up a glass of wine or a cup of coffee.'

I followed him across the hall. 'I'm fine, thanks.'

'When did you last eat?'

The question caught me off-balance. 'This morning?' I suggested.

He eyed me thoughtfully before pulling out a chair. As always in my company, he was careful to give me space, stepping away before inviting me to sit down. 'Take a pew.'

'Thank you.'

He resumed his place at the other side of the table. Lunch was a microwaved pasta meal, still in its plastic container. 'I use a plate when I know people are coming,' he said, picking up his fork. 'Anyone who rings the bell on spec doesn't count. Has Jess been bringing you food from the farm?'

I nodded.

'Do you eat it?'

I nodded again.

He didn't believe me, but he didn't make an issue of it. 'So what can I tell you about Jess? Which particular part of that extraordinarily irritating personality do you want me to explain?'

I smiled. 'How do you know it's Jess I'm interested in?'

He filled his fork. 'I was two hundred yards behind you when you turned in through her gate. Did you find her at home?'

'I watched her grease her baler then she took me inside and showed me around. Presumably you've been in the house?'

'Too often to count.'

'So you've seen the corridor of family photos?'

'Yes.'

'The big room with the screens?'

'Yes.'

'What do you think?'

He didn't answer until he'd dealt with the last of his food and pushed the pot aside. 'I change my mind from time to time but, on the whole, I think it's a good thing Jess never finished art school. She was at the end of her first year when the accident happened, and she had to jack it in to take on the farm. She still regrets it . . . but she'd have wasted three years if she'd stayed.'

I was unreasonably disappointed. If anyone could see she had talent it was surely Peter, because he seemed to have more empathy with her than anyone else. 'You don't think she's any good?'

'I didn't say that,' he corrected mildly. 'I said if she'd stayed at art school she'd have been wasting her time. Either she'd have conformed and lost all her individuality . . . or she'd have been at permanent war with her tutors and done her own thing anyway. If you're lucky, she might show you her paintings one day. As far as I know she hasn't touched a brush since the accident, but the work she did before was exceptional.'

'Did she sell any of it?'

He shook his head. 'Never tried. It's sitting in a studio at the back of the house. I doubt she'd accept money for it, anyway. She's of the painting-for-profit-is-bad school . . . thinks any artist who panders to what the buyer wants is a mediocre hack.'

'What sort of subjects did she paint?'

'Landscapes. Seascapes. She has a very individual style – more impressionist than representational – creates movement in the sky and the water with minimal paint and sweeping brushstrokes. It didn't go down too well with her teachers, which is why she's so intolerant of other people's opinions. They told her she was looking back towards Turner instead of embracing the idea of conceptual art, where a piece is created in the mind before it becomes concrete. The sort of artist they liked was Madeleine's husband.'

My disbelief must have been obvious, because Peter laughed.

'He used to be a lot more interesting than those canvases on Lily's walls. He conceptualized irrationality in physical form . . . quite different from the abstracts he's doing now.'

I tried to look intelligent. 'Jess said you have one of his early paintings. Can I see it?'

There was a small hestitation. 'Why not? It's hanging in my office . . . second door on the right. You shouldn't have any trouble identifying it. It's the only painting in there.'

This picture was detailed and busy, like Hieronymus Bosch, with the same nightmarish visions of a world gone mad. Living houses thrust out massive roots with gnarled lianas burrowing through the brickwork. The painting had a high sheen, as if layer upon painstaking layer of paint had been applied to produce it, and the style bore no resemblance to the looser work at Barton House. There was a whirling madness at its heart. None of the houses stood true, but leaned drunkenly in all directions as if gripped by a hurricane. Hundreds of tiny people, quite out of scale with the buildings, populated the rooms behind the windows, and each face was a meticulous replica of Edvard Munch's *The Scream*. Outside, similarly tiny animals foraged among leaf matter, with no distinction in size made between species, all with the pale, tapered, human faces of the Munch.

I was prepared to accept that it was conceptualized irrationality (whatever that meant – it sounded like an oxymoron to me) but, without a title, I hadn't a clue if a particular piece of unreason was being expressed or if it was unreason in general. Why living houses? Why so many people trapped inside them? Why animals with human faces? Was it man's fear of nature? Or was it closer to Hieronymus Bosch – a vision of hell? I had an uncomfortable feeling that if Jess were there she'd say my opinion was subjective, and therefore irrelevant. It didn't matter how disturbed and powerful I found the vision, the meaning belonged to the artist.

Peter was standing in front of the kettle when I returned to the kitchen. 'I hope you like your coffee black,' he said, pouring water into two mugs. 'I'm afraid I've run out of milk.'

'I do, thank you.' I took the one he offered me, successfully manoeuvring my fingers to avoid his. 'Does the painting have a title?'

'It won't help you. *Ochre*. What did you make of it?'

'Honestly? Or will you bite my head off like Jess? I felt her breathing down my neck in there, telling me not to be so pretentious.'

Peter looked amused. 'Except she hates the thought police more than you do. She calls it the emperor's-clothes syndrome. If someone like Saatchi's prepared to pay a fortune for an unmade bed, then it must be good . . . and it's only idiots who don't get it. Try honesty,' he encouraged.

'OK, well, it's a damn sight better than anything at Barton House, although I haven't a clue what it's supposed to represent. It has a surrealist feel to it. What I really can't get my head around is how Madeleine lives with the artist who painted it. I mean, she's *so* middle-class and conformist . . . and Nathaniel appears to be hovering off the planet somewhere. How does that work exactly?'

He gave a snort of laughter. 'Nathaniel painted it before he married her. The stuff he does now is very tame. Jess describes it as marshmallow buildings with window-boxes. Which is about right. He hardly sells at all these days.'

'How much did you pay for yours?'

Peter pulled a face. 'Five thousand quid eleven years ago, and it's worth hardly anything now. I had it valued for the divorce. In terms of investment, it was a disaster . . . but, as a canvas, it still fascinates me. When I bought it, Nathaniel told me that the clue to what it represents is the repetitive Edvard Munch face – the angst-filled scream.'

I waited. 'OK,' I said after a moment. 'I recognized it in the faces . . . but it doesn't help me much. Is it Hell?'

'In a way.' He paused. 'I thought you might recognize the emotions. It depicts a panic attack. Munch suffered anxiety most of his life and *The Scream* is usually described as an expression of intense anguish or fear.'

I lifted a wry eyebrow.

'You didn't see that?'

'Not really. Why are the houses alive? Why make them unstable? I thought agoraphobics saw them as places of safety. And why put human faces on the animals? Animals don't suffer anxiety . . . or not to the extent that humans do.'

'I don't think you can apply logic to it, Marianne. Panic's an irrational response.'

The 'Marianne' caught me off-guard as usual. I still thought of it as my mother's name and did a mouth-dropping double-take whenever it was used. I think it was on the tip of Peter's tongue to admit he knew who I really was but I spoke before he could. 'He can't have painted it during an attack . . . it's too detailed and meticulous. At the very least, his hands would have been shaking.'

Peter shrugged. 'Who says it was *his* panic attack? Perhaps he witnessed someone else's.'

'Whose?'

Another shrug.

'Not Madeleine's,' I said in disbelief. 'She doesn't have the imagination to worry herself into a box. In any case, if she was his inspiration, wouldn't he still be painting like that?'

'I don't know what his themes are now. Madeleine talks about abstract reflections on the human condition . . . but I don't know if that's her or Nathaniel speaking. Whichever, it's a fairly desperate spin to make up for a spectacular loss of talent. He makes a living from teaching at the moment.'

'How old is he?'

'Mid-thirties. He was twenty-four when he painted the picture I have.'

'And Madeleine's what? Thirty-nine . . . forty? When did they marry?'

'Ninety-four.'

Ten years ago. I did a few sums in my head. 'Which makes him a bit of a toy-boy. Perhaps she's not as conventional as I thought. Jess said she has an eleven-year-old son. Is Nathaniel his father?'

'As far as I know. They married a few months after he was born.'

'What did Lily think about that?'

'Exactly what you'd expect,' Peter said with a smile.

'She'd have preferred a wedding and grandchildren in the correct order?'

He nodded.

'Most mothers would.' I gave a rueful shake of my head. 'It just shows how wrong you can be about people. I'd have put money on Madeleine marrying a rich older man and popping her baby out after a respectable nine months. So where did she and Nathaniel meet? I don't get the feeling she's been hanging around art exhibitions all her life.'

'Here,' said Peter dryly, tapping the floor with his foot. 'About where you're standing. I was having a chat with Nathaniel when Madeleine turned up. He didn't stand a chance once she found out who he was, although I don't know what he saw in her . . . unless it was undiluted admiration. She couldn't tell one end of a paintbrush from the other, but she certainly knew how to flatter him.'

Once she found out who he was . . .? 'Did he live in Winterbourne Barton?'

'Not exactly.'

'What does that mean?'

Peter stared into his coffee. 'Work it out for yourself – it's hardly quantum mechanics.'

I must have been extraordinarily dense, because I couldn't see what he was getting at. 'Why can't you tell me?'

'Hippocratic oath,' he said with a good-humoured grin. 'I'd lose patients if I couldn't keep a still tongue in my head . . . particularly in a place like this where gossip spreads like wildfire. In any case, life's too short to fight other people's wars.'

Wars . . .? 'I've only met two people who seem to be at each other's throats – ' I broke off as the penny dropped. 'Oh, I see! Art school . . . panic attacks . . . Did Madeleine take Nathaniel from Jess? Is that why they loathe each other?' I saw from his expression that I was right. 'No wonder Jess doesn't like flattery. It must be a hell of a sore point if Madeleine laid it on with a trowel.'

'It was her own fault,' Peter said unsympathetically. 'She was far too free with her criticism of Nathaniel's work, and that's not an easy thing to live with. Madeleine's tea and sympathy was much more attractive.'

'If he's lost his edge, then maybe he needed the criticism.'

'Without a doubt . . . but he's a weaker character than Jess. He sulks when his ego's not being massaged.'

'He sounds a pain in the arse,' I said bluntly, remembering one or two men in my past who were similar. 'How long were they together?'

He didn't answer immediately, apparently weighing up how much he could tell me with a good conscience. 'It's hardly a secret. Two years. She met him in her first term. It might have lasted if she'd stayed in London, but there wasn't much hope for it after the accident. She set up a studio for him at the farm but he stopped using it by the summer of ninety-three.' He took a thoughtful sip of his coffee. 'The only reason she took his departure badly was because he left her for Madeleine. She wouldn't have turned a hair if it had been anyone else.'

'What did Lily say?'

His eyes creased with amusement again. 'Why are you so interested in Lily's reactions?'

I shrugged. 'I'm wondering why Jess remained so close to her. If Madeleine had stolen a man of mine, I wouldn't have gone on mowing her mother's lawn. Supposing Madeleine and Nathaniel had turned up while I was doing it? Imagine the embarrassment. I'd be afraid they were laughing at me behind my back.'

'I'm not sure Jess would care. She's completely impervious to what people say about her.'

'*Now*, maybe, but not then. If she was never fazed by anything, she wouldn't have had panic attacks,' I pointed out.

Peter ran a thoughtful hand around his jaw, as if I'd reminded him of something he'd forgotten. 'Lily never spoke about it,' he said, 'but she did say once that Madeleine judged worth by how highly something was valued by someone else.'

It sounded like a good description. 'So does Nathaniel still get undiluted admiration,' I asked curiously, 'or did he lose his shine when his sales dropped off?'

'Pass.'

I laughed. 'I'll take that for a yes. I'll bet he's regretting his decision now. Did Lily like him?'

'She never really knew him. Madeleine always visited on her own.'

'You must have some idea.'

'Not really. Lily was a very discreet woman where her family was concerned, which is probably why she got on so well with Jess. I don't think Jess blamed her for Madeleine's behaviour, but I doubt they ever talked about it.'

'Except Jess slit her wrists in Barton House,' I pointed out, 'which, at the very least, suggests she wanted Lily to know she was hurting.'

The good humour vanished immediately from Peter's face. 'Who told you that?'

'Madeleine.'

He looked angry. 'In future I'd advise you to take anything she tells you with a hefty pinch of salt. She rewrites history to suit herself.' He took a breath through his nose. 'I hope you haven't repeated it to anyone.'

'Of course not. Who would I repeat it to?'

'Jess?'

'No.'

He relaxed a little. 'If Madeleine heard that story from her mother, she must have misunderstood what

Lily was saying.' A carefully evasive statement, I thought.

'It's not true then?'

He couldn't bring himself to give a straightforward 'no', so he equivocated. 'It's a ridiculous suggestion. No one looks for an audience in those circumstances.'

They do if they want to draw attention to themselves, I thought. There was a long history of fanatics killing themselves in public for the sake of a cause, and the shock waves were always tremendous. Perhaps that had been Jess's motive, for I didn't doubt the suicide bid was true. Even without the scars on her wrists, Peter's obvious discomfort at my knowing would have persuaded me.

I made some banal remarks in agreement, while wondering if he thought I was the only person Madeleine had told. I had the impression that it was he who had divulged the secret, and not Lily, which is why he was so uncomfortable. I found his question about whether I'd repeated the story to Jess particularly strange. Did he think she was unaware that Madeleine knew about it? Or was he worried that reminders of suicide might push her into trying again? I thought of the casual way she'd referred to my interest in her wrists and her indifference to rebutting accusations of 'knifing strangers'.

'You're living in cloud-cuckoo-land if you think Jess doesn't know the secret's out,' I said abruptly. '*I* didn't mention it but *she* did. She talked about the scars on her wrists, and Madeleine spreading her poison, and how she's given up trying to convince people that she has no plans to knife them.' I paused. 'I expect Madeleine's worked her version up to put Jess in a bad light, but she was bound to gossip about it. There's no love lost between them.'

'What else did she tell you?'

'Jess or Madeleine?'

'Madeleine.'

'That Jess's family was poor . . . that her grand-mother emigrated to Australia to get away from her son . . . that Jess is a lesbian.' I watched the anger gather in his face again. 'She also said she was a stalker . . . that she makes threatening phone calls and takes revenge when she's rejected. Oh, and she's appalled that you didn't warn me how disturbed Jess is.' I smiled slightly. 'Should you have done?'

'No.'

'*Does* she take revenge? Madeleine told me to check with Mary Galbraith at Hollyhock Cottage.'

Peter gave a frustrated shake of his head. 'Well, you'll certainly get confirmation from Mary,' he said. 'She's convinced Jess is out to get her and her husband.'

'Why?'

Another frustrated shake of the head. 'Ralph Galbraith drove into the back of Jess's Land-Rover in the middle of the village, and Jess called the police when she smelt drink on his breath.' He nodded at my questioning look. 'Three times over the limit, lost his licence and was ordered to retake his test at the end of the ban. Mary was very upset about it. She said there was no reason for the police to be involved – it was a small shunt and no one was hurt – and it's only because Jess is vindictive that they were called.'

I remembered her confiscation of my car keys. 'She has draconian views on dangerous driving.'

'She has draconian views on everything,' he said. 'Compromise doesn't exist in her vocabulary. In this case, a blind eye would have been kind. Ralph Galbraith's over seventy and never drove more than twenty miles an hour, or farther than Tesco's and back, so he was a hardly a danger to other drivers. Plus he's unlikely to pass the test again at his age, so he and Mary have to rely on friends and taxis to take them shopping. I'm afraid most people thought Jess behaved badly . . . me included. She could have left them their independence.'

I decided to keep out of that argument. Everyone's feelings would have been very different if Ralph had run over a child at twenty miles an hour when he was three times over the limit. 'Why would Jess be out to get them? Shouldn't they be out to get her?'

He gave an abrupt laugh. 'You can't apply logic to it. The Galbraiths are one of the couples who found Lily in their bed, and Jess accused them of cruelty because they drove her home and abandoned her without offering to help. The car incident was the icing on the gingerbread – gave her the chance to shop Ralph to the police – or that's how it's viewed in the village at least.'

'When did it happen?'

'Four or five months ago.'

'How long have the Galbraiths lived here?'

'Eight years. Why do you ask?'

'Just trying to understand where stalking fits in.' I repeated as nearly as I could what Madeleine had said about Jess's fixations and her vindictive reactions when she was rejected.

'I'm surprised you went to see her,' Peter said with heavy irony. 'Weren't you afraid of being her next victim?'

'I might have been if I'd believed Madeleine. I'd have given her the cold shoulder . . . which is what everyone else seems to do.' I watched him. 'Except you. Is that because you're her doctor or because you're better informed?'

'About what?'

I shrugged. 'Nathaniel? Does anyone else know he used to be with Jess?'

He moved back to his chair and folded his tall frame on to the seat. 'Presumably anyone who was around at the time does . . . but it was a fairly private thing. If Jess had worn her heart on her sleeve, it might have created a few waves, but she couldn't have shown less interest at losing him. Which is why you shouldn't place too much weight on Lily's remark about value . . . or not where Jess is concerned at least. Boyfriends come and go at that age. Do you even remember the names of the ones you had at twenty?'

'I do, as a matter of fact, even though none of mine lasted longer than three months. I'd certainly remember a man I spent two years with.' I eyed him with amusement. 'Your experience might be different, though. Perhaps you never knew the girls' names in the first place.'

'Ouch!'

'What other reason is there for Jess and Madeleine to hate each other?'

He rested his chin on his hands. 'I've no idea, but whatever it is existed long before Nathaniel jumped ship. He was just a bone in an endless dogfight. It's Lily they've been squabbling over . . . not Nathaniel.'

'Perhaps it's sibling rivalry,' I suggested ironically. 'They're not half-sisters, are they? Could Lily have slept with Jess's father?'

Peter gave a snort of laughter. 'Not unless she was drunk. His mother was her maid, for God's sake. It'd be like touching pitch.'

'It happens.'

'Not in this case,' he said positively. 'Frank Derbyshire wouldn't have done anything so crass. He was far too fond of his wife.'

'What about the other way round . . . Madeleine's father and Jess's mother?'

He shook his head. 'Jenny Derbyshire had better

taste. In any case, it would only be sibling rivalry if *Lily* was Jess's mother . . . and she wasn't. I can guarantee that Jess is a Derbyshire through and through.' He said it firmly, as if the idea of anything else offended him. 'The jealousy's mostly on Madeleine's side. She had no time for her mother until Jess took an interest, then suddenly she was all over her . . . and Lily wouldn't play. I'm sure the remark about value was in reference to herself. Madeleine was never so fond of Lily as when Jess took to visiting Barton House after her parents' death.'

'Why wouldn't Lily play?'

'She knew it wouldn't last. As soon as Madeleine was top dog again, she'd have dropped her like a hot cake. I think Lily felt she'd be better off setting them against each other.'

'She was probably right.'

Peter shook his head. 'She enjoyed stirring too much . . . and it backfired on her. She used to refer to Jess as her "little stalker" in front of Madeleine, and to Madeleine as her "little parasite" in front of Jess. It wasn't very clever of her. If they'd liked each other, they'd have treated it as a joke, but as they didn't – ' he smiled rather bitterly – 'it just added fuel to the flames.'

'So how did the lesbian rumours start? I mean, if Jess had a relationship with a man, why does everyone assume she's a dyke? Has she had affairs with women?'

A look of distaste crossed Peter's face. 'I don't think that's anyone's business but hers.'

'Why on earth not?' I asked in surprise. 'It's perfectly legal . . . and she's told me about your affairs. You're not homophobic, are you?'

He glared at me. 'Of course not.'

I shrugged. 'There's no "of course" about it. Everyone else in Winterbourne Barton is homophobic. It's like Zimbabwe – fifty years out of date and deeply ignorant. Robert Mugabe won't tolerate gays so no one else does either . . . not if they want to keep a head on their shoulders.'

Peter rubbed his eyes. 'She has two women working for her – Julie and Paula. They live together as an openly gay couple, and it may have something to do with that. The younger one, Julie, is Harry Sotherton's granddaughter – he's the old boy who used to work for Jess's father and still helps out at the farm – and he asked Jess to take Julie on about ten years ago. She was twenty-five and married, but she left her husband a year or so later and moved herself and her children in with Jess. They stayed for about two months, then she set up home with Paula . . . which is when the tongues started wagging.'

'Why?'

His mouth twisted cynically. 'Jess was the facilitator. She introduced them, and took Paula on to the payroll so that Julie could work flexitime around her children. Now she and Paula box and cox mornings and afternoon so that one of them's always free to do the school run. It works very well.' He looked as if he was about to add a 'but', then changed his mind.

'But Winterbourne Barton doesn't approve of lesbians bringing up children?'

'Harry's wife certainly doesn't. She's had a lot to say on the subject . . . and she lays the blame at Jess's door.'

'For enabling them to work?'

'For initiating her granddaughter into moral turpitude and depravity. She won't accept that Julie's a lesbian and thinks Jess "taught" her – ' he drew quote marks in the air – 'then handed her over to big, butch Paula to finish the job. Julie's very feminine, and looks as if butter wouldn't melt in her mouth.'

'What does Harry say?'

'Nothing, just turns up for work every day and goes to see the great-grandchildren on his own. Julie won't let Mrs Sotherton near them.'

'Which makes Mrs Sotherton worse, I suppose?' Peter nodded. 'What about Lily? Presumably she didn't condone moral turpitude in Winterbourne Valley?'

He smiled again and this time the smile reached his eyes. 'Quite the reverse. She took it all in her stride. She said Jess was too inhibited to sleep with women, but she quite saw that Julie might, and had no doubts at all about Paula. I think she quite envied them as a matter of fact. She told me once that her life would have been very different if she'd had a loving wife instead of a ne'er-do-well husband.'

'Maybe she wasn't so bad after all.' I paused, but he didn't say anything. 'Where did Jess's "loner" tag come from? It's a very schizophrenic view that has her offering beds to women and children on the one hand . . . and acting like a morose recluse on the other.'

'Pass.'

'Weirdo?'

'Spends her time with weasels . . . has photos of the dead on her walls . . . dresses like a man.' He spread his hands at my frown of impatience. 'Best I can do. If she smiled or said good morning once in a while, it would do more to change people's opinions than anything else.' He steepled his fingers in front of his nose. 'But you'll be wasting your breath if you tell her. She's even more dismissive of advice on her lifestyle than she is on her art. Lily was constantly trying to change her, and it had no effect whatsoever.'

I wondered if he knew how obvious his feelings were. 'You really like her, don't you?'

He gave a muted laugh. 'If you mean Lily, then, no. She was an evil-minded old bitch when the mood was on her.'

'I meant Jess.'

'I know.' He glanced at his watch. 'I'll have to be making tracks soon. Was there anything else you wanted?'

It was smoothly done, but just as final as Jess's

earlier injunction to keep my mouth shut. I took the hint with good grace and left, but as I headed back to Barton House I couldn't help wondering if Peter had made his soft spot for Jess as obvious to Madeleine. If so, it might explain a few things.

From:	connie.burns@uknet.com
Sent:	Thur 29/07/04 10.43
To:	alan.collins@manchester-police.co.uk
Subject:	Scan

Dear Alan,

Re: Scan of O'Connell's documents

No. Even allowing for the poor quality of the original fax,
the man in the photo is NOT MacKenzie/Harwood.
MacKenzie is thinner-faced, thinner-lipped and his eyes
are much paler. This man has dark eyes. Also, he looks
younger. I can't make any useful comments re the facts
in the documents since they don't relate to MacKenzie.
NB: With the name and contact address for next of kin
blacked out, this man could be anyone. Bill Fraser only
has Alastair Surtees's word that it's Kenneth O'Connell.

Could you stress very strongly to Bill that I do not believe
MacKenzie was wrongly identified to me? Our Iraqi guide
took care to note the correct office, and I have no reason
to think he made a mistake or that the academy's
records were out of date when I was told the next day
that Kenneth O'Connell was still working there. The
press corps was guaranteed free access to anyone at

the academy, and several of my colleagues elected to do one-on-one interviews which were speedily arranged. Had O'Connell been wrongly identified as MacKenzie, then there was no reason for O'Connell not to speak to me. But if O'Connell was MacKenzie then he had every reason not to speak to me. Not least because he was using a fake identity.

I realize this casts major doubt on Alastair Surtees's role – not to mention BG's head office in Cape Town – but private security firms are making a fortune in Iraq, and none of them wants to kill the golden goose through the adverse publicity of an investigation. For this reason, I'm deeply sceptical about these 'documents', and my guess is Bill's been sold a 'dummy'.

FYI: At the suggestion of my boss in Baghdad, Dan Fry, who's interested in pursuing the story, I've tracked down a Norwegian photographer who was in Sierra Leone in 2002. I remembered him doing a photo-montage of Paddy's Bar – to show the post-war multinational interest in Freetown – and I hoped he might have a shot of MacKenzie. He's sent through two prints with MacKenzie in the background, and a friend here is enhancing the best one to produce a workable and recognizable headshot.

Dan's idea is to show it round the academy to see if

anyone identifies it as Kenneth O'Connell. Clearly, if he succeeds, he will have a story on Alastair Surtees and BG's operation in Iraq and Cape Town, although he's willing to share any information with Bill before he breaks it. If Bill wants to contact him in advance his email address is: Dan@Fry.ishma.iq

Finally, if Bill is serious about nailing MacKenzie, would it be worth looking for the Mary MacKenzie on the envelope? She must be related to him, and I'm as sure as I can be that the address was Glasgow. NB: All the Brits in Freetown described Harwood's accent as Glaswegian. I realize it'll be like looking for 'Mary Smith' in London, but if the rest of the family's anything like Keith – i.e. violent – they might be known to the Glasgow police.

Hope this finds you well. I shall keep my fingers crossed for your son's A levels. Does he want to be a policeman like you?

Best, Connie

PS. By far the easiest way to identify MacKenzie is by the winged scimitar at the base of his skull – not unlike the one David Beckham has, but smaller. Mackenzie seems to have a thing about feathers. Did I tell you he called the prostitutes in Sierra Leone 'devils' feathers'?

From:	connie.burns@uknet.com
Sent:	Tues 03/08/04 12.03
To:	Dan Fry (Dan@Fry.ishma.iq)
Subject:	MacKenzie photo
Attachments:	DSC02643.JPG; *W* cb_surtees (28 KB)

Dear Dan,

We have lift off! I can't claim much credit for this –
there's a woman here who's a computer/photo whizz –
and she's finessed the end result to perfection. I sent the
finished version to an Australian mate who was in Sierra
Leone at the same time, with the tagline: 'Do you
recognize this face?' And he emailed straight back: 'I'm
surprised you've forgotten. It's the woman-hater from
Freetown, John Harwood.'

I know I've committed you to sharing information with Bill
Fraser in Basra, but it is important, Dan. Please don't let
me down. You'll still have your story on the Baycombe
Group, but it will give Bill a chance to locate MacKenzie
before Surtees spirits him out of the country, or he's
spooked into running himself. It may already have
happened, but Bill should at least be able to find out
where he's gone and what name he's using now. If I'm
wrong, and O'Connell isn't MacKenzie, then I'll apologize

to everyone for wasting their time. If I'm right, you'll have a good, exposing piece on the lax vetting procedures of UK security firms.

Time's fairly short as Bill leaves Basra at the end of this month, and I doubt his replacement will be as sympathetic/interested as he is. Also, I'd rather you didn't give information to Jerry Greenhough in Baghdad. 1) He's leaving at the end of September; 2) A fake UK passport isn't his problem; 3) He won't include you in the loop, and by default me.

I'll keep fingers crossed for a speedy result, and please keep watching your back. Of *course*, I'm worried about you. I'm worried about all of you out there.

Love,

Connie

From: Dan@Fry.ishma.iq
Sent: Wed 11/08/04 10.25
To: connie.burns@uknet.com
Subject: Good news/bad news

Good news: 3 positive IDs of the photo as Kenneth O'Connell.

Bad news: Alastair Surtees now claiming that, 'following concerns raised', he conducted his own in-house investigation and 'gave Kenneth O'Connell his papers two weeks ago'. He has no idea where he went or what name he travelled under, but he allowed him to keep the O'Connell passport as he had no authority to confiscate it. Bill Fraser predictably furious and now going hammer and tongs at Surtees. As am I.

Will forward my copy on the Baycombe Group ASAP.

NB. There's no record of a Kenneth O'Connell/John Harwood/Keith MacKenzie flying out of Baghdad airport, but Bill thinks he probably hitched a lift with an army vehicle and drove out through Kuwait. Frankly, with Iraq's borders so porous, he could have left through any of them.

Bill seems to think it was my idea to show the

photograph at the academy. I haven't disabused him, but is there anything you haven't told me about MacKenzie/ O'Connell? Did he have anything to do with your abduction, Connie? Because despite your assurance that he didn't, I'm having doubts.

Do you still not trust me?

Love, Dan

From:	Brian.Burns@S.A.Wines.com
Sent:	Thur 12/08/04 08.52
To:	connie.burns@uknet.com
Subject:	Telephone calls

Darling,

Written in haste. I'm in a meeting all morning but will call this afternoon when I'm back at my desk. Your mother's terribly upset about the row last evening re the nuisance phone calls. When she asked if Jess Derbyshire could be making them, she meant, *was it possible* – i.e. had you given Jess our phone number or might she have seen it written down somewhere? (Be fair, C. It was you who planted the seed a couple of weeks ago, otherwise the idea of Jess making them would never have occurred to Mum.)

From the way you flew off the handle, I suspect you're more worried than angry, but I don't think there's any reason to assume these calls are aimed at you. An adviser at British Telecom suggested they're the result of random dialling – probably a man – who punched in numbers until a woman answered, and now uses 'redial' for the thrill of it. We've had numerous calls from people trying to contact you, and we've followed your instructions to the letter – said you were out of London and taken their names and numbers to pass on to you. We've refused to be drawn into further detail, even when we've recognized the voices of your friends.

This is particularly true of this nuisance caller. Whoever's doing it only rings during the day, and your mother hangs up as soon as she's greeted by silence at the other end. In fact, she has no idea whether it's a man or a woman as they never speak. There were some 20 calls between Monday lunchtime and yesterday p.m., but dialling 1471 doesn't help as the caller's number is withheld. I've now asked British Telecom to bar all withheld numbers, which means calls from abroad will be automatically rejected. It's a bore in the short term, but hopefully this pest will lose interest when there's no response.

Poor Marianne wouldn't have mentioned the calls if she thought you would react the way you did, and now we're concerned that you're not coping as well as we thought. *We both feel we should advance our visit.* She's asked me to talk to you about it as she thinks you're more likely to say 'yes' if I make the request. I'm not sure that's true, C, but I will phone as soon as I'm free. In the meantime, will you call your mother? You know how she hates falling out with anyone – but particularly you.

All my love, Dad xxx

From:	alan.collins@manchester-police.co.uk
Sent:	Fri 13/08/04 16.19
To:	connie.burns@uknet.com
Subject:	Keith MacKenzie

Dear Connie,

I had some difficulty understanding your email. If you re-read you will see that it's very confused. However, there seem to be three things worrying you: 1) MacKenzie has left Iraq. 2) He'll come looking for you. 3) Your parents have been receiving nuisance calls.

Re 1) I can't see MacKenzie returning to the UK. His most likely course is to go back to Africa where he knows he can find work. That being said, I posted him some time ago for passport-related offences, and Glasgow has your photofit and his 2 known aliases. Ditto Customs & Excise, who will pick him up if he tries to enter the country under any of those names.

Re 2) You say he must know you accused him of serial murder because of the emails you copied to Alastair Surtees. In fact Surtees denies showing them to him because he thought your allegations were malicious. Bill Fraser doesn't place much reliance on this but, in either event, I believe you're worrying unnecessarily. You're the one person who can identify MacKenzie, so he'll stay as far away as possible from you – whether his crime is rape and murder, or merely forging passports. It is not in his interests to draw attention to himself.

Re 3) Coincidences do happen, and it would be wrong to assume the timing of these nuisance calls to your parents suggests MacKenzie is in the country. Your parents should report the problem to the police as it sounds as if someone's casing their property, but without very good evidence that MacKenzie: a) knows their phone number; b) their location; c) is in the UK – then giving his name as a suspect will confuse the issue.

Re the clear alarm in your email. You understand that my advice/conclusions are based on the information you've given me. In order that neither of us is in error about that information, I have it listed as follows:

1. Following the serial murders in Freetown, John Harwood's attack on a prostitute and my remark about 'the foreign contingent', you began to wonder if Harwood was responsible for the women's deaths.

2. You mentioned your suspicions to some of your colleagues, who threw cold water on your ideas, and you didn't take them any further. Shortly afterwards you left Freetown, but not before Harwood showed you an envelope with the name 'Mary MacKenzie'. At

8. Your mobile and laptop were stolen during your abduction. *Therefore*, any information stored on them – contact details of family and friends, notes/emails re the murders in Freetown and Baghdad – is available to your abductor(s).

9. You are now terrified that MacKenzie is looking for you.

At the risk of repeating myself, Connie, you know how to contact me if there's anything you wish to add. I cannot *force* you to say anything. If I could, I would have done it when you returned to England.

I won't pretend I can guarantee a positive result on a crime/crimes committed abroad but, if MacKenzie is as dangerous as you claim, there's everything to be gained by trying. *Not least for your sake.* Fear of retribution is a powerful disincentive to speak out, but I hope you know by now that anything you say to me will be treated in confidence.

Kind regards as ever,

Alan

DI Alan Collins, Greater Manchester Police

that point you remembered he was calling himself
Keith MacKenzie in Kinshasa.

3. Two years later, you recognized him in Baghdad but
   were told his name was Kenneth O'Connell. When
   you raised the issue with Alastair Surtees, you were
   dismissed as unreliable and malicious.

4. You searched the Iraqi press for similar murders to
   those in Freetown. You found two, attempted to raise
   interest among Iraqi journalists, got nowhere, so
   informed me and by extension Bill Fraser.

5. You copied those emails to Alastair Surtees.

6. Shortly afterwards, you were abducted on your way to
   the airport by an unknown group who released you
   three days later. You were blindfolded the entire time
   and were unable to give the police any useful
   information. Because your abduction was unlike any
   other, and because you've refused to talk about it,
   this has led to you being branded 'a faker'.

7. On your return to the UK, you went into hiding and
   have never told your story. As far as I know, I am one
   of the few people in contact with you – certainly the
   only policeman as you refuse to give your email
   address to Bill Fraser – but you have not made me
   party to your address or telephone number.

The Cellar

Ten

IT WAS FRIGHTENING how quickly panic re-entered my life. My mother had thought I was angry when she asked if Jess might be her silent listener, but it was fear that made me shout at her, and asphyxia that made me slam the phone down. I knew exactly who her nuisance caller was. Perhaps I wouldn't have been so certain if Dan hadn't told me that MacKenzie had left Iraq, but I doubt it. I'd bolstered my courage through foolish mantras, and the hope that Bill Fraser would find MacKenzie before MacKenzie found me. But I'd been deluding myself.

Looking back, I'm shocked at how Pavlovian my responses had become. How could three days in a cellar override behaviour patterns that had taken thirty-six years to develop, or negate my careful planning of the last few weeks? Why bother to locate every light switch, oil the door locks, arm myself with torches and devise exit strategies if my conditioned response to terror was to curl into a ball in the corner with my eyes closed? Just as the mutilated victims had done in Freetown.

In the end, even petrified animals move when they find themselves still alive, so I did, too. But only as far as the kitchen, where I could lock the door to the corridor as well as the one to the scullery. For some reason, I decided that sitting in the dark would be safer, even though every other light in the house was ablaze. Perhaps the blindfold had habituated me to it – I'd come to like the fact that I couldn't see who or what was in front of me – but it did at least jolt my brain into some sort of limited reasoning.

I adopted the same siege mentality that I'd used in my car when I first arrived. As long as I stayed where I was, I was fine. If I tried to leave, I'd be in danger. I had access to food and water. I could barricade the window by laying the kitchen table over the sink, and I could use carving knives to defend myself. At no point did I think of calling for help. Peter says I'd trained myself to believe there was none available, but that doesn't explain why, when the dawn broke and I saw the phone on the kitchen wall, I remembered there was a world beyond me and my fear of MacKenzie.

Of course it was Jess I called. Like Lily, I'd come to rely on her. She was a trusted Man Friday who didn't expect, or *want*, to be wined, dined and rewarded with trivial conversation. It was curiously restful once I accepted her way of doing things. If she was in a talkative mood, we talked. If she wasn't, we didn't. I hadn't appreciated how conventional I was until I learnt to sit through Jess's silences. I was the type who rushed to speak for fear of seeming boorish, and changing that habit did not come easily.

I gave up trying to work out what made Jess tick after she resumed her visits. She turned up at inconvenient times of the day, as she'd done before, but I found it less irritating the second time around because she didn't take offence if I said I was busy. As often as not, she'd go outside to mow the semi-circle of formal lawn at the back of the house then leave without saying goodbye, but when I pointed out that I didn't expect her to shoulder my responsibilities, she merely shrugged and said she liked doing it. 'Years ago, when Lily had a gardener, he cut the grass all the way to the boundaries and the wildlife vanished. Now they live in the long grass, and you can see their tracks where they come in and out of hiding. You've got a weasel here, if you're interested. He goes to the fishpond to drink.'

'What else lives here?

'Mice, voles, squirrels. A badger's been through recently.'

I pulled a face. 'Rats?'

'Hardly any, I should think . . . not unless you're leaving rubbish out. Your weasel will have their babies if it can, and there's a colony of tawny owls in the valley who prey on them.'

'Do you have rats at the farm?'

She nodded. 'All farms do. They go for the grain stores and the livestock food.'

'What do you do about them?'

'Make life as difficult as possible, keep animal feed in bins and grain stores in good structural order. They only set up home and breed if they have access to food and water, and find cavities and holes to hide in. They're like any other animal. They thrive in conditions they can exploit.'

Like MacKenzie, I thought. 'You make it sound so simple.'

Jess shrugged. 'It is in a way. You only get infestations if you're lazy or careless. It's an open invitation to a rat to leave food and rubbish lying around. They like easy pickings, the same way people do.' She paused. 'Which isn't to say I don't use poison from time to time, or reach for my airgun when a fat one comes nosing around. They can pass Weil's disease and leptospirosis to humans and animals, and prevention's a damn sight better than cure.'

This matter-of-fact approach to pest management was appealing, but I couldn't see her being so sanguine if a plague of locusts descended on her fields. It's one thing to monitor your own premises for vermin, quite another to look death in the face as your crop is taken by a swarm that has bred and gathered a hundred miles away. In those circumstances, you weep and pray to God for deliverance because there's nothing on earth that can help you except the charity of foreign governments and NGOs.

When I said this, she replied rather scathingly that

BSE and foot-and-mouth were no different. 'I lost Dad's whole herd to BSE when cattle over thirty months had to be incinerated – whether they had the disease or not – and it's taken me eight years to build another herd half the size. It's wrecked the beef and dairy industry in this country but you don't hear much sympathy for farmers.'

'Weren't you compensated?'

'Nowhere near what each animal was actually worth. It took Dad years to build his herd – he was always winning prizes at the shows – and none of them had BSE. I got an extra sixty quid for every animal that was killed unnecessarily when the tests post-slaughter proved negative. It was a joke . . . and bloody upsetting. I was pretty fond of those cows.'

'I'm sorry.'

She nodded. 'You get on with it. Did your dad lose crops to locusts?'

'Only the human variety. Mugabe took his farm.'

'How long had your family been there?'

'Not long enough,' I said ironically. 'Three generations – four if you count me – about the same length of time as Madeleine's has been in Barton House.'

'How does that make it not long enough?'

'Wrong colour,' I said harshly. 'If you're black, you've been there for centuries . . . never mind you were born in Mozambique or Tanzania. If you're white your ancestors stole the land from the indigenous people.'

'Is that what your family did?'

'No. My great-grandparents bought ours fair and square, but deeds of title don't count for much when Zanu-PF thugs turn up your doorstep.' I shrugged. 'There are rights and wrongs on both sides, but stealing the land back again hasn't solved anything. It's just made it worse . . . turned Africa's breadbasket into a dustbowl. Ten years ago, the white farmers were producing enough food –' I broke off.

'Go on.'

'No,' I said with an abrupt laugh. 'It makes me too angry. Like you and your dad's herd. I wouldn't mind so much if the farm had gone to our workers, but it's been appropriated by one of Mugabe's cronies and hasn't produced anything for three years. It's a crazy situation.'

'Will you ever go back?'

'I can't,' I said unwarily. 'I'm excluded indefinitely because of what I've written about Mugabe.'

There was a beat of silence before Jess changed the subject. She'd done it before when I made rash comments about myself, and I did wonder if Peter had told her I wasn't who I said I was. It was noticeable that she never called me Marianne, preferring to wait until she caught my attention before saying anything. I had every intention of coming clean – certainly before my parents arrived, as two Mariannes in the same family would need explaining – but I kept postponing it. I wasn't ready to talk about Baghdad – not then, not ever, perhaps – so I carried on with the pretence because it was easier.

There was no question Peter had told Jess that I knew about her relationship with Nathaniel because she made a reference to it the morning after I'd spoken to him. This left me deeply curious about *Peter's* relationship with Jess. Had he been to her house the previous evening? Had he phoned to say I'd visited him? I wasn't worried by the breach of confidence, because I hadn't asked him to keep it to himself, but I was intrigued to know why he'd felt it necessary to inform Jess. At the very least, it implied a closer friendship than either of them was admitting to.

'It takes a crisis to show you what a person's really like,' she said, jerking her chin at one of Nathaniel's paintings. 'He behaved like a complete tosser after my parents died.'

'What did he do?'

'Holed up in London rather than face the emotion down here. It worked out for the best in the end. I might have sold the farm if I'd listened to him. He wanted me to buy a house in Clapham with a studio upstairs.'

'For him?'

'Of course. He had visions of living in Bohemian bliss in some claustrophobic tenement.' She smiled slightly. 'On my parents' money . . . with him as the charismatic artist and me doing the washing-up.'

'Were you tempted?'

'Sometimes . . . at night. Come the mornings, I always had the sense to see it wouldn't work. I need to be on my own with lots of space around me, and he needs an audience.' She paused. 'I gave him the boot when I realized I wasn't cut out to be a servant.'

Interesting choice of words, I thought. 'Is that when he took up with Madeleine?'

'Nn-nn. He'd been sleeping with her for ages. She sprogged two months after I said I never wanted to see him again.' Jess gave one of her rare laughs at my expression. 'That's how Lily reacted. It was about the worst thing that could have happened . . . her only child getting pregnant by a Derbyshire cast-off. The way she carried on, you'd think Nathaniel and I were related. I thought it was pretty funny, myself.'

'Because Lily looked down on you?' It wasn't my idea of humour.

'No. I liked the idea of Madeleine playing servant for the first time in her life.'

I'm sure it was at that point that I gave up trying to understand Jess. There were innumerable questions I wanted to ask, not least why she'd remained close to Lily, but instead I resorted to banality. 'You're well out of it.'

'I know,' she said, staring critically at Nathaniel's painting, 'but *he* isn't. I feel quite sorry for him sometimes. He comes to the farm every so often, wanting to put the clock back, but I haven't seen him since I told him I'd shoot his dick off if he tried it on again.' There was a glint of humour in her eye.

She really did have the capacity to surprise. 'Does Madeleine know?'

Jess gave an indifferent shrug. 'I shouldn't think so. They hardly speak any more, which is why she wants this house. It's her best chance to get rid of him . . . and she'd have done it by now if Lily hadn't stymied her. Lily didn't approve of divorce.'

'Why did Madeleine tell her?'

'She didn't. *I* did.'

I might have guessed that, I thought. 'Not a bad revenge, then?'

'Except I didn't do it for revenge. I did it to protect Lily. Madeleine would have killed her, or stuck her in the cheapest home she could find, if Lily hadn't reassigned the power of attorney. The only thing that stops her shoving a cushion over Lily's face is because a solicitor's involved. She'll be worth a fortune when she inherits this place . . . as long as she gets shot of Nathaniel and the son first.'

*

There's no question Jess was my protector when she roared up the drive within ten minutes of my phone call. It was a little like having a knight on a white charger come to the rescue, except there was no chivalry and very little TLC. When I unlocked the back door her dogs came bounding in behind her, and she snapped at me angrily as I shrank against the wall. 'I'm not facing an intruder on my own,' she hissed, following the mastiffs into the kitchen. 'Wait there.' I heard her unlock the door to the corridor and then the swish of the green baize as she and the dogs disappeared into the body of the house.

It was only when she came back alone five minutes later that I saw she was carrying a gun. She broke it across her knee and put it on the table. 'You're OK. No signs of a break-in, and I've left the dogs in the hall. So what happened?'

I can't remember what explanation I gave, other than to repeat that I thought I'd seen someone in the garden the evening before. The truth was too complicated, and I was too tired to pick my way through the minefield of revelation. Jess was unimpressed. 'Why didn't you call the police? That's what they're there for.'

'I don't know,' I said, sinking miserably to my haunches in the corner. 'I didn't think of it.'

She reached down impatiently and hauled me to my feet. 'Stop being so bloody pathetic and show some guts,' she growled, pushing me on to a chair. 'I know you've got them.'

I wondered if this was how she'd treated Nathaniel. If so, it was hardly surprising he'd preferred Madeleine's flattery. I don't know what I'd expected from her – sympathy and a little affection, perhaps – but it never occurred to me that she might be frightened. It should have done. I should have guessed that my mention of an intruder would take her straight to MacKenzie's photo.

At the time she'd worked on the headshot, I'd expected her to bombard me with questions. She hadn't, although I do remember her asking what the man's name was and why I was doing it. She used the computer at the farm, with me sitting beside her, and she seemed content with the answers I gave – that it was someone I knew by sight, who was wanted in Africa for passport offences. The only comment she made was that it was surprising I was ignorant of his name when I remembered his face so well.

'Was it that man?' she demanded now.

I stared at my hands.

'Who is he? Why would he come looking for you?' When I didn't answer, she reached for the cordless phone and held it out to me. 'Call the police . . . I'll give you the number of the local station. The person you should ask for is Steve Banks. He's our community bobby, and this is his area. He's a good bloke.' She put the receiver on the table in front of me. 'You've got one minute to make up your mind, then I'll do it myself.'

I pulled the phone towards me and cradled it against my chest. 'There's no point. I didn't see anyone.'

'Then why tell me you did? Why lock yourself in here?'

'You wouldn't have come if I'd said I'd locked myself in for no reason.'

She turned on the tap and ran some water into the kettle. 'You look like shit,' she said severely. 'Do you want to go upstairs and sort yourself out while I make some coffee? I'll shut the dogs in the back room so you don't throw a panic attack when you see them.' She flicked me one of her penetrating gazes as she switched on the kettle before heading for the door to the corridor. 'And don't start feeling sorry for yourself. If you take longer than half an hour, I'll be gone . . . and I won't come back. I really *hate* weepy women.'

*

Denial's a wonderful thing. You can survive for ever if you say 'no'. It's 'yes' that puts you at risk. Yes, I'd like a job. Yes, I'll go to Baghdad. Yes, I know who abducted me. Yes, I can identify MacKenzie. I had a great-aunt who said 'no' to everything. She died a virgin at ninety-eight and her death was the most interesting thing about her. She said: 'What was I thinking of?' just before she died, and we've been wondering ever since.

Jess was right about my appearance. I did look like shit. Red-eyed and haggard, and easily as old and desiccated as a ninety-eight-year-old virgin. As I washed my face and tugged a brush through my hair, I asked myself what *I* was thinking of. I'd hardly written anything since I'd arrived – except emails to

Alan and Dan – and the only people I spoke to on a regular basis were my parents, Jess and Peter. My days were spent surfing the net, researching information on psychopaths and deviants. My nights were spent dreaming about them.

> '**Stalker types**: *The delusional stalker often has a history of mental illness which leads him to fantasize that his victim is in love with him. The vengeful stalker – the most dangerous – seeks revenge . . .*'

> '**Sadist Rapist**: *One who seeks to punish a woman by the use of violence and cruelty. The victim is typically only a symbol of the source of his anger. He is usally very deliberate in his rapes and plans each one carefully. The victims are often traumatized, suffer extreme physical injuries and, in many cases, are murdered . . .*'

> '**Torturer**: *One who inflicts extreme physical and mental pain for the purpose of punishment or obtaining information. Abuse may include: blindfolding; enforced constant standing or crouching; near drowning through submersion in water; near suffocation by plastic bags being tied round the head; rape . . .*'

When John Donne wrote 'no man is an island entire of itself' he can't have known about genuine introverts like Jess or sociopaths like MacKenzie. Such people might live within communities – albeit on the fringes

197

– but their reclusiveness, their reticence, even their indifference to what others think, means, at best, that they're only semi-attached to the 'continent' of mankind. If they engage with the rest of us at all, it's on their own terms and not on ours.

MacKenzie's isolation had turned him into a predator, although it's arguable which came first – his sadism or his alienation. It's unlikely he was born with sadistic fantasies – what baby is? – but a harsh childhood might have led to them. By contrast, Jess's introversion seems to have been inherited from her father, although the tragedies in her life may have exacerbated it. Sometimes, particularly when she refused to speak, I felt there was an autistic element to her personality. She was certainly a gifted artist, and gave the same obsessive commitment to her work that savants show.

In her own way, she was charismatic. She inspired affection and loyalty in those who chose to interact with her, and a disproportionate dislike among those who didn't. There was no middle ground with Jess. You loved her or loathed her, and in either case accepted her detachment as part of the package.

All of which persuaded me back downstairs within the half-hour limit because I needed her a great deal more than she needed me.

Extracts from notes, filed as 'CB15–18/05/04'

. . . The police in Baghdad suggested that my alleged 'ignorance' might be due to Stockholm Syndrome – I'd developed a bond with my captors to stay alive and was withholding information out of gratitude for my release. They told me it was nothing to be ashamed of. It happens to most hostages because their lives depend on their captors, and it's a classic self-protection measure to befriend the one who threatens you. When I denied it, they lost sympathy with me.

. . . The only bond I developed was with the footsteps. I longed for them because I was afraid I'd been left to die of slow starvation and dehydration . . . and feared them because it meant I'd be taken out of the crate. I certainly developed a psychological attachment to sounds. I was owned for three days – and still am.

. . . I was never going to give details of what happened. How could I explain my smiles to strangers? Did I ever say no? Did I ever *think* about saying no?

. . . Do all sadists understand the power they wield? Are all victims programmed to respond in the same way to fear and pain?

. . . I wish I could believe that. At least it's an excuse
for cowardice. Why am I alive? I don't understand that
at all . . .

Eleven

MY RETURN DOWNSTAIRS was a replay of my arrival. When I pushed open the kitchen door, Peter was sitting at the kitchen table and Jess stood mutinously by the Aga, staring at the floor. I hadn't heard Peter's car, and I stiffened with anxiety as soon as I saw him. He gave me a reassuring smile. 'I won't take offence if you give me my marching orders, Marianne. Jess told me to get my "arse over PDQ". She said it was an emergency, but, as I'm sure you know by now, diagnosis isn't her strong point.'

Jess scowled at him. 'You need to talk to someone,' she told me bluntly, 'and Peter's probably the best person. Just don't let him put you on drugs. If he turns you into a zombie, you'll be easy meat for any psycho that comes calling.'

Peter frowned a warning. 'Shut up, Jess. If that's your idea of tact it's no wonder your social circle consists entirely of weasels.'

'It's what she's afraid of.'

He stood up and gestured towards the other chair. 'Please come in, Marianne. You have my word there's no one here except me and Jess. Against her better judgement, I've persuaded her that now is not the time to cure you of your fear of dogs . . . so you don't even have mastiffs to contend with.'

Jess turned her scowl on me. 'It's up to you, but you'll be better off with a dog to guard you. I'm happy to lend you Bertie. He used to be Lily's till she couldn't cope any more, so he'll settle back fine once you start feeding him . . . as long as you don't go spastic and start flapping your hands around. You only need to learn a few commands and he'll stand between you and danger.' Her expression relented a little. 'Think about it, anyway. He'll be a lot better for you than anti-depressants.'

Peter smiled rather grimly. 'You can be a real pain in the arse at times.'

'I'm just giving some options.'

'No, you're not. You're blasting off with half-baked theories as usual. I suggest we revert to plan A – ' he spoke through gritted teeth – 'which was to give Marianne the chance to tell us if there's any way we can help her.' He caught my gaze and made a valiant effort to suppress the irritation in his. 'Can I persuade you to come in? Or would you rather one or both of us left . . .?'

I knew the irritation wasn't directed at me, but it was enough to set a flutter of alarm knocking at my ribcage. My response to any display of male impatience or displeasure was a rush of fear. There were too many associations, and not just with MacKenzie. During the police interview in Baghdad – where the questioning became increasingly brusque – I'd started shaking so badly that the American adviser called a halt and asked if I'd prefer to speak to a woman.

I declined so vehemently that a puzzled frown creased his forehead. 'But you seem distressed, Connie. I thought you might be more comfortable with a member of your own sex.'

I reached for a glass of water, then changed my mind because I didn't want the rim rattling against my teeth. 'I'm tired,' I managed out of a dry mouth, 'and if I start again with somebody new, I'll miss my plane. I really want to get home to my parents in England.'

He wasn't unkind. In other circumstances I'd have liked him. 'I understand that, but I've no wish to upset you, and I have the feeling I'm doing that. Would you care for a female officer to sit in on the session?'

I shook my head. I was afraid of a woman's sympathy, even more afraid of her instincts. It was easier telling lies to men. I ran my tongue round the inside of my mouth and manufactured a convincing smile. 'I'm OK. Just exhausted. It was frightening . . . you don't sleep when you're frightened.'

He watched my expression as Dan put an arm across my shoulders to comfort me. I kept the smile in place – just – but I couldn't stop my eyes widening. Perhaps men are as instinctive as women, because the frown returned immediately. 'I'm not happy about this, Connie. Are you sure you've told us everything?'

All I could do was stare at him. My whole body was rebelling at Dan's closeness. That was the first time I had difficulty breathing, although it was more an enforced holding of my breath – a twenty-second freeze – than the panic that came afterwards. It seems to take time for the bombshell of terror to start exploding without warning. Perhaps we function on automatic pilot in the immediate aftermath of trauma, and only experience anxiety when the body needs rest and the brain overrules it for fear of being caught napping again.

Dan spoke for me. 'Give her a break, Chas. She's told you all she can. The men who took her from the taxi wore ski masks, and she was duct-taped and hooded from the off. When I found her, she'd been in darkness so long she couldn't open her eyes . . . and that was less than four hours ago. Be grateful she agreed to talk at all. If I'd had my way, she'd have been on the first plane out and you'd have been asking London for information.'

'I appreciate that.'

'I don't think you do. You heard the doc. He suggested a twenty-four-hour recuperation period before she answered questions, so letting London do the honours would have made more sense. You'd still have got your information . . . but the delay would have reduced its value. Connie understood that, which is why she's here.'

'I *do* appreciate that, Dan, but, unfortunately, Connie hasn't been able to tell us anything.' He shifted his attention to me. 'Do you know if a video was made of you? The home movie seems to be the hostage-takers' trademark . . . they want their fifteen minutes of fame just like westerners do. Do you remember hearing a camera going?'

I managed to say 'no', and smile while I did it, but my heart was going like a hammer. The whole concept was too devastating to deal with. I could have maintained a pretence of dignity if there'd been no record of what I did. He took close-ups – '*show you're enjoying it, feather*' – so there'd be an identifiable human face, even with taped eyes, on the obedient, rag-doll body.

What was he planning to do with the tape? How many people would see it? Was I recognizable as Connie Burns? Would Dan see it? My parents? My friends? My colleagues? All other invasions seemed trivial compared to a public unveiling in the Baghdad bazaars, or, worse, through al-Jazeera TV or the internet. Is life worth living when you've had to beg for it? How do you function without self-esteem? How do you find the courage to go out?

'Why do you think you were released so rapidly, Connie? Dan's told us he wasn't involved in any negotiations because he didn't know who was holding you. Nor did we . . . nor did any of the religious groups. So why did they let you go?'

'I don't know.'

'The current average is two weeks. At the end of that time, depending on how much pressure has been brought to bear, hostages are either released or beheaded. We think most are being taken to Fallujah – or one of the other no-go areas – but you appear to have been held in Baghdad . . . then released after three days without any active intervention. It doesn't fit the patterns we've seen, Connie.'

'I'm sorry.'

'I'm not blaming you,' he said with a sigh. 'I'm trying to demonstrate why we need as much infor-mation as you can give us. Our only lead was your driver – and he's vanished – so we've no idea what we're dealing with here. It may be the beginning of a new pattern . . . or the emergence of a new group, whose only saving grace is that they haven't learnt to kill yet.' He watched my eyes grow wider as Dan gave my shoulder a clumsy squeeze in solidarity. 'Do you want someone else to suffer your fate, Connie?'

I couldn't have spoken even if I'd wanted to.

'What sort of a question's that?' asked Dan angrily. 'You know damn well your chance of catching these bastards is zero. Zarqawi's got a ten-million bounty on his head . . . and no one's turned him in. If you increase it to twenty-five million, they still won't. What can Connie tell you that's going to change that?'

'Nothing, as far as Zarqawi's concerned. I'm willing to accept she was taken for onward sale, but in that case why didn't he buy her?' He held my gaze for a moment, then turned back to Dan. 'There's a lot of mileage to be made out of female journalists. They're known to their fellow professionals, and women under threat make good copy. Connie and Adelina Bianca have inspired more column inches between them than any other hostages.' He flicked another glance in my direction. 'Why would Zarqawi – why would *any* terrorist – turn down publicity like that? It sure as hell doesn't make any sense to me.'

It didn't to Dan either, but he fought my corner as he'd promised he would. My only leverage was the fact that we'd known each other for years. I'd first met him in South Africa when I joined the *Cape Times* as a rookie sub-editor from Oxford, and he was a columnist. We overlapped for a year before he moved abroad to join Reuters, but we knocked into each other regularly when he was sent to cover an 'Africa' story. He came from Johannesburg, but his primary place of residence – according to his tax returns – was County Wexford, Eire, where he 'lived' with his Irish wife, Ailish, and their daughter, Fionnula.

It was a strange relationship. His visits to Ireland were even more intermittent than the occasional postings that brought him and me together. I asked him once how he came to marry an Irish girl, and he said it was a shotgun wedding when she fell pregnant. 'She was a student in London and was frightened to go home without a ring. Her father believes in hellfire and brimstone. He'd have kicked her out to fend for herself.'

'Why didn't she have an abortion?'

'Because Ailish believes in hellfire and brimstone more than her old man does.'

'It didn't stop her sleeping with you.'

'Mm . . . except some sins are smaller than others – ' he grinned – 'and my charm might have had something to do with it. It's worked out for the best in the end. Fee's a grand kid. It would have been a crime to abort her.'

'If you feel like that why don't you make more of an effort to see her?'

He shrugged. 'It causes too many problems. The only time the family argues is when I'm there. They all approve of the monthly cheque but not the lodger.'

'Does Ailish live with her parents?'

'Not quite. Three houses down. They're a close-knit bunch. She has three brothers within a two-mile radius who turn up in force every time I visit to make sure I'm not going to renege on my responsibilities. I feel a bit like Daniel entering the lions' den whenever I go there.'

It all seemed very peculiar to me. And rather sad. 'Do you still sleep with Ailish?'

His eyes crinkled at the edges. 'She lets me stay in the spare room, but that's about as far as her hospitality goes . . . apart from keeping her lover at arm's length for the duration.'

'You're crazy,' I said in disbelief. 'Why don't you get a divorce?'

'What for? There's no one else to marry . . . except you . . . and you won't have me.'

'You can't cook.'

'Neither can you.'

'Precisely, which is why we'd make a lousy couple. We'd starve.' I bared my teeth at him. 'Are you sure it's not a scam to avoid paying income tax? Everyone knows writers and artists are zero-rated in Ireland.'

'Only creative writers . . . and you have to spend six months a year in the country to qualify. Journalists are excluded.'

I couldn't see that stopping him. He'd worked on a Reuters financial desk at one stage in his career and claimed to know every tax-dodge going. 'Are you planning to live there when you write the great novel?'

'It's crossed my mind.'

'With Ailish?'

Dan shook his head. 'I'd rather have a cottage in Kerry, overlooking Dingle Bay. I took Fee there the last time I was over, and it was beautiful. We walked along the beach.' He paused. 'By the time I take the plunge – *if* I take the plunge – she'll be a grown woman. What do you think she'll make of her father then? Will she still want to walk in the sand with me?'

It was said in the same amused tone that he'd used throughout, but the words suggested something else. A feeling for his child that he wanted reciprocated. It surprised me. I thought he was like me, determinedly unwilling to commit as the only way to stay sane in a life that was nomadic. Perhaps his daughter had given him roots. I envied him suddenly.

And I envied Fee. Did she know how Dan felt about her? Did she know who he was? What he'd done? What he'd written? How he was viewed outside the narrow confines of her mother's family?

'She'll be a strange woman, if she doesn't,' I said. 'It's feminine nature to be curious . . . comes from centuries of having nothing to do except analyse male behaviour. As to what she'll make of you – ' I paused – 'I hope you'll always be a mystery to her, Dan. That way, she'll keep coming back for more.'

He made a passing reference to that conversation as he waited with me at Baghdad airport. 'How am I going to get in touch with you? The only contact number I have is your mobile . . . and that's gone. I'm beginning to realize how little I actually know about you, Connie. I need your parents' details.'

I forced a smile. 'I wrote their address and number on the pad in your flat when I called home,' I lied, 'but you can always find them in the personnel files under next of kin.' In fact I hadn't updated the details since my parents left Zimbabwe, so the only address on record was Japera Farm, and I couldn't see Mugabe's crony forwarding correspondence.

Dan nodded. 'OK. And you're happy with the arrangements? Harry Smith will meet you at Heathrow and steer you through the press conference. After that, he'll ask for you to be left alone . . . although you'll certainly be chased for quotes if and when Adelina Bianca's released.' He reached for my hand. 'Can you cope with all of that?'

I tried not to show how much I hated being touched. 'Yes.'

'You'll be asked about the length of time you were held. That's the issue that's going to interest them. Why only three days? Were you given the reason for your release? Who negotiated it? Was any money paid?' He gave my hand a reassuring squeeze. 'It might be worth thinking it through on the plane. You can legitimately plead ignorance on most things, but they'll want to know what you said to your kidnappers and whether you think that influenced your treatment.'

Twenty feet away, a woman smacked a toddler on the back of his head. I couldn't see what his offence was, but the heavy-handed blow seemed disproportionate to any crime a two-year-old could have committed. I felt a rush of sadness in my throat – the precursor to tears – but I'd lost the ability to cry and gazed dry-eyed at Dan as I slipped my hand from his and hunched inside my borrowed jacket. Underneath, I was still wearing my 'abduction' clothes, a cotton skirt and shirt, which I'd washed before Dan took me to the police station. I'd accepted the jacket from a female colleague in case it was cold in London.

'Are you asking me to make something up?'

He looked away. 'I'm suggesting you get your story straight, Connie. You told the police you couldn't speak because of the duct tape over your mouth . . . but in the next breath said you were given water regularly. That can only have happened if the tape was removed, so why didn't you speak then?'

'Because it wouldn't have made any difference. If they'd wanted to kill me they'd have killed me.'

'Then, yes,' he said with sudden impatience. 'I'm suggesting you make something up. You know the deal. It's all about column inches, so give them the best story you can.'

I dug my hands into my pockets. 'Otherwise what?'

'They'll compare you with Adelina, Connie, and look for bruises. They'll ask for the doctor's report – clean bill of health, with minor bruising on your wrists and some redness round your mouth and eyes from the duct tape – and they'll want to know why you got off so lightly. What are you going to tell them?'

I ran my tongue across my lips. 'That I don't know.'

'And when they ask what you were wearing – which they certainly will – how are you going to answer that?'

I pulled the jacket tighter around my waist and hips. 'What I've got on.'

'Then stick to the story we gave the police . . . that I had your clothes laundered because you had nothing else to wear. I'll take the flak again,' he finished rather grimly, 'even though it makes me look like a bloody idiot.'

He'd been given a rough time by Chas for allowing me to clean myself and my clothes before going to the police station. It was bad enough that he'd kept my release secret for three hours, worse that he hadn't considered the implications of destroying evidence. There was some excuse for my behaviour because I was traumatized, but none for Dan. He should have known better. How were the authorities expected to secure convictions without forensic corroboration?

Dan had stood by me – in so far as he took the criticism on the chin and kept it to himself that he'd tried to stop me – but he made no secret of his suspicions now. 'Why did you need to wash those clothes, anyway?'

'They were dirty.'

But we both knew they weren't. They hadn't even smelt dirty, which was why I'd washed them. I'd toyed with saying I'd been given an orange jumpsuit, similar to the one Adelina wore on her video, but I was afraid of provoking further questions. Why were there no orange fibres on my skin or in my hair? Why bother to dress me as a prisoner if no video was made? It was less traumatic to be accused of destroying evidence than admit to wearing nothing.

I wondered if Dan had guessed the truth because he didn't pursue the issue. Instead, he told me what he planned to say when he announced my release to the press corps in Baghdad. There was heavy emphasis on my cooperation with the police, my refusal to say too much for fear of jeopardizing Adelina's chances, and my undoubted 'courage and professionalism'. It was a clear instruction to stay 'on message' in London so that Reuters in Baghdad wasn't ambushed out of left field.

I sent surreptitious glances towards the clock on the far wall, ticking off the seconds before I could reasonably head for the departure gate. The only luggage I had was a fabric bumbag (borrowed from Dan) which held my ticket stub, boarding-pass and emergency passport (paid for by Reuters), and £25 in precious English fivers from the Baghdad bureau coffers.

'Are you listening to me, Connie?'

I gave another nod. But as I had no intention of performing for the press, it was irrelevant whether I listened or not. If I failed to appear, the only source of information would be Dan's press conference and, with no photographs, the coverage would be limited to a box somewhere. There might be speculation about why and where I'd gone into hiding, but it wouldn't amount to much. Stories without legs and pictures died on the editor's floor.

I'd made the decision to bolt when I phoned my parents from Dan's flat to tell them I was safe. My mother answered in Swahili. Literally. As a child, she'd learnt the language from Adia, her Kenyan nanny, and had passed on what she remembered to me. She spoke before I could say anything. 'Jambo. Si tayari kuzungumza na mtu mie.' *Hello. I can't talk to anyone at the moment.*

It was a device we'd used when things became difficult at the farm. My father was convinced there were physical and wire-tap eavesdroppers. Swahili isn't commonly understood in Zimbabwe, where English is the official language and Shona and Ndebele the native ones. In this case, I guessed my mother was expecting a call from my father, and was warning him there was someone in the room with her.

I answered: 'Jambo, mamangu. Mambo poa na mimi. Sema polepole!' *Hello, my mother. Everything's fine with me. Be careful what you say!*

There was a brief pause. 'Bwana asifiwe. Nakupenda, mtoto wangu.' *Thank God. I love you, my child.* There was a catch of emotion in her voice which she quelled immediately. 'Sema fi kimombo.' *You can speak in English.*

In the weeks after my release, that was the closest I came to breaking down. Had she been in the room,

I would have become her 'mtoto' again, stolen into her warm embrace and told her everything. By the time I saw her in London, that opportunity was gone. I took a breath. 'Who's with you?'

'Msimulizi.' *A newspaper reporter.*

'Oh, Christ! Don't let on it's me!' I could hear the tremors in my voice. 'No one knows I've been released yet . . . except Dan . . . I'm in his flat. I need time to . . . Do you understand?'

'Ni sawasawa.' *It's OK.* She sounded so reassuring that I think she must have been smiling at whoever was in the room. 'Nasikia vema.' *I understand perfectly.*

'I'm flying out this evening via Amman, and should be in London early tomorrow morning.' I glanced towards the door of the room, wondering if Dan was listening. 'Is this reporter a one-off or are they plaguing you?'

Another pause while she worked out a strategy. 'Yes, indeed, it would be much easier in English. I'm very touched that you're calling from Connie's newspaper in Kenya. We've had interest from all over the world. As I speak, there are journalists and photographers in the road outside . . . all of whom are publicizing Connie's plight. We're deeply grateful for everyone's support and assistance.'

My heart sank. 'Are they making life hell for you?'

'Yes.'

'How's Dad bearing up?' I amended that immediately because I knew she wouldn't be able to answer it. 'Don't worry. I can guess.' After the events at the farm, my father had developed a short fuse when it came to intrusion. He particularly hated being questioned about what had happened, as if other people had a right to pry into his humiliation. 'Is he losing his temper with them?'

'Yes. In fact my husband is at the Zimbabwean High Commission today. The British government refuses to talk to hostage-takers, but there's a possibility Robert Mugabe might intervene because Connie has dual nationality. Andrew is trying all avenues.'

'Oh, *God*!' My father would cut off his arm rather than ask Mugabe for help. He hated the thieving little dictator more than any man on earth. 'I'm so sorry! What a bloody awful mess!'

'Haidhuru. Kwa kupenda kwako.' *It doesn't matter. He's doing it because he loves you*. Another pause. 'I wonder if it would be better if you spoke to Andrew? He can tell you far more than I can. Do you have a number that he can call when he returns? Perhaps a mobile?'

'No . . . it was stolen . . . and I don't know where I'll be in the next few hours. Can you wait till I land in London?' I looked at the door again. 'Dan's organizing a press conference at Heathrow – ' I broke off, praying she'd follow up on why.

'Will that be difficult for you?'

'Yes.'

'Is your colleague with you now?'

'I'm not sure. Possibly.' I paused. 'Reuters are holding back the news of my release until the press conference ... which means I need you to keep pretending you haven't heard from me. It's important, Mum. I don't want cameras filming me as I come into the arrivals hall. Will you promise not to say anything till you hear from me?'

'Of course. All either of us wants is Connie's safe return.'

I wished I could tell her that I couldn't go to the flat while photographers were in the street, but I didn't know if Dan was listening or how good his Swahili was. Instead, I hoped she would pick up a hint. I gave a shaky laugh. 'I'm beginning to understand how Dad felt when you left the farm. Do you remember what he said the worst thing was?' (*Talking about it. What am I supposed to say? Does it make people feel better when I admit to being scared?*)

My mother hesitated for a moment before she repeated: 'Nasikia vema.' *I understand perfectly*. 'You'd like a private interview ... in a hotel perhaps ... bila wasimulizi na maswala (*without reporters and questions*). Is that right? Have I understood your wishes correctly?'

'Yes.'

'My husband will be waiting for your call. I guarantee he'll help in any way he can. Our daughter needs all the support she can get.'

I took another breath to stop the tremors. 'I really am fine, you know . . . so don't start imagining things . . . all that happened was that I was blindfolded for three days. Give Dad a hug from me, and I'll see you tomorrow.'

'Tutaonana baadaye, mtoto wangu. Nakupenda.' *We'll see each other soon, my child. I love you.*

It's fairly devastating at thirty-six to recognize that you have a greater empathy with your mother than with the man you've been giving your body to for the last fifteen years. I wondered what would have happened if the roles had been reversed, and it had been Dan on the other end of the phone. Could he have matched my mother's subtlety or understanding? Or would he have waded in blindly with hobnailed boots, as he was doing now?

'I know you're not going to like this, Con, but a few tears wouldn't go amiss. There's been a lot of sympathy shown you over the last three days and it'll ebb away PDQ if you refuse to play along for the cameras. No one's going to believe you've been gagged and blindfolded for the last three days if you don't show a little frailty.'

I dragged my attention back to him. 'Don't worry. I'll do it when the time comes. I'm good at play-acting.'

He frowned. 'Am I supposed to know what that means?'

I shrugged. 'I do a good impersonation of a mistress,

Dan. No demands. No expectations. No drain on the wallet. No interference in the love life when I'm not around. No cause for concern.' I smiled at him. 'You should trust me to put on a good show. I've seen more bloody victims than you ever have.'

He made a ham-fisted attempt to put his arms around me, but I stepped out of reach. 'Are you going to tell me what's going on?' he demanded. 'I've done everything you asked . . . and I get treated like something the cat's brought in. What's up? Is there something you haven't told me?'

'No.'

'Then what's the problem?'

'Nothing,' I said carelessly. 'I'm a recovering hostage.'

He sighed. 'Then talk to me about it. You know I'll listen.'

We'd been through this in the flat. He'd fussed all over me, encouraging me to voice my fears, telling me he'd ask London to organize counselling, running through his own feelings of guilt after his friend died in front of him. Even if I'd been tempted to tell him the truth – which I hadn't – his swamping insistence would have stopped me. What would I have had left once he – once *anyone* – had dragged every last secret out of me?

'There's nothing else to tell. It was frightening while it lasted, but I was luckier than Adelina.' I managed another smile. 'Which is why I might not be able to

produce crocodile tears for the cameras, Dan. I'm alive
. . . I'm in one piece . . . and nothing much happened
to me. It would be shabby to pretend otherwise, don't
you think?'

'Yes,' he agreed slowly. 'I guess it would.'

And that's how we left it, with fifteen years of
sporadic intimacy dead on the floor of a war-torn
airport. Dan went through with his press conference in
Baghdad, and I dodged mine by slipping past Harry
Smith in a group of tourists from another flight. The
interest died very quickly. Apart from the announce-
ment of my release, there was very little else other than
speculation in some of the Iraqi newspapers that I'd
faked my abduction. I didn't mind. I discovered very
quickly that it was easier to live with myself when
everyone thought I was lucky . . . or a fraud.

The trouble was I couldn't live with anyone who
believed it. It's a form of betrayal when people close to
you accept what you tell them at face value.

Shouldn't they know you better than that . . .?

Extracts from notes, filed as 'CB15–18/05/04'

. . . I never realized how fragile trust is. Can a single person really destroy another's faith in everyone and everything?

. . . When I dream of revenge it's always in retribution for my stolen relationships. What gives anyone the right to make me suspicious of people I've liked and loved? Or them of me?

. . . I can rationalize as much as I like but I *know* that nothing will ever be the same again. Whatever happens, I am not the person I was . . .

Twelve

PETER MADE NO comment when I finally entered the kitchen, but he resumed his own seat before I sat down. He shifted it back immediately, as if aware that proximity might worry me. I don't recall in any great detail what I said that morning, although I do remember telling them that my name was Connie Burns and that I'd been held prisoner for three days by a man called Keith MacKenzie whose story I'd investigated. I said he was a serial murderer who'd threatened to come looking for me if I ever spoke about what had happened.

Peter, who had a surgery he couldn't miss, urged me to talk to the local police but I refused, saying it would only confuse the issue as there was a detective inspector in Manchester who was already working on the case. Jess took a more practical approach. She agreed to stay with me until lunchtime, when Peter promised to come back and talk to me at more length. Meanwhile her dogs would patrol the garden.

I was asked afterwards by a Dorset policeman what Jess and I had discussed during the five hours she spent with me, and I said I couldn't remember because it wouldn't have been anything important. Jess wasn't the type to ask questions, and I had already said more than I wanted to. Jess wouldn't have remembered either . . .

*

I remember the conversation I had with Peter later. He had no such inhibitions about asking questions, particularly when Jess wasn't present. He'd already filled in most of the gaps from what he'd read about my abduction, and reached a number of valid conclusions from my behaviour since.

He told me that my fear of him had been very pronounced from the beginning, although I didn't seem to realize I was showing it. It was an involuntary withdrawal – holding myself in a rigid posture, always maintaining a healthy distance, crossing my arms as soon as I saw him, never sitting down when he was standing – yet I showed none of the same aversion towards Jess.

At times I even allowed her to sit beside me, although never close enough for accidental touching. According to Peter, an immature woman, who had difficulty expressing emotion, was my perfect companion. I might have longed for someone with more sensitivity and insight, but I couldn't have coped with the threat they posed. 'If that had been the case you'd have stayed with your mother,' he pointed out. 'She'd have put her arms around you and coaxed out the truth . . . but that's not what you wanted.'

'Sometimes I think Jess is the most perceptive person I've ever met. She always knows when not to be curious.'

'But she's still a virtual stranger to you, Connie . . . and you're not worried what strangers think. Few of us are. Self-image is about how the people we know and love perceive us, not the passing acquaintance who we're never going to meet again. For most of us the universe is very small.'

I thought how wrong he was. 'Until your life is deconstructed across the pages of a newspaper.'

'Is that what you're worried about?'

I didn't answer immediately. His questions reminded me of Chas and Dan in Baghdad – *'But you seem distressed, Connie'* – *'Talk to me'* – and I understood why my father lost his temper when well-meaning people poked him with well-meaning sticks. There's so much arrogance in curiosity. It suggests that nothing can surprise the listener, yet how would Peter have reacted if I'd let out the scream that had been in my head for weeks? How would Dan have reacted?

I hunkered down in my chair. 'I keep thinking of all the proverbs to do with retribution. Reap what you sow . . . live by the sword . . . an eye for an eye. I wake up in the middle of the night with them churning round and round in my head. It seems so inevitable.'

'Why?'

'Because I've made a career out of exploiting other people's anguish. I keep remembering a Sierra Leonean woman who'd watched her family being slaughtered by rebels. By the time I met her she was so disturbed she was raving, but I didn't think twice about using her for a story.' I paused. 'It'll be an apt punishment if the same thing happens to me.'

'I can't agree with you.'

'You should. Everyone gets what they deserve in the end. It'll happen to you, too, Peter. We all get paid in our own coin.'

'What's yours?'

'Death. Disaster. Other people's misery. I'm a war correspondent, for Christ's sake.' I dug my fingers into my eyes. 'Not that it makes much difference. It would be the same whatever kind of correspondent I was. There's no such thing as a "good news" story. Who gives a damn about happiness? It makes readers jealous to learn that someone's better off than they are. Build 'em up 'n' cut 'em down . . . that's all your average Joe wants. If *he* can't make it, why should anyone else?'

'That's very cynical.'

'But I *am* cynical. I've seen too many innocent people die for nothing. Every tinpot dictator knows that the quickest way to control a country is to whip up hatred and fear of a bogeyman . . . and how does he do that without using the press? Journalists are for hire, just like anyone else.'

He watched me for a moment. 'Obviously you know your own trade better than I do,' he said carefully, 'but you seem to be taking the most pessimistic view of how you're going be treated.'

I felt a spurt of irritation at his complacency. 'You would, too, if one of your old ladies died, and her relatives said you were responsible. Supposing Madeleine decided to accuse you of neglecting Lily? Then it'd be *you* being deconstructed on the inside pages . . . divorce, affairs and all . . . on the basis that your mind wasn't on the job.'

But he wouldn't accept that I'd be 'outed' in that way, and argued patiently that however bad the press was – and 'gutter' was the adjective he used to describe it – UK newspapers always protected victims. If the sexual secrets of politicians and celebrities were exposed, it was because they were fair game. They controlled publicity to advance their careers, and only objected when the control was wrested from them.

'You're not in that category, Connie. On the one occasion when you might have milked publicity to advance your career, you deliberately avoided it. Why should your colleagues destroy you now?'

I appreciated what he was trying to do – chop away at the paranoid struts that supported the logic of my hiding under an assumed name for the rest of my life

– but he was naïve and he spoke in clichés. 'Because the public has a right to know about MacKenzie.' I sighed. 'And I agree with that. The public *does* have a right to know. If MacKenzie starts killing women over here, it'll be my fault.'

'But that's not true,' he protested. 'From what you said this morning, you've done everything you can to bring him to police attention. If he's caught, it'll be down to your efforts.'

'Which is when I get to be in the newspapers,' I said with a twisted smile. 'Life's a bitch. If he goes on trial, I'll have to give evidence.'

'You won't be named, Connie. Rape victims are granted automatic anonymity in this country.'

'I didn't say he raped me,' I said curtly. 'I didn't say anything about what he did.'

Peter let a beat of silence pass. 'You described him as a rapist this morning. You called him a serial rapist and murderer of women.'

I couldn't remember what I'd said now. 'It won't make any difference. It's not just names that identify people. If I were writing it, it would go something like this: "Yesterday, at London's Old Bailey, a 36-year-old newswire journalist sensationally revealed details of her Baghdad kidnap. Far from the lucky-to-be-alive version she gave at the time of her release, it was a three-day ordeal of torture and sadism that persuaded her to change her name and go into hiding. Claiming to be deeply scarred and still in fear of her life, the blonde Zimbabwean named the defendant, Keith MacKenzie, as her attacker. She described how she was held blindfold in a cellar for seventy-two hours. Asked by defence counsel if she'd ever seen her assailant – "' I broke off abruptly.

'Did you?'

'No . . . so it'll all be for nothing because he won't be convicted.'

Peter propped his chin on his hands. 'As a matter of interest, how many other versions of that report have you rehearsed in your head? Have you tried one that doesn't reveal who you are? Or better still . . . paints you in a good light?'

'How about, "In detailing the effect this traumatic experience has had on her life, the *attractive* blonde, 36, explained how she sought refuge in the West Country. She spoke of her gratitude to the local GP, 45. 'Without his tireless support,' she said, 'I wouldn't have had the courage to testify' "?' I made a beckoning gesture with my fingers. 'Give me your best shot. What will you tell them when they shove a microphone in your face?'

'How will they know it's me?'

'If I'm still living here, I'll be asked to give my address. If not, someone will work it out. Probably Madeleine. It doesn't take Einstein to put blonde writer, Zimbabwean accent and West Country GP together.'

'There's not much I can say without breaching

patient confidentiality . . . except to applaud your bravery.'

'Boring. It's been done already. My boss in Baghdad shouted my courage from the rooftops to disguise the fact that I hadn't shown as much as Adelina Bianca. They'll keep pestering you until you give them something new.'

'Like what?'

'Whatever they persuade you to say. How, when, where and why did we meet? "Dr C was called to the terrified woman when she broke down after being surrounded by a pack of dogs. She locked herself in her car and refused to get out. 'She was trying to manage her fear by breathing into a paper bag,' he said."'

'What then?'

'Door-stepping. Phone calls. Pictures. They'll argue that my anonymity's been blown because anyone with a surf engine will have worked out who I am from the internet, so I might as well pose for the cameras rather than be taken unawares by a telephoto lens. And that's before the twenty-four-hour news broadcasters muscle in on the act and force a press conference.'

He let a short silence develop before he said: 'Is that it? Or does it get worse?'

'MacKenzie walks away scot-free and I get labelled a sick fantasist. I've already been accused of faking the abduction.' I leaned forward, hugging myself. 'He didn't leave any marks, so I can't prove it happened

. . . and now it's a bit of a blur. If you can't see, you don't seem to record events so well.' I glanced at him. 'There's no way I can give evidence on that basis. I'll be torn to shreds by any half-way decent barrister.'

Peter took some stapled pages out of a folder on the table in front of him. He'd brought it with him, along with a couple of reference books, when he returned from morning surgery. I was suspicious that he wanted to start a file on me, but he said it was just some research he'd done. 'I'm a bog-standard GP, Connie. I have some experience of post-traumatic stress disorder because of Jess, but I need to consult the literature if I'm going to be of any real help to you.'

Oddly enough, I found that reassuring. I tend to have more confidence in people who admit the limitations of their knowledge, which was ironic in view of Jess's tedious insistence that Peter's answer to everything was chemical intervention. In fact, I felt it was she and Dan who were the more blinkered. Dan remained convinced that a few weeks' sympathetic counselling was the cure to all ills; while Jess clung to the tougher approach of facing your fears and using a paper bag to deal with the after-effects. Perhaps it's human nature to assume that if something works for you, it will work for everyone.

Peter pushed the sheaf of pages towards me. 'Have you ever heard of the Istanbul protocol? It's a set of international guidelines for the investigation and documentation of torture, and it's used to evaluate and prepare evidence for trial. I've printed this copy off the net.'

'I didn't say I'd been tortured.'

'I'd still like you to read it. It might help convince you that you'll be taken seriously. Among other things, it contains a comprehensive list of the psychological consequences of ill-treatment and abuse. I've jotted down some of the commonest responses on the front page – you've shown a fair number of them in the last fifteen minutes – although your panic attacks are the clearest indicators that something catastrophic happened.'

I inched forward to read what he'd written. '*Flashbacks. Nightmares. Insomnia. Personal detachment. Social withdrawal. Agoraphobia. Avoidance of people and places. Profound anxiety. Mistrust. Irritability. Feelings of guilt. Loss of appetite. Inability to recall important aspects of the trauma. Thoughts of death.*'

'Jess shows a fair number of those,' I pointed out, 'and she's not claiming abuse.'

'So? The trauma of losing her family was considerable.'

'Then any trauma can produce similar symptoms. It doesn't prove that my version of events happened. Perhaps I'm more easily frightened than most people, and just being blindfolded for three days led to panic attacks.'

'Why are you so determined that no one's going to believe you?'

'Because I didn't report it at the time.'

'It doesn't matter. There's usually a delay before a victim can talk about what's happened. You may find that document difficult in places – particularly where it refers to physical incapacitation and disintegration of the victim's personality – but the more you inform yourself about how evidence is taken in conjunction with testimony, the more confident you will feel about being believed.' He paused. 'For what it's worth, I'd say you're stronger than most people – certainly mentally stronger – which is why you've managed to keep this bottled up for so long.'

'That's not strength,' I said bleakly. 'I'm scared stiff. I thought, if I didn't talk about it and no one knew where I was, I'd be OK . . . and now I wish I hadn't called Jess. I've been jumping at shadows all morning. It's the old saying, three can keep a secret as long as two of them are dead.'

'What about the inspector in Manchester?'

'He only knows bits.'

'So which secret are we talking about? Your location . . . or what happened to you?'

I didn't answer, and Peter watched me with a concerned frown as I hunched deeper in my chair.

'I'm sure you've worked out a hundred reasons why keeping the details to yourself is better than speaking out,' he went on carefully, 'but not being believed is the least convincing. I'm assuming you've told us only half of what happened . . . less than half perhaps . . . but Jess and I aren't doubting you. Nor are we –' he sought for a word – '*condemning* you. Whatever you did, you were forced to do . . . but being ashamed of that simply reinforces this man's right to control your life.'

Simply? What was simple about shame? How many times had Peter woken up in the middle of the night, drenched in sweat and reliving every minute of humiliation? It was worse not being able to remember it properly, or even have a picture in my mind of what it might look like to a third party. In my imagination, my capitulations were eager and extravagant, my actions degrading and repulsive, and my body something to mock.

'He made a video of me. I keep checking the net to see if he's posted it somewhere. If he's arrested . . . and still has it . . . it'll be shown in court.'

'Not necessarily.'

'It's the only proof of what he did. Of course it'll be shown.'

Peter was too perceptive. 'But you're more concerned that it's proof of what *you* did?' He paused, waiting for a reply. 'Do you mind if I say that you're very optimistic to assume that no one else down here has put blonde Zimbabwean and writer together? At the time, you were headline news, and you haven't changed that much from the photograph that was used. There was a lot made of your parents being forced from their farm, and you've been quite honest about that part of your history.'

I felt goosebumps crawl up my arms. 'Does Madeleine know?'

'It doesn't matter if she does, there's no mileage to be made out of you. A small community like this is bound to be curious about a new arrival, but there's no interest anywhere else. The last mention I could find was a brief reference to you when Adelina Bianca was released.'

He was so naïve. I could picture Madeleine dropping my name all over London. Do you remember Connie Burns? The Reuters correspondent who was taken hostage but never told her story? She's rented my mother's house in Dorset for six months in order to write a book. We're *such* good friends.

'In that respect, you've achieved what you set out to achieve, Connie. Your kidnap wasn't – ' he echoed the word I'd used earlier – 'sensational enough to make it worth anyone's while to track you down, otherwise the phone calls and the doorstepping would have started long ago.' He made a reassuring gesture with his hand. 'You understand the point I'm making? If anyone thought you had a story to tell, you'd have been put under pressure already . . . but you haven't.

MINETTE WALTERS

So it's up to you how much you want to reveal, or whether you want to reveal it at all. No one's going to force you.'

I felt like throwing his psychological pap back in his face. It's my genetic link to my father, this inability to take patronizing comments on the chin. Did Peter have a higher IQ than I? Was he better educated? Wider read? So arrogant about his own abilities that he assumed I was incapable of working it out for myself? Of *course* I knew I had control of my story. What did he think I'd been doing for the last three months, other than make damn sure no one else had access to it?

If I wrestled with anything, it was Peter's all-too-accurate observation that MacKenzie controlled me. And through a video. I could have been as brave as a lion if it were my word against that of an ignorant Glaswegian rapist. I could have said anything. That I'd screamed, argued, refused consent, fought for my life. I could have pretended some dignity. Who was going to believe MacKenzie without pictures?

Me.

'They showed a clip of Adelina's video on the television the other day,' I told Peter then. 'They used a close-up of her face – with the black eyes – to give viewers a taste of what's likely to happen to a Korean woman who's been taken. I know Adelina quite well. She's only about five feet three tall – rather like Jess –

but she looked so . . . indomitable. How did she do that?'

'She didn't,' Peter said bluntly. 'I saw that clip, too, and I saw a frightened woman. You're imposing something from your imagination that wasn't there. Adelina was terrified, and rightly so. She had no idea what was going to happen next, and it shows in her face.' He leaned forward. 'Why would hostage-takers release a video showing a victim looking indomitable, Connie? Pictures are propaganda, and terrorists are only interested in portraying terror.'

'She makes jokes about it now.'

'Because she can. None of her worst fears materialized. In any case, a black eye is a visible badge of honour. It proves you've taken some punishment.' He pressed his forefingers together and pointed them at me. 'Think how much easier it would have been for you if you'd come out with bruises. You might not have wanted to explain them – but they wouldn't have gone unnoticed. The police would have insisted on a photographic record, and that evidence would have survived until you gave an explanation for them.'

I folded my arms across my chest and tucked my hands under my armpits to avoid lashing out at him. Why did he keep stating the obvious? Why keep implying that I was too stupid to think these things for myself? I thought him intolerably smug, but feared that any display of irritability would bring a self-satisfied 'I told you so.' The screams that swooped around my head were all about what I should have done.

'Say it,' Peter encouraged.

'What?'

'Whatever you're thinking.'

'I was thinking how debased language has become. "Collateral damage" for civilian deaths, "shock and awe" for relentless bombing, "coalition of the willing", "surgical strike" – *that's* propaganda. It's all designed to put a spin on the truth. Do you know that every time I wrote "Iraqi resistance fighters" the subs changed it to "insurgents". The words are synonymous but the connotations of "resistance" are laudatory. It makes people think of the French Resistance, and the coalition didn't want that connection made.' I fell silent.

'Go on.'

'Words are meaningless unless you know why they're being used. In the context of war, "collateral damage" ought to mean the accidental killing of your own side, but the US military invented "friendly fire" or "blue on blue" for that.' I held his gaze for a moment. 'MacKenzie's favourite expression was "shock and awe". He defined it as "softening up" and really loved the juxtaposition of the two ideas – terror linked to reverence. He felt it was the natural order of things that the weak should kow-tow to the strong.'

'And your role was to give him the illusion of strength?'

'It wasn't an illusion,' I said. 'It was a reality. I was his devil's feather.'

'What does that mean?'

'Whatever you want it to mean. That I was to blame . . . that I was crushable . . . that I was something of no account.'

Peter let a silence drift before he tried again. 'You were a prisoner. The reality is that you were put in a position of weakness by a man who couldn't control you any other way. I'm not trying to minimize your response to that, but at least recognize that he was acting out a fantasy of dominance.'

'It wasn't a fantasy. He's incredibly intimidating, and knows it. Everyone was afraid of him in Sierra Leone.'

'Except other soldiers. Didn't you say it was a couple of paratroopers who forced him to pay compensation to the prostitute?'

I tucked my hands tighter under my arms. 'Yes . . . well, soldiers are braver than journalists. I expect it helps if you have some rudimentary knowledge of unarmed combat.' I took a deep breath. 'Look, this is all fairly pointless, Peter. Believe it or not, I really do have quite a good grasp of where I am and what I need to do. I appreciate your help, and I'll certainly read this protocol – ' I nodded towards the papers on the table – 'but, just at the moment – ' I pulled up sharp as fear shot a spurt of adrenalin into my bloodstream. 'Oh, *God*!'

In retrospect, Peter's reaction still surprises me. I'd have expected some sort of intervention, if only a verbal one to instruct me to 'calm down'. But he did nothing except fold his hands on the table and stare at them while I dragged a paper bag from my pocket and sucked air in and out of it with my eyes starting out of my head. Eventually, when my breathing had slowed enough for me to lower the bag to my lap, he looked at his watch.

'That's not bad. One minute thirty-five seconds. How long does it normally take?'

My face was burning and I had runnels of sweat dripping down my cheeks. 'What would you care?' I gasped.

'Mm. Well, there's always anti-depressants. If you insist on feeling sorry for yourself, I might even prescribe them.'

'Jess was right about you,' I snarled, fishing in my pocket for some tissues. 'You're about as much use as tits on a bull.'

He smiled. 'How long have you had nosebleeds?' he asked, as I put my head back and pressed the wodge of paper to my nostrils.

'None of your business.'

'Do you want some ice?'

'No.'

'What did he use to stop you breathing? Plastic bags?'

It was exactly the way I would have asked that question. In the same uninterested tone and with the same lack of emphasis. And I fell for it because I wasn't expecting it. 'Usually drowning,' I said.

From:	connie.burns@uknet.com
Sent:	Sat 14/08/04 10.03
To:	alan.collins@manchester-police.co.uk
Subject:	Additional information

Dear Alan,

I've spent all night thinking about this email. There are numerous reasons why I don't want to write it, and only one why I do – because it concerns my parents. Despite the pieces I've written over the years, highlighting the tragedies of women and children in war, I honestly believe I'd have allowed a thousand anonymous women to die before I said anything. It's the old morality tale of the death-ray and the elderly Chinaman. Do you know it?

A rich man shows you a death-ray machine and promises you a million pounds if you push the button. The bad news is an old man in China will die if you do; the good news is no one will know it was you who killed him. The victim will be the only loser. His family are tired of looking after him, and pray regularly for his death, while you have only the rich man's word that the machine can kill anyone – let alone a man you've never met. You have three choices: press the button and spend the rest of your life a million pounds richer, convinced the whole thing was a scam . . .

press the button and spend the rest of your life a million pounds richer, with a murder on your conscience . . . or refuse to press the button and forgo the million pounds. Which do you choose?

I think the moral is that the first choice is impossible because there's no such thing as a free lunch. You will always be plagued by doubt about it's being a scam, and the rich man will always own your soul. The second and third choices are the only honest ones – to accept payment for murder, with all its consequences, or to refuse.

I've been trying to implement the first choice. Take the reward (my life) and convince myself that I have no responsibility for anyone else's death – but I've failed because it's not the choice I made. I opted for number two – took the reward, knowing full well I had a responsibility, but hoping I could live with the consequences. I can't do that either. Not because my conscience is pricking me – it's been pretty much dead since I switched my energies to survival – but because my parents are involved. Perhaps we can all kill from a distance – it's how we fight war now – but it's different when we know the faces of the victims.

Although this information is certainly redundant – I think you've always known the truth – please add the following facts to the ones I've already given you:

1. Keith MacKenzie aka John Harwood aka Kenneth O'Connell was my abductor. He had at least two accomplices – the driver of the car and one of the men who pulled me out of it. I can describe the driver because I saw his face in the rear-view mirror – fairly dark-skinned, no moustache, aged about thirty. The other two men wore ski-masks. I can't tell you what nationality they were, as the only one who spoke was the driver (to confirm in accented English that he was driving me to the airport). However, from the build of one of the masked men, I suspect it was MacKenzie.

2. I remember something being held to my mouth (ether? chloroform?). The next I knew, I was in a crate/cage/kennel, stripped, gagged and blindfolded, with my hands tied behind my back. I have no idea where that was or how I got there. From then on, the only person I had any dealings with was MacKenzie, although I never saw him because my eyes were taped throughout.

3. All the bindings felt soft. I have since seen photographs of other hostages who had lint fastened over their eyes with duct tape, and I believe that's how all mine were done. Despite trying several times to loosen my hands, the doctor who examined me afterwards found only 'minor bruising of the wrists – similar to Chinese burns'.

4. On several occasions, the lint over my eyes became saturated with water and was replaced – presumably to prevent the tape losing adhesion – but I have no recollection of when and how that was done. (Sedation?)

5. Similarly, I have no recollection of being taken to the bombed-out building where Dan Fry found me on Monday morning. Dan described me as 'wobbly and disorientated' but, by the time the doctor examined me three hours later, the effects had worn off.

6. I may have been held on or near a dog-handling establishment. When I saw MacKenzie at the Baghdad academy, he was instructing dog-handlers, and dogs were brought to the cellar regularly during my captivity. Also, the only consistent sound from outside was barking. NB. In Sierra Leone, it was widely known that a Rhodesian ridgeback patrolled MacKenzie's compound.

7. My best guess is that I was held either in the cellar/ basement of wherever MacKenzie/O'Connell was living at the time of my abduction; or the cellar/ basement of an empty building which he 'inhabited' for the duration of my stay. The length of my captivity was approx 68 hours, and I believe I can recall ten distinct occasions when he came to the

cellar. I am having some difficulty isolating specific episodes so that number may be higher. It was not LESS than ten.

8. Allowing for the time he spent with me (I estimate a minimum of 45 minutes for each episode) no more than 6 hours elapsed between visits, assuming they occurred at regular intervals during the 68 hours. While it was not impossible for him to drive away and return within that time-frame, it seems unlikely, as coalition patrols/check-points would have recorded the regular movements of his car. Nor do I think he would have attempted such trips after curfew which would have drawn more attention to him. NB. I heard a vehicle leave and return on only *two* occasions.

9. At no time did I sense anyone else's presence in the building. The barking of the dogs was audible, but there was no 'human' noise – e.g. conversation, radio, television, mobile ring-tone, footsteps, moving furniture, etc. Shortly after the two occasions when I heard a vehicle, I was given something to eat. These were the only times I was fed during my captivity. NB. In Sierra Leone, no one went near MacKenzie's compound because he was notoriously hostile to visitors/workers. His habit was to eat 'out', usually at Paddy's Bar.

10. MacKenzie made a video of my captivity. Assuming the microphone was switched on, his voice will be heard as he issued numerous instructions to me and the dogs. I believe this video was a 'trophy' item for his own private pleasure because it doesn't seem to have appeared anywhere. If so, he may have it on him if/when he's arrested.

11. As the only things returned to me on my release were the clothes I was wearing to travel, MacKenzie certainly knows my parents' address and telephone number, which were stored in my laptop and mobile. If he wrote those details down, they may also be in his possession if/when he's arrested. NB. I can supply a list of the contents of my suitcase/haversack/bag in case he kept anything else.

12. My hotel bedroom was entered regularly in the days before my abduction. I had no proof it was MacKenzie but, after one such intrusion, my laptop was open and my letter to Alastair Surtees, giving details of the Sierra Leone murders, was on the screen.

13. I believe the intention behind entering my hotel bedroom was to scare me into dropping the story and leaving Iraq (possibly to make a hijack easier). It succeeded. I believe the intention behind the

abduction was to stifle any interest I might have in pursuing the story in the UK. To date, this, too, has been largely successful.

14. I cannot visually identify MacKenzie as my abductor because I never saw him. Nor did he identify himself to me by name. However, I recognized his voice and he used certain phrases that recalled a conversation I had with him in Freetown. Viz: 'I'm calling in that good turn you owe me.' 'Do you like me now, Ms Burns?' 'I warned you not to cross me.'

15. There is nothing I can say at trial that won't be contested by the defence. At some stage prior to releasing me, he took me outside and hosed me down on some plastic sheeting to remove every last trace of my confinement/contact with him and the dogs. When Dan Fry found me, the binding had been removed from my wrists, the tape on my eyes and mouth had been changed (with the lint removed) and my clothes laundered. Bar a slight reddening where Dan ripped the duct tape away, I had no visible marks to indicate 68 hours of incarceration.

16. I am as convinced as I can be that my parents' nuisance caller is Keith MacKenzie, and that he knows I was responsible for his photograph being made public. It's too much of a coincidence that he

should 're-emerge' shortly after Dan had the photograph positively ID'd as O'Connell. Which means that, if Surtees is telling the truth about handing MacKenzie his papers at the end of July, then MacKenzie is still in close contact with staff/ students at the academy, or colleagues in BG, or Surtees himself. My guess is it was Surtees and he knows where MacKenzie is and how to contact him.

17. It's possible MacKenzie was phoning from abroad but, in case he's already entered this country, I've persuaded my parents to leave their flat and remove anything showing my current address/whereabouts. I was most concerned about my mother's safety, as MacKenzie would have killed her if he'd broken into the flat while she was there. Unfortunately, my father's office details were also stored in my laptop and mobile, but, since I alerted him to the possible danger, he has cleared his desk/computer of all personal information and is planning to take circuitous routes to their temporary address. Their visit to me has been postponed indefinitely.

18. My father feels he should notify his local police but I've made him promise not to. They will ask for more explanation than he can give. He knows only what I've told him – the rest he's taken on trust – and I'm

not willing to go to London to talk to the police
myself or let Dad divulge my address so that they
can come here. What I've said in this email is all I
can say at the moment, and I don't want to appear
'evasive and unconvincing' by refusing to answer
every question that's put to me.

That's it, Alan. I can't accept that you'll protect my
confidence because you won't be able to – you'll be
duty-bound to pass on all my revelations – therefore,
before I say any more, I will need some cast-iron
guarantees that: a) MacKenzie is in custody and b) my
evidence is necessary to convict him.

Otherwise, I shall have passed my secrets to the wind to
no purpose.

Best wishes,

Connie

PS. I'm assuming you won't be in till Monday, but I'd
appreciate some suggestions re my parents and the local
police when you have a moment. Please don't bother
with advice on counselling because I won't take it, and
please don't waste your time trying to think up tactful
phrases. It isn't necessary. I know you wish me well
without your having to say it.

From:	BandM@freeuk.com
Sent:	Sat 14/08/04 12.33
To:	connie.burns@uknet.com
Subject:	Your stalker

Dear C,

This is the new address for my laptop. It's been a
nuisance setting it up, so I hope it was necessary. I hear
what you say about this man passing himself off as one of
our friends because you had some of their names and
addresses in your laptop, but I'm not so gullible as to
answer unsolicited emails, even if they do purport to come
from Zimbabwe. However . . . as your concern is for your
mother, I've gone along with it.

Now that the dust has settled a bit, I would appreciate a full
explanation. We're staying in a very cramped room in a
mediocre hotel, and it would help to have a time-frame.
Your mother's idea of packing was to include our good
stuff and leave out anything comfortable, so we're dressed
to the nines on a Saturday morning and extremely bad-
tempered. Our only other choice is to stay in pyjamas all
day, but we're liable to kill each other if we don't go out.

We're not happy, C. We've done as you asked because
you used emotional blackmail to achieve it, but we'll

need some very good reasons to continue. Your mother's worried and depressed because she doesn't know why you're afraid of this man, and I feel powerless to do anything for the same reason. I'm inclined to overrule you and take it to the police. You may have me over a barrel, in that I can't give them his name, history or full description, but I *can* give them your address, C, and I may still decide to do that in your own interests.

I'm sorry to be a grouch but you're asking a lot of us. *You* may be used to living out of a suitcase, but we're well past the age of finding it amusing. In case you've forgotten, your mother turns sixty-four at the end of the month, which is another reason why she's cross. Apart from the fact that we won't be coming to stay with you, the light in the hotel bathroom is less forgiving than the one at home(!).

Please don't do what you normally do, and leave this sitting in your inbox for days on end. I will not go away if you ignore me. If I don't receive a reply by tomorrow, with an explanation of why all this is necessary, I shall go to the police. And that's not emotional blackmail, it's a threat.

This is emotional blackmail. If we have to remain in this room much longer, you'll be responsible for your parents' divorce.

All my love, Dad xxx

From:	alan.collins@manchester-police.co.uk
Sent:	Sat 14/08/04 14.19
To:	connie.burns@uknet.com
Subject:	Additional information

Dear Connie,

In fact I'm working a weekend shift, so I received your email this a.m. May I quote something my father taught me when I was nine years old and being bullied at school? *'The secret of happiness is freedom; and the secret of freedom, courage.'* When I pointed out that I didn't have any courage, my father said, 'Of course you do, son. Courage isn't about trying to hit someone who's bigger and stronger – that's foolishness – it's about being scared to death and not showing it.' He was a self-educated coalminer who died of emphysema when I was 15. I'll tell you about him one day. He's never going to make the history books, but he was a good man who spoke a lot of sense.

If Dad was talking to you now, he'd say it was courage that kept you alive, but he'd also tell you that the downside of putting on a brave face is that you have to work through your fears on your own. And the mind has a dangerous habit of distorting facts.

I expect you've worked out numerous reasons why
MacKenzie didn't kill you – all of them discounting your
own contribution. In abusive situations, victims invariably
underestimate themselves and exaggerate the intellect
and power of their abuser. He thought Surtees would put
two and two together? He didn't trust his accomplices?
You'd falsely accused him and he's not a murderer at
all? They're all hogwash, Connie. Any man prepared to
imprison and brutalize a woman is certainly capable of
murder, and there was nothing to stop him following his
well-tested MO of disfiguring (even beheading) you,
leaving Iraq, changing his identity, and letting terrorists
take the blame.

I wish you'd see yourself for what you were – a prisoner
without power – but I fear you're rewriting history to show
yourself in the worst light. I may be wrong, but I'm
guessing you were forced to do certain things you're
ashamed of, and now your imagination is busy
exaggerating your willingness to cooperate. Will you think
I'm belittling your experience if I say these feelings are
common to every woman, man or child who's been
abused, raped or sexually assaulted? It's extremely hard
to retain a sense of self when the intention of abuse is to
reduce the victim to the level of slave.

Since it's obvious MacKenzie failed in that purpose –

you wouldn't have contacted me/produced the photograph if he hadn't – can I suggest that the reason you're still alive is because you won his respect? The way you reacted, however that was, worked in your favour. I'm sure you'll believe it's because you cooperated – all surviving victims do – but you'd be wrong to assume that, Connie. There's no question the two murdered women, whose corpses I saw in Sierra Leone, began by cooperating. Any trained SOCO could read that from their rooms – from the lack of evidence of fettering to the clear indications that intercourse/rape happened on the beds. They set out to appease, and succeeded only in provoking.

So why didn't that happen to you? What did you do right that they did wrong? I can only assume that he saw you as a person rather than an object. Perhaps you hid your fear better than they did. Perhaps he never fully possessed you. Who knows? But I urge you not to jump to the conclusion that it was because you're white and spoke his language. To a man like that, any defenceless woman represents the means to self-gratification, and he may not know himself why he didn't follow through.

I also urge you not to conclude that because you were blindfolded and came away 'unmarked', he never had any intention of killing you. It'll persuade you that you could/should have rejected some of his demands, and that would be a wrong inference from the facts you've given me. If you reread my report on the Sierra Leone murders, you'll see there are several indicators to suggest the murderer had been in the victims' rooms for some time – last sightings of the victims, rearrangement of furniture, evidence that food had been consumed, etc.

I made the suggestion in the report that the killer 'played' with his victims before unleashing his final attack because he enjoyed watching their responses. It would have been a roller-coaster ride of hope and fear, and the fewer marks he left on them, the greater the hope they would have had of survival. I believe this is what he was doing with you, Connie, and the reason you're still alive is because you played his 'game' better than they did.

In passing, one of the reasons I wanted a pathologist sent out to Freetown was because both the women I saw appeared to have petechial haemorrhaging of the eyes (small spots of blood under the surface). It's possible they were caused by the ferocity of the attack, but petechiae are commonly found in cases of suffocation – as, for example, when a plastic bag is used to obstruct the airways – and I did wonder if the killer's 'play' involved this type of torture. It's favoured by totalitarian regimes because it leaves no marks. Mock drownings are also popular . . . but tend to 'saturate' anything over the victim's eyes.

If it's any comfort, there's nothing you can tell me that I haven't seen or heard before. There's a depressing familiarity about the way deficient men bolster their self-esteem, and it invariably involves the attempted 'humiliation' of another human being. In your case, I'm glad to see that the attempt has proved unsuccessful, despite your (hopefully temporary) belief to the contrary.

Finally, I've passed MacKenzie's details and picture to the Met and asked for heightened alert in the region of your parents' flat and your father's office, and I'm happy to do the same with your county police force if you're prepared to tell me where you are. I have upped MacKenzie's description to 'extremely dangerous and possibly armed' and I urge you to consider that before you 'go it alone' any longer. I understand very well that you feel safer with no one knowing your address, but you'll be isolated and vulnerable if MacKenzie does succeed in finding you.

Yours as ever,

Alan

DI Alan Collins, Greater Manchester Police

From:	connie.burns@uknet.com
Sent:	Sun 15/08/04 02.09
To:	BandM@freeuk.com
Subject:	Correspondence with DI Alan Collins
Attachments:	Alan.doc (356 KB)

Dear Dad,

I'm really sorry to be causing all this trouble for you and Mum, and I don't blame you in the least for being a grouch. I've sweated buckets trying to put an explanation into words, but I can't do it. It's 2 a.m. and I'm exhausted so, instead, I'm attaching some pieces I wrote and my correspondence with a Manchester Inspector called Alan Collins. It's fairly self-evident. FYI: The conclusions in Alan's last email (yesterday) are spot on. He's obviously a very good policeman.

Lol, C xxx

PS. I do NOT need sympathy, so please don't offer it. I shall refuse to discuss this again if you go tearful on me. You know I don't mean that unkindly, but the milk's spilt and there's no point crying over it.

Thirteen

IN RETROSPECT, I'M sure my primary reason for keeping quiet was because I knew how difficult it would be to accept support. Perhaps I'm a deeply contrary person but I started to see everything as a control issue – advice or offers of help were euphemisms for 'I know better' – and I struggled with anger in a way I hadn't before. Yet it was never directed where it should have been, at MacKenzie.

I was still obsessed with the fear that he'd come looking for me, but my new objects of suspicion and dislike were Alan, Peter and my father, who in their various ways spent the following week urging me to step up to the plate. The only one who put it so baldly was Dad, but when I accused him of trying to exorcize his own demons through me, he retired hurt from the battle. Which increased my irritation, because I saw it as a ploy to make me feel guilty.

My mother tried to breach the gap by leaving messages of love on the answerphone; Alan sent well-argued emails, appealing to my intellect, which sat in my inbox; and Peter brought me piles of research until I bolted all the doors and refused to answer the bell. By the end of the week I was so stressed out that I was thinking of doing another vanishing act. In a grotesque way, their generosity and affection were more intrusive than MacKenzie's sadism. I'd survived brutality, but I couldn't see how I could survive kindness.

Jess showed up for the first few days and stood around, saying very little, but she stopped coming when I started ignoring the doorbell. I left a message on her phone, saying it was Peter I was trying to avoid, but she didn't reply or come to the house. It was one of the reasons why I thought about leaving. There seemed little point staying if the only person I felt comfortable with had lost interest. Even if the fault was mine.

*

She frightened the life out of me when she walked into my bedroom the following Saturday. It was seven o'clock in the evening and, as far as I knew, every outside door was locked. I hadn't heard the green baize door open or close, nor her footsteps on the stairs, nor even had a suspicion there was anyone else in the house. It sent me scrabbling to the nearest corner. I'd had my back to the door, sorting clothes on the bed, and in the second between sensing a presence, turning and recognizing her, I thought it was MacKenzie.

'Don't go weak on me,' she warned, 'because I'm

not in the mood to play nursemaid. Supposing I'd been this bloke? Were you planning to cower in the corner and let him jump you all over again?'

I pushed myself unsteadily to my feet. 'You gave me a shock.'

'And you think this bastard won't?' Her gaze shifted to the empty wine bottle beside the bed, her eyes narrowing in disapproval. 'In your shoes, I'd have weapons stashed all over the house and a baseball bat to hand twenty-four hours a day. It's not you who should end up on the floor, it's him . . . preferably with his brains smashed out.'

I nodded to the carving knife on the bed. 'I've been carrying that.'

'Then why didn't you use it?'

'I recognized you.'

'No, you didn't,' she answered bluntly. 'You were backed into the corner before you knew who it was . . . and you never even thought about reaching for the knife.' She stepped into the room and picked it up. 'It's a useless weapon, anyway. He'll have it off you as soon as you get close enough to stab him.' She balanced it on her palm. 'It's too light. You won't be able to put enough weight behind it . . . assuming you have the balls to stick it in, which I doubt. You need something longer and heavier that you can swing – ' she stared at me – 'then it won't matter if you're drunk. You'll still have a fifty-fifty chance of hitting him.'

I steadied myself against the wall. 'I'll get a baseball bat on Monday,' I said.

'You'll have to be sober to do that.'

It was a good thing I wasn't as drunk as she thought I was, otherwise I might have reacted more aggressively. I'd never met anyone who was quite so self-righteous. To a teetotaller like her, a tablespoon of wine represented ruin and perdition; to a hard-headed hack like me, it took several bottles to close me down completely. But in one way she was right. I might not have been paralytic, but I certainly wasn't sober. The tranquillizing effects of alcohol were easier to come by than Valium or Prozac. As long as I paid by credit card to an anonymous call centre, it was delivered by the caseload to my door.

It didn't stop me having a go at her. 'You're such a puritan, Jess,' I said tiredly. 'If you had your way, we'd all be walking around with steel rods rammed up our backsides. There's no joy in your world at all.'

'I don't see much in yours either,' she said dismissively.

I shrugged. 'There used to be, and when I'm feeling optimistic there still will be. Can *you* say that? Will you ever unbend enough to accept someone else with all their frailties?' I stared into her strange eyes. 'I can't see it myself.'

It was like water off a duck's back. 'I'm helping you, aren't I?' she said impatiently. 'I helped Lily. What more do you want?'

What more indeed? Approval? Encouragement? Sympathy? The very things I was rejecting from everyone else, but they seemed more desirable from Jess because they weren't on offer. Perhaps there's always a gap between what we want and what we know we can take for granted. 'Nothing,' I told her. 'This is as good as it gets.'

She studied me closely for a moment. 'When did you last eat? You haven't been out of the house all week, and your fridge was empty when I last put some eggs in it.'

For someone who didn't want to play nursemaid, she was giving a good impression of one. I wondered how she knew I hadn't been out. 'Have you been watching me?'

'Just making sure you were still alive,' she said. 'Your car's growing moss on its wheels because it hasn't moved, and you spend so much time checking your doors and windows that anyone can see you . . . particularly at night when you have all the lights blazing. There might be better ways of saying, "I'm here, I'm alone, come and get me," but I can't think of one off the top of my head.'

Belatedly, I asked the obvious question. 'How did you get in if all the doors are locked?'

She fished a key-ring from her pocket and held it up. 'Spares to the scullery. Lily was worried about falling down and breaking her hip so she put them on a hook behind the oil tank in the outhouse.' She shook her head at my expression. 'But, if they hadn't been there, I'd have come in through the downstairs loo. That's the easiest window to open from the outside. You just need one of these – ' she dropped the knife back on the bed – 'to ease up the catch. Any moron can do it.'

I surprised her with a laugh, although her puritan streak blamed the alcohol and not the absurd waste of time of checking locks every two hours. 'There's not much hope then, is there? What do you suggest I do? Use the knife on myself and save MacKenzie the trouble?' I lifted a hand in apology. 'Sorry. That wasn't a dig at you . . . just tasteless gallows' humour.'

'You can start by eating,' she said severely. 'I've brought some food. If nothing else, it'll help you think straight.'

'Who says I want to?' I asked, sinking on to the end of the bed. 'You don't get panic attacks when you're pissed.'

'Too bloody right,' she muttered grimly, pulling me to my feet for the second time in ten days. 'If you carry on like this, you'll be mincemeat for this animal.' She shook me angrily. 'It won't stop you hurting, though. You'll be sober as a judge the minute he shoves your head in a bucket . . . but by then it'll be too late. He won't be playing with you . . . he'll be killing you.'

*

It was an interesting juxtaposition of ideas. I'd mentioned drowning to Peter but it was Alan who'd suggested that MacKenzie 'played' with his victims. All Jess should have known – assuming the Hippocratic oath and police confidentiality stood for anything – was what I'd told her and Peter in the kitchen ten days before. My abductor was British, I'd unearthed his story, it hadn't surfaced because he was under investigation for serial rape and murder, and the reason for the abduction was to warn me off.

Peter drew his own conclusions about what might have happened – 'You don't warn people off by feeding them grapes for three days' – and returned later with a printout of the Istanbul protocol. Jess left the whole subject alone, and talked weasels and crows until I stopped answering the door. I was prepared to accept that Peter might let drowning slip during one of their conversations – in fact I expected it – but there was no way either of them could have known of Alan's theory.

I stopped on the landing and shrugged Jess's hand off my arm. 'OK. What's going on? Have you been talking to Alan Collins?'

She didn't bother to lie. 'Only your mother . . . but I've read Alan Collins's emails. She forwarded them to me this morning . . . along with the ones you wrote to him.'

'She had no right,' I said angrily, 'and you shouldn't have read them. They weren't addressed to you.'

'Well, I have,' she said without heat, 'so there's nothing to be done unless you want to sue me. Your mother didn't do it to hurt you.'

'How did she get hold of you?'

'Rang directory enquiries. You gave her my name, apparently, and told her I had a farm down the road from Barton House. It wasn't that difficult.'

'You never answer your phone,' I said suspiciously, 'and you never return messages.'

'I did this time. She kept phoning till I answered.' Jess held my gaze for a moment. 'I thought it was you at first because she called herself Marianne. The pitch of your voice is pretty similar but she's got a stronger accent.'

'Is she here?'

'No. That's why she sent me the emails. To explain why I'm having to do this, and not her. She's frightened of leading this bastard to your front door.'

'Do what?'

'Tell you what an arse you're being . . . persuade you to stop feeling sorry for yourself.' Her mouth twisted. 'I told her I wasn't much of a talker, but she wouldn't listen. She doesn't give up easily, does she? She was ready to give me your whole bloody life story if I hadn't said I'd be coming anyway – ' Jess broke off abruptly. 'Your mother gave me a list of things to say. She said you'd want to hear them.'

'Let me guess,' I said dryly. 'My father's deeply hurt, my mother can't cope with his mood swings and

needs me to start phoning again, they hate the hotel
. . . What else? Oh, yes, I'm their only child and all
their love and hopes are vested in me.'

Jess felt in her pocket and took out a piece of paper.
'Nothing so corny,' she answered, unfolding it and
running her finger down the page. 'Your dad's gone
back to the flat. Your mother thinks he's trying to prove
something re demons. He refuses to discuss it and won't
say if the police know. Just keeps telling her Japera was
a mistake and he doesn't want a repeat. He's moved
your mother to a different hotel and banned her from
calling him. He's left the laptop with her, and she wants
you to email or phone. She's given me the number of
her new hotel.' She looked up. 'That's it. She said you'd
understand the references to demons and Japera.'

Angrily, I snatched the page from Jess's hand. 'I
knew I shouldn't have told anyone. It was all OK, as
long as no one knew. What the *hell* does he think he's
doing?'

Jess took a step back. 'The way your mother
described him, he'll be setting traps . . . which is what
you should be doing.'

'He doesn't have a chance,' I hissed. 'He'll be sixty-
five in November.'

'At least he's trying.'

If that was her best shot, the conversation wasn't
going to last very long. '*I* tried, Jess. I told Alan
Collins. And *this* – ' I shook the piece of paper – 'is
the result. My father trying to prove he isn't a coward.

He's ashamed because he thinks he gave up the farm too easily . . . so he's salvaging some pride by behaving like a jerk.'

She shrugged. 'It runs in the family then. That's pretty much what you're doing, isn't it? Being ashamed and behaving like a jerk, except there's not much sign of pride.'

'That's not going to make me do what you want,' I snapped.

'Who gives a shit? You're not my responsibility.' She set off down the stairs. 'I'll be taking my phone off the hook, so if you don't want your mother calling the police when she can't get through, you'd better contact her.'

I think she half-expected me to plead with her to stay, because she paused on the bottom step to look up at me, but when I didn't say anything she disappeared through the baize door. I didn't *need* to say anything. I knew she'd come back.

*

I decided to speak to my father first, since my mother would ask me to do it anyway. I'd have preferred to dodge any conversation with him that evening because it would certainly develop into a shouting match, but I felt responsible for him being there. Nevertheless, I was so paranoid about my landline registering as the last call that I dialled 141 first to withhold it, and only remembered that withheld numbers were being blocked when I heard the message telling me so. I tried his mobile but it wasn't responding.

My choice was to redial his landline without 141 or use my mobile, but there were too many hairs bristling on the back of my neck to take the first option. It wasn't that I expected MacKenzie to be in the flat – I didn't – rather that Sod's Law predicted my number would still be registering when he broke in and took a punt on 1471. At least if I used my mobile, there'd be no exchange code and nothing to show I was phoning from Dorset.

My second choice was whether to rebuild Jess's pyramid in the back bedroom, which I'd dismantled when I'd had broadband installed, or climb into the attic. I chose the attic as the least onerous option, and went in search of the hooked pole that released the latch on the trapdoor. I found it behind the door in the nearest bedroom, and when I picked it up I realized what a good weapon it would make. It was a homemade construction of two hefty wooden rods, designed to come apart in the middle for storage. The top half was capped by the hook and the bottom by a two-inch screw.

Jess would have said they weren't heavy enough, but they started me thinking about what else was in the house – the axe in the woodstore – rakes, spades and forks in the toolshed – a hammer in the scullery – empty wine bottles that could be turned into razor-sharp clubs. I can't explain why none of this had occurred to me before, except that my plan had always been to leave through the nearest exit and find a place to hide.

Peter put it down to MacKenzie's manipulation of my 'fight or flight' response. In simple terms, I'd been conditioned to submit rather than rebel, but that doesn't explain why one of my recurring dreams was an intensely physical one where I bludgeoned Mac-Kenzie to death. The desire to kill him was always there.

Perhaps fear has to be taken one step at a time. Perhaps the mind needs to heal before it can switch from one automatic response to another. Perhaps we all need to suffer the contempt of a Jess Derbyshire before we remember that fighting is possible. Who can say? I do know that I had a new sense of purpose as I climbed the ladder to the attic.

The roof space ran the entire length of the house. I found a light switch beside the trapdoor which lit a series of bulbs that hung from the rafters. Half of the filaments had blown but there were enough still working to lift the gloom. A pathway of planks had been laid across the joists to make access easier, but I still had to navigate my way past two chimney-stacks before I found a decent signal. The whole place was filthy and draped with cobwebs, and from the odd skittering near the eaves I guessed I had bats and mice for company.

In the event, it was a wasted exercise. There was no

answer from the flat or from Dad's mobile. Rather than leave messages, I fished Jess's piece of paper from my pocket and called the number of my mother's new hotel, but when I asked to be put through to Marianne Burns's room I was told she'd checked out.

'Are you sure?' I asked in surprise. 'She was definitely there this morning. I was given this number to call.'

'One moment.' There was a pause. 'Yes, I can confirm Mrs Marianne Burns paid her account at three o'clock this afternoon.'

'Did she say where she was going . . . leave a number for me to call?'

'May I ask what your name is, madam?'

'Connie . . . Connie Burns. I'm her daughter.'

'I'll check for you.' Another pause. 'I'm sorry, Ms Burns. There are no messages and no forwarding address. Is there anything else I can help you with?'

'No . . . yes,' I corrected immediately. 'Did anyone come to collect her?'

'I don't know.'

'Can you find out?'

'We're a big hotel, Ms Burns. Guests come and go all the time. We don't keep track of their movements.'

'Then can you check if there was a phone call to her room? And if so, is there any way of finding out where it came from? I don't understand why she left.'

'I'm sorry,' the man said again with pseudo-regret.

'We can't divulge private information about our guests. Would you like me to make a note that you called in case your mother returns?'

I thanked him and rang off, then redialled the flat and my father's mobile. I left messages on both phones, just saying, 'Please call me', and for good measure sent a text to his mobile: '*Where are you? What's happening? Mum has checked out. Am worried. C.*' I hoped he'd remember to call the landline, but as I climbed down the loft ladder, I placed my mobile on the frame of the trapdoor opening. There was enough of a signal for it to ring, although I wasn't optimistic about reaching it before the messaging service kicked in. It was worth a try, however.

Of course I assumed MacKenzie was involved in some way – I was too paranoid not to – although I didn't understand why that should have resulted in my mother leaving her hotel. How could he know where she was unless my father told him? I had enough faith in Dad to believe he'd sacrifice every fingernail before he put my mother in danger. And why would Mac-Kenzie ask the question anyway? Why bother with my mother when it was me he wanted? It didn't make sense.

I kept telling myself the more likely explanation was that Mum had staged her own little mutiny and decided to go back to the flat. But in that case why weren't they answering the phone? I stood irresolutely on the landing, wondering what to do. Wait a couple of hours in case they'd gone out for a meal? Try to contact Alan? Call the local police and ask them to check the flat? Even Alan wouldn't take me seriously. Only a madwoman reports her parents missing after half an hour's attempt to locate them.

Despite being convinced my mobile would ring the minute I was out of earshot, I went downstairs to see if my mother had emailed. She hadn't. There was nothing new since Thursday afternoon. I played the answerphone in case I'd missed a call but the only messages were those I'd already heard. On the off-chance that she'd decided to return to their previous hotel, I phoned there, only to be told Mr and Mrs Burns had left the previous morning. I even tried my father's office, while knowing that no one would answer at eight o'clock on a Saturday night.

It's said that our minds can process fifty thousand thoughts a day. I've no idea if this is true, or how thoughts can be counted, but I do know that trying to pre-guess events within a knowledge vacuum creates intolerable anxiety. It doesn't matter how many times you tell yourself that 'no news' is 'good news', your brain will always assume the worst. And in the end your instinct goes with what you know to be true.

Shit happens.

Extracts from notes, filed as 'CB15–18/05/04'

. . . I think there were three dogs and I guessed they
were Alsatians because that was the breed I saw in
the office with MacKenzie at the Baghdad Academy.
I could feel their breath against the tops of my thighs
when they stood around me, so they were the right size
for Alsatians. On a couple of occasions he encouraged
them to lick me and I heard the camcorder running

(can't deal with that at the moment)

. . . So much depended on MacKenzie being able to
control them. So much depended on him being *willing*
to control them. I don't know if he was clever enough
to understand the psychology of that, or if he'd learnt
the technique from the torturers and murderers he'd
worked with, but I was ready to do anything rather
than face those dogs. It's why I came to love the crate.
Being in a cage offered safety in a way that nothing else
did . . .

Fourteen

IN THE DYING days of apartheid I wrote a piece on South African gold-miners with silicosis and emphysema. Statistics suggested that more blacks contracted the diseases because they worked deeper in the mines and had a higher exposure to silica dust after blasting, but it was surprisingly hard to find long-term black sufferers although I interviewed a number of elderly white men with the complaints.

When I asked a doctor why whites seemed to survive longer with respiratory problems – expecting to be told they had access to better medication – he explained it in terms of exertion. 'The more demands anyone makes on his body, the more oxygen he needs. If a black with emphysema could sit in a chair all day, and be waited on hand and foot by a maid, he'd survive just as long. When a man can't breathe, it kills him just to get up and cook a meal.'

I thought of that doctor as I waded through treacle, trying to gather weapons together. He should have added that failing to cook a meal will also kill you since any engine will seize up without fuel. On my trip

275

to retrieve the axe, I succumbed to the double whammy of uncontrollable anxiety fluttering in my chest and a two-stone weight loss in three months, and folded wearily on to a pile of logs in the wood-shed. It was laughable to think about whirling an axe at MacKenzie when I barely had the energy to carry it back to the house.

Ahead of me, fifty metres across the grass, was the fishpond where Jess had found Lily. I stared at it for several minutes as something to focus on and, because Lily was less alarming to think about than MacKenzie, I began wondering about her again. What had taken her there on a cold winter's night? Peter had said there was no logic to Alzheimer's wandering – she may have been acting out a memory or following an imperative to feed the long-dead fish – and had slipped and fallen. It could have happened anywhere.

For once, Jess agreed with him. 'If Madeleine had been around, I wouldn't have put it past her to give Lily a push – solve all her problems in one fell swoop – but she wasn't.' She shrugged. 'There used to be fish in the pond but I don't remember Lily ever feeding them. Maybe she just wanted to see if they were still there.'

Because I was sitting in the woodstore, it occurred to me that Lily might have come out to collect logs for the fire. Whatever Peter said about logic, it was the obvious thing to do on a cold night, and the pond would have proved an easy distraction because it was so close. I still didn't understand why she hadn't moved herself into the kitchen. The Aga threw out more warmth than any of the fires and required no effort to keep it burning as long as there was oil in the tank. Why hadn't an instinct for survival triumphed over snobbery and dementia?

I even wondered if some forgotten memory had prompted her to look for water in the well beneath me. It was dismantled and long-redundant, covered over by the wooden planks that the logs sat on, and I only knew it was there because Jess had told me. She said it was her grandmother's job to draw the water and heat it for the family's baths before the house was put on a mains supply. Could Lily's dementia have taken her back fifty years and sent her outside to look for bathwater?

Fate has a strange way of propelling us forward. I was very close at that moment to unravelling Lily's riddle, even closer when thoughts of hot baths reminded me that I hadn't checked the oil since I arrived. It seemed a good time to do it, as the door was just behind me. Perhaps, too, I was curious to see if Jess had returned the scullery keys to the hook behind the tank. Propping the axe against the door jamb, I unlatched the door and pulled it open.

The sun was touching the distant horizon but there was still enough light to show the tank inside the outhouse, though not enough to read the gauge. I felt around for a switch, and in the process dislodged a sheaf of flimsy papers that were fixed to a wooden upright by a drawing-pin. They fluttered apart as they fell, but when I finally located a switch and was able to gather them up again, I saw they were receipts of some sort from the oil supplier. I couldn't believe they were important since one was dated 1995, but as the drawing-pin had vanished, I tucked them into my pocket to take back into the house.

Having satisfied myself that the gauge was registering over half full and there were no keys on the hook behind the tank, I killed the bulb again. But either my eyes had trouble readjusting or night had fallen during the few minutes I was inside. I realized suddenly how little I could actually see. With no artificial light anywhere, not even in the house because the sun had still been shining when I left it, the garden was a place of stygian shadow.

With shaking hands I recovered the axe and turned towards the path. As I did so the overhead lamp came on in the kitchen, and I saw Jess walk past the window. My immediate feeling was relief, until I saw the gleam of her dogs' pale coats in the backwash of light and realized they were between me and the house. With nowhere else to go, I stepped back and felt for the outhouse latch again.

Mastiffs can move with extraordinary speed. They covered the ground long before I had the door open. I doubt I'd have been able to use the axe if they'd attacked me – I wouldn't have had time – but I raised it to shoulder height in preparation. Faced with a visible threat, my brain persuaded me to show some courage for the first time in weeks.

'Get *down*!' I growled. 'NOW! Or I'll beat your fucking brains out.'

Perhaps eyes *are* the key. Perhaps they saw real intent in mine because, amazingly, they dropped to their bellies in front of me. Jess claimed afterwards that it's what she'd trained them to do, but their obedience was so immediate that I lowered the axe. I'd have accepted an indefinite stand-off if one of them hadn't started inching towards me.

I thought briefly about calling for Jess, but I didn't want to alarm the dogs with loud noises, and chose instead to put myself on their level by sitting down. I can only explain it by instinct, because logic was telling me I'd have more authority standing up. I remember thinking I'd appear less afraid if I could hold a rock-steady position on the ground with my back against the outhouse door.

Which is how Jess found me, ten minutes later, shivering, cross-legged with three great muzzles in my lap, and two of the male dogs using my shoulders as leaning posts. I don't recall what I said to them, but it was a long and rather aimless conversation, punctuated by a lot of stroking. In the time I sat there, I became an expert on mastiffs. They have a drooling and flatulence problem, they snort and wheeze, and the boys roll over at the drop of a hat to expose their extremely large testicles.

I watched Jess approach with a torch. 'Are you OK?' she asked.

'MacKenzie knows about dogs,' I told her. 'If I can do this, he'll have them eating out of his hand in a minute flat.'

'They've got you penned in, haven't they? Try standing up.'

'They're too heavy.'

'Point made then.' She clicked her fingers and motioned them to stand behind her. 'They'd have barked if you'd tried to move, and I'd have found you a lot quicker. What are you doing out here?'

I nodded to the axe which was lying on the ground where I'd left it. 'Looking for weapons.'

She stooped to pick it up. 'I'd forgotten Lily had that. I've brought you a few things from the farm. There's a couple of baseball bats that belonged to my brother and a lead-weighted walking-stick. I'd lend you a gun but you'd probably shoot yourself by mistake.' She eyed my rigid posture. 'Are you coming back in?'

'What about the dogs?'

Jess shrugged. 'It's up to you. We can leave them out here or take them inside. But I'll tell you this for free, if you'd had Bertie in the house earlier, I'd never have been able to reach your bedroom without him hearing me.'

'I meant, will they do something if I move?'

'You won't know unless you try.'

'Can't you shut them in the hall?'

'No.' She turned away but not before her teeth flashed in a smile. 'If you can sit with their heads in your lap, you won't have a problem walking past them.'

*

The most dramatic therapy for phobias is 'flooding', where a person is immersed in the fear reflex until the fear starts to fade. It's a form of familiarization. The longer you're exposed to what you fear, the less anxious you feel. It doesn't work for everyone, and it wouldn't work for me if I was locked in a cellar again with some Alsatians, but I did relax with the mastiffs. It's hard to be frightened of an animal that wags its tail every time you stroke its head. 'Is this Bertie?'

Jess glanced sideways from where she was cooking a fry-up on the Aga. 'No, that's Brandy. There are two bitches – Brandy and Soda – and three boys – Whisky, Ginger and Bertie. I wanted Lily to call Bertie 'Jack Daniels' but she wouldn't do it. He's the one with his chin on your feet.'

'Do they fight?'

'The bitches did once . . . frightened themselves so much, they've never tried again.'

'What did you do?'

'Let them get on with it. They'd have had a go at me if I'd put myself between them.'

'Were you frightened?'

'Sure. There's nothing worse than a dogfight. It's the noise – sounds as if they're killing each other – but most of it's for show. They're hoping to scare each other off before they do any real damage.' She broke some eggs into the frying pan. 'Did MacKenzie's dogs fight?'

'Yes.'

'What breed were they?'

'I never saw them. Alsatians, I think.'

'How did he get them to fight?' She glanced at me again when I didn't answer. 'You said in your email to Alan Collins that you thought they were police dogs, but police dogs don't fight. It'd cause mayhem if they started attacking each other in the middle of a riot. They're selected for their temperaments, and the aggressive ones get booted out PDQ. They'll bring a man down but they won't kill him.'

'He threw them something . . . said it was food . . . but it was alive because I heard it screaming.'

'Twisted fucker,' she said in disgust. 'It was probably another dog . . . a little one that tried to defend itself. I've seen a Jack Russell take on a Rottweiler when it was backed into a corner.' She put the eggs on to plates with bacon and tomatoes. 'Did he set the dogs on you?'

'No.'

'But you thought he was going to?'

'Yes.'

She handed me a plate. 'I'd have been frightened, too,' was all she said before joining me at the table and lapsing into her usual silence while she ate.

To break it, I told her about my failed attempts to get hold of my parents. 'I don't suppose the phone rang while I was outside?' I asked.

'Nn-nn. I spotted your mobile when I went up the ladder to see if you were in the loft. If you're expecting them to call on that, you'll have a job hearing it downstairs.'

'I know. Did my mother say anything to you about checking out?'

'Not that I remember, but it'll be on that piece of paper if she did.'

I felt in my pocket for Jess's note, and pulled out a handful of receipts at the same time. 'It just seems so odd . . . and very unlike her. She hates missing calls. And why get you involved? She could have left a message here.' I isolated the note but there was nothing more than Jess had already told me.

'She said you weren't listening to them.'

'I always listen. I don't necessarily answer.'

'Maybe that's what your parents are doing. Teaching you a lesson.'

'It's not their style.'

Jess's response was predictably blunt. 'So phone the police. If your gut's telling you something's wrong, then something's wrong. Talk to this Alan bloke. He'll know what to do.'

'He'll say I'm being ridiculous.' I checked my watch. 'It's barely an hour and a half since I made the first call to Dad. The chances are Ma got bored and went back to the flat, and they've gone out for a meal because there's no food in the fridge.'

'Why are you worrying then?'

'Because – ' I broke off. 'I'll have another go on the mobile.' I stood up and pulled the remaining slips from my pocket. 'I knocked these down while I was in the outhouse. I think they're receipts for the oil. Do you know if they're supposed to be in date order?'

Jess turned the pile to read the top slip. 'They're delivery notes. Burton's driver leaves them by the tank to show he's been, and when the bill arrives you check the delivery note matches what you're paying for. Lily never bothered to bring hers in, so these probably go back years.'

I looked over her shoulder, curious to see Lily's signature. 'Why aren't any of them signed?'

'She never bothered. I don't either. The driver just whacks it in and leaves.' She looked amused at my expression. 'Dorset folk are pretty honest. They might go in for a bit of poaching but they don't try to cheat the oil suppliers. There'd be no point if they ended up on a blacklist.'

'What about the supplier short-changing the customer?'

'That's what the gauge is for. If you don't check it, you deserve to be ripped off.'

'On that basis any victim of theft deserves it. We should all live behind security fences with multiple bolts on our doors.'

'Too right. Or kill any bastard who breaks in.' She eyed me for a moment. 'You get what you ask for in life . . . and victims are no different.'

'Is that a dig at me?'

She shrugged. 'Not necessarily . . . it depends how long you plan to let this psycho mess with your mind.'

As I left her sorting the notes by date, I tried to imagine any other circumstance that would have allowed us to become friends. Assuming she'd been willing to talk to me if I'd met her socially – and I couldn't conceive of that happening except in an interview – her uncompromising attitudes would have had me heading for the door very quickly. Yet the better I came to know her, the better I under- stood that her intention was to empower and not to censure.

She did it clumsily, in bald, clipped sentences which often followed a prolonged silence, and the views she expressed could be woundingly blunt, but there was no malice in her. Unlike Madeleine, I thought, as I reached the top of the stairs and looked at the photo- graph at the other end of the landing. One of the messages on the answerphone had come from her two days ago. It was full of exaggerated emphasis and dripping with innuendo and spite, and I hadn't bothered to respond to it.

'Marianne . . . It's Madeleine Harrison-Wright. I've been meaning to ring for *ages*. Peter's taken me to task for being naughty – ' a playful laugh – 'he says I shouldn't have broken Jess's confidence in the way I did. I *do* apologize. It's difficult to know what's for the best sometimes.' A pause. 'A lot of it was Mummy's fault of course . . . it's not fair to play with people's affections . . . pretending to love them one moment and showing how bored you are the next. It always leads to problems in the long run. *Still* . . . I said more than I should. Will you forgive me? Peter's talking about having a supper party for me when I come down next week. Will I see you there?' Her voice faded into another little laugh. 'I think I've been cut off . . . I'm so bad with these machines. Call me back if nothing I've said makes sense. My number's . . .'

As far as I was concerned it made perfect sense. Roughly translated, it meant: 'Peter and I are so intimate that: a) he talks about his patients; b) he has permission to tick me off for naughtiness; c) he repeated what you said to him; and d) he's planning to wine and dine me, but won't be inviting you. While making a token apology for breaking confidences, I am also confirming that what I said when we met is true. Jess has serious problems. PS. I know exactly how to use these machines but I think it's more attractive to laugh and pretend I don't.'

It made me question Peter's role again. Were he and Madeleine genuinely as close as she was suggesting? And if so, was he two-timing Jess? What sort of relationship did he and Jess have? I could well believe Peter was a serial philanderer on the evidence of the two nurses he'd bedded while he was still married to the inept ex-wife, but I found it harder to believe he'd cheat on Jess with her worst enemy.

It may have been that my brain worked better on a full stomach but, looking at Madeleine's photograph, I thought how all the artistry was Jess's. The setting. The lighting. The captured sweetness of Madeleine's face. Move it on five clicks and the sun would have gone behind a cloud, Madeleine's chin would have been buried in her collar, and the photograph would have been rather more sinister – an unrecognizable, black-coated figure against a raging sea.

'*I only did it to make Lily happy . . .*'

But why would a mother need a photograph of her daughter looking pretty? Were the other pictures unflattering? Was it the only one Lily had? I couldn't work it out at all. I didn't understand either why Madeleine had left it in Barton House. If it had been a portrait of me, I'd have kept it for myself. I asked Jess once if Madeleine had the negative, and she said, no, it was in a box somewhere at the farm.

'Is this the only print?'

'Yes.'

'Why doesn't Madeleine have it in her own house?'

'Why do you think?'

'Because you took it?'

She didn't deny it, merely added: 'Lily refused to have any of Nathaniel's stuff on her walls. I expect that had something to do with it as well.'

'Has Nathaniel ever seen this?'

'Sure.'

'What does he think of it?'

'The same as me. There's too much sweetness in her face. It doesn't look anything like Madeleine.'

'Why should that matter? It's very striking . . . very dramatic. It's not important who the woman is.'

Jess looked amused. 'That's why Madeleine hates it.'

Fifteen

'YOU SEEM HAPPIER,' said Jess when I returned to the kitchen. 'Did you get through?'

'I didn't try. There was a text waiting.' I put the mobile on the table in front of her so that she could read it. *All fine. Ma with me. Nothing to worry about. Call soon. Dad.* 'I'm not sure if he wants me to phone them or vice versa, but at least they're OK.'

'That's good. Do you have any more of these slips in your pockets?'

'No. Why?'

'I thought I'd put them back in order for you . . . but there seems to be one missing.' She turned the pile towards me. 'The last note's dated November 2003, but there should be one from 2004. Lily didn't go into the home until January but the oil tank was full when I lit the Aga for you.'

'I expect it's still in the outhouse . . . or I dropped it on the way back.'

She shook her head. 'I've just checked. There's nothing. It's very odd.'

I noticed the dogs had gone, so I guessed she'd

taken them with her and left them outside. 'Presumably the agent has it . . . or Madeleine . . . or Lily's solicitor. Who would the bill have been sent to?'

'I don't know.' She frowned. 'The solicitor, I suppose – the house still belongs to Lily so he's in charge – but how did he get the delivery note without being here when the driver came?'

'How do you know he wasn't?'

'I don't for sure, but wouldn't he have taken all of these at the same time?' She gestured towards the pile. 'He cleared out everything else. I was here when he did it. He wanted all Lily's papers . . . bank statements . . . receipts . . . the works . . . and it had to be done before Madeleine showed up and tried to burn the evidence.'

I resumed my seat. 'What evidence?'

'Anything that showed what a grasping bitch she was. Old cheque-books, mostly.' She fixed me with her unwavering stare. 'The other odd thing is that the valve was turned off at the oil tank. I should have thought about it at the time but I didn't – I just assumed it was something the agent had insisted on. Like when you hire a car, you get a full tank and there's no arguing about it.' She fell silent.

'Why should that be odd? It sounds quite sensible to me.'

'Because it's pointless. The valve's only there in case of accidents, not to regulate the flow of oil to the Aga. There's a governor near the burner for that.'

She paused. 'Did you ever read those instructions the agent gave you? Did they tell you the valve was closed?'

'I can't remember but it's easily checked.' I nodded to the drawer by her right shoulder. 'They're in there . . . brown envelope. I think I skipped the Aga page because you'd already done it.'

She pulled out the stapled pages and flicked through them. 'OK, here it is. "Aga. Location . . . Functions . . . Recipe books . . . Cleaning . . ." Well, one thing's for sure, Madeleine never wrote this. It's far too organized.' She ran her finger down a few lines. '"Instructions for lighting."' She read them in silence. 'These wouldn't help anyone – they're straight out of a recent Aga manual and Lily bought hers second-hand about thirty years ago. It doesn't say anything about having to open the valve first, which it should do if the agent closed it.'

I couldn't see what she was getting at. 'I expect it's a standard page for all rented property with Agas. If I'd complained at the beginning, they'd have sent someone out to fix the problem, and then rewritten the instructions. You said Madeleine didn't know how to light it, so presumably she never told them there was a trick to it.'

'But who closed the valve?' she asked. 'The solicitor didn't – he never went outside – and the agent didn't or he'd have mentioned it in here.'

I shrugged. 'Perhaps he forgot.'

'Or didn't know.' She looked at the pile of slips again. 'I think it was turned off at the end of November. I'll bet you any money you like that's when the last delivery was made. That's why the tank was full. Lily never used any of the oil because the Aga was out.'

'She wouldn't have had any hot water . . . wouldn't have been able to cook.'

'Right.'

I watched her for a moment. 'So what are you saying, that she turned it off herself? Why would she do that?'

'She wouldn't,' said Jess slowly. 'I doubt she even knew there was a valve . . . she was pretty ignorant about how things worked. In any case, the wheel was stiff when I turned it, and she had arthritis in her wrists – ' she lapsed into a thoughtful silence. 'I suppose she might have started worrying about the cost and asked the driver to do it.'

'But she wouldn't have done that *after* he'd filled the tank. Not unless she'd lost the plot completely. She'd be billed anyway. Surely she'd have let it run dry . . . wouldn't have called him at all . . . just waited till the Aga went out of its own accord.'

Jess ran her fingers into her hair and tugged ferociously at her fringe. 'Then it must have been Madeleine. There's no one else who would have done it. My God! She really *is* a bitch. She probably hoped Lily would die of hypothermia.'

I didn't say anything.

'No wonder she went downhill so rapidly – Peter's never understood that, you know.' Her frown gathered ferocity. 'It would explain why she went looking for warmth in other people's houses. She probably wanted a bath. They said she washed herself.'

There was a perverted kind of logic to it although it posed more questions than it answered. 'Why didn't she tell someone?'

'Who?'

'Peter? You?'

'I stopped coming and told her not to phone me any more. She tried once or twice but I wiped the messages without listening to them.'

'Why?'

She shook her head, unwilling to answer that question. 'She wouldn't have told Peter,' she answered instead. 'She was terrified he'd tell Madeleine she couldn't cope. She was convinced she'd end up in an institution somewhere, wearing incontinence pads and tied to a chair. She kept newspaper clippings about old people being abused in homes after their relatives lost interest. It was sad.'

'Is that why you persuaded her to reassign the power of attorney?'

'I didn't. She thought it up all on her own when Madeleine told her to hurry up and die, and do everyone a favour.'

'When was that?'

'August. She didn't show again until Lily was taken into care . . . probably because she hoped neglect would do the job quicker.'

'But you don't think the valve was closed until November,' I pointed out mildly.

'Madeleine didn't have to see Lily to do that. She just had to go to the outhouse.'

'But she wouldn't want the whole world knowing what she was up to. I mean, you're effectively accusing her of wanting to murder her mother.'

'She's quite capable of it.'

I doubted that but I didn't say so. 'Supposing Peter had been here . . . supposing *you* had been here? Supposing someone had seen her drive through the village?'

'It depends when it was. The Horse Artillery could ride through Winterborne Barton at midnight and none of that lot – ' she jerked her head in the direction of the village – 'would hear them. If they're not deaf, they're probably snoring their heads off.' She crossed her forearms on the table and hunched forward. 'It's the one time Madeleine could have got away with doing something like that. I'm the only person who ever came in here. Everyone else went into the drawing-room. Even Peter.'

I'd learnt from experience that it wasn't worth repeating questions, because Jess never answered anything she didn't want to. The only technique that seemed to work was to point out Lily's failings, which usually provoked her into defending the woman. 'It doesn't explain why Lily didn't do something about it herself. Peter says she was functioning adequately enough to go on living here alone, so why didn't she look up a maintenance man in Yellow Pages? A total stranger wasn't going to have her committed.'

Jess stared at the table. 'She was much worse than Peter realized. As long as she looked neat, and could open the door to him, and roll out a few amusing anecdotes without too much repetition, he thought she was coping. She was pretty good at the airs and graces stuff . . . forgot everything else . . . but not that.'

'Was it you who was making her neat?'

Her dark gaze rested on me for a moment. 'I wasn't going to do it for ever but while she was still – ' she made a small gesture of resignation. 'She was frightened about going into a home . . . made me promise to keep her out as long as possible.'

'Difficult.'

'It wasn't all bad. I learnt more about my family after Lily went senile than I ever knew before.' Her eyes lit up suddenly. 'Do you know, she really envied them? I'd listened to this crap for years about how low-grade we were – straight out of the primeval sludge without a brain between us – then suddenly it's not fair that trolls with congenital syphilis inherit the earth.'

I smiled. 'So what did she say to make you angry?'

'Nothing.'

'She must have done. You wouldn't have abandoned her otherwise. You're too kind.'

For a moment, I thought she was going to come
clean, but something changed her mind. Probably my
mention of kindness. 'She was taking up too much
time, that's all. I thought if I left her to cope on her
own for a bit, Peter would realize how bad she was
and organize proper care.' She gave a hollow laugh.
'Fat chance. He relied on me to tell him if she went
downhill . . . then vanished off to Canada for a
month.'

I shrugged. 'You can't blame him for that. First you
help Lily hide her condition, then you want to expose
her. At the very least, you could have told Peter you'd
stopped visiting. He's not a mind-reader. How was he
supposed to know Lily had lost her safety net? How
was *anyone* supposed to know?'

An obstinate expression closed over her face.
'You're in the same position. Do you want me to send
round a note if I decide to stop visiting you? Whose
business is it except yours and mine?'

'I'm not ill. I can ask for help if I need it.'

'So could Lily. She wasn't completely shot.'

'Then why didn't she?'

'She did,' Jess said stubbornly. 'She took herself to
the village . . . and none of them did a damn thing
about it.'

We'd been this route before. It's where every conversation about Lily ended – with Winterbourne Barton's perceived indifference. I sometimes felt it was Jess's excuse. As long as she could accuse them, she didn't have to address her own part in Lily's rapid decline. Although in truth I couldn't see that anyone was really to blame. There was no law that said Jess had to take the brunt of a demanding woman's care indefinitely, and no law that said her doctor and neighbours should have foreseen their sudden falling out.

It was harder to excuse Madeleine because she was Lily's daughter, but was she any better at guessing from London what was going on than the people on the ground? I was willing to accept Jess's view of her character – grasping, vindictive, spiteful, selfish – but not that she had a supernatural intelligence. 'How could Madeleine have known that she could turn the Aga off with impunity? Did she know that you and Lily had a row? Would Lily have told her?'

'We didn't have a row. I just stopped coming.'

'OK. Would she have told her *that*?'

I saw from Jess's sudden frown that she knew what I was driving at. She could hardly accuse Madeleine of attempted murder if Madeleine was as ignorant as everyone else. She didn't dodge the question. 'No,' she said flatly. 'Madeleine would have wanted to know why.'

I went back to the question she wouldn't answer. 'So what did Lily say to you that made you angry?

And was so awful that she couldn't repeat it to her daughter?' I watched her lips thin to a narrow line. 'Come on, Jess. You play slave to a first-class bitch for twelve years . . . drop her like a hot potato when she really needs you . . . then start defending her the minute she's off your hands. Does that make sense to you? Because it doesn't to me.'

When she didn't say anything, I lost patience with her. 'Oh, to hell with it,' I said wearily. 'Who *gives* a shit? I've better things to do.' I stood up and fetched the axe and her grandfather's lead-weighted walking-stick from beside the door. 'Do you want to help me stash these things or are you going home in a huff?'

If her mutinous glare was anything to go by, she was certainly thinking about it, and it made me angry suddenly. She was like a spoilt child who used tantrums to get its own way, and I found I didn't want to play any more. 'There's only one person who might have turned off the valve, and that's *you*, Jess. Who else knew where it was or what impact it would have on Lily? Who – *other than you* – knew you weren't visiting any more?'

With a funny little sigh, she pulled the pile of notes towards her and started tearing them up.

I made a half-hearted move towards her. 'You shouldn't be doing that.'

'Why not? Who do you want to show them to? The police? Peter? Madeleine?' She picked up the pieces and transferred them to the sink. 'Can I borrow your lighter?'

'No.'

She shrugged indifferently before pulling a booklet of matches from her back trouser pocket. 'It's not what you think,' she said, striking a light and setting fire to the flimsy pile.

'It seems very clear to me.'

She put out an arm to hold me back, although I wasn't thinking of stopping her. I couldn't see the point of getting into a fight over evidence that was certainly duplicated in the oil suppliers' records, and I wondered why Jess hadn't thought of that. She might have been reading my mind.

'No one will check unless you mention it,' she said. 'And if you do, I'll say the valve was open and the level about six inches down ... which is where it should have been. No one's going to take your word against mine. You were acting like a zombie after your panic attack, and Peter will back me up on that.'

We stood in silence as the paper reduced to sooty ash in the sink, at which point she turned on the tap and washed it away. By then, of course, I was extremely curious about why she'd done it, as thirty seconds' reflection told me she wouldn't have mentioned the valve in the first place if it hadn't surprised her to find it off. The whole thing was very strange.

'I suppose you're afraid of me now,' she said abruptly.

'You're not much different from MacKenzie, that's for sure. He was very fond of saying no one would believe me . . . but his threats were a lot more persuasive than yours, Jess.'

She looked uncomfortable. 'I'm not threatening you.'

'You said you'd accuse me of being a zombie . . . and ask Peter to back you up. What's that if it's not a threat?' I hefted the walking-stick and axe again, and headed for the corridor. 'Don't forget to lock the mortise when you leave.'

*

I sat at my desk in the back room, listening for her Land-Rover, but it never left the drive. I used the time to email my parents.

> Text received. Phone on the landline when you're ready.
> Don't want to use mine without 141, and it's a bore
> climbing into the attic to activate the mobile! Too many
> rats and bats!!!! Lol, C.

I was acutely attuned to noises I didn't recognize. Had been for days. I heard Jess's dogs on the gravel once or twice as they circled the house. Heard the sound of a car as it drove down the valley. Half an hour later I listened to Jess's steps across the hall. They were more tentative than usual. 'It's not what you think,' she said from the doorway, as if thirty minutes' deliberation had merely trapped her in a continuous loop of denial.

I turned my chair to look at her. 'Then what is it?'

She came into the room and looked past my shoulder to see what I'd typed on my monitor screen.

How did the Derbyshires end up owning more land than the Wrights?

How could they afford it?

I watched Jess's face as she read the questions. 'You said Lily was envious,' I reminded her. 'Did she resent the way your family acquired the farm?'

She pondered for a moment. 'Supposing I say to you . . . it's old history . . . Lily's in a good place . . . and it's better to let sleeping dogs lie or people will be hurt. Will you drop it?'

'No, but I might agree to keep it to myself.'

She sighed. 'It's really none of your business. It's no one's business except mine and Lily's.'

'There must be someone else involved,' I pointed out, 'or you wouldn't have burnt those delivery slips. I can't see you doing it to protect Madeleine. You might do it to protect Peter – ' I lifted an eyebrow in query – 'except Peter wouldn't have turned off the valve. And that leaves only Nathaniel. I'm betting November was when you threatened to shoot off his dick.'

She capitulated suddenly, pulling up another chair and leaning forward to stare at the monitor. 'It's my fault. I should have guessed he'd do something stupid.

I gave him some ammunition to use against Madeleine, and I think he may have decided to take it out on Lily first. He probably thought it was funny.'

'Bloody hilarious,' I said sourly. 'He might have killed her.'

'People don't die because their Agas go out for a few hours. I imagine he wanted to make her angry, and that was the easiest way to do it. He knew where the outhouse was, so all he had to do was leave his car at the gate and sneak across the grass. Lily hated it when things went wrong.' She pulled a face. 'I should have told him how bad she was, and he wouldn't have done it.'

'Madeleine would have told him.'

'I doubt it,' said Jess. 'They hardly speak these days.'

'According to who? Nathaniel?

'He wasn't lying.'

'Oh, give me a break!' I said crossly. 'The man's a complete shit. He swaps sides at the drop of a hat, dangles his todger in front of any woman who's prepared to admire it, then thinks he can take up again where he left off. Do you think he tells Madeleine where he's going when he comes down here to see you? Of course he doesn't. Cheats never do.'

Jess rubbed her head despairingly. 'You're worse than Peter. I'm not a complete idiot, you know. If you remember, it was *me* who told *you* Nathaniel was a shit. I don't like him. I never have done. I just . . . *loved* him for a while.'

'Then why protect him?'

Jess was full of sighs that evening. 'I'm not,' she said. 'I'm just trying to stop this whole damn mess getting any worse. I don't see that my life is anyone else's property. Haven't you ever wanted to bury a secret so deep that no one will ever find out about it?'

She knew I had.

Sixteen

ONE OF THE dogs gave a sudden high-pitched bark, and we looked at each other with startled expressions. When it wasn't repeated, Jess relaxed. 'They're just playing,' she said. 'If there was anyone out there, they'd be barking in unison.'

I didn't share her confidence. The hairs on the back of my neck were as stiff as brush bristles. 'Is the back door still locked?'

'Yes.'

I looked towards the sash window but the darkness outside was total. If the moon had risen, it was obscured by clouds, and I remembered how Jess had been lit up like an actor on a stage when she was in the kitchen. Now the pair of us were visible to anyone. 'This isn't the best room to be in,' I said nervously. 'It's the only one that doesn't have two exits.'

'If you're worried, call the police,' Jess said reasonably, 'but they won't get here for twenty minutes . . . and I wouldn't advise crying wolf unnecessarily. It's a long way to come for nothing. The dogs will protect us.'

I bent down to retrieve the walking-stick and axe that were lying on the floor. 'Just in case,' I said, handing her the stick. 'I'll keep the axe.'

'I'd prefer it the other way round,' she said with a smile. 'I don't fancy being in a confined space with you and that thing. You'll drop it on your head the first time you try and lift it . . . or you'll drop it on mine. If you have any muscles in your arms I haven't noticed them. Here.' She made the switch and placed the axe on the chair beside her. 'Hold the stick by the unweighted end and swing it at his legs. If you're lucky, you'll break his kneecaps. If you're unlucky, you'll break mine.'

I must have looked extremely apprehensive, because she drew my attention back to the computer screen. 'You wanted to know why we ended up with more land than the Wrights. Which version do you want? My grandmother's or Lily's?'

It was done to distract me, because she never volunteered information lightly. I made an effort to respond, although my ears remained attuned for sounds I didn't recognize. 'Are they very different?'

'As chalk and cheese. According to my grandmother, my great-grandfather bought the land when Lily's father sold off the valley to pay death duties. Everything on this side of the road went to a man called Haversham, and everything on our side to us. Joseph Derbyshire took a loan to do it, and increased our holding from fifty acres to one and a half thousand.'

'And Lily's version?'

She hesitated. 'Her father made Joseph a gift of the land in return for – ' she cast around for a suitable phrase – 'services rendered.'

I looked at her in surprise. 'That's some gift. What was land worth in the fifties?'

'I don't know. The deeds of title are with the house deeds, but there's no valuation and nothing to show that Joseph ever took out a loan to pay for them. If he did, the debt was cleared before my father inherited the property.' She fell silent.

'What kind of services?'

Jess pulled a face. 'Lily called it a disclaimer. She said Joseph signed a letter, promising silence . . . but there's no copy of anything like that with the deeds.'

I was even more surprised. 'It sounds like black-mail.'

'I know.'

'Is that the ammunition you gave Nathaniel?'

She shook her head. 'It's the last thing I'd want Madeleine to know. She'd take me to court if she found out.'

I had no idea where UK law stood on property acquired through coercion fifty years before, but I couldn't believe Madeleine would have a case. 'I'm sure there's nothing to worry about,' I told her. 'The rule of thumb says possession is nine-tenths of the law . . . and if you demonstrate that at least two gener-ations of Derbyshires have farmed it in good faith . . .'

I petered out in face of her glum expression. 'Did your father know?'

'He must have done. The first thing Gran asked me after the funerals was whether Dad had told me the history of the farm.' She rubbed her knuckles into her eyes. 'When I said no, she gave me the loan story . . . and I never questioned it until Lily became confused and started confiding the family secrets.'

'Because she thought you were your grandmother?'

'In spades. Sometimes she'd be rerunning conversations they had after the folks died . . . other times she'd jump back half a century to when Gran was her maid.' She made a rolling gesture with her hand as if to denote a cycle. 'It took me ages to work out that a thank-you referred to the nineteen-nineties and an order meant she was back in the fifties. She kept telling me how kind Frank had been to her . . . and what a sweet wife he'd found in Jenny. How they'd never taken advantage . . . in spite of her beastliness at the beginning. Her biggest regret was that she'd never acknowledged Dad while she had the chance.' She lapsed into another silence.

'In what way?' I prompted.

'As her brother.' This time her sigh was immense. 'If Lily was telling the truth, then my father's father was *her* father, William Wright . . . not Gran's husband, Jack Derbyshire, who died shortly after the war. Which makes Lily my aunt . . . Madeleine my first cousin . . . and me a Wright.' Her stare became very bleak suddenly. 'The Derbyshires don't exist any more except as a name, and I really *hated* Lily for telling me that.'

I was at a loss what to say because I couldn't tell which she thought was worse – to be a Wright or not to be a Derbyshire. 'You don't have to believe it. If it's the word of a confused woman against what your grandmother said twelve years ago, then I'd put my faith in your grandmother. Why would she lie? Wasn't that the one time to tell you you weren't alone – that you still had family?'

'I think Lily asked her not to. She said a couple of times, "Don't tell the girl, *I'll* do it, she's too depressed at the moment."'

'But Lily never did . . . or not while she was still thinking straight.'

'No.'

'Then either there was nothing to tell,' I pointed out, 'or she never intended to do it.'

'I think she changed her mind after Gran died. That's when I did *this*.' Self-consciously, she turned her left wrist towards me. 'I came up here to tell her Gran was dead and she kept saying the wrong things . . . like, it was a good way to go . . . Gran had had a good innings . . . it wasn't the end of the world. And I started shouting at her, which brought on a panic attack.' She shook her head. 'I was so mad with Lily . . . I was so mad with my *family* . . . and I thought

... what's the point? It *is* the end of the fucking world.'

'Were you serious?'

'About killing myself? Not really. I remember thinking how much pain I was in because everyone had died . . . and hoping that other people would suffer a bit . . . but the act itself – ' she shrugged – 'it was more of a scream than anything.'

'Have you ever tried again?'

'No. Once bitten, twice shy. I hated the fuss more than anything.'

I identified with that sentiment more than she knew. 'What was Lily's reaction?'

'Called Peter to try and keep the whole thing under wraps. She wanted him to stitch the wounds himself, but he wouldn't do it – said he'd lose his licence if he didn't have me properly assessed – so I ended up in hospital with psychiatrists and bereavement counsellors.' She rubbed her eyes again. 'It was awful. The only person who remained half-way sensible was Lily. She got me discharged by promising that she'd take responsibility for me, then never spoke about it again.'

'Did you stay with her?'

'No.'

'Then how could she take responsibility for you?'

'She didn't try, just asked for my word that I wouldn't do anything stupid if she left me alone at the farm, then gave me a mastiff puppy.' Her eyes sparkled at the memory. 'Much better medicine than anything the doctors had to offer.'

'But why should any of that make her change her mind, Jess? It seems so odd. The natural thing would have been to open her arms and say, you're not alone, I'm your aunt.'

'Except she wasn't a demonstrative woman, and then the whole thing with Nathaniel happened.' She shrugged. 'I suppose she felt there was never a good time to do it.'

Personally, I doubted if Lily had ever planned to acknowledge Jess as a relative, although she certainly seemed to have had a soft spot for her. Perhaps she discovered she had more in common with her niece than her daughter, preferring Jess's quiet, introverted nature to Madeleine's more extrovert one. Rightly or wrongly, I'd formed an impression of Lily as a self-contained woman with limited friendships, whose only real loves were her garden and her dogs, and in that she was no different from Jess. She may well have been able to put on a 'show' for visitors, but I wondered if it was just that – a show – and in her head she was mentally counting the seconds to their departure.

'So what was the ammunition you gave Nathaniel if it wasn't to do with your family?' I asked curiously.

'I told him Lily had given enduring power of attorney to her solicitor.'

'I thought you said it was ammunition *against* Madeleine. Wouldn't that have helped her . . . given her a chance to come down here and persuade Lily to overturn it?'

Jess pulled her mouth into a wry twist. 'I half-hoped she would, as a matter of fact. Money was about the only thing that might have persuaded her to pull out her finger for the first time in her life . . . but I didn't think Nathaniel would tell her. I was only trying to give him a head start before the shit hit the fan. Madeleine kept up a pretence of harmony as long as she thought this place was within her grasp . . . but she's probably throwing saucepans at him by now.'

'I don't understand. A head start on what?'

'Divorce . . . ownership of their flat . . . custody of the kid. If he'd moved quickly enough, he might have been able to persuade Madeleine to sign everything over – including her son – *before* she found out she'd been bypassed. She'd already agreed in principle as long as Nathaniel made no claims on Barton House or Lily's money.' She smiled at my expression of disgust for the child. 'She uses Hugo as a bargaining chip because she knows Nathaniel won't leave without him. I wasn't joking about the saucepans, you know.'

'But – ' I couldn't get my head round it. 'Are you saying he wants a divorce and she doesn't?'

'Not exactly. She'll divorce him like a shot when she gets her hands on this place, but not before. Otherwise they'll have to sell the flat and split the proceeds, and she won't do that.'

'Why not?'

'Because she'll end up in somewhere like Neasden with her half. At the moment they're in Pimlico. She'd rather live with people she hates than move down the social ladder. It's not as if she's got Lily's allowance any more. At least Nathaniel's salary – ' Jess came to an abrupt halt as five throaty barks split the silence outside. 'OK,' she said calmly, seizing the axe in both hands. 'We have a visitor. What do you want to do? Find out who it is, or sit tight and phone the police?'

I stared at her in horror. Was there a choice?

'It's up to you,' she said, her eyes glittering danger-ously as the dogs kept up their continuous barking. 'Do you want to beat the shit out of the fucker . . . or let him go on thinking women are easy meat?'

I wanted to say we could do both – call the police *and* beat the shit out of the fucker. I wanted to say it might not be MacKenzie. I wanted to say I was completely terrified. But she was half-way across the room while I was still weighing options, and I could hardly leave her to face whoever was out there alone. So I picked up the walking-stick and went along with her. What else could I have done?

*

It's easy to be wise after the event, but that's to ignore the froth of adrenaline that spurs you on at the time. I had so much confidence in Jess and her mastiffs that I didn't think we were behaving in a particularly reckless fashion. Despite everything she'd told me – about her panic attacks and the wrist-slitting episode – and my experience of her obvious alarm on the day I phoned her from the kitchen, I never thought of her as someone who was easily frightened. That was *my* role. It was Connie Burns who cowered in corners, not Jess Derbyshire.

The idiocy was, there was nothing to be afraid of. It was Peter surrounded by mastiffs, not MacKenzie, and predictably Jess gave him hell for scaring us. She called off the dogs and lambasted him for not phoning first to say he was coming. 'I could have brought this down on your head,' she said furiously, brandishing the axe in front of him.

He looked equally furious in the light spilling out from the open back door and the kitchen window. 'I would have done if I'd realized you were planning to set those blasted animals on me,' he said. 'What's got into them? They've never barked at me before. It's bloody terrifying.'

'It's supposed to be,' she retorted scathingly, 'and you've never come sneaking up on them before. What do you want, anyway? It's nearly eleven o'clock.'

He took several breaths to calm himself. 'I was on my way home from a medical do in Weymouth, had no luck at the farm, saw Connie's lights were still on and thought you were probably here.'

'You'd have frightened the wits out of her if I hadn't been,' Jess snapped.

'Your Land-Rover's in the driveway. Where else

would you be?' He turned to me. 'I'm sorry about this, Connie. Would you rather I left?'

I shook my head.

He relaxed enough to smile. 'To be honest, I could do with a double whisky after being savaged by that pack of brutes.'

I put a hand on Jess's arm to forestall another tirade. 'Let's go back inside. I don't have any whisky, I'm afraid, but I do have beer and wine. Have you had anything to eat?'

If I'd stopped to think about it, I'd have remembered how easy it was to be lulled into a sense of false security. Fear has such strange effects on the human body. It keeps you at a pitch of concentration while danger's in front of you, then sends you into carefree mode afterwards. I think I was the first to laugh because Jess looked so disapproving when I offered her a glass of wine, but within a few minutes even she'd lightened up enough to smile. Hysteria was very close to the surface in all of us.

Tears came into Peter's eyes when I tried to explain what the plan had been. 'So let me get this straight. You were going to break my kneecaps while Jess sank an axe in my head? Or was it the other way round? I'm confused. Where do my goolies come into it?'

I snorted wine up my nose. 'They get chopped off along with your dick.'

Laughter ripped out of him. 'What with? The *axe*?'

He turned a twinkling gaze on Jess. 'What do you think I've got between my legs? An oak tree?'

The spark between them was unmistakable. It fizzed like an electric charge. Jess came as close to giggling as I'd ever seen her. 'More like a Christmas tree,' she retorted. 'The balls are for decoration only.'

Peter grinned at her. 'You can't chop men's dicks off, Jess. It's not the done thing at all.'

I tittered into my drink, happily playing gooseberry. I couldn't tell how successful Peter's courtship had been – they might never have got beyond the teasing stage, or they might have been rogering each other stupid every night – but they were comfortable to be around because I didn't feel excluded. It reminded me of the relationship I'd had with Dan – easy, affection-ate and all-embracing – and I wondered if he and I would ever be able to rekindle that closeness, or if I'd killed it through lack of trust.

'Penny for them, Connie,' said Peter.

I looked up, conscious suddenly that the banter had stopped. 'I was thinking about a friend of mine. You remind me of him . . . same kind of humour.' I should have stopped there, but I didn't. For some reason, I felt I had to give Jess a push in the right direction. 'You're mad, Jess. If Peter makes you laugh, you should nail him to your floorboards immediately.'

There was a brief silence.

'So now we're into hammers,' said Peter lightly.

'Is there any abuse you're not prepared to inflict on me?'

Jess pushed her chair back. 'I need to check on the dogs,' she said gruffly. 'I'll go out the front door. There's some food for them in the Land-Rover.'

I pulled a wry face at Peter as she disappeared at speed down the corridor. 'Sorry. I've obviously put my foot in it big time. What did I say that was so awful?'

'Don't worry about it. Relationships terrify her. As far as she's concerned, they're all doomed to death or failure.' He refilled his glass. 'It's not surprising if you consider her history. Even Lily's effectively dead to her now.'

'I should have been more sensitive.'

'It wouldn't have made any difference. She sees herself as a jinx. Anyone who grows too fond of her dies . . . simple as that.'

'Nathaniel didn't.'

Peter flicked me a mocking glance. 'But he wasn't fond of her. If he *had* been he wouldn't have left her for Madeleine.'

I held his gaze. 'Presumably that's Jess speaking, and not you?'

He nodded. 'Nathaniel would have her back in the blink of an eye if she showed the remotest interest – he's been down here to promote his cause more times than you've had hot dinners – but either she can't see it or she's genuinely uninterested.'

'She's comfortable with indifference,' I murmured. 'She's also the most determined walker-away that I've ever met. It makes sense if she has a fear of relationships. I thought she was trying to control me, but maybe she's afraid of being sucked in. Is that why she does nothing to correct her image? Because it's safer being disliked than having to give anything of herself?'

Peter looked amused. 'Possibly, but it's also her character. She's hard work . . . always has been. Lily was the same. You have to chip away at the armour plating if you want to reach the person underneath, and not many people are prepared to do that.'

I wondered if he knew about Lily's claim to be her aunt. 'It must be a gene then,' I said.

His amusement turned to surprise, but he didn't try to feign ignorance. 'My God! You're either a damn good journalist or you've convinced her you won't repeat it. Is there anything she *hasn't* told you?'

'A great deal, I should think, but if you give me a list of what there is to know, I'll tell you if I know it.'

He laughed. 'No chance. Hippocratic oath, remember.'

I thought I'd challenge him on that, but I didn't want Jess to hear me do it. I cocked an ear for her footsteps returning. There was only silence. 'Except you seem to use that oath at your own convenience,' I said. 'There's a message on my answerphone from Madeleine telling me you took her to task for talking

317

out of turn about Jess's wrist-cutting episode. You can listen to it, if you like. It's still there.'

He shook his head. 'No thanks. I get enough of them on my own damn machine.' He toyed with his glass. 'She's telling the truth. I did repeat what you told me. I'm sorry if that upsets you but I wanted her to know how angry I was.'

'I'm not upset,' I told him. 'I'm *curious*. The implication in the message is that it was you who told Madeleine about Jess . . . and I remember how uncomfortable you were when I first mentioned it in your kitchen. You tried to convince me it was Lily who'd spoken out of turn, but I don't think that's true, is it?'

'No.' He took a mouthful of wine. 'It was me. I thought if Madeleine knew how desperate Jess felt about the loss of her whole family, she'd give the poor kid a breathing space and back off the affair with Nathaniel.' He paused. 'I should have known better.'

I didn't answer. Instead, I listened for footsteps. At the back of my mind I must have been wondering why there was no sound from outside, because I recall being incredibly conscious of an oppressive silence. At the very least, we should have heard the crunch of gravel and the Land-Rover door opening.

'The first thing she did was tell Nathaniel,' Peter went on. 'He was in London when it happened, so Madeleine had free rein with her interpretation of events . . . which was a souped-up version of what she told you, with Jess as a paranoid schizophrenic. It scared Nathaniel off completely.'

I was more interested in the continuing silence. 'Shouldn't we have heard something by now?' I asked, turning towards the window. 'What do you think Jess is doing?'

'Looking for the dogs, I expect.'

'Then why isn't she calling for them? You don't suppose – ' I broke off, unwilling to put the thought into words.

Perhaps Peter, too, was uneasy. 'I'll go and check,' he said, standing up, 'but for Christ's sake stop looking so bloody worried. You'd have to walk on water to get past those animals of hers.' He smiled. 'Trust me. I've still got the bruises.'

Seventeen

HOW LONG DO you wait in such circumstances? In
my case, a very long time. I told myself Peter and Jess
were having a heart-to-heart, and the best thing I
could do was leave them to it, but I remained glued
to the window, watching Jess's dogs patrol the garden.
At one point a couple of them spotted me through
the glass and ambled over, tails wagging eagerly, in
the hope of food. Could someone have got past them?
Logic said no, but instinct had every hair on my body
standing to attention. If MacKenzie knew about anything, he knew about dogs.

I remember trying to light a cigarette, but my hands
were trembling so much that I couldn't bring the
flame anywhere near the tip. Knowing how easily
panicked I was, would Peter really abandon me for
Jess without calling out that everything was fine? And
why couldn't I hear them? His wooing technique was
based on gentle teasing, and he was incapable of
speaking to Jess for more than a few minutes without
laughing.

In the end I decided to call the police. The chances

were they'd arrive to find Jess and Peter in flagrante delicto on the sofa but I couldn't have cared less. I was happy to pay any fine they liked for wasting official time, as long as I didn't have to walk down that corridor on my own.

*

Woody Allen once said, 'My only regret in life is that I'm not someone else.' It's funny if you don't mean it, and desperate if you do. I'd rather have been anyone but Connie Burns when I tried for a dialling tone on the kitchen phone and discovered it was dead. I knew immediately what it meant. The line had been cut some time after I emailed my parents. In the vain hope of a miracle, I tugged my mobile from my pocket and held it above my head, but unsurprisingly the signal icon refused to appear.

Panic came back in waves, and my first instinct was to do exactly what I'd done before, lock myself in the kitchen, turn off the lights and crouch out of sight of the window. I couldn't face MacKenzie on my own. The fight had been knocked out of me when he'd rammed himself into my mouth and told me to smile for the camera. I couldn't go through that again. His smell and taste still had me bursting out of nightmares every night. What did it matter if he killed other people, as long as he didn't kill me?

I can't pretend it was courage, or a sudden flush of heroism, that took me outside. Rather, the memory of my email to Alan Collins re elderly Chinamen, death-rays, and the difficulties of coping with the guilt. Any problems I had now would be magnified tenfold if I had to live with Jess's and Peter's blood on my hands. My plan was to run as fast as possible for the nearest hillside and dial 999. But when I opened the back door, I was met by the dogs, and I had a strong sense that taking to my heels would be the wrong thing to do. Either they'd bark and alert MacKenzie, or they'd bowl me over.

Instead, I walked slowly towards the outhouse in the hope that they'd lose interest and let me cut across the grass to the main road. They didn't. Each step I took was mirrored by five rippling shadows. For big animals they were extraordinarily quiet. The only sound any of them made was the brush of paws over grass. I couldn't even hear their breathing, but that may have been because mine was noisy enough for all of us.

I stopped after about twenty metres, seriously doubting that MacKenzie was in the house. How could he have got past these dogs unless he'd broken in before Jess brought them? In which case, why had he waited? And why only cut the telephone line after I'd emailed my parents? I'd been alone all day, and for a good hour between Jess's first and second visits. He could have done what he liked and left. It didn't make sense to involve other people.

From there, it was a small jump to the absolute conviction that I was doing what he wanted – putting myself at his mercy by leaving the house. It's hard to think logically when you're frightened. I turned rather wildly to head back towards the kitchen and found myself looking at MacKenzie.

He was sitting at my desk with his hands linked behind his head, staring at my computer screen. He laughed suddenly and swivelled the chair to talk to someone behind him. With a dreadful sense of inevitability I caught a glimpse of Peter's face before MacKenzie completed the turn and blocked Peter from sight again.

*

The same policeman, who'd asked what Jess and I had talked about during our five hours alone the previous week, suggested I might have acted differently if MacKenzie had shown her the same respect that he showed Peter. 'I'm assuming it was this man's mistreatment of Ms Derbyshire that persuaded you to confront him? Was it seeing her in trouble that took you back into the house?'

I shook my head. 'Jess wasn't visible from outside. The first time I saw her was when I reached the hall.'

'But you guessed she was in distress?'

'I suppose so. I saw that Peter was frightened – which almost certainly meant Jess was, too.' I couldn't see the point of his questions. 'Wouldn't you be scared if someone broke into your house?' I paused. 'I knew he'd kill her . . . he liked hurting women.'

'So why weren't *you* scared, Ms Burns?'

'I was. I was terrified.'

'Then why didn't you continue with your original plan – ' he glanced at his notes – 'to run for the nearest high point and use your mobile? Wouldn't that have been more sensible than going back inside?'

'Of course it would, but . . .' I shook my head. 'I don't understand. What do you want me to say? That I was stupid to do it? I agree with you. I was the fool that rushed in. I acted first, thought later.'

'You thought long enough to take an axe with you,' he pointed out mildly.

'So? I was hardly going to tackle MacKenzie empty-handed.'

*

I crept down the corridor on bare feet and eased the baize door open a crack before sliding through and letting it close silently behind me. MacKenzie had turned up the volume on my computer and I could hear my own voice coming through the speakers. I knew then what he was looking at. There was no mistaking my begging tone even if the only words I could make out were a repetitive 'please don't . . . please don't . . . please don't . . .'

The sound died suddenly. 'Is that you, Connie?' he

said in his familiar Glaswegian accent. 'I've been expecting you, feather. Will you show yourself to me?'

How did he know I was there? I hadn't made a sound. I didn't make a sound.

'You know what'll happen if you don't,' he warned with a grunt of amusement. 'I'll have to make do with your friend. She's an ugly little bitch but her mouth seems to work.'

My flesh crawled in response to his voice, and it took considerable will-power to move into the open doorway. I hated the way he spoke. It was mangled vowels and glottal stops and exploded any myth that 'Glesca patter' was attractive. No printed words can convey the ugliness of his accent or the effect it had on me. I associated it with his smell and his taste, and nausea flooded my mouth immediately.

He was still sitting at my desk, and Peter was where I'd seen him from outside, in the chair Jess had perched on earlier. He was fully clothed and his eyes were uncovered, but there was duct tape across his mouth, and his hands and feet were bound. Mackenzie had half-turned the chair towards the desk so that Peter could see the images that were flickering on the computer screen, and beyond them Jess, who was standing in the far corner.

I hardly looked at Peter because I was focusing all my attention on MacKenzie, but I saw the panic in his eyes before I picked out Jess at the edge of my vision. She was naked, blindfolded, gagged and bound, and balanced precariously on a footstool. I felt a lurch of panic for her because I knew how frightening that was. Unable to see, and without being able to move your hands or feet, your only point of reference is the wall behind you. If you lose contact with it, you fall. The strain of concentration is unbearable.

I've no idea if MacKenzie's intention was to frighten me into complying – or if the degradation of women was irresistible for him – but Jess's frailty shocked me. Without its normal covering of a man's shirt and jeans, her body looked too small and child-like to take the kind of punishment that MacKenzie liked to inflict. I was aware of an object on the carpet in front of her. I couldn't see it properly because I didn't want to lose sight of MacKenzie for a second, but the serrated outline reminded me of one of my father's homemade stingers.

They were short planks with nails hammered through them, and he'd used them anywhere on the farm where he found rustler or poacher tracks. His favourite trick was to bury the wooden base in the dry earth and leave the nails poking half an inch above the surface. Occasionally he caught elderly vehicles which were abandoned when their tyres burst, but the more usual result was bloody footprints in the dirt. No one died from having his feet pierced but it was an effective deterrent against stealing from my father.

Where had it come from? Had Dad made it?

I ran my tongue round the inside of my mouth. 'How did you find me?'

'The world's smaller than you think.' He took note of the axe that I was holding across my chest. 'Are you planning to use that, feather?'

Dad always used two-inch nails . . . They'd kill Jess if she fell on them . . . 'Don't call me that.'

MacKenzie smiled. 'Answer the question, *feather*. Are you planning to use that?'

'Yes.'

His smiled widened. 'And when I take it off you and use it on Gollum over here – ' he tilted his head towards Jess – 'what will the plan be then?'

'To kill you.'

I think my expression must have shown that I meant it, because he was in no hurry to move. 'I persuaded your father to tell me where you were. He didn't want to, but I gave him a choice . . . you or your mother. He chose your mother.' There was a glint of humour in his pale eyes. 'How does that make you feel?' He pronounced 'father' in almost the same way as he pronounced 'feather' – '*fay-ther*' – a rasping, grating sound.

My fists tightened round the axe. 'Flattered,' I said from a dry mouth. 'My father has faith in me. He knows I can survive you.'

'Only if I let you.'

'Where is he? What have you done to him?'

'Taught him the facts of life. It was sad. It's always sad when old men fight.'

'You wouldn't have taken him on if his hands had been free. You won't even take on a woman unless she's bound, gagged and blindfolded.'

MacKenzie shrugged indifferently and took my father's mobile from his pocket, turning it towards me so that I could see it. 'Recognize it? Remember this? "All fine. Mum with me. Nothing to worry about. Call soon. Dad." Your text came through while I was still on the road. I thought I'd put your mind at rest by answering.' He studied my face for a reaction. 'I'd have sent another one but I lost the signal when I reached the valley. Why would you want to live in a dead zone, Connie?'

I moistened my mouth again. 'How do you think I sent the text? It depends which server you use.'

'Is that right? So why doesn't this guy have a signal?' He nodded at Peter's mobile which was on the desk. His eyes narrowed speculatively. 'You wouldn't have come looking for me if you'd been able to call the police. Am I correct, feather?'

'Yes.'

He didn't like that, yet how strange that it was the truth that made him uneasy. I think he wanted me to bluster and pretend, because no one in my position would admit so readily that help was unavailable. I don't even know why I did it, since my hope had been to persuade him the police were on their way.

He darted a suspicious look at the hall behind me. 'You'd better not be lying.'

'I'm not,' I said with as much sincerity as I could muster. 'How could I have called them without a signal? The landline's not working. You know that.'

It was the smallest of hits – a nervous toying with my father's mobile as he confirmed the lack of signal – but it seemed to hand me an advantage. A fear that he hadn't read the situation as well as he believed. My difficulty was that I couldn't see how to exploit it, as I had no idea how long he'd been in the house or what he knew, and his doubts would vanish, anyway, when the cavalry failed to appear.

'They know about you,' I said. 'Your mother's made a statement.'

He stared at me. 'You're lying.'

Was there doubt in his voice?

'If you go into my inbox, you'll find it as an attachment to the last email from DI Alan Collins.' I could hear the clicks as my tongue rasped against my dry palate. 'I remembered her name from the letter you asked me to post.'

The flicker of recognition, brief though it was, was unmistakable.

'I told Alan Collins she was called Mary MacKenzie, and had probably been . . . or still was . . . a prostitute. He passed the information to Glasgow and they found her quite easily.'

I wasn't committing myself to much. If he denied

his mother was a prostitute, or that Mary MacKenzie was her name, I'd say my information had been wrong and the police had located her another way. He didn't. He was more interested in the axe. 'You'd better not take me for an idiot, Connie. Do you think I'll turn my back on you? It's no matter, anyway. My bitch of a mother's been dead to me for years. Tell me what her statement says.'

Oh God! Such tiny steps and each one had to be understood and profited from immediately or Mac-Kenzie would smell a rat. I shouldn't need thinking time to recall a statement. It helped that I'd given some thought to his mother, helped that I'd trawled the net for information on sadists and rapists. I'd even had the idea of trying to find her myself, either by using a private detective agency or going to Glasgow and searching through the local newspaper archives. It seemed incredible to me that a man of his violence hadn't shown up in the courts before he left his native city, or that his hatred of women was unassociated with his mother.

I gave a passable attempt at a shrug. 'She blames herself for the way you are . . . says it was her being on the game that started you off. You found school difficult and started truanting . . . and she talks about thieving and drunken fights.' There was enough of a reaction to make it worth trying something I'd found on a website – the term Glasgow prostitutes use for the red light district. 'She says she was more frightened of you than going on the drag.'

'That's crap,' he grated angrily.

'It's what she says. There've been seven unsolved prostitute murders in Glasgow since 1991, and she's told Strathclyde police she thinks you're responsible. It's all in her statement.'

He didn't know whether to believe me or not. Would a Zimbabwean know that Strathclyde police was the over-arching force for Glasgow or that files were still open on seven prostitutes from the drag? The murders had happened, although they weren't thought to be linked to a single individual. Did MacKenzie know that?

He sent a darting glance towards the computer screen. I kept my eyes on his face, but at the edge of my range I could see Peter struggling to release his hands. I knew from experience that it was wasted effort but I prayed for a miracle, anyway. 'It's your mother who provided the photograph,' I said.

I was afraid that might be a step too far. Would Mary MacKenzie have a recent picture of her son? Apparently so, because he didn't question it. I wasn't entirely clear where it took me, except that it seemed to keep his unease alive. My real hope was to persuade him that taking out his anger on me, Jess and Peter would achieve nothing if it was his mother who had given most of the information to the police.

'Your photograph has been posted with every police force in the UK, along with a warrant for your arrest on suspicion of the Glasgow murders. Once you're in custody, Alan Collins and Bill Fraser will be given time to question you about the Freetown and Baghdad murders. You came under UK jurisdiction as soon as you entered the country . . . which means you can be questioned about crimes anywhere in the world.' Carefully, I adjusted my grip on the axe. My palms were so wet I could barely hold it. 'It's all in Alan's email.'

If I could indeed tempt him into turning his back, I would certainly hit him, but I had few illusions about my ability to do any serious damage. I was more likely to miss him completely and bury the axe in my monitor. At least I'd kill the awful repetition of my own tearful entreaties, followed by mute obedience, that filled the screen behind him. The images, many in close-up, were worse than anything I'd imagined.

I had to try twice before any words came. 'They've done a psychological profile on you that says if you filmed me, then you'll have filmed the women you murdered as well. They say you're an addictive trophy killer . . . you hang on to evidence that will convict you because you need to keep reminding yourself – '

The speed with which MacKenzie's fist whipped out to flick a knife blade in front of Peter's face stopped me in my tracks. 'Stay where you are,' he warned. 'I don't give a shit for this man's sight . . .

but you probably do.' With his other hand, he felt behind him for the CD Rom button. 'You talk too much, Connie,' he said, glancing round to retrieve a disk from the open tray. 'All women talk too much. It does my fucking head in. I liked you better when your tongue was tied.'

He played the point of the knife between Peter's terrified eyes while he slid the DVD into his pocket. 'What else does this profile say?'

Christ! Which was better? Back off or keep going? How much did he know about psychological profiling? What was more likely to tip him over the edge? Something anodyne or something brutal? I dredged facts from the research I'd done. 'That you're an organized killer . . . a vengeful stalker who blames women for your inability to make relationships . . . that you target your victims carefully and plan your murders to avoid detection.' I kept my eyes on the blade. 'That your socio-economic group is at the lower end of the scale . . . you're unlikely to be married . . . possibly delusional . . . have no interest in personal hygiene . . .' I fell silent because his aggression suddenly vanished.

He lowered the knife to the table and assessed me critically. 'You're skin and bones, feather,' he said gently. 'What happened to you?'

'I haven't been eating. I feel sick if I put something in my mouth.'

'You think about me then?'

'All the time.'

'Go on,' he encouraged, placing the knife on the desk to reach for a canvas bag that I hadn't noticed within the embrasure of the desk. I watched him pull back the flap to put my father's mobile and the DVD inside, and with a small shock I recognized it as my own bag.

'At night, I wake up screaming because I'm afraid you're in the room,' I said in a monotone. 'During the day I have panic attacks because I see a dog or smell something that reminds me of you.' Inside the bag, I could see a pair of miniature binoculars that I was sure belonged my father. 'There isn't a single minute in twenty-four hours when Keith MacKenzie doesn't fill my mind.'

I lapsed into silence again because I didn't know what he was doing. Part of me wondered if he was preparing to leave; the other part remained intensely suspicious. His only way out was past me, but I wasn't so naïve as to lower the axe to let him pass. Nor was I prepared to separate myself from Jess and Peter. However incapacitated they were, I drew a confidence from their presence that I wouldn't have had if I'd faced MacKenzie alone.

My concern now was Jess. She was beginning to tire. On the fringes of my vision, she kept jerking her head back to keep her shoulders in contact with the walls. Peter's fear for her was intense. He doubled his efforts to free his hands, and I saw his desperation every time he looked from her to me.

MacKenzie saw it, too, and smiled as he jerked his head towards the stinger. 'It's a neat little thing, isn't it? I assume it was meant for me, feather. If your friend's unlucky, the nails will get her in the belly. I've seen more soldiers die of gut wounds than anything else. The filth from the intestine infects the blood.' He gave an indifferent shrug. 'It's your choice. You can come in and move the trap . . . or you can let her fall. I'll even make a deal with you. As soon as you're through the doorway, I'll leave.'

Peter nodded violently, begging me to obey. I forced my tongue across my lips so that I could generate some noise. 'JESS!' I cried. '*Listen* to me! You *must* concentrate! I *can't* come in. Do you *understand*?' Her head ducked a millimetre in response. I went on more calmly: 'I don't care how tired you are or how much it hurts, you stay upright. At least you're on your feet and not cowering in a corner. *Understand*?' Another dip of her head.

I don't know when I realized that I wasn't as afraid as I'd expected to be. I showed physical signs of it in my parched mouth and sweating hands, but that had more to do with fear of being taken by surprise than fear of MacKenzie himself. Rightly or wrongly, I felt it was he who was isolated, and I who was in control.

He was smaller than I remembered and a great deal seedier, with stubble on his jaw and a shirt that looked as if it hadn't been changed for days. I could smell it from ten metres away. It stank of dirt and sweat and caused my only genuine falters when the nausea of memory scorched the back of my throat. For the most part, I wondered how someone so unprepossessing could have gained such a hold over my imagination.

The policeman who interviewed me later asked me why I hadn't accepted MacKenzie's offer to leave. 'Because I knew he wouldn't,' I answered.

'Dr Coleman's less sure.'

'Peter was frightened for Jess – it's what he wanted to believe. All I could see was that we'd all be more vulnerable if I did what MacKenzie wanted. While I was free and barring the exit, he was the one in the trap . . . but if I'd entered the room the dynamics would have changed completely.'

'Weren't you worried that Ms Derbyshire would fall?'

'Yes . . . but I felt she could hang on a bit longer. In any case, I couldn't have moved the trap easily. I'd have had to look at it – which would have meant taking my eyes off MacKenzie – and he'd have jumped me immediately. I don't see I had a choice except to stay where I was.'

'Even when Dr Coleman was threatened?'

'Even when,' I agreed. 'It's easier to understand if you think of it as a game of chess. As long as I controlled the doorway to the hall, MacKenzie's moves were limited.'

The policeman eyed me curiously. He'd introduced himself as Detective Inspector Bagley and, despite my request that he call me Connie, he insisted on the more formal Ms Burns. He was ginger-haired and stocky, not much older than I was, and, though he remained courteous throughout, his suspicion of me was obvious. 'Were you that cold-blooded at the time?'

'I tried to be. It wasn't always easy ... but I couldn't see what good it would do any of us if I didn't stay one step ahead of him.'

Bagley nodded. 'Did you and Ms Derbyshire make the stinger, Ms Burns? Was that part of the plan to stay one step ahead?'

'No.'

'According to Dr Coleman, MacKenzie said the stinger was meant for him. Are you sure you didn't plan a trap that went wrong?'

'No,' I said honestly. 'In any case, I don't think Peter heard MacKenzie right. He speaks with a very strong accent. The way I heard him, he said it was meant for me.'

'So it was MacKenzie who made it? Along with the other five we found?'

'He must have done.'

Bagley consulted some notes. 'Dr Coleman says you told MacKenzie that your plan was to kill him.'

'Only when he asked me what I'd do if he used the axe on Jess. I didn't have any plan when I first went into the hall except to try to convince him the police were on their way.'

'That's not the impression Dr Coleman received, Ms Burns. He says you knew what you were doing from the moment you appeared in the doorway. He also says MacKenzie had the same impression.'

I shrugged. 'What *was* I doing?'

'Looking for revenge.'

'Is that what Peter thought?'

'He certainly believes MacKenzie thought it. He says he was frightened of you.'

'Good,' I said dispassionately.

*

Being clothed made a difference. Even a flimsy cotton top and sarong felt like body armour compared with the shameful exposure of nakedness. When I made the decision to stay in the doorway, I wiped each palm down the side of my skirt while I balanced the axe in the other, then tucked my hem into my knicker elastic to give myself more freedom of movement.

Being able to see changed everything. For the first time, I understood how fear had distorted my perceptions of the man I was up against. For all the violence that I knew MacKenzie could generate, I saw him as a little man, not much taller than I was. And he couldn't disguise what was going on inside his head. His eyes darted to and fro, checking and double-checking that he still had control of his environment; but whenever he looked at me now, it was with doubt.

Did I still recognize his authority? How much did I care about the other people in the room? Was my hatred of him greater than my loyalty to them? How frightened was I? How much sympathy did I have for Jess's plight?

'She'll not be able to stand there all night,' he told me, 'and neither will you. Better do as I say, Connie.'

'No.'

He raised the knife to Peter's face again. 'Shall I cut the doctor?'

'No.'

'Then come in.'

'No.'

He placed the tip of the blade under Peter's right eye. 'One flick and he's blind. Do you want to be responsible for that, feather?' Peter cringed into the back of the chair. 'Look at him,' MacKenzie said in disgust. 'He's even more scared than you were.'

'Then untie him and see if he's as scared when his hands are free.'

'You'd like that.'

'Of course,' I agreed unemotionally. 'You ought to be able to take him easily if you were in the SAS. But you never were, were you?'

He didn't rise to the bait, but I hadn't expected him to. Instead, he stared at Peter with contempt. 'Your father showed more spirit than this creep.'

It was a tactic he'd used with me, and I'm sure on every other victim. The more a person's belittled the harder it is to retain a sense of worth. I tried the same ploy on him. 'What do you think I'm going to do if you use that knife?' I asked with as much scorn as I could muster. 'You can't really be stupid enough to think I'll suck your cock again. Or maybe you are? Your mother's IQ was measured at retard levels.'

It was like water off a duck's back. He played the point of the blade between Peter's eyes again. 'You'll do what I want I you to do, Connie, the way you did before.'

Peter's terror was so intense I could feel it. It palpated the air. And I *was* cold-blooded. I remember thinking you haven't begun to experience what I experienced, Peter, or even what Jess is experiencing now. I was angry with him, too, because his fear was feeding MacKenzie's confidence.

I managed to produce enough saliva to project a globule of spit on to the floor. 'That's what I think of you, you little fucker,' I growled at MacKenzie. 'You try anything on me and you're dead. You should listen to the voices in your head that tell you how frightening women are. You daren't go near them if their hands are free.'

That didn't seem to trouble him either.

'Do you know what the prostitutes in Freetown called you?' I said with an abrupt laugh. ' "Zoo Queen." They thought you were gay because you hated women so much . . . and the story went that you shafted dogs because you couldn't afford pretty boys. Why do you think the Europeans gave you such a wide berth? The first thing any of us learnt was, don't shake hands with Harwood or you'll catch whatever his ridgeback has.'

I had his attention.

'I told the police you could only get a hard on when dogs were present,' I went on, fishing for anything that would provoke him. 'Nothing *I* did excited you. Look at you now. You're far more aroused by Peter than you are by me or Jess. You can only do it with women when they're tied up and subservient. They remind you of your mother . . . grunting and sweating under any man she brought home.'

He didn't answer, just stared at me.

'You have to blindfold women so they won't see the size of your dick,' I went on, 'and you force fellatio on them so you won't have to come into contact with anything intimate. Breasts and vaginas scare the shit out of you. You can fuck an anus, but you sure as hell can't fuck a vagina.' This time the hit was a very direct one if the momentary shock in his eyes was anything to go by. 'It's all in your profile. They call it "stage fright" because you can't hold an erection – '

'Shut up!' he hissed, making a convulsive movement of his hand and stabbing the point of the knife
towards me. 'You're doing my head in!'

I swallowed desperately to find more saliva. 'You're
a *joke*,' I grated back. 'Your mother's turned you into
a laughing-stock. She said you never had much of a
penis and it made you obsessional – '

His pale eyes gleamed with sudden hatred, and
he launched himself out of his chair, charging at me
like a bull. I couldn't have been readier. The minute
he moved, I was out of the door and running for the
green baize door. I flung the axe under the stairs as I
passed because I knew I wouldn't be able to use it,
and grabbed the brass doorknob with both hands. For
one sickening moment my damp palms slid around
the metal instead of turning it, and it was desperation
that prompted me to scream as I dug my fingers in
and wrenched at the handle for all I was worth.

Eighteen

INSPECTOR BAGLEY WOULDN'T believe that my recollection of what followed was as poor as I claimed. Yet the truth is I don't remember it in any great detail. It remains a blur of noise and bodies, and a realization somewhere along the line that quantities of blood were pouring on to the flagstones.

I tried to explain to Bagley that if I'd known screams were all that was needed to incite mastiffs to attack a stranger, I'd have taken them with me in the first place instead of leaving them in the corridor to the kitchen. Why confront MacKenzie alone if I could have launched a cohort of giants at his throat? *Because I had more faith in his ability to turn them on me than mine to turn them on him.* Indeed, my only expectation when I left them behind the green baize door was that they'd create some confusion when I released them into the hall.

There hadn't been time to plan. I think I gambled on winning a breathing space for us all to escape or, at the very least, that Jess would be able to issue commands herself and use the dogs to herd MacKenzie into a corner. Everything I did was ad-libbed, and based entirely on my certainty that I'd fail with a weapon. It was immaterial which I selected – axe or walking-stick – MacKenzie would have it off me as soon as I took the first swing.'

'Then why remain in the hall?' Bagley asked. 'Why retrieve the axe from under the stairs?'

'I don't know. There was so much noise I couldn't work out what was happening. It's weird. The dogs never made a sound while they were in the corridor . . . but when I opened the door they went ballistic . . . straight for MacKenzie. But why him? Why not me? It wasn't that long since they'd had me pinned against the outhouse door.'

'He was in front of them.'

'How did he get past them in the first place?'

'Are you sure he didn't break in before Ms Derbyshire came back?'

'Pretty sure. The phone line wasn't cut until after I emailed my parents . . . and the only unlocked window you found was the one in the office. Yet I remember looking at that catch while Jess and I were in there earlier, and it was definitely closed then.'

'He certainly came in that way. He scraped the paint when he used his flick knife to slip the catch . . . and left traces of mud and grass on the carpet. It's also the window where the phone line enters. The whole operation – cutting the wire and forcing the lock – wouldn't have taken more than a couple of minutes.

We think the most likely explanation is that he'd been watching you for some time from outside the garden and took advantage of Dr Coleman's arrival to break in. While the dogs were distracted, he had plenty of time to circle round. He would have seen how straightforward that window was if he'd been watching you and Ms Derbyshire through binoculars.'

I pulled a face. 'We made it easy for him.'

Bagley shook his head. 'If he was determined to get in, he'd have found another way.' He went back to what had happened after I'd released the dogs into the hall. 'Dr Coleman said you were screaming all the time. He was afraid you'd been wounded.'

'I don't remember.'

'Please try, Ms Burns,' he murmured patiently. 'The explanation you gave Dr Coleman was that you thought the mastiffs were fighting over a cat. But there is no cat at Barton House.'

I do remember freezing. The roaring and snarling shot iced water through my veins and I stood in petrified fear for what seemed like an eternity. The echoing guttural noises were amplified by the stone floor and the high ceiling above the stairwell, and my response was to do what I'd done in the Baghdad cellar – stand like a pillar of salt until the frenzy died down.

If I was screaming, I wasn't conscious of it, although I'm not convinced that Peter's recollection of events was any clearer than mine. All he really saw was MacKenzie's sudden leap from the chair in pursuit of me, and he developed the rest out of an overactive imagination. For example, he persuaded the police that I gave the dogs commands – first to attack, then to stand back – but as I kept telling Bagley, I couldn't have been screaming and giving commands at the same time. In any case, Jess hadn't taught me which commands to use.

'I can't accept that, Ms Burns. You're a resourceful woman. You didn't have a statement from Mrs MacKenzie either, yet you were able to give a plausible account of what might have been in it. The same with the non-existent profile.'

'It was all very vague. I was only repeating generalizations from case studies I found on the internet.' I paused. 'I knew quite a lot about him already . . . which is the part Peter forgets. MacKenzie gave away more than he realized in Baghdad.'

'I think you'll find Dr Coleman stands in awe of your investigative abilities,' said Bagley with a small smile. 'As far as he's concerned, you'd have discovered how to control Ms Derbyshire's dogs within half an hour of knowing her.'

'I'm phobic,' I protested. 'Tonight's the first time I've been able to go within ten metres of a dog. I'm sure Dr Coleman's told you that.'

'Indeed, but you're not deaf and blind, Ms Burns.'

'What does that mean?'

'You've spent three months watching and listening

346

to the commands Ms Derbyshire gives. Did you learn nothing from that?'

I might have been flattered by Peter's glowing description of my ascendancy over psychopaths and mastiffs if it hadn't resulted in prolonged questioning about my motives. It was explained to me in no uncertain terms that under UK law a home owner or tenant had the right to defend his property and himself against intruders. For the purposes of the law 'himself' included any family and friends who were under his roof at the time and whose lives he believed to be threatened.

However, the level of force used against the intruder had to be "reasonable", and premeditation of any kind – be it setting traps, inflicting further punishment on a man already disabled, or pursuing him for the purposes of revenge – was a criminal offence. In simple terms, a pack of mastiffs could be used to corral an intruder but not to tear his throat out; homemade stingers, placed about a house with the intention of maiming and wounding, were illegal; as was the use of an axe against an intruder who was already subdued.

Bagley's biggest question mark was over why I'd re-entered the house when my obvious course of action was to do what I'd planned and run to the nearest hillside to phone the police. 'Revenge' hung over my head like a bad smell. I'd known Peter was alive because I saw him, and there was nothing to indicate that Jess was in the room, let alone in trouble.

Indeed, at the point I turned round, I had no reason to believe that either of them was being threatened since I admitted I hadn't noticed the duct tape on Peter's mouth.

'It's a ridiculous law,' I said with considerable indignation. 'In Zimbabwe we were taught that an Englishman's home is his castle.'

The Inspector wasn't impressed by my playing the colonial card. 'It is,' he assured me, 'and he's allowed to defend it as long as he doesn't use disproportionate violence.'

'It's an open invitation to burglars to bang their heads against the wall every time they're caught,' I said crossly. 'That way, they never leave empty-handed. They might not get away with the stereo system, but they can sure as hell sue for compensation on the grounds of unreasonable force.'

'You obviously read your newspapers.'

'I'm a journalist.'

'Mm. Well, I don't disagree, Ms Burns, but it *is* the law . . . and I *am* obliged to enforce it. Why did you retrieve the axe?'

'Because I saw blood on the floor.'

A great deal of blood. It was like a war zone. Whoever was injured was pumping pints of the stuff on to the flagstones. I didn't gave a thought to its being MacKenzie. Fate was never so obliging. I knew immediately that it was one of Jess's dogs, and that MacKenzie's flick knife had found an artery. I don't know what was in my mind when I picked up the axe. Perhaps I did want revenge. I do remember thinking it was incredibly unfair.

'You talk as if I know how dogs behave,' I told Bagley, 'and I don't. I've spent years avoiding them because everywhere I go there's rabies. It's a different world. You learn to be wary around animals in hot climates. They lose their tempers in the heat just as people do.'

'You saw blood,' he reminded me patiently.

'I thought they might react like sharks – go into a feeding frenzy because of the smell.'

He eyed me doubtfully. 'You mean eat MacKenzie?'

'Rip apart,' I corrected him, 'the way hounds rip foxes.'

'So you picked up the axe to protect him?'

'And myself. It was all happening only a few feet away from me.'

'Did you know it was a mastiff that was dying?'

'Yes. I saw Bertie collapse.'

He glanced at some notes. 'Do you recall what you did next?'

'Not really. All I could think about was trying to stop the fight.'

'So your plan was to use the axe on the mastiffs?'

'I didn't have a plan. I just knew I had to do something.'

He held my gaze for a moment then returned to the notes. 'According to Dr Coleman you screamed "bastard" then ordered the dogs behind you and brought the axe down on Mr Mackenzie's right hand ... the one that held the flick knife. Dr Coleman's impression was that you wanted to defend the dogs from further damage ... *not* Mr MacKenzie.'

I shrugged. 'I don't know what to say except that Peter's investing me with a level of control that I didn't have. It's true I hit MacKenzie's hand, but it was a complete fluke. If I repeated the action a thousand times, there'd be a thousand different outcomes. I can't even use a hammer properly ... so how on earth could I expect to hit what I was aiming at with an axe?'

I could have proved the point better by telling him that my target had been MacKenzie's head and I'd missed it by a yard, but that would have been a spectacular own goal since I was doing my best to persuade him that undue violence had never been part of my agenda. Or Jess's. Or my father's.

'And where were the dogs when this happened, Ms Burns?'

'Milling around MacKenzie. It's a miracle I didn't hit one of them.'

'Indeed,' he said with heavy irony. 'Perhaps MacKenzie's hand was protruding conveniently from the pack.' He didn't seem to expect an answer because he went on: 'I'm having trouble understanding how someone with a phobia of dogs had the courage to wade into the middle of a fight between grown mastiffs. At a rough guess their combined weight must have been in excess of six hundred pounds . . . and by your own admission you thought they were engaged in a feeding frenzy. What you did was either very brave or very stupid.'

'Very stupid,' I assured him. 'About as stupid as going back into the house in the first place . . . but you don't think straight when you're frightened.'

More irony. 'That's certainly true of most people.' He smiled slightly. 'Tell me why the dogs decided to draw back.'

'I don't know. I think the sound of the axe striking the stone might have startled them. Only the top half of the blade hit MacKenzie . . . the bottom half cracked one of the flags.'

He consulted his notes. 'At which point you decided to tie him up?'

'Yes.'

'Even though he was wounded?'

'Yes.'

'Using his own duct tape . . . which meant you had to go back into the office?'

'Yes.'

'But you didn't think to release Dr Coleman and Ms Derbyshire?'

'I didn't have time. I was frightened of leaving MacKenzie free even for the seconds it took me to run in and out of the office.'

'May I ask why?'

'Because I was sure he was only winded. His eyes were open . . . and he was groaning. He called me a bitch when I kicked the flick knife away.' Wearily, I massaged my temples with my fingertips. 'I thought about bashing him on the head to knock him out, as a matter of fact, but I didn't how much force would be needed. I was afraid of killing him by mistake.'

'Mm . . . Dr Coleman mentions the groans. He says they stopped after you retrieved the tape. Did you decide to gag him as well, Ms Burns?'

'Does Peter say he was gagged?'

He shook his head.

I chose to take that as a firm negative. 'He passed out when I bound his hands together. If I'd realized I'd broken his fingers, I might have been a bit more careful . . . but, at that stage, I didn't even know I'd made contact with them. Wouldn't you expect an axe to chop them off . . . instead of just mangling them?'

'It depends when the axe was last sharpened.'

'I know that now. I didn't at the time.'

'Wasn't it obvious to you that he was incapacitated? He'd been savaged by a pack of dogs and attacked with an axe.'

I took a few seconds to order my thoughts. 'No, it wasn't obvious at all. I agree he looked a bit of a mess because he had Bertie's blood all over him, but I'd seen him in fights in Sierra Leone and I knew he could take punches. I'd have been mad to risk it.'

The Inspector's expression was sceptical. 'Surely a

more normal reaction would have been to get a doctor to him as fast as possible . . . particularly as there was one less than fifteen metres away?'

'That's effectively what I did,' I said mildly, 'and Peter agreed I was right to tie him up first. None of the blood was MacKenzie's. He had the broken fingers and some bruising on his arms where the dogs had held him through his shirt, but no puncture wounds.'

'Did Ms Derbyshire ever tell you that's how she trained her dogs? To terrify and restrain rather than inflict damage?'

'No. All she ever said was that I had no reason to fear them, but she didn't specify why.' I produced my most ingenuous smile. 'If she *had* done, I'd have known MacKenzie wasn't in any danger from them.'

'But you knew MacKenzie had a flick knife, so you knew the dogs were in danger from him. Presumably you also knew how angry the death of one of her mastiffs would make Ms Derbyshire?'

'Not really,' I said apologetically. 'I'm not a doggy person.'

His scepticism grew. 'Why did you release Ms Derbyshire before Dr Coleman?'

'Because she was the most vulnerable. If she'd lost concentration she'd have fallen on the nails.'

'Then why didn't you release Dr Coleman directly afterwards?' He consulted the notes again. 'He says you and Ms Derbyshire left the room and it was several minutes before you came back again . . . which contradicts your earlier assertion that you took Dr Coleman to Mr MacKenzie as fast as you could.'

I sighed. 'Only if you accept Peter's estimate of how long anything took . . . but I honestly believe he's given you some very exaggerated timings. You said he thought it was half an hour between him leaving the kitchen and my appearing in the office doorway, yet my estimate would be more like fifteen minutes. And as for the dogfight, there's no way it lasted the five minutes Peter's claiming. More like sixty seconds. In five minutes, MacKenzie could have killed every one of them.'

'Dr Coleman's used to emergencies, Ms Burns. It's his job. Why should his timings have been any less accurate than yours?'

'Because I have more experience of frightening situations. You learn very quickly in a war zone that everything becomes inflated . . . ten minutes under mortar bombardment seems like ten hours . . . a hundred-strong mob with machetes looks more like five hundred.' I leaned my elbows on the table. 'I left Peter just long enough to see Jess to the top of the stairs – one minute max. She was very shaken and she didn't know what MacKenzie had done with her clothes – so I told her to put on something of mine till we found them. Then I went back down and released Peter.'

The Inspector nodded as if he could accept that.

'These being the clothes that were dropped outside the office window?'

'Yes. Jess thinks he did it to confuse the dogs in case they picked up his scent where he came in.'

'You should have left them there for the police to examine, Ms Burns.'

'I couldn't. Jess had nothing else to wear. Everything of mine was too long, and she needed her boots.'

Another nod. 'Was Ms Derbyshire in the hall when Dr Coleman examined Mr MacKenzie?'

'No, she was still upstairs.'

'Where were the dogs?'

'With Jess. She wanted to check them over for stab wounds.'

'Excluding – ' he checked his notes – 'Bertie. He was already dead?'

'Yes.'

'Who decided he was dead, Ms Burns? You? Or Ms Derbyshire?'

In view of the doubt I'd thrown on Peter's ability to estimate time, I suspected a neat little trap. 'You only had to look at him,' I said flatly, 'or *smell* him. His sphincter muscle had relaxed and the contents of his rectum were on the floor. I'm sure in other circumstances Jess would have tried for a pulse, but she was more concerned about the others. They were covered in blood as well.'

'What did you do while Dr Coleman examined Mr MacKenzie?'

'Watched.'

I left out that Peter's self-control deserted him and he swore like a trooper for a good minute after I removed his gag. At that stage he didn't know who to blame for his perceived shortcomings. MacKenzie for humbling him? Me for being strong? Jess for taking most of the punishment? Himself for being frightened? His devastation increased when he saw Bertie, as if Bertie had somehow been sacrificed on the altar of his cowardice. Of course these 'shortcomings' were his own creation – much as mine had been – for neither Jess nor I saw him in such terms.

Nevertheless, the result of this orgy of self-flagellation was that he set out to paint me and Jess in glowing colours. I became the iron lady who took control and exercised it – Peter even used the word 'revenge' after describing what he'd seen on the DVD, claiming anything I did to MacKenzie was 'reasonable'. Jess became the martyr figure who refused to give in to exhaustion or threats, and retained an icy composure even after the death of one of her dogs.

It left Bagley with the impression of two tough and determined women who, for different reasons, had wanted MacKenzie dead. An impression not helped by the various weapons hidden around the house, particularly Jess's baseball bats and my carving knives. To Peter's credit, he tried to set the record straight as soon as he realized the damage he'd done, but by then it was too late. If both Ms Burns and Ms Derbyshire were subject to panic attacks and agoraphobia, Bagley asked, why had we shown no evidence of it that night?

'You *watched*,' he echoed now. 'Yet I understand Dr Coleman asked you to call the police and an ambulance. Why didn't you do that?'

'The landline wasn't working.'

'But you knew your mobile worked in the attic.'

'I didn't think it was a good idea to leave Peter alone with MacKenzie.' I rested my forehead on my hands and stared at the table. 'Look, what I'm going to say isn't very kind, but it *is* true. Peter was petrified from beginning to end of the whole thing. I didn't blame him – I don't blame him now – but I guarantee MacKenzie would have freed himself somehow if I hadn't stayed.'

'How?'

I dropped my hands into my lap. 'Probably by pretending to be more injured than he was. Peter was uncomfortable about the way I'd bound his hands behind his back, particularly when he realized the fingers were broken. He wanted me to retie them at the front while MacKenzie was still unconscious.'

'But you refused. Why?'

'Because I wasn't as convinced as Peter that he *was* unconscious.'

'You think a doctor would make a mistake about something like that?'

I shrugged. 'It's hardly difficult to fake but, in any case, it wasn't a risk worth taking. I couldn't see Peter leaping to my rescue if MacKenzie decided to grab me round the throat and throttle me. There'd have been a lot of hand-flapping and not much action. He made a hell of a fuss about getting Bertie's blood on his trousers.'

It wasn't a very fair description of Peter but it seemed to strike a chord with the Inspector. 'Dr Coleman certainly seems to have found the experience more – ' he searched for the appropriate phrase – '*soul*-destroying than you and Ms Derbyshire.'

'You don't know much about women then,' I said flatly. 'If it'll bring an end to this, I'll happily burst into tears and throw hysterics. Is that what you want me to do? It's easily done . . . almost as easy as MacKenzie pretending to be unconscious.'

A gleam of humour appeared in his eyes. 'I'd rather you told me why you persuaded Dr Coleman to go back to his own house and call the emergency services from there. That puzzles me.'

'It didn't happen like that,' I demurred. 'It was Peter's idea . . . I merely agreed it was sensible.'

The Inspector consulted his notes. 'Dr Coleman has the roles reversed, Ms Burns. I quote: "When I told Connie we needed the police and an ambulance as a matter of priority, she pointed out that MacKenzie had cut the telephone line. She said the only option was for me to go home and call from there. I agreed."'

'I honestly don't recall it that way . . . but does it matter?'

He frowned. 'Of course it matters. There were five working mobiles in the house, yours, Dr Coleman's and Ms Derbyshire's . . . plus Mr MacKenzie's and your father's. We've already established there's a perfectly good signal in the attic, so why not send Dr Coleman upstairs? Why tell him going home was the only option?'

I shook my head. 'I don't remember doing that . . . but, even if I did, how does it make me the bad guy? Peter knew about the signal in the attic. He could have thought it through just as well as I could. It wasn't a normal situation . . . we weren't exactly sitting around, discussing the best way to proceed, you know. We were both shaking like leaves . . . and all *I* recall is jumping at the first suggestion that was going to bring us some help.'

'In fact Dr Coleman expressed surprise when we told him it was possible to use a mobile at Barton House.'

'Then he's two-faced,' I said crossly. 'He knew all about the pyramid Jess built in the back bedroom so that I could use my laptop when I first arrived. You can ask my landlady. It was Peter who told her about it when I asked permission to install broadband.'

The Inspector steepled his hands in front of his mouth and studied me reflectively for several seconds. 'He recalls that now,' he agreed, 'but not at the time. And you didn't remind him.'

'Then I can only apologize for a blonde moment,' I said sarcastically. 'Has Peter apologized for a *senior* moment? It all happened very fast. As soon as he made up his mind to go, he ran for the door.' I folded my hands on the table. 'I wish I could make you understand how disorientated we all were . . . but maybe you've never had a psychopath break into your house and take you prisoner.'

He didn't rise to that bait either. 'So what happened next? When did Ms Derbyshire join you in the hall?'

'Almost immediately. She heard Peter's car on the gravel and came down to find out what was happening.'

'Were the dogs with her?'

'No. She left them in the bedroom . . . she was worried they'd start sniffing around Bertie.'

'What was she wearing?'

'My dressing-gown. It was too long for her and trailed across the floor. She knelt down to stroke the dog, and – ' I sighed. 'It all got very messy.'

'What was on her feet?'

'Nothing. None of my shoes fitted her. Which is why she asked me to find her boots.'

'But you weren't wearing shoes either.'

'No, I took them off before I went into the hall. I didn't want MacKenzie to hear me coming.'

Bagley nodded. 'What made you look for Ms Derbyshire's clothes outside the office window?'

'Because they weren't in the office. MacKenzie had kept her knickers – he'd put them in the bag – but there was no sign of anything else. Then Jess told me she'd heard the window open and close after he put her on the footstool . . . so I raised the sash and spotted them immediately.'

'And you went through the kitchen to retrieve them?'

'You know I did. You found my bloody footprints.'

'Mm. And during the time it took for you to go outside and return, Ms Derbyshire was alone with Mr MacKenzie?'

'Yes,' I said wearily. 'We've been over this twice already. I ran – you can measure my strides – and when I returned, the only thing that was different was that Jess was sitting in the armchair under the stairs. If you spray it with Luminol I'm sure you'll get a reaction from the bloodstains on my dressing-gown.'

'You're very knowledgable about crime scenes, Ms Burns.'

'I've covered a fair number of trials over the years. It's amazing how much information you pick up from hours of police evidence. You should try it yourself some time.'

It was impossible to provoke him to anything other than displays of polite scepticism, except when it came to MacKenzie's disappearance. On that subject, his disbelief was total. Yet again, he took me through the sequence of events.

'You say MacKenzie was lying on his side and you could see the duct tape was still firmly in place.'

'Yes.'

'You then handed Ms Derbyshire her clothes and suggested she have a bath to wash off Bertie's blood because it was clearly distressing her. She went directly upstairs, and shortly afterwards you heard the water running.'

'Right.'

'You were also distressed by the dog's blood, so you chose to wash in the kitchen sink before changing into a skirt and T-shirt that were waiting to be ironed in the scullery. And to avoid the blood setting on your stained clothes, you left them soaking in a bleach solution in the sink . . . because they were "whiteish" and made out of cotton.'

'Yes.'

'Did you expect it to work?'

'Not really, but it seemed worth a try. My wardrobe's hardly bursting, and it *was* only dog's blood. The pathologists will prove me right. I'm sure I've read somewhere that DNA is still recoverable after a garment's been washed.'

'Except we're not talking about washing, Ms Burns, we're talking about *bleaching* . . . and all the literature says bleach *destroys* DNA.'

'Really?' I murmured. 'I didn't know that.'

'Why did Ms Derbyshire do the same thing? Why did she leave your dressing-gown in a bleach solution in the bath? Was it your suggestion? Did you take the bleach to her after you'd finished in the kitchen?'

I dropped my chin on to my clasped hands. 'It's "No" to the last two questions, and "That's what women do" to the first two. Every woman in the world has a problem with bloodstains on her clothes. You should watch African girls spending hours at the rivers, hammering away with stones to get rid of them. We're all programmed to do the same thing . . . never mind our cultures. Do you have a wife? Ask her.'

'Did you take the bleach upstairs, Ms Burns?' he repeated.

'I've already said I didn't. There was a bottle of Domestos beside the lavatory in the bathroom. Look – ' I paused, wondering if it was wise to continue – 'you must see how ridiculous this line of questioning is.' *What the hell!* I was exhausted. 'Peter wasn't away more than twenty minutes . . . and the police and ambulance arrived shortly after he returned. How could Jess and I kill MacKenzie and get rid of his body in that short time?'

'You couldn't.'

'Then why keep implying we were in some sort of conspiracy? Has Jess told you a different story?'

'No. Her account matches yours. MacKenzie was still tied up when she went for a bath, and she only learnt he'd gone when Dr Coleman started shouting in the hall.'

Nineteen

POOR PETER. HE became intimately acquainted with panic that night. His first idea when he found the front door wide open, and no MacKenzie on the floor, was that he was about to be jumped again. His second was that Jess and I were probably dead. His third – not very sensible in view of the first two, as they suggested MacKenzie was hovering around with the axe – was to start hollering for us.

His voice was high-pitched and uneven, and I heard it in the kitchen. 'Connie! Jess! Where are you? Are you all right?'

I called back that I was in the kitchen, but when it became obvious that he hadn't heard me, I dried my hands and went down the corridor. Peter described me as behaving 'with extraordinary calm'. Indeed, I was so relaxed that when I urged him 'to get a grip', he came to the strange decision that Jess and I had moved MacKenzie somewhere else.

'But you hadn't?'

'Of course not. Peter told me to leave him where he was until the ambulance arrived. How could we have moved him, anyway, without releasing his feet? We couldn't have carried him.'

'Two of you might have been able to.'

'Where to?' I asked reasonably. 'You've searched the house three times, and he's not here. And you've tracked every one of our footprints.'

'Those we can find. Blood dries quicker than you think, Ms Burns. We've found your outward tracks through the kitchen when you went for Ms Derbyshire's clothes, but there's nothing to show you returned.'

'Except that I must have done since she was wearing them by the time the first police car arrived.'

I think he found my composure as frustrating as Peter had done. They both felt that hand-wringing and breast-beating suited the mood better than hardheaded analysis. Peter lost it completely in the middle of the hall when he asked me what I'd done with MacKenzie. He even accused Jess and me of 'doing something awful' since MacKenzie couldn't have freed himself without assistance.

'And did you, Ms Burns?'

'No.'

'Then how *did* he free himself?'

'I don't know. At a guess, he used Jess's Leatherman. She said he took it off her. If it was in his trouser pocket, he might have been able to move his arms enough to wriggle it out.'

'Hard to pull out a blade with broken fingers.'

'He had quite an incentive,' I said dryly. 'He was about to be arrested.'

Bagley studied me for a moment. 'Why weren't you as worried as Dr Coleman when you saw that Mac-Kenzie was missing? He could have been anywhere . . . upstairs with Ms Derbyshire, for example.'

'Jess arrived on the landing about the same time as I came into the hall . . . and Peter's voice was so far up the register that most of what he said was incomprehensible. I'm not sure I even realized Mac-Kenzie *was* missing until Peter started to calm down . . . and then we heard the sirens. It was all very quick.'

'You're an observant woman, Ms Burns. You must have noticed the floor was empty.'

'I was looking at Peter.'

But Bagley couldn't accept that. 'As soon as you realized Dr Coleman was frightened, you'd have checked on MacKenzie as a matter of priority.'

I shrugged. 'This would be a lot easier if Peter hadn't given you such an inflated opinion of me. You seem to think I have an immediate grasp of what's going on in any situation. Well, I *don't*. I may have seen Bertie out of the corner of my eye – a *shape* – and assumed it was MacKenzie . . . although I don't remember doing it, and I don't remember thinking about it.' I tugged a cigarette out of my pocket and lit it with relief. 'Just out of interest, why isn't Peter being put through the third degree? He's far more likely to have freed MacKenzie than Jess or I.'

'What makes you say that?'

'Because he was worried about MacKenzie's hands. Perhaps he decided to loosen the duct tape when he came back in.'

'I don't think so.'

I absorbed as much nicotine in one shot as I could, then blew the smoke in Bagley's direction. 'Is that a bloke thing, Inspector? The fact that you're willing to believe a man, but not a woman?'

He took it in good part. 'Ms Derbyshire heard Dr Coleman's car come back. She says there was a few seconds' time lapse between that and his shouting. I haven't ruled out that he did what you suggest but it seems unlikely. He didn't have a knife on him when we searched him, and he'd have needed one to cut through the duct tape.'

'Perhaps MacKenzie took it off him.'

'Did Dr Coleman look as if he'd been in a fight?'

'No . . . but if he had any sense he'd have relinquished the knife and run out the front door before he got slashed with it.'

'Leaving MacKenzie to collect his bag and disappear through the office window? Is that what you're saying happened?'

'Why not? It's what you're suggesting Jess and I did, isn't it?'

'We think he left through the front door . . . and, from the impressions on the floor, he appears to have been on bare feet.' Bagley smiled slightly. 'We have a lot of bare feet, Ms Burns. It's quite confusing.'

'All different sizes . . . and with different toe-prints.'

'Prints don't register well on stone. There was a lot of skating done through the blood. It's hard to say who went where when.'

'Only in the hall. Have you found MacKenzie's prints anywhere else?'

He wasn't going to answer my questions. 'One line we're pursuing is that he managed to ease his shoes off in order to slip out of the duct tape round his ankles. You told us you wrapped the tape round the bottom of his trousers. Do you recall how many turns you made and whether he was wearing socks?'

I thought back. 'Not really. About four, perhaps. I just wound it till it seemed tight enough. I don't remember seeing socks.'

'What sort of trousers were they?'

'Denims.'

'Do you remember Dr Coleman undoing the fly to help him breathe?'

I nodded.

'So all MacKenzie had to do was slide out of the trousers to free himself?'

I saw criticism immediately. 'I'm damned if I'll take the blame for that,' I said indignantly. 'It wasn't me who unbuttoned his stupid trousers. Blame Peter. He could have worked it out just as well as I could.'

'I'm not blaming you, Ms Burns, I'm pointing out what might have happened. Did you bind his hands in the same way? Was the duct tape over his cuffs or against his skin?'

I was very tempted to say it was over his cuffs but it wouldn't have been true. 'Against his skin. The cuffs were rolled back.'

He'd obviously been told the same by Peter because he nodded. 'He had more opportunities once his feet were free, of course. Do you remember what happened to the flick knife?'

'I kicked it away from him. As far as I remember, it went under the stairs.'

'We haven't found it.'

I shrugged, suspecting another trap. By his twisted logic, victims were probably required to retrieve all pieces of evidence and line them up for inspection when the police arrived.

'A flick knife would have been easier to manipulate than Ms Derbyshire's Leatherman . . . but, in either event, he seems to have taken them with him. We haven't found the Leatherman either.'

I drew in a lungful of smoke. 'Why didn't you tell me this at the beginning? Why accuse me of murder if you've known all along how he freed himself?'

'No one's accusing you of murder, Ms Burns.'

'Well, it feels like it,' I said. 'The only difference

between you and one of Mugabe's henchman is that I still have some fingernails left.'

He lost patience with me. 'Interviewing witnesses is a necessary part of any criminal inquiry, and it's not police policy to exempt women. I agree it can be a stressful experience . . . however, given your views, I'm surprised you feel unequal to it.'

I grinned. 'Ouch!'

He took an irritated breath. 'Did you or Ms Derbyshire move MacKenzie's canvas bag from the office to the hall, Ms Burns?'

'*My* bag,' I corrected. 'He stole it from me in Baghdad.'

'Did you move it?'

'Yes. I handed it to Jess on my way to collect her clothes so that she could check the pockets. He'd put her knickers in the flap, but I thought he might have taken her bra as well. He was that kind of pervert.'

'Do you remember what she did with it?'

'I think she left it on the chair.'

'Did either of you take anything out of it?'

'I can't speak for Jess, but *I* didn't.' I stubbed out my cigarette. 'I should have done. My father's binoculars and mobile were in it. Why do you ask?'

'Just tying up loose ends.' He saw my frown. 'The SOCOs found your imprints on the office floor, but none that matched those by the front door. We wondered why, since you and Dr Coleman both said the bag was by the desk.'

He was very thorough, I thought. 'Have you found the bag? Why did you think we might have removed something?'

'It was a hope, Ms Burns. If you'd kept something of MacKenzie's we'd have a better chance of extracting some DNA.'

'Oh, I see.'

'We have foot- and fingerprints but nothing else. There might have been saliva traces on your father's mobile or an eyelash on the binoculars, although the most likely source would have been your clothes, since you came into contact with him when you tied him up. If Ms Derbyshire's dogs had drawn blood or the axe had broken his skin – ' he shrugged.

'What about Jess's clothes or Peter's clothes?'

He shook his head. 'If you'd left Ms Derbyshire's untouched, we might have found a rogue hair, but there was too much moving and handling . . . and Dr Coleman lost anything on his way back to his house.'

'Do you need DNA evidence if you have his fingerprints? Peter and I can both identify him.'

Bagley smiled rather grimly. 'It depends if he's recognizable when we find him, Ms Burns.'

*

Chaos followed hard on the arrival of the police and the ambulance. I remember the terrible clamour as the sirens wailed into the drive, and the ensuing confusion as Peter tried to explain that the 'patient' had vanished. We all had different priorities. Mine was to find out what had happened to my parents, Jess's was her dogs, and the police wanted a clear picture of events before they did anything at all.

In the first instance, they wanted to know whose blood was all over the floor and why it had been trodden in so freely, and they weren't prepared to accept that it had all come from Bertie. Neither could I when I looked at it through the objective eyes of startled newcomers. What the dogs hadn't flicked around in the immediate aftermath of Bertie's death, Peter, Jess and I had tracked across the flagstones in our movements to and fro. It looked like a bloodbath and felt like a bloodbath, and the police chose to view it as one until tests proved different.

We learnt later that Bertie suffered massive haemorrhaging from his carotid artery where MacKenzie had slashed the flick knife across one side of his throat. Jess's grief was that he didn't die immediately but continued to pump blood until his heart gave up. Mine was that I hadn't used the axe sooner to split MacKenzie's head open. In the great scheme of things, Bertie's contribution to life, liberty and happiness so outweighed MacKenzie's that there was no contest between which of them deserved to live and which deserved to die.

Much to Jess's and my annoyance, we were relegated to second place behind Peter. While he was invited into the dusty dining-room to give the first account of what had happened, we were instructed to wait in the kitchen under the eagle eyes of a WPC. By that time, several more police cars had arrived and the house and garden were being scoured for MacKenzie. I kept trying to raise the issue of my parents but no one wanted to hear. 'One thing at a time,' I was told. In the end Jess threatened to punch the WPC if she didn't whip up some action, and instructions were finally given to alert the Metropolitan police.

Inspector Bagley was curious about why I hadn't used my mobile to contact my parents myself. If they were such a priority, he argued, I'd have headed for the attic as soon as Peter left the house. 'You could have phoned Alan Collins,' he pointed out. 'He knew the history, and he was already in contact with the Met.'

I did understand his dilemma. An obsessive need to clean seemed a poor excuse when the lives of well-loved parents were at stake. Predictably, we disagreed about how long Jess and I had been alone with MacKenzie – the Inspector favoured forty minutes (Peter's assessment), while I favoured twenty. We compromised on thirty when police records showed that the time lapse between Peter's 999 call and the arrival of the first police car was just over twenty-three minutes, allowing seven minutes for Peter to drive home from Barton House. But, in the Inspector's view, even thirty minutes suggested I hadn't accounted for all my actions.

'That's a mighty lot of washing, Ms Burns, and it doesn't explain why you only remembered your parents when we arrived. You admit you saw your father's binoculars in the bag. Why didn't they prompt you to contact him?'

His suspicion wasn't helped by the fact that I didn't tell him DI Alan Collins of the Greater Manchester Police had a file on MacKenzie. Alan only entered the equation when he contacted Dorset police himself at lunchtime on Sunday, after hearing via the Met in London that my father had been rushed to hospital at three o'clock in the morning after being found, brutally attacked, in his sitting-room. With no details of what had happened at Barton House, the Met simply informed Alan that Keith MacKenzie was a suspect in the assault, and the request to check the flat had come from Dorset police.

In the belief that MacKenzie would head straight for me, but unable to warn me because he didn't have my address or number, he rang Dorset's Winfrith headquarters. What he told them subsequently of my history with MacKenzie, which was a great deal more detailed than anything I'd said, persuaded Bagley that I was not only well-practised at withholding information but also made a habit of it.

'Why didn't you tell me that you failed to report this man to the Iraqi authorities, Ms Burns? Or that it's only in the last two weeks that you've divulged any information at all about your captivity?'

I toyed with saying, 'You didn't ask,' but decided he wasn't in the mood for flippancy. 'There hasn't been time. I've tried to fill in some of the gaps, but most of your questioning has been about what happened here.' I looked him straight in the eye. 'I suppose I could have insisted on talking about Baghdad, but wouldn't that have made you more suspicious?'

His eyes didn't drop, but a perplexed frown puckered his forehead. 'I can't make you out at all,' he said. 'From Dr Coleman's description of the video, you suffered the most appalling abuse at this man's hands . . . Alan Collins says you were so frightened of him you wouldn't divulge his identity and went into hiding . . . Ms Derbyshire says you haven't eaten or been out for a week . . . your parents are in hospital . . . MacKenzie's still free . . . yet you're sitting here in front of me as cool as a cucumber.'

'Is that a question?'

He smiled in spite of himself. 'Yes. Why are you so calm?'

'I'm not sure a man would understand.'

'Try me.'

'In the first place, my parents aren't dead,' I said.

There was no mystery about how they both ended up at the flat as MacKenzie's prisoners. My father did exactly as Jess described, set out to lure MacKenzie into a trap, using himself as bait. Afterwards, he was given the same lecture I received about vigilantism and revenge but, as Dad took most of the punishment, no charges were brought despite question marks over his purchase of wood and nails on Friday morning.

He wasn't very forthcoming about the details of his plan – claiming only that his intention was to confine MacKenzie and call the police – and denied knowledge or responsibility for the homemade 'stingers' that ended up in Barton House. Of course Jess and I did, too, which left MacKenzie as the guilty party. I told Alan privately that my father had made them, and MacKenzie had brought them to Barton House; but, with the law as it was, none of us was going to admit to it publicly.

Initially, my father had some difficulty agreeing with Met detectives that his idea of an ambush was ill-considered and naïve, but under pressure from my mother he ate humble pie. Perhaps it was a mercy he could only nod his agreement, because the air would have turned blue if he'd been able to speak. The only detail he genuinely conceded was that, had he entered the flat accompanied by a police officer, MacKenzie wouldn't have taken him prisoner so easily.

It's unclear how long MacKenzie had been there – several hours if his intensive search of the place was anything to go by – but my father had no inkling of danger when he let himself in on the Friday evening. The last thing he remembered was stooping to collect the post; the next, waking up trussed and helpless in the sitting-room. He's even less communicative about this experience than he is about Mugabe's thugs, but when he reached hospital sixty hours later, he had five fractured ribs, a dislocated jaw and so many bruises his skin was a uniform purple.

My mother says he refused to tell MacKenzie anything and would probably have allowed himself to be punched and kicked to death if she hadn't decided to go back to the flat herself on Saturday afternoon. 'I knew something was wrong,' she said. 'I tried phoning him at the flat and on his mobile, but both went straight to voice messaging. Then I called you and the same thing happened.' She smiled rather ruefully. 'I could have murdered you that morning, Connie. I was so worried.'

'Sorry.'

She squeezed my hand. 'It all worked out for the best in the end. If you *had* answered . . . or if Jess had passed on my message a little more promptly . . . you'd have persuaded me to stay in the hotel. And where would your father be then?'

Six feet under, I thought. There's a limit to how much punishment anyone can take, and MacKenzie's frustration would have killed him eventually. He's a good old boy, my Dad – a *tough* old boy – but he's lucky one of his ribs didn't snap completely and puncture a lung. I asked my mother why she hadn't called the police, instead of going to the rescue herself, and she said it would have required too much explanation.

'Did *you* get the vigilante lecture?' I asked her.

She shook her head with a twinkle in her eyes. 'I burst into tears and said how foolish I'd been . . . but then I'm not as bull-headed as you and your father.'

In fact, despite a gut-feeling that Dad was in trouble, she was more inclined to think there was a rational explanation for the phones not being answered. As I had done, she wondered if he'd gone out for food or was refusing to answer because he'd instructed her not to contact him.

'I expected to have my head bitten off for meddling,' she admitted, 'but I couldn't let the nonsense go on. You must have known he'd do something silly when you refused to talk to him. There isn't a cut-off point when a man like your father stops trying to prove himself, Connie . . . any more than there is for you. I wish you'd learn that caring what others think is a form of slavery.'

Her safety net in the event of trouble – a little simplistic as things turned out – was to ask the taxi driver to wait while she went inside for his money. As he wouldn't leave until she paid him, she must either return with her wallet or force him to come knocking on the door. 'I was as naïve as your father,' she said. 'I should have realized the driver wouldn't care who handed over the money as long as he got it.'

MacKenzie must have been watching from the window because he was waiting behind the front door when Mum opened it. As soon as she was over the threshhold with her suitcase, he slammed it shut and had her mouth and hands bound with duct tape before she even reached the sitting-room. When the knocking began and an angry voice demanded payment, he calmly bundled her out of sight, took her wallet from her bag and paid up. 'He's not stupid,' she said reluctantly. 'Most people would have panicked.'

'Did *you*?' I asked her.

'I did when I saw your father. He looked terrible – face all bruised and misshapen – body curled into a ball to protect himself. He started crying when Mac-Kenzie threw me on the carpet beside him.' She shook her head. 'That's the only time I felt I shouldn't have gone back. Poor love. He was devastated. He'd tried so hard to protect me . . . and there I was.'

She had no qualms about bargaining my address against their lives. 'It would have been madness to do anything else,' she said. 'While there's life there's hope, and I knew you'd worry if you couldn't get me at the hotel. I prayed you'd phone that policeman friend of yours in Manchester. Your father was unhappy about it . . . but – ' she squeezed my hand again – 'I was sure you'd understand.'

I did. I do. Whatever nightmares I still have would be a thousand times worse if I was carrying my parents' deaths on my conscience. My mother believes my father's 'unhappiness' related entirely to his fears for me, but his concerns were rather more practical. He was appalled at her naïve assumption that a man like

MacKenzie would honour a promise to leave them alive if she gave him the information he wanted.

He tried to dissuade her, but his dislocated jaw had seized the muscles in his face, making speaking difficult. To stop any further attempts, MacKenzie muzzled him completely by winding several turns of duct tape round his head. The ironic upside was that, with his jaw supported, my father's pain lessened, and he survived the next twelve hours in considerably more comfort than he would otherwise have done. The downside was that it increased my mother's concern for him, thereby encouraging compliance.

'Weren't you worried that MacKenzie would kill you anyway?' I asked her.

'Of course . . . but what could I do? He threatened to strangle your father in front of me if I refused. At least there were slivers of hope if I betrayed you . . . none at all if I betrayed Brian.' A small crease of doubt furrowed her brow. 'You do see that, don't you, darling? It was a card game . . . and you were my only trump. I had to use you.'

I didn't know how to answer. *Absolutely . . .? Don't worry about it . . .? I'd have done the same . . .?* They were all just anodyne forms of words that meant nothing if she didn't believe them. 'Thank God you had enough faith in me,' I said bluntly. 'Dad wouldn't have done. He still thinks of me as a little girl in pigtails who screams every time she finds a spider in the shower.'

'Only because he loves you.'

'I know.' We exchanged smiles. 'He was very brave, Mum. Is his tail wagging now? It damn well ought to be.'

Her smile played around her eyes. 'You're so alike, you two. You both assume the only way to win is to show no weakness. You should have played bridge with Geraldine Summers. I've never known anyone conjure so many triumphs out of hands that contained nothing.'

'By bluffing? Is that what you did with MacKenzie?'

'I couldn't do anything until he removed my gag because he wanted the password to your father's laptop. Before that, he went through my suitcase. I told him he wouldn't find your address in the computer, but I suggested he read the email you sent to Alan Collins. I hoped he'd realize how pointless it would be to kill any of us.'

'What did he say?'

'That you'd chosen a good parallel in the story of the death-ray and the Chinaman. The only point of killing was to gain from it. He wasn't very talkative – I doubt he spoke more than twenty sentences from the moment I arrived – and he became extremely agitated when I asked what *he* gained from killing? That's when he said he'd strangle your father if I didn't tell him what he wanted . . . and the gain would be the look on both our faces when it happened.' She shook her head. 'And I'm sure he was telling the truth . . . I'm sure that's why he does it.'

I felt a shiver of goosebumps on my arms. 'Then why didn't he go ahead with it?'

'Because your address was my trump card, darling. Supposing I was lying? He had no way of checking unless he phoned you – which would have alerted you – so I persuaded him to take me along as security. It was the only bargaining chip I had . . . and it meant your father and I stayed alive for a few more hours. I felt I'd won the trick when he produced the car keys and demanded to know where the car was parked.' She laughed suddenly. 'Poor Brian! I don't know which offended him more . . . my pandering to the brute or the brute driving his precious BMW.'

'You know damn well,' I said severely. 'He was worried sick for you.'

Again, my father never speaks about the hours he lay on the sitting-room floor, except to say that his lowest moment was when I left my message and he couldn't answer. I know he imagined the worst – we all do when situations are outside our control – but it wasn't until the police broke into the flat in the early hours that the search began for my mother. She doesn't dwell on those hours either, several of which were spent in the BMW's boot, but her cramps were so severe by the time she was found that she had to be given morphine before her back and legs could be straightened out.

'It's only when the bidding starts that you realize how many cards you have,' she went on. 'The wretched man had to free me to walk to the car, and my price for not attempting to escape or draw attention to myself was that we left your father alive. If he could have put me in the boot immediately, I'm sure he'd have gone back to finish Dad off, but – ' another laugh – 'I've never been so glad of street parking before. You can't mistreat women with half of Kentish Town watching.'

There wasn't much else she could tell. She recalled MacKenzie tucking my father's mobile and binoculars, together with their two wallets, into a canvas knapsack, which he tossed on to the back seat of the BMW. Then he taped her hands and feet again and told her he was going to move her to the boot as soon as they were clear of built-up areas. He warned her to keep her mouth shut until he did or he'd tie her up so tight she wouldn't be able to breathe, but it wasn't until they'd passed the Fleet service station on the M3 that he left the motorway and made the transfer on a quiet country road.

He must have rejoined the motorway because my mother remembered constant traffic noise but, as happened to me in the cellar, she quickly lost track of time. She remembered one other stop of about ten minutes, which was probably when he sent me the text, and her last contact with him was five minutes after the engine died for good. She'd been in darkness for so long that, when the boot suddenly opened, she had to close her eyes against the daylight.

'He apologized,' she said. 'It was very strange.'

'For shutting you in?'

'No. For the fact that, if I'd given him the right address, he was going to come back and burn the car with me in it.' She gave a muted laugh. 'I presume he wanted me to panic but, you know, I was so tired by then I fell asleep . . . and the next thing I knew, the alarm was going like the clappers, and a rather jolly policeman was wrenching the boot open with a crowbar.'

It was all lies. She couldn't possibly have slept with the level of cramp she had when she was found, any more than my father could have passed 'a half-way reasonable night'.

From:	Dan@Fry.ishma.iq
Sent:	Sun 22/08/04 17.18
To:	connie.burns@uknet.com
Subject:	MacKenzie

Of course I'm upset that you didn't tell me at the time. I'm not made of stone, Connie.

What did you think I was going to do? Invoke your contract and force you to write the story with all the salacious details? Write it myself? Sell you to the highest bidder? I thought we trusted each other, C. I thought we loved each other . . . but maybe that was all on my side. Jesus! I'm not some fly-by-night. When have I ever not been there for you?

* * *

OK, I've calmed down a bit. I wrote that first paragraph three hours ago after reading your email. Now I've had some time to think, I realize I'm being unfair. I've decided not to delete the para because I want you to know that I *am* hurt. I wouldn't have done anything differently if you'd told me the truth . . . except perhaps protect you a little harder. Reading between the lines, I wonder if that's what you were afraid of? I'm sure it's no accident that the only person you felt you could trust in the last few months was a woman.

The newswires are short on detail. They're all naming MacKenzie and describing him as extremely dangerous and wanted for questioning re abduction and murder in the UK, Sierra Leone and Baghdad. But there appears to be a blackout where you're concerned. Is this at your request? Or is it something the police have imposed because you're still being questioned?

An answer ASAP would be helpful, as I'm already fielding questions re my piece on the Baycombe Group which named MacKenzie/O'Connell re passport fraud. How little/much should I say? Do you want it known that MacKenzie held you in the cellar? Or have you asked for anonymity under UK rape legislation?

AAGH! I can't believe what a tosser I was. I keep remembering that I told you to play-act some tears and milk the sympathy vote. I am SO sorry, C. Will you see me if I come to England? Or have I burnt my boats? I'm due some time off.

Love, Dan

PS. Sorry to be the journalist but do you have any updates on MacKenzie? Have there been any sightings, or do they think he's fled the country?

Twenty

'WHAT'S THE SECOND REASON?' Inspector Bagley asked, after reminding me that I'd said a man wouldn't understand why I was so calm. 'You said, "In the *first* place, my parent's aren't dead." What comes next?'

'Jess and Peter?' I suggested. 'I wouldn't be remotely calm if anything had happened to them.'

'No one would. Why should a man have trouble understanding that?'

'He wouldn't. It's what I thought of MacKenzie that he might have problems with. For a kick-off, I couldn't get over how *small* he was. He'd been in my head for so long as something monstrous that to find he was just a dirty little runt was ... strange. That doesn't mean he wasn't frightening ... but I had him in perspective for the first time, and it felt good.'

'Was?' he echoed. 'Had? Felt? Is he dead, Ms Burns?'

We'd been this route several times already. 'I don't see how he can be,' I said. 'I might wish it ... I might earnestly pray for it ... but he was alive the last time

I saw him. It depends on whether broken fingers can kill you . . . but I wouldn't have thought so.'

'If that's all that was wrong with him.'

I shrugged. 'Peter said it was.'

'You and Ms Derbyshire were alone with Mac-Kenzie for thirty minutes. A man can suffer a lot of damage in that time.'

'Then where is he? Why haven't you found him?'

'I don't know, Ms Burns. That's what I'm trying to discover.'

I showed my irritation. 'How about I turn the questions on you? What sort of police force allows a man to escape as easily as MacKenzie seems to have done? He can't have left the house much before you arrived . . . but it was two *hours* before you started searching the valley. He could have been anywhere by then . . . on a ferry out of Weymouth . . . on the train to Southampton airport. Have you checked those places?'

He gave an impatient nod as if the question didn't warrant an answer. 'We're more interested in your father's BMW, Ms Burns. That was his obvious choice of transport. It was parked less than half a mile down the valley – he could have been out of the area before anyone knew it was missing – yet he didn't return to it. I find that strange.'

'Me, too.'

Bagley hated it when I agreed with him. He seemed to think it was a form of mockery. 'Perhaps you have an explanation,' he murmured sarcastically. 'You seem to have explanations for everything else.'

'I expect he got lost,' I said. 'It happens to me all the time . . . and I only go walking in the daylight. It's a big valley. If you lose your bearings and take the wrong footpath, you end up at the Ridgeway instead of in the village. I suppose you've checked the empty houses in Winterbourne Barton? Perhaps, he's holed up in a weekender's cottage, eating their food and watching their telly. Or maybe he went the other way and fell off a cliff?'

There's no question Jess and I sparked an intense suspicion in him. He knew we couldn't have magicked MacKenzie out of existence in half an hour, but our attitude offended him. I was too glib, and Jess was too mute. According to Peter, who heard it from a friend on the force, she was no more forthcoming with the police than she was with anyone else.

What happened when you left the kitchen, Ms Derbyshire? I was jumped. *Can you be more explicit?* No. *Did you know who your assailant was?* I guessed. *Who removed your clothes?* He did. *Did you think he was going to rape you?* Yes. *Even with Dr Coleman and Ms Burns in the house?* Yes. *Did MacKenzie speak to you?* No. *Then why did you think he wanted to rape you?* He took my clothes off. *Can you be more explicit?* No. *Were you upset by your dog's death?* Yes. *Did you want revenge for Bertie?* Yes. *Did you want revenge for yourself?* Yes. *Did you take it?* No. *Why not?* There wasn't time. *But you would have done if the police hadn't arrived?* Yes.

Our worst fault seemed to be that we weren't frightened enough. With MacKenzie on the loose, we should have demanded round-the-clock police protection or seclusion in a safe house, but neither of us did. Jess refused to leave the farm because she couldn't rely on Harry and the girls to run it alone, and with search teams scouring the valley, I effectively had police protection anyway.

*

It was an odd few days. Although Jess and I were never arrested or charged with anything, we were both treated like suspects in a murder investigation. I was asked several times if I wanted a solicitor present, but I always refused on the basis that I had nothing to hide. I believe Jess did the same. The silver lining was that the press was held at bay while every nook and cranny of Winterbourne Valley was painstakingly examined, and the police withheld our names – including Peter's and my parents' – after Jess and I invoked our right to anonymity because of the nature of the crimes against us.

I was allowed to see my mother briefly in Dorset County Hospital before she was transferred back to London to be near my father, and I was able to speak to Dad on the phone. Because of his jaw, I did most of the talking, but he gave a couple of grunting laughs and seemed pleased when I suggested he and Mum come to stay as soon as the brouhaha died down. He managed a few sentences that I understood. 'Did we win? Are the demons dead?'

'Dead and buried,' I said.

'Good.'

Perhaps it was a mercy no one overheard that little exchange, because it would certainly have been misinterpreted. As would my conversation with Jess when the police finally ackowledged we'd had no hand in MacKenzie's disappearance. We were warned to expect further questioning if and when MacKenzie was taken into custody, but in reality it was a green light to pursue our lives as normal.

I hadn't seen or spoken to Jess since the early hours of Sunday morning. There was no official ban on our communicating with each other, but, with the continuous police presence in Barton House, neither of us felt inclined to do it. The telephone line was repaired almost immediately, more for police convenience than mine, but I was given permission to operate my laptop in the back bedroom when I explained that my boss in Baghdad deserved an explanation before MacKenzie's name appeared on the newswires.

For three days, the back bedroom and the kitchen were the only areas I was allowed to use. Even the bathroom was sealed off for forty-eight hours while the U-bend was taken apart for forensic examination. The same happened in the scullery. I asked Bagley what he was expecting to find since both drains had had bleach down them, but he said it was routine. I pointed out that it was routine for me to take regular baths and wash my clothes, and with bad grace he ordered the plumbing to be reinstated on the Monday afternoon.

On Wednesday evening, I watched Jess's Land-Rover nose up the drive less than half an hour after Bagley had taken his leave. I remember wondering how she knew he'd gone, and half-suspected she'd been squatting in her top field with binoculars. The one thing I knew about Jess was that her patience was inexhaustible. It had taken one hundred hours of filming to capture the antics of weasels on a fifteen-minute video loop.

'I hope you understand why all this was necessary, Ms Burns,' Bagley said as he left, offering me his hand in a gesture of peace.

I shook it briefly. 'Not really. Is it a job's-worth thing? Do policemen get chopped off at the knees if they don't go through the motions?'

'If that's how you want to see it.'

'I do,' I assured him. 'Peter tells me he's only been questioned twice . . . once to give his version . . . and the second time to confirm or deny what Jess and I said. That doesn't seem fair when we were all witnesses to the same crime.'

'What happened before Dr Coleman left isn't in

dispute. It's how MacKenzie freed himself and van-ished into thin air that interests us.'

I shrugged. 'Perhaps he used his SAS training.'

'I thought you believed the SAS claim was a lie.'

'I do,' I agreed, 'but it doesn't mean I'm right.'

There was a moment's silence before he gave an abrupt laugh. 'Well, that's something I never thought I'd hear.'

'What?'

'Ms Burns admitting she might be wrong.' He eyed me for a moment. 'I hope you and Ms Derbyshire know what you're doing.'

I felt the familiar flutter round my heart. 'In what way?'

'Staying put,' he said with mild surprise. 'I'm not sure either of you is strong enough to face MacKenzie again . . .'

*

There was something immensely reassuring about Jess's scowl as she stomped into the kitchen and put a bulging carrier bag on the table. 'I hate that bastard,' she said.

'Which one?'

'Bagley. Do you know what his parting shot was? "You've been thoroughly obstructive, *Ms* Derby-shire – "' she screwed her mouth into a Bagley sneer – ' "but Dr Coleman tells me you lack communication skills so I've given you the benefit of the doubt." Bloody wanker. I told him to get stuffed.'

'Peter?'

'Bagley.' Her eyes gleamed with sudden amusement. 'I'm holding Peter on ice. Christ knows what he said to them, but it sure as hell didn't do us any favours. Bagley seems to think we're a pair of Amazons. Did he ask you what your sexual orientation is?'

'No.'

'I suppose I have the idiots in the village to thank,' she said without animosity. 'He asked me if I thought it was worse for a lesbian to have her clothes taken off by a psychopath? What kind of question's that?'

'How did you answer?'

'Told him to fuck off.' She started unpacking the bag. 'I've brought you some food. Have you been eating properly?'

'Mostly sandwiches. The police have been ordering them in by the cartload.'

'Champagne,' she said, producing a bottle of Heidsieck. 'I don't know if it's any good . . . also, smoked salmon and quail's eggs. It's not the kind of thing I usually have but I thought you'd like it. The rest's off the farm.' She handed me the bottle. 'I reckon you've earned a little celebration.'

I couldn't resist a nervous look over my shoulder towards the drive. What would Bagley make of this? I wondered.

Jess read my mind. 'Bertie deserves a toast,' she said, taking some glasses from the cupboard, '*and* your parents. I don't see why we shouldn't remember them just because Bagley's got bees in his bonnet. Go on, open it. We'd all be dead but for you.'

That's not how I saw it. 'It was me who put you in danger in the first place,' I reminded her. 'If I'd never come here, it would never have happened.'

'Don't go feeble on me,' she said scornfully. 'You might as well blame your father for going back to the flat . . . or Peter for showing up when he did . . . or me for leaving the kitchen. You should be on cloud nine.'

'Keep talking like that and I will be,' I said more cheerfully, peeling the wire from the neck of the bottle. 'It's unnerving to have you ply me with drink and compliments, Jess.' I popped the cork and poured froth into one of the glasses. 'Are you going to have some?'

She inspected it as if it was devil's brew. 'Why not? I can always walk home.'

'When did you last have champagne?' I asked, wondering how drunk it was going to make her.

'Twelve years ago . . . on my mother's birthday.' She clinked her glass against mine. 'To Bertie,' she said. 'One of the good guys. I buried him in the top field under a little wooden cross with "For valour and gallantry" on it, and that bastard, Bagley, got his men to dig him up again to see if MacKenzie was underneath. Can you *believe* that? He said it was normal procedure.'

'To Bertie,' I echoed, 'and a plague on Bagley. What did you say to him?'

She took a tentative sip and seemed surprised when she didn't drop dead. 'Called him a grave robber. Peter was there when they did it, and he gave Bagley hell . . . kept asking him how I could have smuggled MacKenzie's body out of Barton House without anyone noticing. I don't think he realized until then what a bloody great hole he'd dug for us. You know he repeated our conversation about chopping MacKenzie's dick off? I got more questions about castration than anything else.'

I watched her thoughtfully over the rim of my glass. 'Mine were all about manipulation and control. Peter told them I knew what I was doing . . . even to the extent of giving your dogs commands.'

For the first time ever, Jess defended him. 'He was trying to give praise where praise was due. It backfired spectacularly . . . but he meant well.'

'What did they tell him *we* were saying?'

She flicked me an amused glance. 'Men are a waste of space.'

'Well, that didn't come from me. I might have thought it, but I didn't say it.'

She nodded. 'It was Peter quoting Bagley quoting me. I said something like "Men are useless in a crisis" but Bagley milked it for all it was worth. Did you accuse Peter of releasing MacKenzie?'

'Not exactly. I asked why he wasn't being given the third degree when he'd had the same opportunities that you and I had.'

'It was presented as a full-on accusation. According to Bagley, you bust a gut to implicate Peter, and it was only my evidence about timing that exonerated him.'

I took a mouthful of champagne. 'Is Peter upset about it?'

Jess shrugged. 'I don't know. He's being a bit odd at the moment.' She changed the subject. 'Madeleine phoned him to say she's coming down tomorrow. She spoke to someone in the village and they told her MacKenzie targeted you because you knew him from before. Now she wants to talk to whoever's in charge of the inquiry.'

'Why?'

Jess shrugged. 'Maybe she thinks there's money in it.'

'How?'

'Cheque-book journalism.' She rubbed her thumb and forefinger together. 'You're back in the news – or could be if your anonymity's blown. She'll sell your story like a shot if Bagley gives it to her. She was pumping Peter for all he was worth over the phone. Who was MacKenzie? Where had you met him? She said she'd read that he was wanted for abduction in

Iraq . . . and it wasn't difficult to put two and two together.'

'What did Peter say?'

'That he's been warned to keep his mouth shut in case it jeopardizes a future trial.' She picked up her glass and examined it. 'He says Bagley's bound to give her the details of what happened . . . if only to winkle out any information she might have.'

'What kind of information?'

'Anything. Madeleine lived here for over twenty years, don't forget. I'm sure she'll be asked if she has any ideas where MacKenzie might have gone. That's the only thing Bagley's interested in.'

Maybe champagne was as potent for me after four days of alcohol-abstinence as it was for Jess after twelve years, because my first instinct was to laugh. 'Do you have any idea how much it would piss me off to have Madeleine muscle in on the act? People might think we were *friends*.'

Jess grinned. It was the widest smile I'd ever see on her face. 'She told Peter she's coming here first to see how much damage was done. Do you want to play my trump card?'

It might have been my mother speaking. Was bridge a metaphor for life? 'Which one? You hold so many. Cousinship . . . Lily . . . Peter . . . Nathaniel . . . What matters most to her?'

Jess tapped her foot on the quarry tile floor. 'Barton

House,' she said. 'Lily rewrote her will at the same time she reassigned power of attorney to her solicitor. She gave him complete freedom to realize any of her assets to pay nursing-home fees, but if on her death Barton House still remains in her estate it's to come to me.'

I looked at her amazement. 'So what does Madeleine get?'

'Whatever money's left after all the bills have been paid.'

'I thought you said there wasn't any money.'

'There isn't . . . but there would be if the solicitor sold the house and invested the capital. It's worth about one point five million, and as soon as it's converted to cash it becomes part of Madeleine's inheritance, not mine.'

'God!' I took a swig of alcohol to oil my brain. 'So why is she blocking the sale?'

'Because she doesn't know the will's been changed. Neither of us was supposed to know. Lily only told me because she thought I was Gran. She said Madeleine would win or lose depending on how greedy she was . . . and if the house ended up with me then so be it.' Jess tugged at her fringe. 'I told you it was a mess,' she said ruefully. 'I tried to get Lily to change her mind, but it was too late by then. She didn't know what I was talking about five minutes later.'

'Are you sure she wasn't inventing it? Perhaps it was a fantasy will . . . something she'd like to have done, but never did.'

'I don't think so. I phoned the solicitor and said, if it was true, I didn't want to be involved but, instead of denying it – which he could have done – he said I had to take it up with Lily.'

'Did you tell him she was gaga?'

She sighed. 'No. I was afraid he'd come piling in to take charge and the will would have been set in stone. I thought if I stayed away Lily might have some lucid days, and Madeleine would get back into favour. I even wrote to the silly bitch and told her I'd fallen out with her mother . . . but she didn't act on it. If anything it encouraged her to neglect the poor old thing even more. She really did want her dead, you know.'

I wondered why she thought I needed convincing. It would take a lot to make me doubt Jess's word on anything. You don't face danger with someone only to start mistrusting them afterwards. 'Why don't you want the house?' I asked curiously. 'It's worth a bob or two. You could sell it and buy more land.'

Another shake of her head. 'I can't manage any more. In any case, Madeleine's bound to contest it . . . and what kind of hell will that be? I'm damned if I'll have a DNA test to prove I'm related to her. I don't even want it known.'

'Have you told Peter?'

She shook her head. 'I haven't told anyone.'

'Not even Nathaniel?'

She took another sip of champagne, but I couldn't tell if her look of disgust was for the liquid or for Madeleine's husband. 'No, but I think he guessed. When I told him about the power of attorney, he kept asking if the will had been changed as well. I said I didn't know – ' she broke off in irritation. 'He really bugged me that night . . . said I owed him a second chance because he'd supported me through the folks' death. Bloody joke, eh?'

I was tempted to ask, why that night in particular? Nathaniel Harrison would have bugged me *every* night. Instead, I said: 'Was this before or after your letter to Madeleine?'

'After.'

'Then I'll bet she put him up to it . . . or, more likely, came with him. Maybe they started on Lily and couldn't get any sense out of her, so Nathaniel tried you. You take everything he tells you on trust, Jess, but – *seriously* – what kind of man would leave an old lady to freeze to death just because he was annoyed with her? At the very least, he should have had a rethink the next day and phoned you or Peter to check she was all right.'

'I know,' she agreed, 'and I'm not trying to defend him, but if he told Madeleine about the power of attorney why didn't she do something about it?'

'Maybe she did. Maybe she and Nathaniel put the

fear of God into Lily to make her change her mind. If you want to coerce an old woman into doing what you want, turning off her heating supply is a good place to start.' I paused. 'I've been thinking about this a lot over the last few days, Jess, and whichever way I look at it, I'm convinced Madeleine knows there's a relationship between you. She's too OTT about your family. If you're not Down's syndrome, syphilitic or servants, you're tenants with bad genes who die young.'

'She got all that from Lily.'

'*And* the rest,' I said slowly. 'Perhaps Lily felt lonely after her husband died and wanted to reconcile with her brother . . . and made the mistake of thinking her daughter would feel the same. Perhaps that's what the allowance was about . . . compensation for being related to plebs.'

Jess threw me a withering look.

'It's how Madeleine sees you. Lily, too, if you're honest.'

'I know.' She glanced back down a bleak corridor of time. 'She treated my father like dirt until Robert died, then she was all over him. Do this . . . do that . . . and he did it. I remember telling him he was embarrassing us. It's the only time he shouted at me.'

'What did he say?'

Her eyes narrowed in memory. 'That he'd expect a remark like that from Madeleine, but not from me. God! Do you suppose that's what he had to put up with – Madeleine screaming and yelling and calling him an embarrassment? Poor old Pa. He wouldn't have known what to do. He always ran away from arguments.'

'Did he know Lily asked you to take the photograph?'

She nodded. 'He put pressure on me to do it because he said it would be kind. Lily was at the farm one day and saw some of my other stuff. She asked if I'd be willing to do one of Madeleine before she left for London. She wanted a portrait shot – the sort of things studios do – ' Jess injected scorn into the words – 'but I said I'd only do it if I could have the sea in the background.' She lapsed into a thoughtful silence.

'And?'

Jess shrugged. 'Madeleine spent most of the time scowling or simpering – all the other negatives are crap – but that one came out OK. It's weird. I started off being half-way nice to her, but it wasn't until I told her what I really thought of her that she turned and gave me that smile.'

'Perhaps she took it as proof that you didn't know you were related to her. That would make her smile, wouldn't it?' I raised inquiring eyebrows. 'She was probably worried sick while you were being nice . . . particularly if it was out of character.'

Jess's frown was ferocious. 'Then she's even more stupid than I thought she was. What makes her think I'd admit to having a talentless slapper for a cousin?'

I hid a smile. 'So stop bellyaching. Move on. Let her go.'

'Is that what you'd do?'

'No.'

'What would you do?'

'Get her to retract every bit of slander she'd ever spread about me and my family, then tell her to go fuck herself.' I tipped my glass to her. 'Personally, I can't see it matters a damn whether you're a Wright or a Derbyshire – to me you're *Jess*, a unique individual – but if the Derbyshire name means something to you then fight for it.'

'How can I?' she asked. 'The minute I admit I'm a Wright, the Derbyshires cease to exist.'

I don't know if it was a good thing or a bad thing that I couldn't identify with this view. I certainly wasn't as sensitive towards her turmoil as I might have been, but I've never viewed labels as much of a guide to what's in a package. 'If you want to be pedantic, Jess, they ceased to exist when your father was born. The last surviving member was your great-grandfather, an alcoholic blackmailer who saw an opportunity to grab some land and took it. It was probably the single most effective thing a Derbyshire ever did, but I guarantee the farm would be a wasteland today if your father hadn't come as part of the deal.'

She stared unhappily at her hands. 'That's worse than anything Madeleine's ever said.'

'Except the Wrights are no better,' I went on. 'The

only one who had any get-up-and-go was the old boy who bought the house and the valley, but his successors were a useless bunch – lazy . . . mercenary . . . self-obsessed. By some fluke, probably because your grandmother's genes were so strong, your father didn't inherit those traits – and neither have you – but Madeleine has them in spades.'

'So? It still doesn't make me a Derbyshire.'

'But it's a good name, Jess. Your grandmother, father and mother were happy with it . . . your brother and sister, too, presumably. I don't understand why you're so unwilling to fight for it.'

She rubbed her head in confusion. 'I am. That's why I don't want any of this to get out.'

'It won't,' I said, 'not if you keep it between you and Madeleine.'

Her unhappiness grew. 'You mean blackmail her?'

'Why not? It worked for the Derbyshires last time.'

Twenty-one

I HAD TO admire Madeleine's flair for duplicity. She appeared with a concerned smile at eleven o'clock the next morning and said she'd just come from Peter, who'd been telling her about the awful events of the previous weekend. She looked cool and pretty in a white cotton shirtwaister, and I thought how well she confirmed my mother's advice that no one should judge a book by its cover.

'I had no idea you and Barton House were involved until I spoke to Peter,' she said with convincing sincerity. 'The papers talked about Dorset, but didn't specify where. You must have been terrified, Connie. This man sounds appallingly violent.'

She used my name with casual ease, even though it was only a few days since she'd left a message calling me Marianne. 'Come in,' I invited, pulling the door open. 'How nice to see you.' She had no monopoly on duplicity.

Her eyes darted about, looking for anything unusual, and she found it immediately. Despite the efforts of a professional cleaner, brought in by the police, and further attempts by me and Jess the previous evening, the bloodstains on the unsealed flagstones and porous fifties wallpaper refused to come out. They were more the colour of mud than freshly spilt haemoglobin, but it didn't take much imagination to work out what they were.

Madeleine clapped her hands to her mouth and gave a little cry. 'Oh, my goodness!' she squeaked. 'Whatever's happened here?'

It was a girly response – the sort of thing clichéd actresses do – but it was genuine enough to persuade me that Peter hadn't told her much. If anything at all. Jess had been certain the previous evening that, when it came to taking sides, he'd pick me and her over Madeleine, but I wasn't so easily convinced. In my experience he had verbal diarrhoea where Madeleine was concerned.

I led her towards the green baize door. 'Didn't Peter tell you?' I asked in surprise. 'How very strange of him.'

'Is it blood?' she demanded, her heels pecking across the flagstones behind me. 'Did someone die?'

I shook my head, pushing open the door and ushering her through. 'Nothing so dramatic. Jess's dogs had a fight and one of them was wounded. It looks worse than it is.' I shepherded her down the corridor. 'Would you like a coffee?' I asked, pulling out a chair for her. 'Or are you caffeined out on Peter's espressos?'

She ignored me to wave her hand rather wildly towards the hall. 'It can't stay like that,' she protested. 'What will prospective tenants think?'

I retreated to the worktop. 'I'm told the flagstones will come up good as new if the top layer is sanded off,' I said, ostentatiously lighting a cigarette. 'I'll have it done before I leave.'

'What about the walls?'

'Those, too.'

She looked suspiciously around the kitchen and I wondered if she'd noticed the faint hum that was coming from the scullery, or the two loops of fabric tape at either end of the Aga rail. 'What were the dogs fighting about?'

I shrugged. 'Whatever dogs usually fight about. I'm not much of an expert, I'm afraid. Should I stick to the same colour scheme, or would your mother's solicitor prefer something different?'

'I don't –' she stopped abruptly. 'Did it happen while this man was here?'

'Didn't Peter tell you?'

She folded herself on to the chair, placing her bag on the floor beside her feet. 'Not every detail. I think he wanted to shield me from the worst.'

'Why?'

'Presumably because he didn't want to worry me.'

'I see.'

She had trouble with short answers. In her world everyone played the game and readily divulged their scrubby little pieces of gossip. She forced a smile. 'Peter's so sweet. He kept it as low-key as possible to avoid upsetting me but the truth is, I'd rather have had the details. It is my house, after all.'

'Oh dear,' I murmured, tapping ash into the sink, which brought an immediate scowl to her face, 'that means I've given the wrong information to the police. I told them it belonged to your mother. I believe Peter did as well. He even supplied them with the solicitor's address ... the one who has power of attorney.'

She kept the smile in place. Just. 'It's the family home.'

I nodded. 'You told me last time.'

She opened her mouth as if to say, 'Well then,' but seemed to think better of it. 'The papers said this man – MacKenzie – held three people captive then escaped before the police arrived. Was Jess one of the three? You said her dogs were here.'

'I said they a had fight,' I corrected mildly.

'While MacKenzie was here?'

'Jess's mastiffs are better guard dogs than that.'

Her impatience got the better of her. 'Then who *was* here? You must see how worrying it is for me to know that a man broke in so easily with three people on the premises. Did one of them let him in? What did he want? Was he after something in the house?'

'Why don't you ask your mother's solicitor?' I suggested. 'I'm sure he'll be able to set your mind at rest. Or even the police. I can give you the name of the detective leading the inquiry.'

'I already know it,' she snapped. 'I've asked to see him this afternoon.'

'Then there isn't a problem,' I pointed out reasonably. 'He'll tell you as much as he can.'

She stared at me for a moment, trying to assess if there was any mileage in continuing, then with a shrug reached for her bag. 'You'd think the crown jewels had been stolen the way everyone's behaving.'

'Well, you can be reassured on that front at least,' I said with a small laugh. 'MacKenzie didn't think there was anything worth stealing ... so your husband's paintings are still here.'

She threw me a look of dislike. 'Perhaps he was targeting my mother's antiques. Perhaps he didn't know she'd left.'

'That was Inspector Bagley's first idea,' I agreed, 'which is why he wanted a list of anything that had struck me as unusual since I took over the tenancy. I said there were several things ... but I didn't think they were connected with Saturday's events.'

Madeleine froze. Only briefly, but enough for me to notice. 'Like what?'

I blew a ring of smoke towards the ceiling. 'The water had been turned off.'

It was a guess, much like the guesses I'd made about MacKenzie's mother, but as I'd said to Jess the previous evening, why stop at turning off the Aga?

Why not the water? I couldn't get it out of my head that Jess had found Lily beside the fishpond. Or that memory might have told her there was a well under the logs in the woodstore? What was she doing outside at eleven o'clock at night? And why did she go to other people's houses to clean her teeth and have a cup of tea?

'That wasn't me,' Madeleine said abruptly, searching through her bag so that she wouldn't have to look at me. 'It must have been the agent. The stopcock's under the sink. All you had to do was turn it back on again.'

'I didn't mean it was off when I arrived,' I told her. 'The taps in the kitchen were fine. The problem was upstairs. There was so much air in the water pipes to the bathroom taps that they all started banging. It scared the living daylights out of me.'

'It's an old house,' she said carefully. 'Mummy was always complaining about the pipes.'

'I called in a plumber because I was so worried, and the first thing he did was check the stopcock. According to him, air gets into a system when the main supply is interrupted and people keep trying the taps because they don't understand why nothing's coming out. Water runs out downstairs and air fills the void upstairs. He said it could only have happened while someone was living here . . . and that must have been your mother because the house was empty till I took it on.'

She took a tissue from her bag and touched it to the end of her nose. 'I don't know anything about the water system. All I know is that Mummy said the pipes were always banging.'

I was relying very heavily on the fact that she knew nothing about the water system. Or any other system. My 'oddities' were courtesy of Jess. 'Try Madeleine with the electricity as well,' she said. 'The night I found Lily, the house was in darkness and I couldn't get the outside lights to work. That's the main reason I took her back to the farm. I didn't want to waste time trying to find out which of her fuses had blown. Everything was working fine the next day, and I rather forgot about it.'

'Something else that was unusual,' I went on, 'was that several of the fuse cartridges had been removed from the electricity box. If Jess hadn't been here, I'd have spent my first night in darkness because none of the lights in the bedrooms worked. It was only when she checked the box that we discovered why. They were laid in a row on the top of the case . . . and as soon as they were plugged back in the lights came on.'

Madeleine played with her tissue.

'Do you know who might have done that? The police are wondering if an electrician did some work. If so, how did he get in? They're very keen to find anyone who's had access to the house in the last six to nine months. They're wondering if your mother let him in . . . but why would he leave her in darkness?'

She shook her head.

'The *really* strange thing,' I said, reaching into the sink to turn on the tap and drown my fag end, 'is that the valve on the oil tank was turned off but the gauge was reading full. And that doesn't make any sense, because Burton's last delivery was at the end of November . . . and your mother didn't go into a nursing-home until the third week in January. It meant she had no hot water or cooking facilities for the last two months she was here.' I paused. 'But how could that have happened without you knowing? Did you not visit her during that time?'

Madeleine found her voice at last. 'I couldn't,' she said rather curtly as if it was a criticism she'd faced before. 'My son was ill and I was helping Nathaniel prepare for an exhibition. In any case, Peter came in regularly so I would have expected to hear from him if anything was wrong.'

'But not from Jess,' I said matter-of-factly. 'She'd already written to tell you that she'd withdrawn her support from Lily.'

'I don't recall that.'

'I'm sure you do,' I said, taking a copy of Jess's letter from my pocket. 'Do you want to remind yourself of what she said. No? Then I'll do the honours.' I isolated a passage. ' "Whatever's gone before, your mother needs your help now, Madeleine. Please do not go on ignoring her. For a number of reasons, I can no longer visit, but it's in your interests to come

down and organize some care for her. Without support, she cannot stay at Barton House alone. She's
more confused than Peter realizes but if you allow
him or anyone else to decide on her competence you
might regret it."' I looked up. 'All of which was true,
wasn't it?'

She abandoned denial in favour of protest. 'And
why should I believe it when Mummy's GP was saying
the opposite? If you knew Jess better, you'd know that
stirring up trouble is her favourite pastime . . . particularly between me and my mother. I wasn't going to
take her word against Peter's.'

I showed surprise. 'But you and Nathaniel drove
down as soon as you received this letter . . . so you
must have given it some credence.'

There was a brief hesitation. 'That's not true.'

I went on as if she hadn't spoken: 'You sent
Nathaniel to find out from Jess what "regret" meant
while you stayed here and tried to prise it out of your
mother. Did she tell you? Or did you have to wait for
Nathaniel to come back with the bad news about the
power of attorney?'

I watched her mouth thin to a narrow line. 'I've no
idea what you're talking about. The first I heard about
the solicitor being in charge was when Mummy was
taken into care.'

'That's good,' I said encouragingly, 'because when
I told Inspector Bagley about the utilities being turned

off, he said it sounded as if Lily had been subjected to a terror campaign. He's wondering if it had something to do with MacKenzie.' I paused. 'I told him it couldn't have done – MacKenzie was in Iraq between November and January – but, as Bagley said, if not MacKenzie, who? What kind of person deprives a confused old lady of water, light, heat and food?'

Perhaps I should have predicted her answer – Jess certainly did – but I honestly hadn't realized how slow-witted Madeleine was. The old adage about tangled webs might have been written for her. She was so caught up in the knowledge of what she and Nathaniel had done that the obvious answer – 'There was nothing wrong with this house when I prepared it for let' – escaped her.

The intelligent response would have been surprised disbelief – 'a *terror* campaign?' – and a finger pointed straight at Lily and her Alzheimer's: 'It must have been Mummy who did it. You know what old people are like. They're always worrying about the cost of living.' Instead, she offered me her pre-prepared 'culprit'. In some ways it was laughable. I could almost hear her brain whirring as she produced the 'line' that she and Nathaniel had rehearsed.

'There's only one person in Winterbourne Barton who's that disturbed,' she said, looking me straight in the eye. 'I tried to warn you but you wouldn't listen.'

Her eagerness to implicate Jess was faintly disgusting.

She looked pleased, as if I'd finally asked a question that she knew the answer to. 'Jess?' I suggested.

'Of course. She was obsessed with my mother. She was always creating problems so that Mummy would have to call her up. Her favourite trick was to put the Aga out because she was the only one who knew how to relight it.' She leaned forward. 'It's not her fault – a psychiatrist friend says she probably has Munchausen's syndrome by proxy – but it never occurred to me she'd go as far as turning off the water and the electricity.'

I smiled doubtfully. 'So why didn't she follow through?'

'On what?'

'Milking the benefits. Munchausen's by proxy is an attention-seeking syndrome. It needs an audience. Sufferers make other people ill so that they can present themselves in a caring light.'

'That's exactly what she did. She wanted Mummy to be grateful to her.'

I shook my head. 'It's not the *victim* who's the audience – victims tend to be babies and toddlers who can't speak for themselves – it's the sympathy and admiration of neighbours and doctors that sufferers want.'

Annoyance hardened her eyes. 'I'm not an expert. I'm merely repeating what a psychiatrist told me.'

'Who's never met Jess, and doesn't know that she's so reluctant to attract attention to herself that hardly anyone in Winterbourne Barton knows her.'

'You don't know her either,' she snapped. 'It was Mummy's attention she wanted – her *undivided* attention – and she lost interest as soon as the Alzheimer's took over. She was happy being the constant companion but she wasn't going to play nursemaid. That's what that letter was about – ' she jerked her chin towards the piece of paper – 'shuffling off the responsibility as soon as it became arduous.'

'What's wrong with that? She wasn't even related to Lily.'

There was the shortest of hesitations. 'Then she had no business to insist on Mummy being sectioned. Why was it done in such a hurry? What was Jess trying to hide?'

'Peter told me it was social services who ordered it, and they did it for her own safety. It was a temporary measure while they tried to locate you and her solicitor. Jess wasn't involved . . . except to give them your phone number and the name of the solicitor.'

'That's Jess's story. It doesn't mean it's true. You should ask yourself why Mummy had to be silenced so abruptly . . . and why Jess was so keen to accuse everyone else of neglecting her. If that's not attention-seeking, I don't what is.'

If you repeat a lie often enough people start to believe it – it's a truism that's seared into the brains of tyrants and spin doctors – but of all Madeleine's lies, the most pernicious was her use of 'Mummy'. She used it to paint a picture of innocent love that didn't exist, and I was amazed at how many people found it charming. Most of those who condemned Jess as unnatural for hanging pictures of her dead family on her walls never questioned whether Madeleine's relationship with Lily was healthy and close.

'But Lily *was* neglected, Madeleine. As far as I can make out, she lived here for seven weeks in the most appalling conditions until Jess found her half-dead beside the fishpond. Peter went away . . . the surgery safety net didn't work . . . the neighbours weren't interested . . . and you stayed as far away as possible.' I took out another cigarette and rolled it between my fingers. 'Or *claim* you did.'

'What's that supposed to mean?' she demanded.

'Only that I find it hard to believe you didn't keep tabs on what was going on.' I tucked the cigarette in my mouth and lit it. 'Weren't you and Lily close? You always call her "Mummy". The only other middle-aged woman I know who does that phones her mother every day and visits at least once a week.'

Her eyes narrowed to unattractive slits at being called middle-aged but she chose to ignore it. 'Of course I phoned her. She told me everything was fine. I realize now it wasn't true, but I didn't at the time.'

I smiled doubtfully. 'It must upset you, though. I'd be mortified if my mother didn't feel able to tell me she was in trouble. I can just about understand why she wouldn't ask strangers for help . . .

although she seems to have tried by going to the village. But her *daughter*? Wouldn't she have been straight on the phone to you as soon as the water failed?'

'You should ask Jess that question. She was always the first person Mummy called in a crisis. Why didn't *she* do anything?'

'Who was the second?'

Madeleine frowned. 'I don't understand.'

'Who did your mother phone when Jess wasn't available? You?'

'I was too far away.'

'So Jess turfed out every single time. For how long? Twelve years? And before that her father? Was either of them ever paid?'

'It wasn't a question of payment. They did it because they wanted to.'

'Why? Because they were so fond of Lily?'

'I've no idea what their reasons were. I always found it rather sad . . . as if they couldn't get over the class barrier. Perhaps they felt they had to follow in Jess's grandmother's steps and play servant to the big house.'

I gave a snort of laughter. 'Have you ever actually been to Barton Farm, Madeleine? The house is marginally smaller than this, but it's in a lot better repair. At a rough guess, and with all the land she has, I'd say Jess's estate is worth two or three times your mother's. If she ever sold up, she'd be a millionairess. Why on earth would someone like that want to play servant to impoverished gentry?'

She smiled faintly. 'You're assuming she owns the property.'

'I'm not assuming anything. I know it for a fact. I believe you do, too.' I took a thoughtful puff of my cigarette. 'But why does it matter to you so much that everyone should think she's a tenant?' I went on curiously. 'Does it stick in your throat that her family built on their successes while yours frittered theirs away?'

As a lure, it almost worked. 'They wouldn't have anything if it hadn't been for – ' She clamped her mouth shut suddenly.

I tapped more ash into the sink to ratchet up her irritation. 'You're lucky she's so self-effacing. If Winterbourne Barton knew she was the richest woman in the valley, you wouldn't get a look-in. They'd be queueing up to lick her arse.'

If looks could kill, I'd have had a dagger in my chest. 'There wouldn't be room,' she snarled. 'They'd have to get you out of the way first. Everyone knows you're her latest conquest.'

My eyes watered as I choked on some smoke. 'Do you mean her latest *fuck*? I might have thought about it if she wasn't shagging Peter every night. Wouldn't you say that's a fairly good indication that she prefers cocks to cunts?'

'You're disgusting.'

'Why?' I murmured in surprise. 'Because I said she shags blokes? Surely Nathaniel's told you what a good lay she is? I gather they went at it like rabbits before you muscled in on the act. He's down here all the time, trying to resurrect the good old days. He was even here the night Jess found Lily.'

A flicker of something showed in her eyes. Fear? She looked away before I could decide. 'That's rubbish.'

'Then who turned the utilities back on before Lily's solicitior and social services came in?'

It was like pressing the 'on' button. As long as I fed her questions she'd prepared for, she could produce her rehearsed answers. 'Jess, of course,' she said confidently. 'She was the only one who knew Mummy had collapsed. Everything she did was designed to cover her tracks. She could have phoned for an ambulance or put Mummy back to bed herself and called a doctor . . . but instead she drove her to the farm and waited till the morning to bring in social services. Why did she do that if it wasn't to give herself time to put things straight at Barton House?'

'It was too cold to wait for an ambulance, so Jess took Lily back to the farm and called the surgery as soon as she got there. A locum turned up an hour later – by which time your mother was cleaned, fed, warm and fast asleep – and he advised Jess to leave her where she was until the morning. I thought you knew all this.'

'Why at the farm, though? Why not here?'

'Because it would have meant carrying your mother fifty yards just to get her to the back door, and she couldn't see anything because none of the outside lights were working,' I said patiently. 'Instead, she drove the Land-Rover on to the lawn and lifted Lily into it. Her first plan was to take Lily to hospital herself, but as soon as your mother was in the warmth of the cab, and wrapped in the dogs' blanket, she perked up and asked for food.' I eyed Madeleine curiously. 'Peter told me all this within a week of my arrival. Did he not tell you? I thought you were such friends.'

'Of course he did,' she snapped, 'but he's only repeating Jess's story. He doesn't know it for a fact because he wasn't here.'

I shrugged. 'Then what did the locum say in the messages he left on your answerphone? Or social services? Did they give different explanations?'

'I didn't listen to them all. The only one that mattered was Mummy's solicitor saying she'd been taken into care . . . and I responded to that as soon as I got back from holiday.'

'So you didn't hear the message that Jess left at twelve-thirty to say your mother was at the farm? The locum was with her when she did it. She told you you had twelve hours to take charge before the surgery alerted social services.' I folded my arms and watched her closely. 'She gave you every chance, Madeleine, but you didn't take it.'

'How could I? I was away.'

'Nathaniel wasn't.'

'That's not true. Nathaniel wasn't in the flat either. He took our son to visit his parents in Wales. It's something he does every year. Ask my in-laws if you don't believe me.'

'It's quite easy to pick up messages from a distance . . . and most of Wales is no farther from Dorset than London is. At a guess, it was you who turned the utilities off and Nathaniel who raced down here to put them back on before social services came in the next morning.'

'That's ridiculous,' she said, her breath hissing angrily through clenched teeth.

'No one else had a reason to make Lily's life miserable.'

'*Jess* did.'

'I can't see it,' I said. 'I don't think the police will either. She wouldn't have written to you if it meant you'd find out she'd been mistreating your mother.'

'What reason did *I* have?'

'I'm not sure,' I said honestly. 'At first I thought you were trying to coerce her into reassigning the power of attorney . . . but now I think it was straight-forward cruelty. You punished her because she wasn't mentally competent to do what you wanted . . . and then found you enjoyed it. Simple as that. It's why most sadists do what they do.'

She stood up abruptly. 'I don't have to listen to this.'

'I suggest you do,' I said mildly, 'otherwise you'll be hearing it from Inspector Bagley. So far I've told him very little, but only because your mother didn't die. If she had, we wouldn't be having this conversation . . . you'd be at the police station answering questions about murder. You'll just answer different ones if you walk out now.'

'No one's going to believe you.'

'I wouldn't rely on that. It just needs a chink of doubt.' I tossed my still smoking butt into the sink. 'Your problem's the Aga. Burton's delivery notes prove it was off for two months. But if Jess had been responsible for that she'd have relit it . . . because she's the only one who knows how.'

Madeleine shook with suppressed anger. 'I suppose she put you up to this. She's always hated me . . . always told lies about me.'

'Is that right? I thought lies were your specialty.' I ticked my fingers. 'Predatory lesbian . . . stalker . . . obsessive . . . mentally ill . . . servant mentality . . . tenant farmer . . . syphilitic grandmother . . . hates men . . . only has sex with dogs. What have I left out? Oh, yes. Your grandfather had a yen for maids and raped every poor girl who entered his service, including Jess's grandmother.'

She looked shell-shocked. 'I'll sue you for slander if you repeat that.'

'The bit about the rape? Is that not true? I thought he handed over fifteen hundred acres in compensation after his son was born? It was cheap at the price . . . the land cost him nothing and his reputation would have been in ruins if Jess's grandmother had gone to the police.'

'It's all lies,' she hissed. 'There was no saying who the father was. Mrs Derbyshire was a tramp . . . she slept with anyone and everyone.'

I shrugged. 'It's easily proved by a DNA test. The closest match will be Jess and your mother.'

'I won't allow it.'

'It's not your permission to give. Lily handed that right to her solicitor.' I smiled at her. 'It'll make a grand story. Skeletons rattle in Wright closet as DNA proves link. Abuse jumps a generation as failed artist's wife seeks to silence mother. Career scrounger cites class as justification for sadism . . .'

Jess had predicted she'd take a swipe at me if I provoked her enough – *'Lily was afraid of Madeleine, and her kid's completely terrified'* – so I should have been expecting it. But she still managed to take me by surprise. I've come to the conclusion that I'm really quite naïve about the levels of violence that some people are prepared to use. I shouldn't be – I've seen too much of it in Africa and the Middle East – but my experience of war is different. I've always been a bystander, and never a participant.

MacKenzie should have taught me the dangers of complacency. And he did, as far as he was concerned. But it never occurred to me that a twisted psychopath, who raped and mutilated women, had anything in common with a Dresden china blonde in high heels and an elegant shirtwaister. I should have paid more attention to Jess. From day one, she had described Madeleine as a manipulative, narcissistic personality of shallow emotions, who demanded instant gratification, resorted to bullying when she didn't get it, and showed no remorse for the impact her behaviour had on others.

And that's as good a definition of a psychopath as you'll find.

Twenty-two

I'D EXPECTED A slap across the face, not an all-out assault on my eyes with crimson fingernails. I was on the floor, shielding my head from her kicking shoes, almost before I knew she'd attacked me. It was very fast and very noisy. I remember her screaming 'Bitch' as she grabbed me by the hair and spun me round so that she could aim at my face, but I curled into a tight ball and took most of the punishment on my arms and back.

She wasn't fit enough to keep it up for long. The kicks became less frequent as her mouth took over. How dare I question her? Didn't I know who she was? Who did I think *I* was? It was an interesting insight into her character. At no point did she consider the consequences of what she was doing or whether my provocation had been deliberate. Quite simply, a red mist descended and she went ape.

I won't pretend it wasn't painful – her shoes were leather with pointed toes – but it was a walk in the park compared with Baghdad. Her balance was precarious, her aim was bad, and her foot had very little weight behind it. I put up with it because anger, like alcohol, loosens tongues, and she thought my refusal to fight back meant she had nothing to fear.

'It was the best day of my life when the Derbyshires died . . . the only one left was the runt . . . and she was so feeble she tried to kill herself. I told my mother she should have let her bleed to death . . . and do you know what she said? Be *nice* . . . you *owe* it to her . . . you have *Nathaniel*. God, I hated her! She couldn't keep her mouth shut . . . *had* to talk to her brother . . . *had* to apologize . . . wanted *me* to call him uncle. I said I'd rather die than admit I was related to a slut's bastard . . . and he *laughed* and said the feeling was mutual. Then he had the nerve to beg my mother to keep the secret . . . for the sake of *his* children . . .'

She referred obliquely to the cruelty she and Nathaniel had inflicted on Lily. 'I told Nathaniel no one would help her . . . she was such a bitch they never went near her. Even Peter wasn't that bothered . . . he said the troll would always tell him if things got worse. Blame *her* for neglect . . . she's the one who walked away and left me to deal with it . . . as if *I* was the servant . . .'

I'd have let her run her head even farther into the noose if she hadn't decided to grind her heel into my hip bone. Enough was enough. I was out from under her heel and on my feet while her gabby mouth was still flapping about her status in life, and she wasn't ready for the pile-driving charge that drove her against the Aga rail and knocked the wind out of her.

I don't think she noticed when I slipped her right wrist through a fabric loop and pulled it tight, but she certainly struggled as I grabbed her left wrist and yanked it the other way. 'My God, you really are a piece of work,' I said in disgust before raising my eyes to the webcam on a cupboard next to the sink. 'Did you get all that, Jess?'

Jess pushed the scullery door wide and the sound of her hard-drive fan intruded noticeably into the kitchen. 'The camera in the hall failed,' she said, coming in, 'but the three in here worked perfectly. Are you OK? It looked pretty bad on screen but as you didn't yell – ' she broke off to stare at Madeleine. 'I don't think she's ever taken on anyone of her own size before . . . just frail old ladies and children.'

I rubbed my shoulder gingerly where a bruise was beginning to form. 'Not so different from MacKenzie then. I wonder what else they have in common.'

'Arrogance,' said Jess, examining the other woman curiously as if she'd never seen her before. 'I should have guessed it was Dad who wanted it kept secret. He used to say if any of us pretended we were better than we were, he'd disown us. I thought it was because we came from working stock, but now – ' she jerked her chin at Madeleine – 'I think he was terrified we'd turn into this.'

*

Madeleine's ignorance of Jess's proficiency in computer technology and film-making meant we could only convince her of what we had by moving Jess's hard-drive and monitor into the kitchen, playing the scene again from the perspective of three different cameras, and demonstrating how easy it was to copy the images to disk. She harangued us fluently throughout, accusing us of blackmail and kidnap – both of which were true – but when I retrieved a pack of envelopes from the office and started addressing them to the inhabitants of Winterbourne Barton, she quietened down.

'You can have a go at persuading the neighbours it was a joke or a piece of play-acting,' I told her, 'but it doesn't show you in your best light, does it?' I glanced thoughtfully at the muted monitor. 'I wonder what your smart friends in London will make of it.'

Madeleine stopped trying to wrestle her wrists free and took a deep breath. 'What do you want?'

'Me personally? I'd like to see you charged with attempted murder of your mother and assault on me but – ' I gestured towards Jess – 'your cousin's even less inclined to admit a relationship with you than her father was . . . and she won't have a choice if we send these disks out and the police become involved. The easiest solution will be for you to instruct Lily's solicitor to sell this house. That way you can cut your ties with Winterbourne Barton and Jess can keep the secret.'

She gave an angry laugh. 'Is this some sort of joke?'

'No.' I wrote on another envelope.

She wrenched at the fabric tape again. 'I'll have you prosecuted for this.'

'I doubt it. You may be the stupidest woman I've ever met, but you're not *that* stupid.'

'Go ahead,' she spat. 'Make as many copies as you like. There's no better proof that you set out to blackmail me. What does a film prove? I'll say you held me prisoner and forced me to do it.'

'The cameras are still running,' I said mildly. 'Every word that comes out of your mouth is being recorded.'

'Yours, too,' she hissed. 'Are you going to try and claim this isn't blackmail?'

'No. We'll give you one hour to make up your mind – we'll even let you consult with Nathaniel via loudspeaker phone – but if you don't call your mother's solicitor at the end of it . . . and if he doesn't confirm to Jess that the house will be up for sale at the end of my tenancy – ' I put my hand on the envelopes – 'these will be on everyone's doorsteps in the morning. Including Bagley's.'

'What if I refuse? Are you planning to keep me prisoner for ever? What do you think Nathaniel's going to do when I tell him you've tied me up?'

'Give you some good advice, I hope. We'll let you go at the end of the hour whatever you decide. You can have your interview with Bagley and say whatever you like about us. You can do the same in the village. You'll have twelve hours to convince everyone that we forced you to implicate yourself before we mail-drop our version.'

'You're mad,' she said in disbelief. 'The police won't let you.'

'Then take the gamble,' I urged. 'You've nothing to lose.'

None of us spoke again until Jess had connected the loudspeaker phone from the office to the socket in the kitchen. She set the dialling tone buzzing through the amplifier. 'Is he at the flat?' she asked Madeleine. 'OK.' She punched in a series of numbers from a piece of notepaper. 'Your hour starts as soon as he picks up.'

Madeleine wasted the first five minutes by gabbling at high speed and high volume about being taken prisoner by me and Jess, forced to say and do things for blackmail and being threatened with the sale of the house. It made sense to her and us, but none at all to Nathaniel. He could hardly get a word in edgeways, and when he did her strident voice overrode him, ordering him to listen.

I was interested by Jess's reaction. She sat impassively, staring at the monitor, apparently uninterested in the exchange until Madeleine called Nathaniel a moron. With a hiss of frustration, she picked up the receiver and spoke into it. 'This is Jess. The situation is this . . .' She explained it succinctly in a few sentences, then put him back on loudspeaker. 'Now you can talk to Madeleine again. You've got fifty minutes.'

There was a short hesitation. 'Are you listening, Jess? Is the other woman listening?'

'Yes.'

'Are you recording this conversation?'

'We're filming it.'

'Christ!'

'Stop being – ' Madeleine began.

'Shut up!' he ordered her. 'If you keep digging you're going to be in real trouble.' Another pause. 'OK, Jess, have I understood you right? You've got some film of Madeleine abusing your friend and some kind of admission that she also abused her mother. In return for keeping that under wraps, you want her to approve the sale of Barton House. Is that correct?'

'Yes.'

'And if she refuses you'll release her to say whatever she likes, then you'll send out copies of the DVD to anyone who's interested.'

'Yes.'

Madeleine tried again. 'They won't be able – '

'*Shut up!*' A longer silence. 'Can I talk to the other woman? Is it Connie? What do you really want?'

'Exactly what Jess has told you. Madeleine can approve the sale or she can explain the DVD. It's up to her. Either way she won't be able to stay in

Winterbourne Barton. She's given too many details of how you and she terrorized Lily.'

'That's a lie,' Madeleine called out. 'I said hardly any – '

'*Jesus!*' Nathaniel shouted down the line, showing real anger suddenly. 'Will you keep your mouth shut? I'm damned if I'll let you drag me into this. There's only one devil in this family . . . and we all know who that is.'

'Don't you dare – '

'You say *one* more thing, Madeleine, and I'll hang up. Do you understand?' He let a beat pass. 'OK,' he went on more calmly, 'I want to hear what you've got, Jess.'

'You don't have time for it all,' she told him, 'so I've keyed in the seven minutes that matter. You'll hear Connie's voice at the beginning saying: "You know, what really surprises me", then – '

Nathaniel cut across her. 'How come you've already keyed it in?'

'I knew you'd ask for it.'

'How do I know it hasn't been edited?'

'No time, but in any case I ran a clock on the three cameras. For the DVD, I'll do a split screen to show the action synchronized.' She pointed to the bottom right-hand corner of the screen. 'I'm showing Madeleine the digital numbers so that she can tell you if any of them are out of sequence.' She clicked her mouse. 'Running now.'

Madeleine and I went through our motions again on screen, but, to me, the more I saw the clip, the less convincing it became. Madeleine won hands-down on the photogenic front. Even at her most furious, she remained elegant and pretty, and it was hard to believe that her Jasper Conran designer shoes were doing any damage at all. I just looked ridiculous. Why hadn't I fought back instead of allowing myself to be kicked?

I don't know if Jess was aware of my dejection, but when the clip ended she spoke before anyone else could. 'The images are graphic and don't flatter your wife, Nathaniel. She's enjoying it too much. If I decide to run the fight in slow-motion, which I will for the DVDs, it'll be even more obvious. No one'll believe she didn't do the same thing to Lily. You said she's done it to the kid.'

'That's a lie,' Madeleine shouted.

Jess glanced at her briefly then leaned towards the telephone speaker. 'Was it, Nathaniel? You told me you can never leave her alone with Hugo . . . which is why he never comes to Dorset with her. Is that true or not?'

We all heard him take an audible breath through his nose. 'True.'

'*Liar!*' Madeleine stormed. 'Don't you try and blame – '

Nathaniel cut in again. 'I had nothing to do with any of this, Jess. You've got to believe that. My only involvement was to pass on what you told me about the power of attorney and phone Madeleine when I picked up your message about social services.'

'Connie thinks you came down the night I found Lily.'

'No. The last time I came down was when I spoke to you in November. Hugo and I didn't see Madeleine at all for most of December and January. We thought she was looking after Lily – it's what she *said* she was doing – playing the dutiful daughter in the hopes of reversing the power of attorney. If I'd guessed – ' he broke off abruptly. 'Lily was supposed to die of hypothermia that night, Jess. Madeleine was furious when you turned up and took her away.'

There was a short silence.

Jess stirred herself. 'She was *here*? She was *watching*?'

'All the time.'

'Staying in the house?'

'Yes. She couldn't abandon Lily completely. Anyone could have arrived out of the blue, and there'd have been hell to pay if they'd found Lily drinking from the fishpond. Madeleine switched the water on and off as it suited her . . . sometimes Lily had water . . . sometimes she didn't . . . the same with the lights.'

'He's lying,' Madeleine said. 'It's all lies.'

'She made Lily take cold baths, then locked her in her room in the dark. The only thing she couldn't turn on and off at will was the Aga, so she booked herself into a hotel some nights to have a bath and a decent meal. That's when Lily got out and went looking for help in the village.'

There was a horrible logic to it. 'Why did no one see Madeleine?' I asked.

'Because she was only going to show herself if someone came to the door. Her story would have been that she'd just arrived and discovered Lily *in extremis*. It never happened.' He gave a hollow laugh. 'She said it wouldn't. She said if her mother died, the body would lie in the house for weeks until Jess went in.'

I glanced at Jess's bent head. 'Why didn't she show herself when Jess found Lily outside?'

'Too scared. She'd parked her car in the garage at the back so that no one would see it . . . and she never did that normally. In any case, the house was in darkness, and she had no explanation for why she hadn't turned on the lights to look for her mother as soon as she arrived.' He paused. 'You let her off the hook by taking Lily to the farm, Jess. If you'd stayed and called an ambulance, Madeleine would have been trapped in the house.'

When Jess didn't say anything, Nathaniel spoke again. 'I can't see her being prosecuted for it. It's maybe what you want but – ' he faltered briefly as if deciding how honest to be – 'I don't think you'd be doing this if you had any real evidence.'

'We do now,' I said. 'You've filled in the gaps.'

'I can't swear to any of it – I wasn't there – and

Madeleine will deny it. I've only said as much as I have because I'm hoping you'll back off for Hugo's sake.' He appealed to Jess. 'You know what'll happen if you go public, Jess. Madeleine will accuse everyone but herself – me included – and the only person who'll suffer will be the child. I really don't want that.'

'If I go straight to the police – ' Madeleine began.

'You'll be screwed' he told her harshly. 'Can't you *see* that? Whatever you do, you'll be screwed. If you try to justify yourself in advance, Jess will quietly dispose of the film and leave you to hang yourself on your own . . . and if you call her bluff, and she sends it out, you'll be in the police station with her answering questions. Maybe she and Connie will get done for blackmail but it's nothing to what'll happen to you if you can't keep your stupid trap shut.'

Jess raised her head. 'It's not blackmail if we only show it to the police,' she said. 'It's evidence.' She looked at me with troubled eyes. 'What should I do? I'm not sure any more.'

Neither was I. The idea had been to give Jess some leverage over Madeleine so that she could be rid of the woman with a clear conscience. Lily's will would allow Madeleine to inherit the money eventually, and none of the history of the two families need ever come out. We also hoped we could scare her back to London without talking to Bagley. There was a canvas bag and a DVD that I'd successfully hidden from the police – both of which I regarded as my private property – but, in any case, I resented the idea that my story might be handed to a woman who would certainly sell it, or use it to enhance her standing. She'd drop my name and the details of my captivity all over London if she thought it would earn her some kudos.

Jess had been sceptical when I proposed the idea the previous evening. 'Even if she does say something damaging, she'll never agree to the sale of Barton House. What do we do then? I don't mind filming her and threatening her with blackmail – ' her eyes lit with mischief – 'I'll even enjoy it – but we can't do it for real. She'll be into Bagley's office like a rat down a drainpipe.'

'Then you'll have to come clean about Lily's will,' I said cheerfully. 'Just give her an hour of hell before you do it. Think of it as Lily's revenge. Yours, too, if you like. At least let Madeleine know what you think of her before you hand her a million and a half quid on a plate. Personally, I'd rather see you inherit this house – I'm sure it's what Lily wanted – but there'll be no keeping quiet about the Derbyshire–Wright connection if you do.'

Neither of us had expected to hear revelations of attempted murder. Jess had felt she could live with the knowledge of absentee cruelty and neglect – *'It's what Madeleine's been doing all her life'* – but that was a far cry from sending a confused old lady into the cold and standing idly by while she succumbed to hypothermia.

What stuck in my throat more than anything was the idea that Madeleine might profit from what she'd done.

I reached across Jess for the mouse and double-clicked on the live feeds. 'Are they off?'

'Yes.'

'OK.' I put my thoughts in order. 'I don't think my conscience will let me do this, Jess. Madeleine's *dangerous*. For all I know, her creep of a husband is as well. If he was truly interested in protecting his child, he'd have reported her himself. What if she has another go at Lily? Could you live with that . . . because I certainly couldn't.'

'No.'

'We have to report her.'

'I know,' she sighed. 'But who to? Bagley?'

'Not necessarily,' I said. 'We can do what Lily would have done . . . send everything to her solicitor and let him decide.'

The angry protests that erupted simultaneously from Madeleine and Nathaniel sent Jess reaching for an envelope. It seemed they were considerably more worried about the man who held the purse strings than they were about the police.

From:	alan.collins@manchester-police.co.uk
Sent:	Thur 26/08/04 10.12
To:	connie.burns@uknet.com
Subject:	Your extraordinary resilience

Dear Connie,

I'm impressed by your resilience, though not as
impressed as Nick Bagley seems to be. After what
you've been through, he's astonished by your
determination to stay put and carry on. I explained that
you've been in worse situations and survived them but
with MacKenzie still on the loose, Nick feels you should
be more afraid. Your response appears to be 'out of
character for a woman'. I might have cast aspersions
against Dorset ladies, but he says your friend Jess is
being equally bullish.

I've had several conservations with Nick re MacKenzie's
disappearance. He tells me there've been a number of
sightings across the south-west although none is reliable.
He's interested in MacKenzie's alleged SAS training (still
to be corroborated) and asked if I thought it possible/
likely that the man *never left* Winterbourne Valley. I said
I thought it unlikely as I understand the entire area was
swept twice and no trace of him was found. *I hope I'm*

correct, Connie. If not, please take extra precautions. The consequences could be extremely serious for you if MacKenzie is still in the vicinity.

I was sorry to hear that one of Jess's mastiffs died trying to protect you. It's not a breed I know much about except that they're large and extremely powerful. Nick tells me the 'Hound of the Baskervilles' was a mastiff – he referred to it as 'a huge beast that hunted men and ripped their throats out' – and I know he views Jess's pack with the same alarm. He keeps a close eye on them, although he's surprised they're now confined to their enclosure when Jess's previous routine was to exercise them daily across her land.

Finally, Nick is surprised that you didn't destroy the DVD of your captivity when you had the chance. From the concerns you expressed both to me and Dr Coleman about being filmed (and Dr Coleman's description of what he saw), Nick wonders why you seem so indifferent to the fact MacKenzie still has it. I presume you aren't, and that you're still anxious about it?

Yours as ever,

Alan

DI Alan Collins, Greater Manchester Police

From:	connie.burns@uknet.com
Sent:	Fri 27/08/04 08.30
To:	alan.collins@manchester-police.co.uk
Subject:	My extraordinary resilience

Dear Alan,

Thank you. I deeply appreciate the thoughts behind your email.

So . . . for your reassurance. . .

Nick Bagley would have been no less suspicious if Jess and I had folded ourselves into heaps and demanded 24-hour protection. Peter Coleman's evidence about our courage was so OTT that a sudden collapse afterwards would have looked very odd. We can only be what we are, Alan, and there was no sense assuming different personas to satisfy Bagley's view of how women ought to behave. You know very well I could have kept up a sham for as long as I liked – I've done it successfully in the past – but Jess is too honest.

I took your Thucydides quote to heart. 'The secret of happiness is freedom; and the secret of freedom, courage.' I've tried to explain to Bagley that merely confronting MacKenzie was a liberation. I saw him for what he was – not what my imagination had made of him – and I'm a great deal happier for it. I can't, and won't, pretend a fear I don't feel any more. Bagley's given me a panic alarm, but I'm sure MacKenzie won't come back. He seemed far more frightened of me that night than I was of him.

In so far as anyone can guarantee anything, I guarantee that MacKenzie is NOT in the valley. Dorset police searched it twice from end to end, and there was no sign of him on either occasion. He may have holed up somewhere else but I'm sure the more likely explanation is that he left the country under a different passport. He seems to have unlimited access to them.

FYI, Dan has requested a filter on all Reuters files to pull out anything relating to unexplained murders, so if MacKenzie starts again somewhere else we may be able to spot him.

Re the Hound of the Baskervilles. Conan Doyle describes it as a mastiff/bloodhound cross, the size of a small lioness with phosphorus flames dripping from its jaws (!), and trust me, even Bagley's interesting imagination would have trouble embroidering Jess's soft-mouthed mutts into anything so exciting. It's true you can't move when they sit on you, but their favourite occupation is to drool saliva into your lap, not grab you by the throat and shake you. She's keeping them in for the moment because Bertie's buried in the top field and she's worried they'll dig him up. Once the turf has grown over the grave, they won't be interested. She explained this to Bagley but, unfortunately, it seems to have made him more suspicious.

Re the DVD. It never occurred to me to destroy it. Am I still anxious about it? No. If I'm honest, I'm rather proud of it. I even wish Bagley could see it. It might help him to understand why I'm so jubilant about taking MacKenzie on a second time. As a wise man once said: 'Winning is everything.'

You've been a good friend, Alan, and I hope I've set your mind at rest. In passing, if I ever do kill MacKenzie I won't bother to hide his body. There'll be no point if I can hack him to death in the hall with a blunt axe and plead self-defence. Maybe I should have done it when I had the chance!

With my love and thanks,

Connie

Twenty-three

I DON'T KNOW if Madeleine kept her appointment with Inspector Bagley. If she did, he never referred to it. He fell into the habit of dropping in unexpectedly, both at Barton House and Barton Farm, sometimes making two or three visits in a day. He usually found me working at my computer, but invariably missed Jess who was out in her fields, bringing in a late harvest after one of the wettest summers for years.

On several occasions she discovered his car in her drive and the man himself poking around in her outhouses, but she took it all in good part, even though he didn't have a search warrant. She told him he was welcome any time, and suggested he keep checking the back garden so that he could satisfy himself the only bones there were beef bones. Her dogs lost their suspicion of him once they learnt the sound of his engine, but he never lost his suspicion of them.

I, too, remained wary around them. Some phobias aren't susceptible to logic. I could cope with one dog at a time but the four en masse still alarmed me. It was clear they missed Bertie. Outside, they patrolled their wire enclosure looking for him, and, inside, sat by doors, watching for his return. Jess said they'd do it for a month before they forgot him, but Bagley didn't believe her.

'They're not waiting for the other dog to return,' he told me one morning, 'they're trying to get out.' He was standing behind me, reading what was on my computer screen, a complicated paragraph on post-traumatic stress statistics. 'You haven't got very far with that, Ms Burns. You've only added one sentence since last night.'

I clicked 'save' and pushed my chair back, narrowly missing his foot. 'It would go a lot faster if you didn't keep coming in and breaking my train of thought,' I told him mildly. 'Can't you ring the doorbell once in a while? At least give me a chance to pretend I'm out.'

'You said I could walk in whenever I felt like it.'

'I wasn't expecting you to take up residence here.'

'Then shut your back door, Ms Burns. It's an open invitation to anyone to enter.' He offered me a cigarette. 'After what happened, I'm surprised you're so unconcerned about unwanted visitors.'

It was a variation on a question he'd asked a hundred times already. I accepted a light. 'I'm not unconcerned,' I answered patiently, 'but the alternative is to turn this place into a prison. Is that what you want me to do? I thought modern policing was all

447

about persuading victims to get back to normal as fast as possible.'

'But this isn't normality for you, Ms Burns. Normality was checking the locks on the doors and windows every two hours.'

'And a fat lot of good it did me,' I pointed out. 'It raised my stress levels, and MacKenzie got in anyway.' I fingered the panic alarm round my neck. 'In any case, I now have this. It's given me confidence that the cavalry will turn up . . . which was the intention, wasn't it?'

He smiled rather sourly as he dropped into the armchair beside the desk. 'Indeed, but I suspect it's a waste of taxpayers' money. Are you ever going to use it? Ms Derbyshire refuses to wear hers.'

'There's no point when she's out in the fields. It needs a landline or a telephone signal to work.'

He cast his usual glance around the office as if something would suddenly show itself to him. 'I had a word with Alan Collins last night. He said you're too clever for me, and I might as well give up now. He also said he won't be shedding any tears if Mac-Kenzie's never heard of again. If anyone deserves what he gets, it's your attacker.'

I doubted Alan had said anything so crass, particularly to an opposite number in a different county. 'Really?' I asked in surprise. 'I've always thought of him as such a stickler for the rule of law. I can't imagine him ever going on record with favourable views about summary justice and vigilantism.'

'It wasn't on record,' Bagley said. 'It was a private conversation.'

'Still . . . will he repeat those remarks to me, do you think? I like the one about my being too clever for you. If I were to broaden that out into a general piece, contrasting IQ levels among the police with those of prison inmates – ' I raised an eyebrow. 'What do you think?'

'That you're probably the most annoying person I've ever met,' he said grimly. 'Why doesn't it worry you to be interviewed, Ms Burns? Why doesn't it make you angry? Why don't you have a solicitor? Why isn't he arguing police harassment?'

'*He*? If I had one, don't you think he'd be a *she*?'

Bagley flicked ash irritably into the ashtray on the desk. 'There you go again. Everything has to be turned into a joke.'

'But I enjoy your visits,' I said. 'Winterbourne Barton's a black hole as far as social interaction's concerned.'

'I'm not here to entertain you.'

'But you do,' I assured him. 'I love watching you poke around the garden looking for clues. Have you found anything yet? Jess says you keep going back to her granary, so presumably you're wondering if we buried MacKenzie under a ton of wheat? It wouldn't have been easy, you know. Grain's like quicksand. We'd have had trouble lugging a corpse on to the heap without sinking in ourselves.'

'She's added another ton in the last couple of weeks.'

'And it's all about to be shifted to a commercial grain store. Don't you think someone will notice if a body tumbles out?' I watched his mouth turn down. 'I don't understand why you can't accept that he freed himself and took to his heels. Is it because *you'd* have killed him if you'd been in our shoes?'

He took a thoughtful drag of his cigarette. 'I'm sure you dreamt of revenge.'

'All the time,' I said with a small laugh, 'but it did me even less good than checking the window locks. I lost so much weight over it that I feel like an old hen about to drop off her perch. Look.' I extended a bony right arm. 'If there's any useful meat on me you'd need a microscope to find it. How could *that* – ' I cocked my left forefinger at a grape-sized bicep – 'vanish a corpse in thirty minutes.'

He smiled reluctantly. 'I've no idea. Would you like to tell me?'

'There's nothing to tell, but even if there were you wouldn't be able to use it. You're on your own and there's no recorder. Anything I said would be inadmissible as evidence.'

'For my own satisfaction then.'

I glanced towards the hall. 'I *wanted* to kill him,' I

admitted. 'I would have done if I'd been a better shot. I was aiming for his head when I hit his fingers . . . and the only reason I didn't take another swipe was because it felt as if I'd been electrocuted when the axe slammed on to the flagstones. I had judders all the way up my arms and into the base of my neck. That's when I decided it would be better to tie him up.'

I squashed my fag end into the ashtray. 'Jess wanted to kill him, too – she was devastated about Bertie – but we couldn't see how to do it. Peter had already left and there wasn't time to work anything out. I suggested we untie MacKenzie and argue self-defence, but Jess said we'd have to corner him to do it – ' I sighed – 'and I had this sudden picture of the women in Sierra Leone . . . all huddled against walls because there was nowhere else to go.' I fell silent.

'Did Ms Derbyshire agree with you?'

'Yes. She said it might have been different if he'd been blindfolded but it wasn't possible after she'd seen into his eyes.' I pulled a wry smile. 'I don't think it's easy killing people. I don't think it's easy killing *animals*. I couldn't kill a rat if it looked at me the way MacKenzie did. I can't even kill woodlice. There's a nest in some of the rotten wood in Lily's drawing-room and the only way I can deal with them is to hoover them up and chuck them outside . . .'

*

H. L. Mencken once said: 'It's hard to believe a man is telling the truth when you know you would lie if you were in his place.' If I'd realized earlier that Bagley shied away from killing animals, I'd have introduced rats and woodlice at the beginning. His views on psychopaths and sadists were extreme – they should all be hanged – but he empathized strongly with my inability to crush the life out of vermin. I'm not sure I ever fully understood the logic of his argument, but apparently my clear reluctance to kill anything was more convincing than repeated denials that I'd killed MacKenzie.

In a shameless PR exercise to encourage complete exoneration, I persuaded Jess to release her dogs in front of him. As she predicted, they headed straight up the field for Bertie's grave and began a mournful howling around it. Bagley asked how they knew he was there and Jess said they'd attended the first funeral. Like elephants, they never forgot. Whether he believed that, I don't know, but he declined her invitation to dig poor Bertie out a second time. The remaining dogs showed no inclination to go anywhere else in the valley, and had to be dragged away from the grave on leashes.

After that, Bagley left us in peace. Alan was amused by the motives I ascribed to this sudden end to suspicion, saying it had more to do with an absence of evidence than Bagley being unable to kill woodlice, but I still feel I showed my best side as a woman when I mentioned the hoover.

*

The second week of September saw the arrival of my parents and the beginnings of an Indian summer after the rains of July and August. Jess took to them immediately, and in no time at all my father was up at the farm, lending a hand. My mother worried that he was over-exerting himself after his injuries, but Jess assured us he was only driving a tractor and helping Harry feed the livestock.

The subject of MacKenzie was taboo. None of us wanted to talk about him or what had happened. For all of us, it was done and dusted, and there was nothing to be gained by conducting a ghoulish post-mortem on who had suffered the most. Nevertheless, within a few of days of her arrival, my mother read some signals that were invisible to me and sought out Peter for a long chat.

I'd hardly had any contact with him since the incident, but I assumed he was still making regular visits to Jess. She'd mentioned his attendance at Bertie's exhumation, and defended him for some of the information he'd given Bagley, but, bar a phone call one evening to ask if I was all right, he hadn't been near me. I remember cutting the conversation short when he insisted on beating himself up for sins of omission and commission, but as Bagley arrived shortly afterwards Peter dropped out of focus again.

My mother gave me a hard time over it. I, more than anyone, should have understood how crippling it was to feel a failure. It was worse for men. They were expected to be courageous, and it destroyed their confidence to realize they weren't. Tongue in cheek, I asked her if it would have been better for Peter if Jess and I had failed the bravery test as well, and she echoed Bagley's statement about finding me deeply annoying.

'I don't like to see you gloating, Connie.'

'I'm not gloating.'

'I don't like to see your father gloating either.'

'He's having fun,' I protested mildly. 'Ploughing Jess's fields is a lot more exciting than sitting at a desk all day.'

'He's been cock-a-hoop since you phoned him in hospital,' she said accusingly. 'What did you say to him?'

The demons are dead and buried . . . 'Nothing much. Just that we'd all survived and MacKenzie had run away with his tail between his legs.'

Mum was peeling some potatoes at the sink. 'Why should that please him? He wanted the beastly man dead or behind bars, not free to do the same thing to someone else. I can't understand why you're all so unconcerned about him getting away. Aren't you worried that he'll murder some other poor woman?'

I watched her busy hands and debated the merit of

truth over lies. 'Not really,' I said honestly. 'It's the age of the global village. The story's gone round the world with his photograph, so he'll be found very quickly if he's alive. There are too many people looking for him.'

She turned to look at me. 'If?'

'Wishful thinking,' I said.

'Mm.' A pause. 'Perhaps that explains your father. He's behaving like a schoolboy at the moment.'

'Being on a farm reminds him of home.'

'Except the last time he operated a tractor was twenty years ago,' she said. 'We employed a workforce for ploughing . . . Dad was the boss man who drove a four-by-four and checked the furrows were straight.' She held my gaze for a moment before returning to the potatoes. 'But I'm sure you're right. The simplest explanation is usually the correct one.'

*

One afternoon, Jess said she was going to visit Lily and asked if I'd like to go, too. I knew Jess went to the nursing home regularly, even though Lily had no idea who she was, but this was the first time she'd invited me to accompany her. I went out of curiosity – a desire to put a face to the personality I'd come to know – and I'm glad I did. Even though the fires that had driven her were now absent, Lily's beauty was so much sweeter than her daughter's. It proved nothing – for I firmly believe that looks are skin deep – but I did understand when she smiled why Jess was so fond of her. I'm sure the same bemused affection had been in Frank Derbyshire's smile when his daughter had quietly taken his hand in hers, and stroked it without saying a word . . .

*

If I live to be a hundred I'll never understand my mother's gift for socializing. When she and my father first arrived in London, they were on the Zimbabwean exiles' dinner party list within hours of the plane landing. My father complained about it – '*I hate being trapped at tables with people I'm never going to meet again*' – but underneath he was secretly pleased. He had more in common with ex-pat farmers who had experienced Mugabe's ethnic cleansing at first hand than he did with the London chattering classes who could only talk about their second homes in France.

Suddenly, visitors started appearing at Barton House. I knew a few of them through Peter, but most I'd never seen before, and I certainly wasn't on dropping-in terms with any of them. The first time anyone appeared – a jolly couple in their sixties from Peter's end of the village – Jess was in the kitchen and, despite her best efforts to melt into the background, my mother drew her back out again. I warned her she'd scare Jess away if she wasn't careful, but it didn't happen. Jess turned up each evening with Dad, and seemed content to be quietly included in whatever was happening, albeit on the fringes.

On a few occasions Julie, Paula and their children came too. Even old Harry Sotherton put in an appearance, and had to be driven home by my father after consuming more ale than he was used to. It reminded me so much of life in Zimbabwe where meals were regularly stretched to accommodate anyone who was passing. Jess was never going to be the life and soul of a party, but to see her held in genuine affection by the people who knew her did her nothing but good.

Peter became the most regular visitor. I never did find out what my mother said to him, but she asked me to make the first move by inviting him over. I decided to go to his house and, if necessary, slap a MacKenzie embargo on him, but the subject never arose. He was more interested in Madeleine. 'Listen to this,' he said, pressing the button on his answerphone. 'I got back about five minutes ago and it was waiting for me.'

Madeleine's strident voice filled the speaker. 'Peter, are you there? The bloody nursing home's locked the door against me. I need you to come and tell them not to be so damn . . . *stupid*! They say they'll call the police if I don't leave immediately. How *dare* the solicitor stop me seeing Mummy? He's taken out an *injunction* against me. I'm *so* angry. Oh, to *hell* with it!' There was a muffled shout which sounded like 'I'm going, for Christ's sake,' then silence.

I couldn't avoid a smile and Peter saw it. 'What's she on about? Do you know?'

'The solicitor's obviously given the nursing home authority to exclude her.'

'Why?'

'It's a long story,' I told him. 'You can ask Jess about it.'

'I haven't seen her for days. She's not answering her phone or her door.'

'Nothing new there then,' I said. 'Since when did you have to announce yourself? I thought you always went in the back.'

'I did, but – ' he broke off on a sigh. 'I don't think she's speaking to me any more.'

'I'm not surprised if you keep ringing her doorbell. She probably thinks it's that worm Bagley.' I watched him give a small shake of his head. 'Then it's your fault,' I said bluntly. 'You changed the rules of the game and she doesn't know how to play any more.'

'What rules?'

'The ones that say you have to barge in on her all the time and tease her mercilessly till she laughs. She probably thinks you don't fancy her now that you've seen her naked.'

'That's ridiculous.'

'Mm. About as ridiculous as you hanging around outside her front door like a nervous adolescent.' I gave his arm a friendly buffet. 'We're talking about the most introverted woman in Dorset, Peter. She's been manhandled by a psycho . . . watched one of her dogs die . . . stood up to the third degree from Bagley . . . and suddenly she's supposed to understand why a man she likes doesn't want to tease her any more? You're an idiot!'

He smiled grudgingly. 'That's for sure. I got it all wrong, Connie. I thought we should humour –'

I gave him another buffet, rather harder this time. '*Don't* lay a guilt trip on me. I'm on a roll . . . I'm writing again . . . I'm *eating* again. Life's grand. Does it matter who did what, when?' I smiled to take the sting from my words. 'You helped me from the day I arrived, Peter. You and Jess helped me just by being there that night. If I'd been on my own I couldn't have done it. Can't you feel good about that? For me and Jess . . . but mostly for yourself?'

'You're a nice person, Connie.'

'Is that a yes or a no?'

The smile stretched to his eyes. 'I'm not sure yet. I'll tell you after I've barged in on Jess.'

*

Half-way through my parents' stay I received a letter from Lily's solicitor, asking what my intentions were with regard to the information Jess and I had given him. My father was deeply unimpressed by him. As he pointed out, the man was a typical lawyer. He'd failed to protect his client before the event, but was happy to keep her alive and skim his percentage afterwards.

I didn't disagree, but I took the line of least resistance. Did I care enough about Lily to make myself available for more police questioning? No. There wasn't a sliver of paper to draw between her and her daughter. Lily had been no more willing to acknowledge Jess than Madeleine had. There'd been no public championing of the Derbyshires, and no stamping on Madeleine's libels. Lily had treated her brother and her niece like servants and exploited their goodwill to the nth degree.

Did I think it would do an eleven-year-old boy any good for me to spend days in court, fighting off blackmail charges, in order to separate him from his parents? No. Rightly or wrongly, I accepted Jess's word that Nathaniel genuinely cared for his son, and I hadn't the will or the energy to take responsibility for a child I knew nothing about.

But in the end I kept quiet for Jess's sake. Some debts can only be repaid with loyalty.

BALLDOCK & SIMPSON SOLICITORS

Tower House   Poundbury   Dorset

Ms C. Burns
Barton House
Winterbourne Barton
Dorset

14 September 2004

Dear Ms Burns,

WITHOUT PREJUDICE

*Re: Ms Derbyshire's account of an alleged assault on
you by Madeleine Harrison-Wright; and information
contained in a film purporting to show the incident*

As you know, I act on behalf of Mrs Lily Wright and
I have taken the view that it is not in my client's
interests to pursue charges relating to alleged events
between November 2003 and January 2004. Because
of her frail health, Mrs Wright would be unable to

testify, and I believe this would result in a failed prosecution. Your case is different since you have a film of Madeleine Harrison-Wright's apparent assault on you, and an independent witness in Ms Derbyshire.

I cannot, of course, advise you on what action to take as you are not my client, however I hope you will forgive my presumption in pointing out some likely consequences of proceeding. Madeleine Harrison-Wright will argue that nothing she said can be relied on as there is clear evidence of provocation and coercion. Your own credibility will be questioned because you failed to report your suspicions to the police. The same is true of your witness. In addition, the very existence of the film may result in you and Ms Derbyshire being charged with conspiracy to blackmail.

As my primary concern is Mrs Lily Wright's welfare, I have introduced various measures to ensure her continued welfare and safety. Please feel confident that she is being looked after with kindness, and is as happy as her condition allows. Before her health failed, she gave me certain instructions regarding herself, her family and her estate. Despite, or perhaps because of, the information you and Ms Derbyshire

obtained from Mrs Madeleine Harrison-Wright, I see
no reason to move away from those instructions.

1   For the foreseeable future, Barton House will
     remain in Mrs Lily Wright's estate.
2   Mrs Wright's nursing-home care will continue to
     be covered by income from its rental and income
     from her investments.
3   Should the sale of Barton House become
     necessary, the money will be placed in trust for
     the benefit of Mrs Wright during her lifetime.
4   Upon her death, the benefit will pass to her
     grandson, Hugo Harrison-Wright, with all
     disbursement of money at the discretion of
     trustees.
5   In the event that Barton House remains unsold at
     the time of Mrs Lily Wright's death, it will pass to
     her niece to keep or dispose of as she pleases.

Ms Derbyshire tells me you fully understand the
implications of these decisions, but should you require
further clarification please feel free to contact me. As
per Mrs Lily Wright's instructions, Nathaniel and
Madeleine Harrison-Wright remain in ignorance of
her wishes.

While I accept that you have a genuine grievance

against Madeleine Harrison-Wright, I worry that an attempted prosecution will exonerate her and allow her access to confidential information. For this reason, may I urge you to consider all of the above and let me know if you intend to proceed? You will, of course, be aware that any such action will lead to disclosures about Ms Derbyshire's connection with the family.

Finally, on behalf of Mrs Lily Wright, I would like to thank you and Ms Derbyshire for bringing these matters to my attention. I am distressed that my client was unable to inform me of what was happening to her at the time, but I am advised that her long-term condition would not have been unduly affected by her daughter's mistreatment. Sadly, the progress of the disease was always irreversible.

Yours sincerely,

Thomas Balldock

Twenty-four

SEVERAL RUMOURS SURFACED at the same time, although it wasn't clear where they started. Everyone knew about the injunction preventing Madeleine from visiting Lily, and it was generally assumed that she'd made an attempt on her mother's life in the nursing-home. From that developed the Chinese whispers. I was told variously that Madeleine had been diagnosed with a personality disorder; that she was under compulsory psychiatric care; that she'd been forced to leave the London flat after assaulting her son; that Nathaniel had filed for divorce; and that a restraining order had been imposed to stop her coming within a mile of Winterbourne Barton.

The only whisper I knew to be true (apart from the nursing-home injunction) was the restraining order which Thomas Balldock had applied for on behalf of Jess and myself. I don't know what evidence he presented, but we were told to notify the police if Madeleine or Nathaniel tried to contact us or enter our properties. However, it wasn't until Peter bumped into an acquaintance of Nathaniel's in London that

465

the separation was confirmed. According to the acquaintance, it was Nathaniel and Hugo who'd moved out of the flat, and Madeleine who remained in possession. Father and son were living in Wales with Nathaniel's parents, and Madeleine was struggling to pay the bills.

The residents of Winterbourne Barton were surprisingly honest in their reactions. Most claimed to be shocked by the rumours, but a few said they'd always found Madeleine's charm superficial. I was the recipient of several indirect apologies to Jess for some of the things that had been said and thought about her, but no one was brave enough to make them in person. If they tried, they were met with a ferocious scowl.

I stayed out of it, but I know my mother urged her to be generous since people were 'only trying to be nice'. Jess replied that it was *she* who was being nice, by letting them 'gawp' at her, because the only thing that had changed was their perception of Madeleine. Jess was the same as she'd always been and Winterbourne Barton remained a retirement village for rich, ignorant pensioners who knew nothing about the countryside. Under my mother's emollient balm, she was persuaded to produce the odd smile in place of a scowl, but small talk remained beyond her.

I suggested to Mum that as soon as she and Dad went back to London Jess's brief renaissance would be over. 'I don't want to schmooze the locals any more than she does,' I pointed out, 'and my tenancy ends in December.'

'Jess has a kind heart,' she said. 'If she hears of someone in trouble, she'll help them. She helped you, didn't she?'

'But I didn't impose on the friendship.'

My mother laughed. 'And neither will anyone else. People aren't stupid, Connie. As long as she keeps making social calls, everything will work out fine. It's hard to dislike someone with as much warmth as Jess has.'

Warmth . . .? Were we talking about the same person? Jess Derbyshire? Dysfunction on legs? 'Jess doesn't make social calls.'

'Of course she does, darling. How many times has she dropped in on you since you arrived here?'

'That's different.'

'I don't think so. When Peter tells her one of his patients needs some eggs, she'll be round like a shot. It's her nature to look after others. She'll make an excellent doctor's wife.'

It was my turn to laugh. 'Do you think that's likely? I don't think she's the marrying type.'

'Perhaps not, but she could do with a baby or two,' said my mother matter-of-factly, 'otherwise her farm will go to strangers when she dies.'

I eyed her with amusement. 'Have you told her that? How did she respond?'

'Rather more positively than you've ever done.'

I didn't believe her for a moment. Jess's most likely retort was that giving birth to me hadn't stopped strangers taking my parents' farm in Zimbabwe – it was the answer she'd given when I'd strayed on to the subject of inheritance – but I decided not to argue the point. My mother was too well practised at turning other people's babies into a lecture on my lack of commitment in the same department. In any case, I rather liked the idea of Jess producing little Derbyshire-Colemans. I thought they'd grow up to be as affectionate, competent and well balanced as her mastiffs.

*

I spent a couple of days in Manchester at the end of September, giving Alan Collins a full statement of the events in Baghdad. By then he'd built up quite a file against MacKenzie, which was available to other national and international police forces in the event of an arrest. I asked him if he was optimistic, and he shook his head.

'I think he died the night he came to your house, Connie.'

'How?'

'Probably the way you suggested to Nick Bagley . . . he lost his bearings in the dark and fell.'

'Off the cliff?'

'Unlikely.'

I watched him for a moment. 'Why not?'

Alan shrugged. 'His body would have been found. Nick tells me there's a rocky shoreline along that part of the Dorset coast.'

'Perhaps he went in farther down. Some of the cliffs to the east are sheer.'

'Perhaps,' he agreed.

'You don't sound very convinced.'

He smiled slightly. 'Did I ever tell you I took the family on holiday to Dorset once? We rented a cottage near Wool, about ten miles from where you are. The children loved it. There was a well in the garden with a thatched roof and a bucket painted red. They were convinced there were fairies living at the bottom of it, and they used to climb on the stone surround to look down. My wife was terrified they were going to fall in.'

I folded my hands in my lap. 'I'm not surprised.'

'It was quite safe. It was capped below the parapet to prevent accidents. I asked the old boy next door what he'd done with his well, and he told me he'd filled it in and put a patio over the top. He said he'd had to wait until the late sixties for mains water, and he didn't want any reminders of the back-breaking days. According to him, every old house in rural Dorset has a redundant well somewhere. The big houses usually have two . . . one outside and one inside.'

I squeezed my hands between my knees. 'Well, if there are any at Barton House they were covered over long ago. You could look for ever and never find one.'

Alan watched me while he shuffled his papers

together and tapped them on the desk to square them up. 'Nick tells me the woman who owns Barton House asked for an interview but never turned up. Do you know why not?'

'Lily Wright?' I said in surprise. 'She can't have done. She has advanced Alzheimer's. Her solicitor put her in a nursing home eight months ago.'

'I believe he said the name was Madeleine Wright.'

'Oh, *her*!' I said scathingly, wondering how many conversations he'd had with Bagley, and how much he'd said to him about wells. 'You mean Madeleine *Harrison*-Wright, the double-barrelled daughter.'

He looked amused. 'What's wrong with her?'

'Not my type,' I told him. 'Not yours either, I wouldn't think, unless you like spoilt forty-somethings who expect to be kept all their lives. She doesn't work – far too grand – but she's not above selling a story. She tried to pump Peter Coleman for the gory details on MacKenzie, and when he refused she said she'd ask Bagley.'

'So why didn't she?'

'I don't know for certain. I was told Lily's solicitor became involved, and he read her the riot act on behalf of Jess and me.' I pulled a wry face. 'Madeleine lives in London and never lifted a finger to help her mother . . . which makes her very unpopular in Winterbourne Barton. They're all over sixty-five and imagine their children love them.'

Alan gave a snort of laughter. 'Meaning what? That

you and Jess won the grey vote, and the wrinklies ran her out of town so that she couldn't make money out of you?'

I smiled in return. 'Something like that. They've been very protective of us.'

'And the fact that Madeleine's the only person who knows the ins and outs of Barton House has nothing to do with it?'

'Hardly. If Bagley wants to talk to her, he can always ask Lily's solicitor for her phone number.'

'He's done that already.'

'And?'

'Nothing. She said she didn't keep the appointment because her car broke down, and the only thing she wanted to ask was whether she could go ahead with having the flagstones cleaned.'

I shrugged. 'That's probably right. She told me it all had to be done before I left so that the next tenant wouldn't complain about Bertie's blood all over the place.'

Alan tucked the papers back into MacKenzie's file. 'Will anyone ever ask me for this, Connie?'

'I don't know,' I said lightly. 'Maybe a body will wash up on the Dorset coast one day, and put us all out of our misery.'

'Then let's hope there's salt water in its lungs,' he said, standing up and helping me into my jacket.

*

From Manchester I drove down to Holyhead in North Wales to meet the ferry from Dublin. I saw Dan before he saw me. He looked no different from the day we'd parted at Baghdad airport – big, weather-beaten, slightly crumpled – but the sight of his well-remembered face gave me such a jolt of recognition that I had to retreat behind a pillar until my schoolgirl blush faded.

Back in Dorset, Jess and he tolerated each other for my sake but neither understood what I saw in the other. It was like introducing a boisterous grizzly bear to a cautious feral cat. There were no such problems with Peter. In no time at all, he and Dan were playing rounds of golf together, and stopping off for a jar at the local hostelry. Each told me the other was a 'good chap', and I wondered why men found it easier than women to strike up a casual bond and move on without regret.

I wouldn't be able to do that with Jess. The ties we had ran too deep.

The Abyss

Epilogue

THERE'S LITTLE ELSE to tell. A few days after Dan returned to Iraq, part of an arm washed up on rocks about fifteen miles down the coast. It was spotted by a group of fisherman on their way home from catching mackerel. Enough of a fingerprint was retrieved to link the remains to MacKenzie, and a DNA test, using saliva from a glass in my parents' flat, confirmed the indentification.

There was some debate about how the arm had become detached from the rest of the body, and why it had survived relatively intact after a long immersion in water. It appeared to have been wrenched apart at the elbow but there were no obvious marks on the skin to show how that could have happened, although it was noted that three of the fingerbones were broken. There was talk of shark attacks but they weren't taken seriously. The benign coastal waters of the West Country were occasionally home to plankton-eating basking sharks, but not to man-eaters.

Police divers explored the sea bed for several hundred metres around the rocks, also a couple of areas to the west where experts on tidal-drift suggested Mac-Kenzie might have gone in, but nothing else was found. Jess, Peter and I were asked to attend a rather bizarre inquest, where the arm was pronounced dead from misadventure – along with a presumption that the remainder of the body had died similarly – and both Alan and Bagley closed their files.

There were several column inches in the press, detailing what was known of MacKenzie, but the full story was never revealed. Bagley was satisfied with a verdict of misadventure – any man who was watching his back for a police pursuit could easily lose his footing on the cliffs in the dark – but Alan wouldn't commit himself. As he said, there was nothing to be learnt from a forearm except the name of the owner and the fact that he was probably dead.

'Isn't that what you wanted?' I asked. 'Confirmation.' He, too, had attended the inquest, and I'd abandoned Jess and Peter to take him to a tea shop near the Coroner's Court in Blandford Forum.

Alan nodded. 'But I'll always be curious, Connie. It may be coincidence that he died of drowning after fending off a dog and machete attack . . . but there's an interesting symmetry to it.' He stirred his tea. 'Even his arm was detached in the same place that the prostitute's was broken in Freetown.'

'It wasn't a machete,' I corrected amiably. 'It was an axe.'

'Near enough.'

We were sitting opposite each other and I examined his face to see how serious he was. 'I don't believe in an eye for an eye, Alan. It's a crazy form of justice. In any case, if I'd wanted the perfect revenge, I'd have kept MacKenzie in a crate for three days.'

His eyes creased attractively. 'It crossed my mind.'

I laughed. 'Bagley would have found him. There wasn't an inch of Barton House that wasn't searched at least twice.'

'Mm.'

'You don't *really* think I'd do something like that, do you?'

'Why not? He was a killer. A sadist. He liked hurting people. He boasted about what he'd done to your father . . . humiliated your friend and killed her dog. You're good at hiding your feelings, Connie. You have a brain . . . and you have courage. Why wouldn't you kill him if you had the chance?'

'It would make me no better than MacKenzie.'

Alan took a sip from his teacup and eyed me over the rim. 'Do you know Friedrich Nietzsche's quote about being corrupted by evil? I have it pinned to a board above my desk. Simplified, it says: "When you fight with monsters take care not to become one yourself." It's a warning to all policemen.'

I nodded. 'It goes on: "If you stare too long into the abyss, the abyss stares back at you." How would you simplify that?'

'You tell me.'

'When you're teetering on the brink, step back.'
'And did you?'
'Of course,' I said, offering him a biscuit. 'But MacKenzie didn't. *He* fell in.'